Sour

Uzuri M. Wilkerson

Sour

by Uzuri M. Wilkerson

Paperback | Copyright 2015 © Yellow Leaf Books

Second Edition

Cover by ReBelle Design Studio

www.uzurimwilkerson.com

www.amazon.com/author/uzuriwilkerson

Other works by
Uzuri M. Wilkerson

Bitten:
Sweet
Bitter

Sour

One

THE RED SOX were home after a week of away games. So their win was fantastic. The people who didn't want to elbow their way through the Fenway club crowds went to Cage's, and boy, were there plenty of them.

Celia wiped the sweat from her forehead with a napkin. She pulled out two glasses into which she tipped a couple of mint sprigs. Making mojitos during club nights was time consuming. She informed Bobby of this numerous times but he liked the look of it on his drink menu, especially in the summertime. She had to use a spoon to muddle the mint. After that, she added the sugar and lime juice. The girls who'd ordered the mojitos were too busy yelling to each other over the music about their hair and outfits to take in and appreciate the process.

Celia placed the finished drinks on square napkins. The white napkins were a new addition, showcasing the

Cage's Bar and Lounge logo stenciled in black ink. It was a

simple logo. "Cage's" was written in block letters with "Bar and Lounge" in cursive underneath. A tiny, steel cage was etched behind the words in a faded design.

"That'll be twenty," Celia called.

After giving their change, she looked to the three men who had taken their place.

"Three Terminators cold, and Heinies," the taller one requested.

She nodded with a friendly smile, and faced the array of bottles before her on the back bar. The strobe lights reflected across the clear, blue, and brown liquors.

"What the fuck's a Terminator?" she asked Joni from the corner of her mouth.

Joni stood six feet tall with rubbery, orange skin that made the freckles on her arms and shoulders stand out more. Her permed hair was pinned back and out of her face, though a few curly tendrils fell loose.

She frowned blankly down at Celia with her too-close brown eyes. She then leaned over to Carson on her other side. He told her something and she nodded.

"Shot of Jäger and SoCo," Joni reported.

Celia pulled those bottles down. She paused in pouring the toasty almond liquid over ice in a shaker. Someone had whispered in her ear. Curiously, there weren't any words to decipher, only a soft sound in her ear.

She lowered the Southern Comfort bottle and glanced around. The only possible candidates were Joni and Carson mixing drinks and the harried patrons, whose heads jerked from each of them, trying to capture their attention.

She was distracted as she added Jägermeister, placed the cover on the metal container, and shook. You couldn't even hear the ice clinking against the metal container through the din of the lounge. DJ Mickey was in his booth, bouncing to the dance mix of

"Day 'N' Nite," his headphones slightly askew on his ears. People laughed merrily all around her. How did she hear the whisper?

She strained the liquor into three shot glasses.

Celia.

The one-word command floated over her like a hot breeze. Suddenly, Celia felt itchy, uncomfortable, constricted. Before she realized what was happening, before she had a chance to stop it, she was consumed.

Come to me.

The discomfort eased, leaving her numb. The life drained out of her in that instant. Her face went completely blank.

The silver shaker had started to burn her hand from the cold. She gently placed it onto the well. The three guys frowned at each other, and then after her. See, she was walking away. Celia moved at an even pace, her arms hanging limply at her sides. Joni did a double take when she noticed her absence. She had been handing someone a bottle of Bud Light. After quickly sliding the men's drinks across the bar to complete Celia's order, Joni called her name.

Celia ignored her, continuing on. Bobby, the owner and manager of Cage's, was talking with a tall guy in front of his office. It didn't matter because Celia didn't register him.

Bobby glanced up when she appeared in the hallway. "Celia," he said. "I want you to meet someone."

She went on to the kitchen as if he hadn't spoken.

"Celia!"

The door swung shut.

She went through the kitchen to the back door. It clicked closed behind her. The air was still pretty warm, though it was September now. You could always count on a breeze to keep the temps down a tad in downtown Boston, since it was so close to the water. She didn't shiver in her black shorts and black scoop-neck shirt thanks to the numbness.

Celia headed down the alley toward Washington Street where Cage's main entrance was located. Cage's building was all brick with wide windows that wrapped around the right side. The strobe lights made circles on the glass. A couple was pressed up against a window, making out in one of the booths. Rick went to another booth to demand a drunken girl that was stumbling in her high heels atop the table to get the fuck down. Others laughed on the curb in the fenced-off smoking section.

Celia's body moved with its own volition, as if being tugged forward by that invisible rope that had seized her. She crossed the street to squealing tires and honking horns without breaking stride. She carried on, past the Boston Commons movie theater, whose banner flashed the midnight movies still playing inside. She crossed Tremont Street and continued on Boylston until she came to the opening of The Public Garden.

Celia entered through the wrought iron gate. The park was quiet, aside from the occasional cricket or duck. She passed a man sleeping behind a bench and two women in jogging shorts and ear buds on their late-night run. Streetlights illuminated the path that wound through the trees then around the pond rippling from the few ducks skimming the surface. The weeping willows rustled in the wind, waving as she went.

The little dock was roped off and dark. The four swan boats bobbed slightly. They knocked into the wooden port. Mallard Island was straight ahead in the center of the pond, its lush greenery concealing the many ducks fast asleep. Celia headed toward the stone bridge, where she finally stopped at the paved area underneath. One of the lights was burned out. The lamps from the bridge above provided little illumination.

He was waiting for her, leaning against the foundation. He smiled as he pushed off. Tonight, he wore dark-washed skinny jeans and a black Rock Band shirt with the lead guitar emblem adorned across the chest.

Milo's blonde hair looked like white fire, even when the lighting was so dim. Celia stared at him with brown eyes devoid of any emotion. The vampire beamed, as if she'd just jumped up and down in ecstasy at seeing him.

"Celia, my sweet." He inhaled deeply. "Mm, you smell nice. Did you do that for me?"

She continued to stare. Milo sauntered over and stroked her cheek.

"How are you doing tonight?" he crooned softly, like he cared. "I'm glad you came. Did you like my call? 'Come to me' is such a classic."

Leaning forward, he brushed her lips with his. His mouth was small and didn't quite match hers. She watched the murky water slapping at the edge of the path.

"Kiss me," Milo commanded, so she did. He moaned against her mouth.

"Touch me," he whispered. His breath was on her face. Celia's hand reached up mechanically and caressed his smooth jaw. Her other hand rubbed his chest and stomach.

"Lower," he instructed. Her hand went to his crotch and Milo sighed in pleasure. "That's good," he said unnecessarily. He was bulging against her stroking.

Milo's lips kissed her chin, under her jaw. He shifted her head to the right, revealing the loveliness of her neck. His mouth opened, his fangs slowly lengthening. She didn't flinch when he pierced her skin. He drank from her while squeezing her tit.

After a minute or two, he pulled away with a contented sigh. "Goddammit, I could get used to this."

He flexed his fingers a few times, rolled his neck. He shook out his hands as he visibly shivered with pleasure. He then reached behind him and produced a pocketknife. It flicked open with a soft click. He ran the blade along his wrist.

"Drink."

Celia turned into him, her back to his chest, and brought his bleeding wrist to her mouth. She sucked on it while gazing off at some fallen leaves. His blood was warm. Her cheeks flushed soft pink—a purely physical reaction.

He moaned behind her, his other arm holding her close. His woody pressed against her ass and he moved her hips slowly from side to side. A moment passed. Milo pulled his wrist from Celia, spun her around, and kissed her again.

A large hand cupped her shoulder, shaking her roughly. Celia's eyes fluttered open. She had to blink a few times to get her bearings. The sun shone above, blinding her. The activity around the park was confounding. People ran past. Birds fought over crumbs. The guys prepared the swan boats for the day.

A man adjusting his sneakers across the way peered at her with unguarded curiosity.

That was because of the chubby police officer leaning over her. Celia squinted up at his graying moustache and crinkly blue eyes. She could see every line, every crease in his middle-aged face.

"Miss?" he said. "You need to move it along."

The Garden seemed different in the early morning light. Everything was sharper and the trees impossibly green. The two swans—nicknamed Romeo and Juliet, though they were both boys—paddling alongside the ducks in the pond were the whitest things she'd ever seen.

When her gaze landed on the bridge a few feet away, the events of last night came rushing back. Her breath caught in her throat.

"Miss?" the officer asked, cautiously now that she looked so frightened. "What is it?"

Celia shot up from the bench, her eyes darting all around

her. Logic told her that the vampire wasn't nearby now that the sun was rising. Even so, she could feel his hands on her, she could see his horny smile. The bastard hadn't enthralled her because he wanted her to remember him.

She took a step away from the officer, and then ran flat out in the opposite direction. She easily outran everyone she passed, making them do double takes in wonder. She didn't stop until she made it to her car.

Taco, the stout owner of Taco's Tacos, the Mexican restaurant next door to Cage's, was climbing out of his blue Ford pickup when Celia raced through the lot. He waved with a genial smile because, though he didn't know their names, he recognized many of Cage's employees since he allowed them to park in his lot. His bushy eyebrows pulled together, though, when he saw she was in a panic.

"Ma'am?" he called through his thick accent. "You okay?"

She didn't answer, didn't even stop until she skidded to her door. That's when she realized she didn't have her keys. She had nothing on her since she had just up and left work. Celia stared at the window. Her reflection gazed back with no solutions. Tears prickled her eyes. She pressed the pads of her palms to her forehead as she tried to figure out her next move.

Ignoring Taco's expression of concern, she rushed around the back of Cage's. At the foot of the alley, the loading dock jutted out toward the street. The doors were closed but the overhead light was still on. She hurried up the stairs and leaned on the doorbell, praying someone was inside. She twisted the knobs. The double doors were locked. She rang the bell again. She was too preoccupied to realize that she could probably knock the doors down if she was so inclined.

A minute passed before the locks turned. The left door swung open and a man jumped out, wielding a bat. He was thin, light-skinned, with short, dark hair. Grease and bleach stained his green t-shirt.

His hostility melted into surprise when he recognized Celia and, oh, was she a sight: ashen brown skin; eyes wide and terrified; smudged makeup; ruffled hair and clothes. She had blow-dried her normally curly hair for the night. It was wild around her neck and shoulders.

"Miss Celia?" He lowered the bat.

He was Cesar, a member of the cleaning crew. Sometimes, if they weren't around when the lounge closed, the cleaning crew came in at the ass-crack of dawn to make the place sparkly for the next business day. They needed to make sure everything was in order by eight. That's when whoever was opening the restaurant came in—Bobby, Rick, or head chef, Silvio. Bobby was flexible with their schedule because they got the job done efficiently.

Celia tried not to cry but it was such a relief to see him. She wanted to throw her arms around him in a tight hug.

"I forgot my purse," she stammered. "Is it okay if I come in?"

He nodded, though he looked uncertain. After a small pause, he stepped aside for her. She passed the supply closet and pantry and went to the kitchen. The smell of bleach burned her nose. Bruna was there, sweeping under the stoves. She glanced up when Celia entered.

Celia wanted to give her some kind of recognition, a smile or a wave, but just couldn't manage. Bruna looked to Cesar for explanation. Celia heard them talking in Portuguese after she pushed through the swinging door.

She found her purse in her locker and sighed in relief. She hastened back the way she came, not bothering to say goodbye. The parking lot was empty of people. She climbed into her car. The clock on her dashboard told her it was quarter to seven. She started the car and sped off.

She was gripping the wheel and leaning forward, her eyes flitting around frantically. Her heart was doing that slow thumping thing it did the last time she'd ingested vampire blood. If it weren't for the blood, she was sure her heart would be pounding against her rib cage.

When her phone rang suddenly, Celia shrieked. She fumbled in her purse until her fingers grasped the black phone. A picture of her best friend sticking her tongue out flashed on the display.

The tears that had been stinging her eyes pooled and spilled at the sight of her name. "Trixie?"

"Seal!" she cried into her ear. "What happened to you?"

"It was Milo!" she blurted in a jumble. "He made me leave and made me kiss him and . . . and . . ." She broke off then as sobs racked her body. She was getting tears and drool on her phone, while gasping for air in an attempt to control herself.

"Oh, God, Seal." Trixie's voice was shaky, like she was going to cry, too. "Where are you?"

Celia looked around. She couldn't see anything through her tears, even with her heightened vision.

"I—I don't know. I'm going home."

"Okay, I'll be there as soon as I can."

Celia nodded and let the phone drop to her lap. A car beeped behind her because the light had changed to green. She swiped her hands across her eyes, smearing mascara on her cheeks, and drove on.

When she made it to Washington Street, a main road in Dorchester, a wave of relief had her eyes welling up again. She stopped at the first spot she found. It took five tries for her to park and, in the end, she was crying again in frustration.

Inside, she locked the door and sank into her sofa. An hour later, the buzzer went off. It sounded once, followed by three bursts. Celia sprang up from where she had fallen over. She wiped the sleep from her eyes as she crossed to the intercom.

She pressed the release button for Trixie. She then unlocked the door and stood back. From the stiffness of her spine, you'd think she was waiting for certain death to come through her door. She might've welcomed it if it meant no longer feeling terrified. But it was only Trixie, her ice-blue eyes red around the edges, her cheeks flushed from crying.

"Oh, Seal," she said. Her thick, black hair trailed behind her as she ran to Celia. They held each other for a long while, weeping into each other's shoulders. Trixie finally coaxed Celia to the sofa then rushed to the kitchen to make her a cup of chamomile tea. She handed her the steaming mug and a wet paper towel.

Celia used the paper towel to wipe her face. When she pulled it away, streaks of black and brown were captured on the cloth. She sipped the tea while rocking back and forth.

Trixie, not knowing what to do in this kind of situation, stroked her hair. They couldn't tell the police because of the culprit. Trixie would've asked for more details but seemed to fear she would upset Celia further. So, she sat in silence beside her as the time ticked by.

"What were you doing up so early?" Celia asked after a while. Her voice cracked as it had been some time since she'd spoken.

"I was getting ready for work. You had left so suddenly and Joni said you seemed kind of out of it."

Celia gasped suddenly. "Oh, fuck, how did you get home?" she cried.

Trixie waved her hand. "How can you concern yourself with that?" She looked at her closer. "How are you feeling?"

Celia's eyes dropped. "Like shit."

"Should I call someone? Victor?"

"No, he'll be here at sunset." Victor, Celia's boyfriend, had been making it a habit now to come to Celia as soon as he woke for the night, to make sure she was safe.

"Your aunt, maybe?"

Celia shook her head. "I can't tell anyone because they wouldn't be able to do anything."

Trixie's eyes watered. "How about Jay? He would."

Celia stiffened. She shook her head so vigorously that she might've given herself whiplash.

"No! I don't want him to know."

"But, he could help—"

"No!"

Celia rushed to the bathroom, slamming the door behind her. She stayed in the bathroom after her shower, no matter how much Trixie pleaded through the door. Her kimono robe had been hanging from the hook on the door. She paced the small room, hugging herself around the stomach. Her clothes had been shoved deep down into the hamper. She didn't want them on her skin anymore.

The water and heat made her hair go curly again. She found an elastic band in one of the cabinets and pulled it up into a ponytail. She avoided looking in the mirror, which was considerably easier compared with repressing the memories of last night. Though the touches and smells hadn't registered while under his trance, Celia could feel them now.

His hands had been all over her body. Her hands were on his. His blood had been warm in her mouth.

A wave of nausea rocked her to her core and she dropped to her knees in front of the toilet, where she retched and retched. Nothing came out. She was crying again because the dry-heaving was painful. When she finished, she leaned over the toilet seat, exhausted and miserable.

The buzzer sounded at nine-thirty. Celia's head popped up at the sound. She waited, not even daring to breathe.

"She's in there," she clearly heard Trixie say, thanks to the vampire blood.

The person didn't respond. The newcomer's boots tapped against the hardwood floor. They stopped in front of the bathroom door. The handle jiggled but she had locked it behind her. There was a knock.

"Celia?"

She closed her eyes, her anger rising at the tremor of his voice. She had specifically told Trixie she didn't want Jay to know but she had gone ahead and called him anyway. She didn't want Jay to see her like this, broken and in pain. Trixie was supposed to be her friend. Friends didn't go behind your back and do things you didn't want.

Celia's fury made her jump to her feet so fast, her head spun with dizziness. She swung the door open, ready to fight—and accidentally yanked the doorknob off. The other half clattered to the floor.

Jay was there in wrinkled jeans and a ringer tee. His golden-brown beard was coming in strong; his hair was disheveled. He must've thrown on the first things his hands touched. He looked fully awake though. There was nothing like an early morning trauma to serve as a caffeine boost.

When she saw the mixture of concern, relief that she still had all her limbs and, not to mention, fear in Jay's emerald green eyes, her anger deflated like a balloon. She looked away from his intense gaze and pushed past him. Trixie was standing by the sofa, wringing her hands as she watched Celia.

In the kitchen, the water was still hot in the kettle. She needed something strong. She dropped the doorknob on the counter then headed to the freezer. A bottle of vodka was tucked beside her frozen veggies. Screwdriver it was, even though she hated them. Orange juice and vodka was all she had. She forced herself to gulp the drink down, and then made another.

Jay stood at the threshold of the kitchen. "What happened?" he asked as gently as he could manage.

Celia drank some more, wishing the vodka would make her numb already. She heard Jay approaching carefully. That was different. She was so used to just suddenly feeling Victor's arms around her.

Not wanting him so close, she took a step away, shielding her face and tightening her robe. It was irrational, she knew. Jay was a good guy who had protected her more than once in the past. The vampire he tracked to Boston had found Celia and Trixie one drunken night and he had been there to save them. He'd also helped her against Milo and Clarice.

He wasn't going to hurt her. There was only one person to blame for her condition and he was hidden away somewhere for the day.

Jay placed a hand on her shoulder. When she didn't shrug it off, he slowly slid it along her back so that his arm was around her. She turned into him, burying her face into his chest. His fabric softener was a nice airy scent. It was probably called "Babbling Brook" or something of that nature. Jay squeezed her tightly. She couldn't return the embrace but it was comforting in his arms, so safe and strong and warm.

"What happened?" he asked again. She recounted the story and he listened, though she was sure her voice was muffled. When she finished, he was trembling in rage.

"I'll kill 'im," he growled.

She stepped away to pick up her drink. "Someone better."

"Seal, I'm so sorry," Trixie said. She had come to the kitchen when Celia was talking and now she hurried forward to wrap her arms around her. She kissed her temple, rubbed her back.

Jay's fingers suddenly grazed the left side of Celia's neck, which made her frown and quiver at the same time. She looked at him quizzically.

He glared at her neck like he had been personally offended. She touched where he had. Her fingers brushed the two puncture wounds. In response, her heart rate picked up to a normal pace. If her memories hadn't been sufficient evidence of her trauma, here were two big slaps in the neck.

Trixie looked like she was going to cry again. Jay's lips were pursed together, his fists balled at his sides.

Celia finished her glass. She took her hair down, feeling too exposed. She didn't want the pity anymore. Milo had made a fool of her. He had used her and humiliated her. She wasn't normally a violent person but nothing would please her more than Milo's head on a stake. She'd do it herself if she could.

She turned to Jay with unwavering eyes.

"If you find that son-of-a-bitch," she stated. "I wanna be there."

"When," he corrected, with just as much intensity.

They sat around her coffee table, Celia and Jay on the sofa, Trixie sitting Indian-style at her feet. No one spoke.

Celia's mood had shifted perceptibly. The alcohol seemed to be a factor. She was no longer panicked. Instead, fury curled her hands into tight fists. The change was so sudden that it couldn't be healthy.

Trixie made sandwiches at one. At four, she needed to get ready for work at Cage's.

"I hate to leave. You're not going in, right?" she asked. Celia shook her head in reply. "I'll make up something for Bobby."

Trixie hugged her again at the door. "Jay," Celia said over her shoulder. He was by her side at once, squeezing her arm. "Can you give Trixie a ride home?"

His gaze went to Trixie then back. He didn't want to leave her alone either. Well, that was too bad. She needed space.

"Oh, that's okay," Trixie said quickly. "I can take the bus."

"You won't have enough time."

Jay seemed to understand what she was doing. It didn't erase the tightness in his jaw. He nodded reluctantly. His beard was scratchy against her skin when he leaned down and kissed her forehead.

He headed out with Trixie. Celia closed and locked the door behind them. She shuffled to her bedroom to put some clothes on, again avoiding the mirror.

Jay called a half hour after leaving. She told him she was good. And she was fine for the rest of the afternoon, even when the vodka ran out. She went to the hardware store and repaired the broken doorknob. She made dinner, cleaned the kitchen, sorted her laundry. Her aunt allowed her use of their washer and dryer. She made a mental note to stop by this weekend. She'd been neglecting her family as of late but she wanted to change that. She wanted to start up their Sunday get-togethers of cake and coffee again.

She didn't want to admit that a tiny part of that decision was to find out about her grandmother. Nancy was her name. Besides the fact that she lived out in the western part of the state, Celia didn't know her. She hadn't even known she existed.

It was at six when her resolve to not be sniveling and afraid began to slip. The sun was already setting, as it was getting closer to autumn now, which meant longer nights. She didn't know when Milo rose. What if he decided he wanted another go? What if Victor didn't get there in time? And what if he couldn't stop her from leaving?

Her right hand went to the elastic around her left wrist. She didn't become aware that she was snapping it against her skin until she pulled the band back too far. It slapped her wrist so hard that she cried out.

The sun set at six forty-five. Victor arrived ten minutes later. He appeared in the middle of the living room with a smile and a dozen roses.

"Hey, baby," he said when he saw her sitting on the sofa.

She stood slowly. Yup, that resolution was pretty much kaput now. Her shoulders shook as a round of sobs overcame her. Victor dropped the flowers and scooped her into his arms.

"What's going on?"

She was crying too much to speak. He sat her back on the sofa, hugging her to his chest. Having nothing to do but wait, his nose told him things she couldn't say.

He smelled both Jay and Trixie. It was very strong, their scents imbued in her hair and skin. He detected her shower gel but any other scents weren't discernible. His jaw tensed when he wondered what the hell Jay was doing near her. There was no love lost between Victor and the Texan hunter. They'd both tried taking the other out last month. Victor wondered if Jay was the reason she was such a wreck.

He was contemplating where he'd seen him last because he had plans for him if he had hurt Celia, when he noticed her crying was slowing. She couldn't look at him as she told him what happened with Milo.

Victor stared at her in blank disbelief, though deep down he wasn't surprised. He'd come across plenty of vampires who used their powers to deceive and manipulate humans. That was part of what had drawn him to Boston. Ramsey wasn't into those games, and didn't allow it in his territory. All of the humans in his entourage were willing participants.

Victor had also known Milo for ten years, was there when he joined Ramsey's nest. Therefore, he had a good idea of what he was capable. Victor had never stated explicitly to the other vamps that Celia was his because of what that kind of declaration implied. Even so, Milo knew and should not have drunk from her. One of those vampire rules that, incidentally, he'd broken a few times—once during a fight and twice as a method to obtain information from Jay.

Breaking that rule usually incited a battle to the death. Victor hadn't had the chance with the hunters attacking them. Hearing this latest infraction would just make his death that much sweeter.

Celia noticed he wasn't breathing, plus his grip around her had tightened. She finally looked up into his eyes.

They melted from their normal gray to black in a matter of seconds.

"I'll kill him."

Celia leaned into him again, taking comfort in his words and his arms. His phone rang softly in his pocket. He reached to silence it.

Victor stroked her hair. "Celia," he started gently. "Take my blood."

She frowned. The after-effects of Milo's blood still cursed through her. They had lasted longer this time; probably because it wasn't the first time she'd had his. She was only just now experiencing that peculiar feeling of floating above the ground, when that had occurred almost immediately the first time. Next would be a tingling sensation under her skin, like something with tiny feet crawling beneath. It was an indicator the blood was making its way from her system and that took hours.

She looked up at him, brows furrowed.

"It will break the connection. He won't be able to call you again. I wanted to mention it to you earlier. I didn't know how to bring up the subject." He shook his head darkly. "I wish I had."

Celia hesitated. She didn't know the long-term effects of drinking vampire blood. She knew, however, she did not like this fear that had taken hold of her like it didn't want to let go. It made her sick being this way. Loving a good thrill was one thing. This latest . . . adventure was another level, another game.

She stopped snapping the elastic against her wrist and nodded her consent. Then she shifted on the seat and tilted her head, readying to show her neck. Before she did, she gave him a glare of mock reproach.

"Don't think this gives you hand," Celia declared.

Victor stared at her, not understanding the reference.

"Hand?"

She shook her head. She wasn't feeling the humor either.

"Never mind."

She pushed aside her hair to reveal her throat.

Big mistake.

She had completely forgotten. Victor snarled ferociously at the sight of Milo's bite, his face transforming into a hardened, feral mask. He shot up like a bullet. His fingers gripped the heavy coffee table and flipped it over, scattering magazines and mail and her scented candles. He then flitted to the corner and knocked her television to the floor. He kicked over her brown director's chair and threw her floor lamp to the ground, shattering the halogen bulb.

This all happened in the span of two seconds. Before Celia had time to fill her lungs to scream, the room was immersed in darkness. She gasped instead, staring at Victor in disbelief, her sharp eyes able to cut through the darkness. He stood in the corner, one hand on his hip, the other on his forehead. He was angry that she had been a victim, angrier that he hadn't been there to stop him. He was breathing heavily, trying to control himself. It took a full minute. Celia stayed on the sofa, out of the way.

He went to flip on the overhead light. The reason she preferred the lamp was the light in the living room was fluorescent and way too bright. She squinted because it hurt her eyes. Fluorescent lights in an apartment were like torture under any circumstance.

"Shit," Victor muttered when he saw her discomfort. He turned it off for the light of the kitchen that didn't completely reach the sofa. There was barely a moon tonight. The orange streetlights filtered into the room through the thin curtains, setting a strange contrast of orange and white across the living room.

Victor's phone rang again while he was in the kitchen. It was silenced mid-ring. He came back to the living room and sat beside her somberly. He was still upset but his determination was stronger. His face was blank. The angry beast had withdrawn.

After taking a deep breath, he reached out for her right hand. His cold palm pressed against hers. He turned her hand, facing her palm to the ceiling.

Slowly, gently, he brought her wrist to his mouth. His lips were soft against her skin. He paused for only a second before biting. A tiny whimper escaped her lips. His moans were soft though strained because he didn't want to enjoy this. Tonight was definitely not how he had pictured their first time. She felt his moans vibrating up her arm, tingling her sensitive nerves.

Celia told herself to relax. It really was better not to resist. Her lids drooped as she gave into the lovely pulling.

He was tugging her from the inside in a rhythmic motion. Her free hand combed through his hair and held on tight. Soon, she was shivering and shuddering like she was having a particularly powerful orgasm. Her breath escaped in ragged gasps.

Victor raised his head after laving her wrist. The marks would flush into a light pink and disappear after a minute or two. He sighed; he hadn't wanted to stop. When he faced her, she saw the color rise in his skin. His eyes lightened as well.

He was in ecstasy. He'd always wanted to taste her; he still remembered the little remnants from her neck that night after Milo's first attack. But when he had asked all those months ago, she had said no and he was forced to refrain. It took years for vampires to gain that kind of self-control, especially with feeding and sex always mingled and muddled together in their world. So, he was pretty much like a Zen master or something. Being allowed to sample her had opened a new door and he wished it didn't have to end. Especially with how sweet her blood was—like pure vanilla. He'd never tasted a human so rich. Just a few drags would've maintained him the entire night, he was certain. Except, if he hadn't stopped, he'd have lost his honey. That's when the Zen master who had allowed him to live amongst humans for a hundred years came into play.

Victor held out his left wrist. She watched as he used the sharp nail of his right index finger to make a horizontal slice along his wrist. The blood bubbled and dripped onto the floor. She'd been contemplating changing the rug, and now it appeared there was a definite need. First the love hole he dug into the cream-colored shag carpet a few weeks ago, and now blood.

She took hold of his arm, gave him one last look—a mixture of fear and conviction—before bringing it to her lips. She closed her eyes as his blood warmed the inside of her mouth. It coated her throat as it made its way to her stomach, filling her up like a medicine she hadn't realized she'd needed.

She noted a hint of tartness to his blood, like how lemonade could have that biting effect. Sweet and sour, bonded together.

Victor was moaning again. His manly grunts, the air seeping from him in slow exhalations were sounds she was not used to hearing. See, her boyfriend was not one for verbal affirmations during lovemaking. He'd been trying lately though, of which she was grateful, but it always seemed artificial. The sighs escaping now were very much authentic and she was the cause. She trembled in happiness.

Ugh, maybe it was all the vampire blood.

Two minutes passed and she was still sucking away. Vampire blood was like the finest nectar, and she wondered briefly if it tasted differently to other people.

It appeared Celia was not going to let go. Victor had to place a hand on her shoulder, and when she still dragged from him, he gently shoved her back.

Her breathing was erratic and her head spun. She leaned

back into the fluffy cushions of the sofa. Her finger traced the corners of her lips, catching the lingering droplets and sucking every bit into her mouth. Her eyes closed while she waited for the calm. It didn't come. Instead, she was wired and tingly all over.

After a few deep breaths, her head cleared. Sharp shivers branched from her lower abdomen, igniting between her thighs. She squeezed her knees together as the flood started.

She peeked over to Victor. His head was bent forward, watching the wound on his wrist slowly mend itself. Celia clutched his hair, though she hadn't intended to be so rough. He looked at her, observed the lust in her face, saw her bite her lower lip. She leaned over and kissed him passionately. A trace of her blood lingered on his tongue. She didn't get the big deal; it tasted metallic to her. She shoved him onto his back with enough force to make him grunt.

Celia was on top of him, grinding her hips between his legs. She didn't bother removing her clothes; her shorts were baggy enough to move aside. She straddled his lap, opened his pants. She took hold of him, stroking until he was ready while laying warm kisses down his neck. As always, she fit around him like a warm glove. Her hips twisted in quick circles. He clasped her waist but she had control.

She teased him, lifting and squeezing until just the head of him remained inside her. She held there, her stomach muscles contracting. Victor's fingers insisted she stopped fucking with him.

"Celia," he groaned. A smirk crossed her face. She let her hips meet his.

She kissed him, not caring that his fangs were out, even when she cut her tongue on one. He took care of that with a little suckling. She flicked the tip of her tongue against his. Her quivering breath was on his face. She felt his soft hands on her neck, massaging the muscles and veins. Then he bit and her breath stuck in her chest.

Fireworks exploded inside of her, in her head and her groin. They sparkled and flamed in a good kind of burning, converging in the pit of her stomach and she was floating on the ceiling. Only Victor's strong arms kept her from drifting out the room, up into the night sky with the stars and the round, full moon.

Celia buried her face in his chest. She didn't know what to do. Whenever she moved, the burning stirred up again, making her breath come in quick gasps. She'd have to wait it out, not that it was unpleasant.

What a new experience. She wondered why he had never told her that would happen if she let him drink from her. She had been denying him the entire time they'd been together—about ten months now; though only during eight of those did Celia know what Victor was. He had explained that sharing blood with a vampire could be addictive for the human. Now she understood why.

Victor could get addicted to this, too.

Celia fell asleep in his arms. At three-thirty, she was rustled awake. She looked around to see what was different.

Victor was trying to disentangle his hand from her hold. He must've realized she was awake.

"I'm just going out for a bit," he whispered to the back of her head.

"No," she said quickly and tightened her grip on him. The vampire blood meant he'd have to use full force to get away and he wasn't going to do that. She knew it and he knew it. So he relaxed behind her and she drifted off again.

Two

AFTER DROPPING TRIXIE off at the apartment she shared with her sister in Hyde Park, Jay called Celia to check in. He hadn't seen her in almost two weeks, when Victor had thrown him out of that car. They were all three together because Victor had kidnapped Jay to find out the location of the other hunters. They had just set fire to Ramsey's mansion. All of the vamps were furious. Victor's plans had gone awry after Milo and Clarice showed up with their own hostage: Celia.

Jay had surveyed her for a long time in the kitchen, the realization of how much he missed her hitting him in the gut.

She said she was fine, so he let her be. It wouldn't be long before sunset and her vampire boyfriend came out. He did not want to be around.

He still couldn't wrap his brain around why she'd chosen a vampire; it had even kept him up at night. He tried to convince her to stick with the living, but she was a grown-up who made her own decisions, whether he liked them or not.

Jay went to Snipe's house in Southie. Snipe was the leader of the local hunters. Two weeks ago, they made a truce with the vampires not to hunt them as long as no more suspicious deaths occurred. Correction: a truce with the vampires who were still part of Ramsey's nest. Three of them had broken away, not wanting to deal with lowly humans. You met Milo.

There were only three hunters left.

Jay pulled his trusty Mustang to the curb in front of the white house. It was a '67 G, all black, two squeaky doors, leather interior, shiny rims, rumbly engine and a transmission that would sometimes stick. He loved his baby.

Lauren, Snipe's lovely wife, was in the driveway, unbuckling the two little girls in the backseat of their blue minivan. They jumped down to the pavement wearing matching white sundresses and fuchsia cardigans. Their black curls bounced at their shoulders. The youngest one, Jessa, was the first to spot Jay. She pointed and stared, not cracking even the teensiest of smiles. Morgan looked around to see what had captured her sister's attention.

"Jay!" she called, beaming. She ran to him and leapt into his arms.

"Hey, beautiful."

Jay immediately tucked away all the concerns and worries he had to smile at the precocious little girl in his arms. Being a hunter was a hard existence. Always out, searching and fighting until the break of dawn. Jay envied Snipe's life, with his home and family and minivan.

Well, maybe not the minivan. He was too cool for that shit.

Jay crossed the yard to deposit Morgan at her mother's feet. He greeted Lauren with a chaste kiss on the cheek before taking the bags from her arms. Notebooks, boxes of pencils, and a pink pencil holder among other supplies peeked out from the top of one of the brown shopping bags.

"Is it school time already?" he asked.

Lauren sighed wistfully. "Yeah. I was lucky to find these things. We only just received the supply list from her teacher." She rubbed the top of Morgan's head. "My little girl."

Morgan rolled her eyes. "It's okay, Mommy," she replied formally, sounding older than her six years of age. "You'll be fine."

Lauren gave Jay a forlorn smile that showed just how proud she was of her little girl.

Jay followed behind them up the stairs to the house. Lauren pushed the door open to a bedlam of yelling.

Snipe stood in front of the television, his arms crossed tightly at his chest. He was a tall man with olive skin only marred by the identical scars across his nose and the other along his jaw, interrupting his beard. His shoulder-length black hair was swept back into a ponytail at the nape of his neck.

He was staring at a woman, who was medium height, with reddish blonde hair and a face littered with freckles. She had the same green eyes as the glum boy sitting on the sofa.

Colin wore a black sling on his right arm. A newbie vamp named Trent had dislocated his shoulder. The hunters were trying to put a tracker on him to discover the location of Ramsey's nest. The task hadn't gone as planned.

You couldn't see them, but Colin was also sporting stitches holding together the four gashes on his back, courtesy of another vampire named Annie. That happened when the hunters firebombed the Milton mansion.

He hadn't been able to patrol with the others because of his injuries. Apparently he'd been holed up at Snipe's. His mom stopped by on a whim to find him in a sling and, you best believe, she was pissed.

"Why didn't you tell me he was hurt?" the woman cried. She

pointed to Colin. "Look at him! He's a mess!"

Snipe licked his lips slowly. "Colin had assured me he told you." He threw Colin a harsh look. Colin cringed.

Lauren ushered the girls, who had been staring wide-eyed at the woman, out of the room. Jay placed the bags he'd been carrying on the table in the kitchen, then stood to the side. Colin's mom shook her head vigorously, grasping her hair in her hands.

"You're the adult! You should've called me!"

Snipe nodded. "You're right," he sighed. "I apologize, Linda."

She glared at him some more. "It's real easy to apologize later, isn't it?" she snapped.

"Ma, come on," Colin piped. "Don't yell at him."

"You hush," she cut across him. She turned her fiery green eyes on her son. "You sure as hell should've told me."

Jay frowned at this back and forth. He wondered if Colin's mom knew what he did for Snipe.

"It's nothing," Colin said. "It was just dislocated. No more basketball for me for a while. Lauren's set me up with the physical therapist. I'll be fine in a couple of weeks."

"You are not fine!"

She was getting frantic now, at how they were making his condition out to be no big deal. He was her baby, after all. Tears welled in her eyes as she surveyed him for the tenth time.

"Colin!"

She slapped her hands against her face and shook her head, truly distraught.

Colin struggled out of the seat and stood in front of his mom. "Ma, I'm not a kid. I'll be twenty-one next month for God's sake."

"Don't take His name in vain," she warned, pointing a finger up at him. "You know I don't like that."

He rolled his eyes. "Look, I'm sorry for not telling you sooner."

"And for hiding out here and making me into a basket case?"

"Yes, yes, for all of that too."

She paused a second, her bottom lip trembling. Having nothing more to complain about, she lunged at him and threw her arms around his waist. Colin barely contained a yelp of pain. Jay chuckled to himself; he couldn't help it.

It took another five minutes of convincing and hugging to get Linda to leave. Colin banged his head on the closed door a few times. He must've felt the heat of Snipe's glare because he faced the room reluctantly.

Snipe didn't have to open his mouth. "I know, I know," Colin said, raising his good hand. "It won't happen again, I swear."

Snipe turned and bounded to the hallway that led to the rest of the house. Colin heaved a sigh before giving Jay an apologetic look since he had to witness that display.

"Mothers," Jay replied with a snort. Colin chuckled.

Jay made his way over to Snipe's brown Barcalounger. He was just reaching for the remote to turn on the television when a little hand snatched it up first. He was about to protest when he saw it was Jessa who had claimed control.

He stared at her a moment and she stared right back, challenging him to say something. He sighed, giving up, and slouched into the chair. She was the only entity that seemed to always make him feel defeated. No matter the beatings or injuries sustained from fighting vamps and other things, this little girl had him under her tiny thumb.

Jessa turned the channel to SpongeBob. She did it purposely, just to annoy him. He was sure of it.

No matter. It would be dark out soon. He had plans to search for Milo and his friends. Downtown seemed to be the best place to start since the vamps tended to partake of the clubs there. He really hoped he'd come across Milo. He'd make him pay for what he'd done to Celia, if it was the last thing he did.

***

Celia woke up the next morning at eight. She was alone on the sofa, of course. From her angle, she saw that Victor had righted the coffee table and all of its contents, the director's chair and the lamp. The ruined television and broken bulb were gone.

She sat up and rubbed her head. She took a moment to assess herself. The floating remained, and that was about all she was feeling. She looked at her hands, splayed her fingers out. Turning them over, she saw that Victor's marks were gone. She touched her neck. There were no bumps she could feel.

She glanced around, trying to figure out what to do next. She noticed that Victor had moved the sofa forward to cover the bloodstain. Since the TV was gone, she didn't know how to occupy her time. She knew that if she stayed in the house, she'd go nuts. Even now, after sitting up for a few minutes, even through the effects of the blood, fear whispered in the back of her brain. Her eyes drifted to the kitchen. She was out of vodka but there was beer. Maybe just a sip . . .

As she stood to go to the kitchen, her gaze landed on her purse peeking around the sofa. A better idea came to mind. She bent over and rifled through it until she found her cellphone. The battery was low but she called Bobby anyway.

"Hello, Cage's," he answered.

"Bobby it's me, Celia."

"Celia!" he cried, and he didn't sound annoyed in the least. His relief threw her for a loop. "Trixie told me you had a family emergency. Is everything okay now?"

"Um, yes," she said to keep it vague. "Thank you for asking."

"Do you need tonight off as well? I can find Lynn—"

"No, that's why I was calling. I was wondering if I could come in today as well."

"A double?"

He didn't like to overstaff; she knew this. However, she needed to do something with herself. Plus, she'd missed a busy

Friday shift and wanted to make up the lost tips.

"If that's alright," she added gently.

"Of course," Bobby said finally. "I'll see you in a few."

He was probably feeling sorry for her. She didn't care at the moment however she knew it would bother her later. She didn't need or want anyone's pity.

Celia hung up then hurried to shower. She pulled on black slacks and a black quarter-length shirt with a V-neck. She tossed black shorts and a tank top into a shoulder bag, in case she decided to change for the night shift. Running around behind the bar usually made you work up a sweat.

Outside, she took a deep breath of fresh air and closed her eyes. The air was crisp but the sun was warm and glorious on her skin. She stood on the stoop for a moment only because she knew Milo was nowhere near.

Trixie was surprised to see her come through the door. Celia gave her a tiny smile on her way to Bobby's office to stow her purse in a locker. When she returned, the morning meeting was already underway.

The four servers, a guy Celia didn't know, and Trixie, who was playing hostess today, stood around one of the smaller round tables, near the hallway to the kitchen. Four dishes sat on the table filled with steaming food. Head chef Silvio stood by in his white coat while Bobby explained the specials. He was the same height as Bobby, only leaner and Brazilian. His expression was usually stern, as if he always expected you to ask him something stupid.

Bobby pointed to the last two dishes. "This is the chicken scaloppini and this is the Caprese salad. Maria, what's on the scaloppini?"

Celia slid in beside Trixie, who squeezed her hand.

"Butter, lemon and capers," Maria answered proudly in her Colombian accent. She was one of the older servers, with a husband and family to feed. There were only three "older" ones; the rest were mainly college-age. "It also comes in veal."

He nodded as he looked at his watch. "Okay, doors open in ten. Check your stations and tables."

He cut a piece of the chicken and headed off to his office. The rest of the servers dug in. Celia wasn't hungry so she went to the hostess stand to see where she had been assigned.

A clear, plastic panel covered the top of the podium. A copy of the floor plan was underneath, with the tables labeled by numbers. Bobby, or sometimes one of the more senior servers if Bobby wasn't there for the opening shift, would use a dry-erase marker to divide the restaurant into sections. As patrons came in, the hostesses marked the tables.

Her finger hovered over the floor plan until she came across her name. She had the section in the back, near the restrooms and payphones. It wasn't as bad as it sounded. There was a hallway that separated the restrooms from the rest of the floor, which created an alcove of booths and tables to the side. That was actually one of the most requested sections since it provided privacy.

Bobby must've been feeling really bad for her.

Trixie came up behind her. "Are you okay?"

Celia shrugged. "I guess so."

Trixie rubbed her shoulder. Celia gave her a tight smile before heading off to fold napkins. It was a tedious, boring task but she would take anything to get away from the pity. She stopped at the bar to apologize to Joni for taking off so abruptly. Joni gave her a wary look as she dried glasses, like she was hoping Celia wouldn't get too close. Celia hurried to the kitchen. She hoped her hurt feelings didn't show. Let Joni get enthralled by a heartless vampire and see how much fucking control she has over the situation.

In the kitchen, Celia pulled down a stack of white napkins

and made a space next to Maria at the silver prep table to begin folding.

The unknown guy from the meeting strolled over with his hands in his pockets. He was about six-two, probably Celia's age, with his hair cut close and skin the color of caramel. His arms and shoulders rippled with hard muscles under his black dress shirt. He smiled at them as he approached. A single dent appeared in his left cheek when he spoke.

"Need me to do anything?" he asked Maria.

"We normally fold napkins whenever there is free time. You can make sure everything is all set at our tables. You know, salt and pepper. Make sure the flowers aren't wilting."

He nodded. His hazel eyes shifted to Celia. Maria slapped her forehead.

"Sorry! Celia, this is Michael. He just started yesterday."

Celia looked up at him and tried to smile. He reached out. She shook his hand. As soon as their skin touched, Michael stiffened. He jerked his hand away as if he'd been shocked, though she could've done that herself. It felt like he'd had his hand on a hotplate. She frowned at him, bemused.

"I, uh," he stammered. "I'm gonna check on the tables."

He hurried for the door so fast he almost mowed down Silvio entering the kitchen with the empty dishes. Silvio muttered crossly in Portuguese and continued to the sink.

Celia and Maria exchanged puzzled glances.

"That was strange," Maria said as she picked up another napkin.

That was strange, Celia mused.

***

Victor went to Ramsey's as soon as he fed. Celia hadn't been home; she was obviously his first choice. He also didn't want to pressure her. She had been in an altered state of mind last night. He wasn't sure she'd want to do it again.

There was something different tonight. He was used to sensing the humans he had drunk from—what they were thinking or feeling. It was part of the package. The time in which the connection with that human faded varied based on how much he had taken and how often.

With the intake of blood, his skin was warm to the touch. Vampires didn't necessarily experience coldness when they hadn't fed, even though their skin was like ice. To them, they were just incredibly thirsty and numb. Blood soothed both their hunger and their numbness. The side effects included warm skin.

When he rose tonight, he could feel his fingertips and toes. It was strange because he didn't normally have those sensations until after he had fed.

When Victor arrived at Ramsey's home in Brookline, he found only Elizabeth. She was packing in the living room when Victor appeared behind her. Her wavy hair was tucked behind her ears as she leaned over a brown box, arranging her medical supplies.

"Hey, Victor," she replied without looking up. "Ramsey's in Milton."

He frowned. "Why?"

"Ramsey's young friend has agreed to fix the house." She shook her head. "I hope it works. I don't like it here."

Victor looked around at the homey living room, the buttery leather sofas, and the mantel laden with pictures of the human family that lived there. Ramsey had been renting it to them but when the hunters had desecrated the white mansion in Milton, he moved his nest to the smaller home. Victor didn't know what he said to make them leave, and there appeared to be some connection between Ramsey and the woman of the house. These were all things he couldn't bring himself to ask. He didn't want to overstep their boundaries.

Victor teleported to Milton. The air was still tinged with the smell of burnt wood. The humans had tried to investigate. The mirage of an impenetrable forest kept them from trekking too closely. Otherwise, they would've crashed into the invisible structure, which would've caused even more confusion.

Ramsey was a thick man with sandy-brown hair and soft blue-green eyes. Bryce, the even thicker man with dark hair and brown eyes, stood beside him on the sidewalk with his arms crossed. They were staring down at a girl who looked to be eighteen.

She had short, blonde hair with streaks of bubble gum pink. She was dressed in light jeans with giant holes in the knees and a white hoodie. Her eyes were round like quarters and rimmed with heavy black eyeliner. Her nose was a tad on the large side, which stood out more on her thin face. She was very small and slight, like you could break her if you shook her hand too hard.

Victor approached carefully. He wasn't a member of Ramsey's nest. He didn't want to intrude, though Ramsey didn't mind in the least. The girl jerked her head to him. Her dark blue eyes narrowed suspiciously.

"We just need you to fix the house," Bryce said gruffly. "It's not like we're asking you to cure fucking world hunger."

She cut her eyes back to Bryce with all the hostility her little body could muster. "Well, since it's so easy, why don't you do it yourself?"

In her sudden fit of anger, the pink streaks of her hair darkened to a deep red.

Bryce groaned. "Why do you have to make everything a damn production?"

Ramsey held up his hand to silence him. He looked down at the girl. "Corinna. What's it you want?"

She glowered at him for a moment as she visibly contemplated. She eyed the house then faced Ramsey again.

"I'll do it for fifty thousand."

Bryce gaped at her. "When did you become a goddamn extortionist?"

"Oh please!" Corinna cried. "That's like pocket change to you vampires. Look," she huffed. "If you wanna keep your home a secret, it's gonna cost you. You know how this works."

Ramsey was quiet a moment. "Fifty thousand is reasonable."

A smug grin replaced the scowl on her face. You'd think a smile would soften her. Instead, her arrogance worked to distort her features even more.

"But," he added and her face froze. "If you don't want Sofia to know you're sleeping with her husband, I suggest you take your money and forget you've ever been to this street."

Her eyes widened in terrified surprise. Now it was Bryce who wore the smug grin.

She shook her head furiously. "You . . . you can't prove that."

"No?" Ramsey asked. "I don't have video? I'm sure Sofia would believe me without evidence. She's very suspicious and an extremely jealous woman, you know that."

Corinna gulped at the mention of her coven leader. It would not please Sofia to hear Corinna was using her magic without much regard. Sofia believed that witchcraft should only be used among witches, and definitely not for profit. If Ramsey spoke with her, Sofia would know right away he had solicited Corinna for her magic. Some form of punishment would be in order.

About two years ago, one witch had lost the ability to speak for a month because she had healed a cyclist who'd been in a hit-and-run accident. She was a more advanced witch. The ability to heal came with much practice and the exertion of a great deal of energy. Many said that one had to be born with the gift in order to master healing without causing harm to oneself.

That man would've died if it weren't for the witch. Even so, Sofia had been irate, especially when the man told his story to the local news station. She didn't want the publicity. Because he spoke, the witch was denied her voice.

Now that witch only had the intention of helping an injured man. In the heat of the moment, she hadn't thought of the repercussions of her action. You could imagine Sofia's wrath if she found out one of her witches was blatantly using magic for money. On top of that, she greatly detested vampires, even the charismatic ones like Ramsey.

In that instant, Corinna shrank a little, as if she wanted to run away. Her face took on a pallid nature and she didn't look at them. Fifty thousand was a lot of fucking money though. Her hesitation showed that she had just tossed that number out there. She probably hadn't expected Ramsey to actually agree. It was definitely the most she had ever demanded for her services.

"Fine," she grumbled. "Give me the drawings."

Bryce handed her five sheets of papers. On them were sketches his girlfriend, Annie, had constructed of the mini-mansion the way it used to be. She snatched them from him, and then stalked up the grass to the stone stairs.

Ramsey surveyed her a moment longer before acknowledging Victor. "We didn't see you last night," he commented. "Annie had a lead on Clarice but she was gone when we got there."

"Some shithole in Quincy, near the beach," Bryce added in disgust. "She had humans there. She wasn't taking care of them at all."

He shook his head. Indeed, the three humans—one male and two females—had been on their last legs. Dressed in tatters, laying in their own filth, they had hit rock bottom. When they saw the vampires, incredibly, they begged for them to drink from them. They were junkies to the fullest. Bryce wanted to take them out of their misery but Ramsey instructed him and Annie to bring them to the hospital.

"Milo assaulted Celia Thursday night," Victor said in a

hollow voice. "I was with her last night."

Bryce *tsked* in displeasure. Ramsey squeezed his shoulder. There wasn't much for them to say. They were already on the hunt for the renegade vamps; they'd help Victor find justice.

The air around them suddenly churned and vibrated as it took on a corporeal life of its own. They all looked to the house. Corinna had her hands up, her head bowed. She was chanting but the words streamed out too quickly to decipher. Her hands trembled as a golden haze began to surround the dilapidated structure. It glittered and glowed, flowing in and out of the house, repairing the foundation and the walls and the roof as if it were made of tiny hands and hammers.

After a minute, the haze dissipated and the house was whole again. The white pillars and ornate black door with its flowers and vines engraved in the wood were all intact.

"How come we didn't have those humans pay for this?" Bryce asked. His head was cocked to the side as he scanned the house.

"Don't worry about that," Ramsey replied lightly. He probably didn't want any more issues with the hunters than necessary. Dealing with Corinna was no biggie compared to a fight for money and responsibilities with humans who despised them.

"They could've killed Matt and Hunter, you know." He was speaking of two of Ramsey's groupies.

"I know," Ramsey replied simply, letting him know to drop it.

"Elizabeth will be glad to be back," Victor replied.

Ramsey sighed. "She didn't like that we were in Jennifer's house."

He didn't need to explain further once the name sparked a memory. Victor had heard Jennifer mentioned only once; fifteen years ago, when Victor first came to Boston.

Ramsey carefully spelled out the rules of staying in his territory. At the top of that list: the sanctity of human life. No one was to kill while feeding, nor turn any humans.

Victor interrupted to ask why that was so important to him. He had no intentions of doing either but Ramsey had been particularly passionate on those points.

Ramsey took a step closer to the water's edge. They were outside of Victor's cabin in Plymouth. He rented the place at first with only a temporary stay in mind. He would soon find the peaceful woods too accommodating to leave.

Ramsey stared at the pristine lake. The moon left a silver strip across the surface. A single duck bobbed on a wave.

"Thirty-five years ago, I killed a man. It was the first human death at my hands in almost two hundred years. I found out later he was a father."

Victor didn't understand. Ramsey continued with his back to him.

"A vampire named Nathan had control over this area for nearly a century. He arranged it in a caste system, with him at the top, a few select marshals under him to ensure his power, then everyone else who brought him money, jewels, anything of value. The regular vampires were divided into different groups based on their skills, wealth, and supernatural abilities. Of course, those with abilities were kept near, mostly as marshals. Nathan himself didn't have any powers, except his ability to find your greatest fear and exploit it.

"You had to seek his permission for everything. Moving, mating, who you shared blood with, human or otherwise. Those who took animal blood were condemned. Nathan was a purist. He believed our blood was sacred and meant only for specific types. If they tended to be blonde with blue eyes, he would say that was purely coincidence."

Ramsey sniffed with discord. "He had the Boston vampires under his boot heel. When I came here, there was plenty of unrest. But no one knew how to defeat Nathan. I was the only one to openly defy him. He'd heard of me. How I valued human life. How I lived among them for so long.

"After fighting him hand-to-hand, and almost dying since he let his marshals participate, he told me he would let me live, he would relinquish his throne, if I killed that father."

He looked down at his hands. "Of course it was a trick. I was only able to stake Nathan by catching him before he rose. I conquered him with the help of one marshal named Omari, and his human mate, Rashida. Nathan had been holding Rashida captive. Omari was an extremely powerful tracker and Nathan wanted to harvest his ability to find and kill his enemies.

"After my failed fight, Omari came to me. He knew where Nathan rested, being a tracker and all. I found a witch named Claudia, who gave me a potion that allowed me to stay awake during the day. She had been hesitant. She didn't like vampires and most definitely didn't want one around in the daytime. She was thinking of her family. I explained my cause and she finally relented.

"The potion didn't protect me from the sun. I burned badly. It was easy getting through his human guards, even with my wounds. Once I was inside, though, I had to contend with his slaves. He kept them in his quarters while he rested. You could tell the ones who'd been with him the longest. They were skin and bones, barely able to move.

"Rashida had been with him for five years so you could imagine the damage. She killed the stronger slaves who were trying to attack me for staking Nathan. They had underestimated her instinct to survive. I had too, in all honesty. She took her last breath in Omari's arms."

"He didn't want to bring her over?" Victor asked.

"No. He believed he was preserving her soul."

Victor didn't comment.

"Most of Nathan's underlings," Ramsey continued, "and the ones who didn't want to change, fled. The rest were staked. I had broken his system but I didn't want to lead. I had only been in Boston for six months. I didn't want the responsibility. There are currently three dozen vampires in this area. Back then there were upwards of a hundred.

"That first year, the vampires roamed freely. Without Nathan's tyrant constraints, they didn't know what to do with this newfound freedom. Many died—humans and vampires alike.

"I eventually took reign. I couldn't sit back any longer. I allowed the remaining vampires to stay, allowed them to live freely only if they followed these rules, the rules I have laid out for you."

He crossed his arms at the chest and repeated the rules. "No deaths, no turning humans, stay under the radar. When you join a nest, I must be informed. I must be informed of where you rest. I must be informed of any extended visitors. I must be told if you leave the area."

Victor was quiet for a moment. Instead of answering, he asked, "Why the change of heart?"

Ramsey glanced over his shoulder. The duck had tucked his head under his wing.

"Two months after I killed that father and Nathan was gone, I came across a girl. She was fifteen and angry. I found her getting high behind an elementary school. I knew who she was right off. She had the man's round nose, his small eyes, his same determined look.

"I'll always remember that look. How he almost dared me to kill him. To take him away from the misery Nathan subjected him to. I was wrong, though. He wasn't thinking about his own misery. *He thanked me, before he died. Thanked me because, like me, he thought Nathan would step down. He thought with Nathan gone his family would be safe. If he had to die, then that was the best reason to lose his life.*

"I was furious. There she was throwing away the very life he had given her. Nathan had a thing for killing families, one by one. As much as he enjoyed being a vampire king, he hated that he was taken from his mortal family. I held the girl, got her clean because of Elizabeth. Then I told her what really happened to her father. She cried a lot. She screamed and cursed us. Once she calmed, I vowed my protection for her and her family. She would always be safe.

"She spat on me, and then left. Our relationship—" He broke off with an ironic laugh. *"It was strained at best. Jennifer, her daughter, isn't as contemptuous as her mother was. She lives in her mother's house but insists on paying any bills. She despises me because her mother drilled it into her, but I think she understands. She's thinking of her children's wellbeing. Age does that."*

"Life does that," Victor chimed.

"Right." He faced Victor. "So, that's it. What do ya say?"

The vampires stayed back while Corinna collected herself. When she finished, she returned to the sidewalk at a much slower gait.

"There," she muttered. She shoved the drawings into Bryce's stomach. Though she looked drained, the hostility remained in her eyes.

"Let's take a trip," Ramsey replied. He motioned to his silver convertible parked in the cul-de-sac. The moonlight twinkled across the hood. She didn't budge. She stared at the car like it was a Venus flytrap and she had just sprouted wings.

"My accountant leaves at nine," he said casually.

That made her move. Ramsey opened the door for her. She pointed her large nose to the sky indignantly and plopped down in the seat. He drove out of the circle and down the road. Victor turned to Bryce.

"Any more leads?"

Bryce shook his head. "Nah. I told Annie she needed a break. She's with the Monte Carlos to practice her tracking skills. She's getting pretty good; she finds me every single time."

He was referring to the game they played, where Annie would wait at the house for a certain amount of time, and then find Bryce by following his trail. He liked to mess with her by making paths through smelly alleys, ninety-nine cent stores, and strip clubs.

"I might go to Faneuil Hall to relax a little. Wanna come?"

Victor considered it a moment. He finally declined, figuring he'd go visit Celia at work.

Bryce groaned. "Dammit. I miss Josiah."

He shook his head as he strolled over to a shiny all-black Chevy Camaro. The rims were black, with thin, yellow strips on the edges of the spokes.

Bryce got a new toy. You could almost smell the new car scent from the sidewalk. The engine revved, the bass rattled the roof, and he sped off. Victor glanced up once more at the restored house before vanishing.

**

Celia was very happy that she had decided to go to work. She was so busy that she didn't have time to think, which was just fine with her. The night crowd filled the place by eleven-thirty. Two bussers in black "Staff" shirts pushed their way through the mass, collecting empty glasses and bottles. Trixie and the two other dancers were in their cages, winding their hips to the dancehall beat. The men, even the women below them stared, captivated by their performance and amount of exposed skin. Celia, Carson, and Joni were behind the bar, trying not to run into each other while fielding drink orders.

At twelve-thirty, Joni called her name. Celia was preoccupied with mixing two Amaretto Sours; she only nodded in response.

"You haven't taken a break yet."

"Oh, that's okay. I'm fine."

Joni shook her head. "Take fifteen."

"But—"

She broke off when she saw the no-nonsense look on Joni's face. Celia had been prepared to work the entire night through. It appeared that wasn't going to happen.

She sighed, finished the order, and then left the bar for the quiet of the kitchen. Heading for the teapot, she stopped once she saw the leftover Spaghetti Bolognese on the counter. She hadn't eaten since lunch, when she had forced herself to down two bites of a grilled chicken and eggplant Panini at four. Her stomach lurched with hunger at the sight. She made a plate and ate it cold.

The kitchen door swung open just as she stuffed her mouth full of pasta. She stiffened when she saw Michael.

He had been smiling when he entered. Once he glimpsed Celia sitting at the table, red sauce on her lips, chewing like there was a fucking gun to her head, the smile slipped away. She tried to say hello to clear the air but her mouth was occupied. She couldn't even choke out a grunt.

Michael made a beeline to the pantry where he grabbed a stack of bar napkins. He hurried back the way he came before she swallowed.

She didn't understand his offense. She wondered if she had maybe said something. Except that couldn't be the case. She had only just met him earlier. And he seemed fine until he shook her hand.

She looked down at her palm in search of an answer. All she encountered were familiar lines and creases and a splotch of red sauce.

Not wanting to ponder on it any longer, Celia took a last bite of spaghetti, grabbed a bottle of water and headed back out to her station behind the bar. She was at the far end, where it curved. Victor sat up straighter when she returned. He smiled cautiously, his eyes roaming her for signs of distress.

"Hi," she said when she was closer. He reached across to caress her arm.

"How are you?" he called, though he didn't need to.

But there were people around; a few were watching them since an additional bartender had shown up and they were parched or, more likely, trying to get a female drunk.

"Good."

He was still studying her. She cocked her head to the side with a pointed look. "You're supposed to be able to tell, right? Don't I feel fine?"

He was quiet another moment. He finally sighed. "Not really, but I suppose it'll do."

She squeezed his hand then went back to work. He seemed amused watching Celia's exchanges with the customers. She easily circumvented the guys and the two women flirting with the cute bartender. At the end of the night, she retrieved her paycheck from Bobby and her split of the tips from Joni. She changed back into her pants and zipped her yellow hoodie. Trixie was waiting by the door with a huge grin. Her face was still flushed from the night's activities.

"You know my friend Lee from Verizon?" she asked in a giddy rush. Celia knew his name though she had never met Trixie's coworker. They sometimes grabbed drinks together when Trixie didn't have to work at Cage's. "He came by tonight. He bought me a drink and now he wants to grab something to eat. We're going to Victoria's Diner. Wanna come?"

Celia shook her head, even though she loved the twenty-four

hour diner's pancakes. "You have fun, though."

Trixie let out a cheerful squeal before bouncing out the door. Celia was amazed at her energy. She was usually dragging at the end of doubles. Working from nine in the morning until two-thirty the next morning, and then making time for Victor was draining. Of course, Victor was understanding and usually kept his hands to himself so she could sleep.

Tonight, she was fully awake thanks to Victor's blood. He waited for her outside. He was on his phone and hung up as soon as she came near him. He gave her a peck.

"Mm," he said when he pulled back. "You're happy."

She smiled. "Well, you're a good kisser." Victor kissed her again, took her hand and they headed toward the parking lot. As her car loomed ahead, Celia realized she didn't want to go inside, not just yet. Nighttime meant vampires but Victor was by her side. She had to take advantage.

"Let's walk a little."

Of course, there was more fun ways of making your thighs burn than fucking walking.

They walked for hours, looping through downtown Boston, even over the bridge into Cambridge at one point. They had walked so long that Victor had to remind her that the sun was going to rise in an hour.

"Sorry," she said sheepishly. "I guess I'm kinda wired."

"That's okay." He pulled her closer.

They were near City Hall now, in Government Center. The walk back to Cage's wasn't very long. Their reflections in the tall glass windows followed them past the Planet Fitness gym and Rebecca's Café.

They crossed at the intersection and continued down Washington Street—the downtown one. As they went by a quiet street, a strange noise made them both falter. It was soft but sounded like whimpering. Celia wouldn't have normally caught it; she did tonight. She glanced up at Victor. Of course he heard.

"Stay here," he said.

She kept her grip on his arm. She didn't want to be alone. He saw the panic in her eyes and immediately relented. She gingerly trailed behind him as he followed the sound.

The whimpers grew louder when they neared a green dumpster halfway down the alley. Many different smells that didn't mix well floated from the dumpster, churning Celia's stomach along with her nerves. Suddenly, she gasped.

A pair of legs stuck out beside the dumpster. Slender, women's legs with sexy black stiletto pumps. Celia and Victor stopped because she wasn't moving.

This was like the opening of *Law & Order*, Celia thought ruefully.

The woman's left leg twitched. A wounded groan followed. Okay, maybe *Special Victim's Unit*.

They rushed forward. The light wasn't too good at this part of the street. Even still, Celia could see that the woman was not doing well. Her face was crumpled in pain. Dried blood matted the dark hair around her temples. Celia couldn't help but cringe. The woman's face was swollen and misshapen. Normally, in her condition, she should've been covered with red and yellow bruises. Instead, her skin was deathly white. She had the appearance of being made of very absorptive marshmallows.

Ugly, pale slashes marred her cheeks and forehead. The same marks crossed her forearms and shins. Little wisps of white smoke puffed from the welts around her ankles and wrists, which were bleeding steadily. These were the only wounds that contained any color—a muted pink.

One of the straps of her purple mini-dress was broken, the hem ripped and frayed. She was also sporting lattice-like marks on her knees, like she'd been made to kneel on pavement.

Celia didn't know what to think. She'd never seen anything

like this before. Instinct had her searching in her shoulder bag for her cellphone.

"It's okay," she whispered to the woman as she fumbled with opening her phone. "I'm going to call nine-one-one."

Tears prickled the back of her eyes, but she forced herself to control them, which took substantial effort. Again she was battling her damn emotions. She was sick of it. So now, not only did she want to cry for this battered woman, she was also furious that she was about to cry. She needed a moment to calm herself. The woman, however, didn't appear to have moments to spare.

Celia had just pressed "9" on the keypad when the screen went black. Victor knocked the phone away, an unnecessary move since the battery was officially dead now. She frowned at him in confusion.

"You can't call the police."

"Why not?"

"Look for yourself."

Celia's eyes went to the woman.

Her head lolled from side to side. She opened her mouth slightly, like she was going to speak. In the little bit of illumination the streetlight offered, Celia saw white fangs pressing against her chapped bottom lip. The woman mumbled something she couldn't make out.

Celia turned to Victor again. His jaw was tense.

"What do we do then?" she asked.

He was pondering that. He took hold of the woman's bicep so as not to disturb the welts on her lower arm. When he grasped Celia's hand, she knew what was coming. Even so, there was no way to prepare for the ice-cold tidal wave that always knocked the wind from her when Victor teleported.

She closed her eyes to the street disappearing. When she felt whole again, her breath came out in painful coughs.

"Victor," a woman gasped.

A man's voice was next. "What's going on?"

Celia opened her eyes to the vampires scrambling around her. Her coughing subsided rather quickly, compared to the last few times Victor had teleported her. She was in the living room with the white furniture that could've easily doubled as a swanky lounge. Ramsey and Victor carried the injured woman out of the room. Elizabeth hurried behind them.

Two other people were sitting on a loveseat—a man and woman in their late twenties. She was wearing a flowery maxi dress and a cropped pink cardigan; he was in pressed pants and a nice shirt with shiny black shoes. They had watched the vamps go in silent shock, and now they were staring at Celia in curiosity. She couldn't find enough mental energy to figure out who they were and what they were doing there.

Celia cradled her head as she struggled to her feet. She followed the voices to a spare bedroom across the hall, the same room Victor had recuperated in not so long ago after a fight with two vamps. Those vamps had been hopped-up on a drug the hunters had brewed.

Elizabeth flitted around the room in her pretty sundress at an impossible speed. Celia's enhanced eyes could only barely keep up. Wielding a tongue depressor, the vampire doctor slathered some kind of ointment onto the woman's arms and legs. The odor from the mustard-colored stuff was strong and distinctive, like someone had watered a rosebush with gasoline.

Celia went to Victor, who stood off to the side with Ramsey.

"What's she doing?" she whispered.

"She's treating her wounds with a homeopathic ointment."

"Ramsey," Elizabeth said. "I need that blood in the basement."

Ramsey flashed from the room. He returned a minute later holding three plastic bags of crimson red blood, the kind they hang from IVs in the hospital. He opened one with no effort at all, though Celia was sure that plastic was meant to be impenetrable.

Elizabeth raised the woman's head and Ramsey held the bag to her lips. At first, she wouldn't open her mouth. Her oversized cheeks puffed out more as she pursed her lips together. She tried to turn her head away with a feeble groan. Elizabeth held her in place. Once the blood touched her lips, she accepted it with gusto.

Celia told herself it was only Kool-Aid. It was . . . only . . . Kool-Aid.

She finished all three bags then fell against Elizabeth's arm weakly. Elizabeth adjusted her head on the pillow. She then waved everyone out the room.

"I'm sorry to be so abrupt," she said, closing the door tightly behind her. She smiled warmly at Celia. "How are you?"

Celia tilted her head slightly. She was confused by the tenderness in her voice. "I'm . . . okay."

"Good. I know how traumatic something like this could be."

Celia directed her frown to Victor. "This is Elizabeth," he said evenly. "You've met her before."

His voice trailed off a bit at the end and Celia realized why she didn't remember. She managed to hold her burgeoning anger at bay at recalling when Victor erased her memory after the disastrous meeting in the Adams Street park last month.

"Oh, right," Elizabeth said softly. There was sorrow in her brown eyes. She turned to Victor. "The sun's going to rise in about twenty minutes."

Victor nodded. He took Celia's hand. The cold returned. They showed up in Celia's bedroom and she gasped for air.

"I'm sorry, babe," he said, kissing her cheek. Then he was gone.

She rushed to the kitchen for a glass of water, which helped to ease her breathing. She refilled the glass and headed to her room to crash for a few hours before she needed to be back at Cage's. Unfortunately, her car was downtown; she would need to leave earlier. She was debating whether it was even worth going to sleep when she halted in the living room.

Sitting in the corner where her old, standard tube television used to rest was a brand-spanking-new, fifty inch LCD HDTV. You'd think it would be too large for such a small apartment but it fit just fine. She stared at it in disbelief, like she was afraid it would vanish if she blinked. It was beautiful and, even better, already installed.

She made a mental note to properly thank Victor the next night as she trudged off to lie down for an hour.

Three

*A*FTER HER SHIFT at Cage's the next day, and after loading up her car with laundry, Celia went to her aunt and uncle's house in Lower Mills. She was exhausted but she hauled the canvas laundry bag up the stairs and let herself in.

"Hello?" she called. "Anybody home?"

Of course, the smell of curry chicken was plenty sign that someone was home.

"In the kitchen!" her aunt Meg called back.

Celia dragged the bag down the hall. She paused to gaze at the family pictures hung on the walls, especially the one that captured the mysterious twinkles in her mother's eye.

The washer and dryer were located in a pantry off the side of the kitchen. Her aunt was at the stove, stirring a wooden spoon in a deep pot. She wore a peach tunic, brown leggings, and brown sandals. Her honey-blonde hair was in a braid.

And sitting at the table, reading the paper was Winston,

Celia's older cousin. Celia's mom died of breast cancer when Celia was fifteen. As a result, she moved in with her aunt and uncle. Their oldest son Lyle had already started at New York University then. Winston was a senior at Boston Latin School, on the course to Columbia University.

Celia was used to her cousins visiting though usually during holidays and special occasions. Labor Day had already passed, so this was unexpected.

Winston smiled his toothy grin before crossing over to her. He was about five-ten with dark, wavy hair, a round nose, and marks on his forehead from scratching chickenpox when he was small. His gut had been expanding with time; an effect of Aunt Meg's cooking and relaxed workout regimens. Today, however, he looked very trim.

From his stance and smile, it appeared he was going to hug her. Instead, he wrapped an arm around Celia's neck and used his fist to ruffle her hair roughly.

"Ugh!" Celia cried, swatting him away. "You're such a jerk!"

"Now, Winston," Meg scolded playfully over her shoulder. "Be nice."

"How's it going, cuz?" Winston said. "You miss me?"

"Can't say that I have," she grumbled as she fixed her ponytail. She then continued her path to the washer. He didn't bother giving her a hand. She filled the washer with the first load before going over to kiss her aunt.

"Dinner will be ready in about fifteen minutes. Set the table?"

Celia pulled out the plates and glasses, working around Winston as she arranged the table. He stuck his foot out and tripped her when she went to gather silverware. She slapped the back of his head in retaliation.

Twenty minutes later, Celia, Winston, Meg, and Max sat around the table, dishing out curry chicken and rice and beans.

"Are you in a Jamaican mood tonight?" Celia asked. "Shall we put on the Bob Marley?"

"I say, *eh mon!*" Winston cried with a huge grin. Celia rolled her eyes at his atrocious accent.

"Listen, you two," Meg said suddenly. "I need you to be careful, especially when you're out late."

Winston snorted. "We're not five."

Celia frowned. "What's up, Auntie?"

"There have been some really strange deaths lately. A woman and her husband were found dead in their bedroom. The man was ravaged! Only he didn't have any blood in his body. Neither did the woman, but she was tucked nicely in the bed, like she was asleep. She didn't have any marks on her.

"And there was the woman found in Franklin Park, behind the golf club. She didn't have her blood either."

"How do you know all of this?" Celia asked.

"The news! And remember last week they just found this man in Milton—right, Max? Milton? He was in his shed and he'd been missing for over a week and his daughter finally went out to the backyard for some thing or another and they said it was the worst smell you have ever smelled! He'd been rotting away in there in the hot sun. His neighbors hadn't even noticed, could you imagine?"

Meg shuddered. Celia felt her frown deepen.

"I'd like to think that our neighbors would notice a nasty smell and call the police."

"I'm sure they would," Winston replied. "You don't have to worry about rotting in the hot sun."

Meg glared at him.

Winston chuckled. "Chill, Ma. It sounds like those are all really weird but really coincidental deaths."

"And the couple found in Dudley Square!" she went on. "They thought they were homeless so no one bothered them until the transit police came along to tell them to move and found they were dead! They had been coming home from the airport. It was the same: the man had all of the damage."

"Meg," Max interrupted. "We are already very vigilant. The kids know what to do to protect themselves."

"But Max, those couples—"

"Were the Dudley bums missing blood, too?" Winston asked and you could tell he was holding back his laugh.

"Well . . . no," she said, sounding unsure. "Not all of it anyway. And they weren't bums!"

"Then okay, it wasn't exactly the same. These things happen, Ma. It's the way of the world."

"How can you say that so dismissively? Those are horrible acts."

"Ah, who cares?"

Celia kicked Winston under the table. He jumped with a yelp. His knee hit the table, shaking up their drinks. "Stop being an asshole—"

"Celia!" Meg admonished. "Watch your language."

"Yeah," Winston said with a smirk. He was rubbing his shin. "Watch that filthy mouth."

She had to bite her tongue because what she wanted to say was most definitely unclean. "What are you doing here, anyway?" she snapped at him.

His goofy smile slipped a little. He swirled his fork in his curry. "I'm visiting," he replied. "I can't see my parents?"

She shrugged. "It's just unusual."

"Well, don't worry. I won't be in anyone's way."

She eyed him a moment. His smile had departed, his expression sobered. He was thinking about something, she could tell. She wondered if he was having troubles at work. Even though he acted like a twelve-year-old most of the time, he was serious about his nonprofit job.

Winston was an advocate for homeless teens, running a shelter in Brooklyn. There had been some cutbacks from the state—as most states experienced—and the nonprofits were hit the hardest. Winston would never just up and leave; his coworkers may have made him take a break.

Celia didn't ask. Now that she was sitting, sleep tugged at her insistently. She didn't think she'd get any rest, though. She was still in the floating stage, which was way too distracting to relax. She tried to listen to the conversation—something about Meg's begonias—but she just couldn't concentrate.

Irritatingly enough, her mind switched to Milo and his roaming hands and she thought she might be sick right there at the dinner table. Taking a deep breath that was loud enough for Winston to hear—he glanced her way when she sighed—she pushed the images away. That's what happened when she wasn't busy, when she wasn't distracted by other problems, like what went in a Grand Cadillac margarita or did that guy ask for lemon or lime with his Coke?

After dinner, she began folding the loads that were finished in the living room, content with doing something with her hands. The television was tuned into a CSI marathon. The team was investigating a gruesome murder in a hotel's walk-in fridge. That brought to mind Cage's walk-in fridge and made her shiver. She'd have to make sure the door never closed fully behind her. Or, better yet, send Carson in for supplies, just in case the door decided to stick.

While imagining Carson pounding on the door, she added a shirt to the swaying pile beside her. It was one shirt too many. The pile tumbled forward and onto the floor.

She muttered a curse, dropping down to scoop them up. As she was stacking the clothes back on the sofa, her eyes landed on a blue gym bag that rested on the floor. Her rolled-up black socks had found their way inside the crack of the unzipped bag. She picked up the socks and was going to go about her business when something shiny made her pause.

Brows furrowed, she slowly reached for the bag and pulled back the opening. A silver chain sat at the top, reflecting the light from the television. It was long, wound around a few times and tied off with a string. It looked like a simple chain used for necklaces, not unlike the gold chain around her neck holding the heart-shaped pendent from Victor.

She grasped the bundle and lifted it up. The chain had been resting on top of a dark towel and loose garbage bags. Now that she had a better view, she noticed little flecks of red twisting around the silver. Was that . . . blood?

"What the hell are you doing?"

He startled her so bad that she shot up to her feet, dropping the chain in the process. Her heart pounded in her chest as she stared at her cousin. Winston's eyes were narrowed and his lips pursed into a thin line. Frowning like that brought his chickenpox marks closer together on his forehead.

"I . . ." she started but couldn't find more words.

"Why are you going through my shit?"

She shook her head. "I didn't know it was your bag."

"So that gives you the right to go through it?"

He bounded toward her with such menace that she took a step back. He snatched up the bag from the floor and shoved the chain inside.

She pointed to the gym bag. "What . . . what is that?"

"None of your business," he muttered. He stormed out of the house. Celia stared after him while catching flies with her open mouth.

***

Victor went to Ramsey's at eight-thirty. His cellphone rang from his pocket. He peeked at the display. Knowing full well he needed to deal with that, he sighed regretfully and silenced it.

Ramsey and Elizabeth were in the spare bedroom. The female vamp lay unconscious on the bed. Elizabeth examined her ankles while Ramsey tossed the empty blood bags into a trashcan.

Elizabeth had removed the vamp's coat. With the addition of blood into her system, mean bruises had appeared on her skin. They were blue around the edges, royal purple in the centers.

"How did she do during the day?" Victor asked, coming up to the bed.

"These marks aren't as bad," Elizabeth reported. "We gave her more blood but it'll take time."

"She was drained, right?"

"Almost," she said grimly. Gently, she lifted her left leg to point out the deeper gashes along the interior ankle. The wound was gaping and the skin above it bright pink and threadbare. Whatever was used to bind her had been loose enough to chafe her skin. The good news was the wound was no longer bleeding. That, plus the bruises marring her body, meant she was in fact healing.

"If they had kept her a little longer, I don't think she would heal."

Victor shook his head angrily. "You don't think those hunters . . ." He trailed off because he knew it wasn't them. This wasn't their style.

Ramsey ran a hand over his hair with a deep sigh. "No, I don't think so."

"They used silver to bind her," Elizabeth said. She was wrapping a bandage around the left ankle. "There were traces in her wounds. They wanted the sun to find her."

"Do you have any idea who she is?"

"It's too hard to tell at the moment."

Indeed, her face was still swollen—with an added red bruise taking up residence on her left cheek—and she didn't have a wallet. Victor's eyes scanned her limp form, looking for any signs of identification. There were none. They had more than likely been removed by her assailants.

"I'm going to need blood," Elizabeth said after a moment. She glanced at her watch. "I have to be at work soon anyway. I'll pick some up."

Victor frowned. "Work?"

Elizabeth smiled warmly. "I'm on-call for Beth Israel. I'm covering for a doctor tonight in oncology."

Victor raised his eyebrows in surprise. She checked the woman's vitals one last time before leaving the room. He looked at Ramsey, who seemed preoccupied.

"She's working now, huh?" he asked lightly.

"Hmm?" Ramsey glanced up. "Oh, yeah. I suggested it. She was feeling restless."

Now that was surprising. The vampires seemed to always have money. Even though it kept boredom away, holding down jobs wasn't easy. Suspicions arose when after working for a company for twenty years you still looked twenty-five. The ones who worked usually moved a lot. Victor himself had held a few jobs, ranging from chef to night-class teacher. He taught Latin dance and Spanish. He knew Ramsey wouldn't want to leave Boston, so this newfound interest in the job industry was peculiar. Ramsey's savvy came in handy with Wall Street. Investments and stocks were easier to handle from afar and he kept his seethe supplied when they needed it.

Just then, Victor's cellphone vibrated in his pocket. He thought to ignore it. He knew he couldn't. Stepping into the hall, he finally answered.

"Courtney, you have to stop calling me so much."

"What's going on, Victor? Have you found anything?" Her voice was shaky. He could tell she'd been crying. He closed his eyes.

He spoke as gently as he could. "I told you I'd let you know."

She sniffled. "I'm sorry. I've just been so worried. The police have given up searching for her. They said she wouldn't be able to survive this long without water and food. I know she's alive, Victor. I just know it."

He had no words. He didn't want to get her hopes up. He didn't want to get his hopes up. But it would take about a week for the woman in the spare bedroom to be conscious long enough to speak coherently. Until then, he'd have to keep searching for Courtney's sister, the woman who'd gone missing during a hiking trip three weeks ago.

Her companion, a guy she was dating, had been found dead at the bottom of a cliff three miles up Mt. Monadnock in New Hampshire. His neck was broken, apparently a result of the fall. Courtney's twin sister, Ashleigh, was nowhere to be found. Only small traces of her blood had been detected on the scene, suggesting she may have been carried off. Victor went to the mountain but too much time had passed and he wasn't able to pick up a scent.

Courtney met Victor through a man he had helped two years ago. The man knew what Victor was. Courtney did not. The man's name was Geoff and he seemed to have a sixth sense. He'd known right away that Victor was a vamp.

Victor had been visiting a friend in Greenwich Village for his birthday. He was only celebrating due to her insistence. It was a warm night in May. When he was heading back to her house after a walk, he saw Geoff struggling with one of those reusable, canvas bags. The bag was full of produce and he was having trouble pulling it from the trunk of his beige Cadillac. Victor came to his rescue.

When Geoff heard his neighbor Courtney's story about her missing sister and Courtney's doggedness that she was alive, he told Victor, hoping he could help.

Maybe he knew something Victor hadn't.

"I'll call you," Victor said, a note of finality in his tone because this conversation was going nowhere.

There was a pause before she said, "Okay."

Ramsey closed the bedroom door behind him and stood before Victor. "Sounds like you're working, too."

He shrugged modestly. "I'm helping a friend. You haven't heard of anybody recently turned in the area?"

"Only the woman Phyllis turned by accident." Victor was stunned. Ramsey nodded solemnly. "Yeah, she got a little carried away with the *amor*. She hadn't realized she took too much when she gave her blood. She came to me right away once she figured out what happened."

"What are you going to do to her?"

Ramsey sighed. "She's been exiled for five years with her progeny. I think she went to Amaryllis." She was the vampire queen of France.

"I was sad to see her go," Ramsey said with a shake of his head.

Yes, Victor was not surprised. Phyllis was a talented cellist. She performed often during gatherings and she had a few ties in her Wellesley community. Her students were sad that she had to leave them.

But rules were rules. At least Phyllis's progeny would be able to adjust away from her former life. A newborn vamp was a dangerous thing. They were disoriented and confused as their bodies went through changes and a hunger so strong overwhelmed them. Usually the maker—the vampire who turned the human—was there to help with the transition.

There were times when a newbie wasn't so lucky.

If they became too obvious, too reckless, it was up to the vamps in the area to either take them in or . . . take them out. It was kind of an unspoken rule, unless the area was run like

Nathan's caste system, where the master vampire—or vampires if there was a council—had the final say in who was turned and where that newbie would fit into the pyramid of power.

Humans, for the most part, didn't know of vampires' existence and they tried to keep it that way. Once you became a member of the undead sect, you were meant to disappear. Your life was no longer the way it had always been. You were frozen in time, watching the world change before your eyes.

Victor left the house with the intention of searching for Milo. His body carried him to The Public Garden instead. He wanted to see. He passed a few people crossing through on their way downtown. A pair of geese waddled on the water's edge. The male lifted his head when Victor neared. He moved closer to his mate. His beak opened as if he were summoning a loud scream.

Victor carried on without much notice. His destination lay just ahead. The little niche under the stone bridge seemed harmless.

He stood there in the semi-darkness, replaying Celia's words. It probably wasn't the best idea, especially since his blood was actually boiling in rage. Milo was a dead man walking. Well . . . he was literally a dead man walking but . . . now he was a . . . Oh, never mind.

There was a crunch of gravel to Victor's right. He spun around. Being angry meant less self-control. His back arched, his nails lengthened to sharp talons, and his fangs slid out. He snarled perilously at whoever was interrupting his moment.

"Calm down, Vic."

Victor hissed even more. Jay chuckled softly as he stepped from the shadows of the bridge. He strolled over, his hands in his pockets.

"No nicknames. Good to know," he joked.

"What the hell are you doing here?" Victor grunted, still in the defensive stance.

"Same as you, I 'spect." Jay stopped a few feet away from him and glanced around at the ground, the foundation of the bridge, and the path that wound around a bend, not allowing witnesses. He was probably imagining like Victor had. His face darkened in fury.

"And you don't know where that son-of-a-bitch is?" he demanded.

"Do you think he would still walk the earth if I did?" Victor countered evenly.

Jay shook his head in disgust. "Fuckin' bastard probably thinks he got away with it."

"No, I'm sure he's just hiding out." Victor finally eased up and relaxed out of his stand. They were silent for a moment, alternating glances every once in a while.

Quietly, Jay asked, "How's she doing?"

"Better. I won't have to worry about Milo calling her," he said darkly. Jay paused at that. Victor heard his heartbeat pick up in anger; he refrained from showing his satisfaction.

Jay seemed to swallow his bile and looked away. "Well, that's comforting," he said scornfully.

Just then, Victor's cellphone rang. He held back a groan, assuming it was Courtney again. Celia's frantic voice hit his ear. Victor disappeared at once. When he showed up at her place, he found her cowering by the window of her living room, staring out through the curtain. The phone was still pressed to her ear.

"I—I don't know, maybe I'm crazy," she was saying.

"No, you're not."

She started at the sound of his voice. "I'm sorry." She ran to his arms. "There was a noise outside," she cried into his chest, "and I looked and thought I saw him and I didn't know what to do so I called you and I'm such a baby for this, I'm sorry."

"Shh," he whispered to the top of her head. She smelled of rum. "You're okay, now."

Her anxiety was running through him at the moment and he didn't like it. Her entire body was trembling. He held her tighter until it began to abate. After a minute, he became aware of her lips on his collarbone. Her fingers grazed his sides. He didn't need to feel her arousal although that was simmering under his skin as well.

"Victor?" she murmured, a little sheepishly.

"Yes?"

"Let's do it again."

She didn't have to tell him twice. Victor gripped her thighs and lifted. She wrapped her legs around his waist, hugging him tight—like she was afraid he might let her go. He carried her to the bedroom.

Four

COLIN TOSSED BACK the shot of Wild Turkey. He immediately began to choke. He held his injured shoulder and peeked up at Jay, his cheeks coloring in embarrassment.

Jay chuckled. "Atta boy."

He drank his own shot and placed it on the table with the five empty glasses. He then sipped his Sam Adams. He'd never had the beer before, and was really taking a liking to the Octoberfest ale.

"Dude, that's gross," Colin griped about the bourbon. He shook his head a few times while making a smacking sound with his lips.

"That shit's gross," Jay corrected. Colin gazed at him in wonder. His expression was quite serious.

Colin laughed. Loudly. A few of the people sitting near them glanced their way. He slapped his hand on the wooden table between them, shaking up the condiments and the sign announcing the removal of the tables on club nights in the corner.

"That shit's gross!"

"Fuckin' gross," Jay goaded. "Curse like a man."

"Fuckin' A!"

"Tits. Ass."

Their waitress was a short girl with a silver hoop for a nose ring and her brown hair pulled up into a tight bun. She made her way over, weaving through the crowded tables. Cage's was bustling for a Sunday night. The patrons were either too lazy or just unwilling to cook.

"Pussy!" Colin cried out. He laughed at himself. The waitress stared at him, along with their neighbors. Colin instantly sobered when he saw her, his face dropping to the floor. "I'm sorry!"

She clucked her teeth and removed their empty glasses. She turned briskly without asking if they needed anything.

"I was going to ask for her number," Colin said regretfully.

"You still could."

He balled up a napkin and tossed it aside. "She probably thinks I'm some perv."

"That could work in your favor."

Colin grabbed his own beer for a sad gulp. "I wanna have sex, Jay. I've only done it once but we got caught right at the beginning so that didn't even count. My mom . . . she came home early."

"Once, I was with a girl and I had to fuckin' pee so bad. Do you understand how difficult it is to fuckin' concentrate when you gotta take a piss?"

Colin dropped his head to the table with a groan.

Jay had just smiled to himself and turned back to scanning the crowd when the woman passed them. She was slender with long, dark hair flowing down her back. She wore a skin-tight cheetah print dress that showed off her very long legs. A cute, black leather coat that curved to her form covered her arms. She licked her cherry-red lips. Round sunglasses sat on her nose and her skin was pale, though all he saw was the white glow.

Clarice.

Jay lowered his glass to the table while staring after her. The hunters kept a "Vamp Board," as Colin called it, in Snipe's living room. The bulletin board was overloaded with pictures and descriptions of vampires in the area, separated into categories of "visitors" and "locals." They had the locals narrowed down to Ramsey's bunch plus four others. The hunters had agreed not to pursue Ramsey's nest, but Clarice and Milo were open terrain after breaking away last month.

What was she doing there anyway? Sundays weren't club nights. He looked around until his eyes landed on a booth in the back corner. A woman with short blonde hair was rubbing her neck. Confusion clouded her expression. The skin was pink beneath her hand and her lipstick was smudged.

Jay took another swig of beer, tossed some money on the table, and slid from the booth. "Stay here," he barked at Colin, who looked up at him blearily. He was drunk and injured and would only get in the way.

Jay followed her outside. The night was cool and he adjusted his leather jacket. There was a storm brewing in the south, making its way up the coast. Boston was receiving the headwinds.

Clarice strolled down the street, toward empty Downtown Crossing. The farther she moved from the lounge, the sooner she'd become aware of her tail. Fewer people meant fewer heartbeats to cover his own. It didn't matter. He wasn't going to let her go that easily.

He watched her smooth gait. With her hands in her pockets, she glided silently over the pavement. Her extra-high heels didn't make a peep. Jay passed an older couple holding hands. The wife smiled warmly at him. He said goodbye to the last of his cover.

Clarice stopped to look into the window of the Bath and Body Works at the corner of Washington and Milk Streets. They were showcasing their new line of body butters. Jay kept on at a steady pace. He saw her grin.

She tapped a crimson fingernail to her lip. "Mm, gotta love the smell of hunter," she remarked. "It's so freakin' manly."

She glanced over her shoulder at him. Jay pulled his stake from the holster at his side. He saw the flash of her fangs before she dashed at him at full speed. She was too fast and rammed into him like a football player, knocking him to the ground. His legs went up in the air, which was kind of embarrassing. She barely fussed her hair.

He was still sore from his last ass whooping, thanks to Victor. He groaned as he rolled over to get to his feet. Clarice grabbed his shoulder and jerked him downward to meet her knee. He got it in the gut, knocking the wind out of him. She punched him in the face and he was on the ground again, wincing in pain.

Clarice stooped down next to him. She wasn't wearing panties. That explained the smoothness of her very tight dress. He cringed and looked away. He was still clutching his stake. She reached for it. He swung at her, sinking the wood in her shoulder. She hissed in response. Her knee pressed into his throat. He tried to push her off but he was choking. While he struggled, she knocked his hand off the stake.

"This was my favorite jacket," she spat. She yanked the wooden stick from her shoulder. She turned it around and stabbed him in the thigh. He cried out hoarsely. She chuckled behind her dark shades and pulled the stake out, spurting his blood onto the sidewalk. Her own blood had oozed down her arm. It dripped from her sleeve, mingling with his. She was raising the stake again, this time over his shoulder, when she halted.

"Hmm." She leaned down to kiss his lips. His panting fogged her glasses. "Next time."

And she was gone. She'd even absconded with his stake. Jay slowly sat up. His jeans darkened before his eyes. He started to pull his belt through the loops when he heard running feet on the pavement.

"Are you okay?"

Three men rushed to his side. Jay got his belt loose and attempted to wrap it around his thigh, above the wound. One of the men, a Puerto Rican guy with thick hair and a red-and-blue "B" tattoo on his neck, took hold of the belt and pulled tight. Jay grimaced. The man put his hands up; he was frightened he had hurt him more. The other men stood to the side. One of them was on his phone with the police before Jay could stop him.

"That's okay," Jay tried. "You don't haveta call the police."

"What?" the "paramedic" asked in surprise. "Your fucking leg's bleeding, man."

"I'm good."

He bent his uninjured leg and used the guy's shoulder to pull himself up. The Good Samaritan stepped in his path when he tried to walk away.

"You should really get that looked at by a doctor."

Jay waved him off and limped down the street. He called Colin and told him to meet up at the car. He had to repeat himself three times. Hopefully Colin understood.

It took him twenty minutes dragging his foot to get to his car parked on a side street near Cage's. He let out a sigh as he fell into his seat. His cheek was stinging from Clarice's blow. Colin came tripping around the corner a minute later. He bumped into the fender before fumbling with the handle. Jay had to reach over and open the door for him. Colin plopped into the seat.

"Hey, dipshit," Jay said. "Shut the door."

Lucky for him, Clarice stabbed him in the left leg or he

wouldn't have been able to drive to Snipe's. Colin was no help. He fell asleep as Jay pulled off. When he parked the car in Southie, he shoved Colin. He started awake with a snort. He'd been drooling on his shoulder.

Harold, the barreled-chest, neurotic hunter answered Jay's ringing. He still had the nasty scrape on the side of his face—it was scabbed over and crusty in some parts, smooth and discolored in others. Jay staggered inside and into the kitchen. Colin crashed down heavily onto the sofa. He would regret that in the morning.

Jay rummaged through the cabinet, searching for the bottle of rum he'd seen once or twice before. He found it hiding behind the boxes of instant rice. He poured four fingers of rum followed by Pepsi, since that's what they had in the pantry. It looked more like iced tea than Pepsi and it was warm, which was fucking gross.

"Jay? What happened?"

Lauren entered the kitchen wearing baggy, purple plaid pajama pants and a short-sleeved gray shirt. She rubbed her eyes sleepily as she approached Jay with the first aid kit. Taking hold of his arm, she directed him to sit at the table, sidestepping the drops of blood on her linoleum floor in the process.

Lauren was a nurse in Beth Israel Hospital's triage unit. She tended to patch up the various injuries with which the boys came home. She used large scissors to cut his jeans up to the belt/tourniquet.

Snipe lumbered in just as she was cleaning the wound. It stung like crazy. Jay downed his drink then glanced wistfully at the rum bottle sitting on the counter. Snipe brought it over to him and stood at Lauren's side.

"It's not too deep," she said. "I don't think anything's broken. We should take him to the hospital."

"No," Jay said immediately. "I hate hospitals," he added in a grumble.

Lauren looked up at Snipe in concern. "Jay," Snipe said wearily.

"Just fix it," Jay demanded before he could try to convince him. He refilled his glass, this time omitting the Pepsi. The rum burned his chest as it went down.

Lauren shook her head. "You could have nerve damage or something more I can't see. I'm not a doctor or a surgeon."

"Lauren. Please." He stared down at her, steadfast. "Do what you have to. I'm not going to the hospital."

Lauren wanted to protest more. In the end, she sighed. She did the best she could from what she'd assisted at work and was able to staunch the bleeding. Jay grimaced while she sewed. He noticed that there was more pain in the sewing than in the injury now.

Jay finished half the bottle by the time she placed gauze on his thigh. She held it in place with a tan-colored wrap, the elastic kind that was self-adhering.

"I'll give you some Tylenol in the morning," she said carefully. He was drinking and she didn't want any interactions with anything stronger. No matter, since the alcohol gave him a pleasant numbness.

Jay hobbled to the living room. Colin was out cold. Harold had the spare bedroom and wasn't selfless enough to give up the bed for an injured person. Snipe pulled out the spare bed from its spot in the corner. Down Jay went onto the thin-ass mattress. Loud squeaks responded to the unexpected weight. Lauren pulled out the mop but Snipe sent her off to bed. He took up the task of cleaning so the girls wouldn't wake up to the bloody mess.

Twenty minutes later, he stopped off in the living room. Jay peered up at him, his eyes drooping from fatigue and drunkenness.

"It was Clarice," Jay mumbled. "Downtown. She was at

Cage's."

Snipe nodded. Whether he said anything else, Jay didn't know. He slipped off as soon as he finished speaking.

***

Victor's blood wore off by Wednesday. Celia was at work, feeling like herself again. In other words, jumpy. She was behind the bar during the dinner shift and every short, blonde guy who passed by made her break out in a cold sweat.

Carson had called out, leaving her to run orders by herself. Bobby came around every once in a while to keep her out of the weeds. He stepped behind the bar at nine to relieve her for a break. She went to the kitchen. The chefs were dancing to hip-hop songs from the radio while they cooked. She couldn't help a smile as she made a cup of tea.

She sat in a chair by the prep table where someone had left a Metro newspaper. Picking it up, she scanned the front page. Murders and violence littered the headlines. Great.

Just then, the back door opened. She had a brief moment of panic. It was only the new guy, Michael. He stepped inside, bringing the smell of cigarette smoke and spilled beer with him.

His steps faltered when he saw Celia. The atmosphere in the room shifted, growing thick with tension. She didn't understand the change since none of the other people in the kitchen were paying any attention. His throat clenched as he swallowed noticeably, like he was anxious about being in the same room as her. He ducked his head and started for the door.

"Hey!" she called. He halted. The chefs glanced around, too, since she had been kind of loud. Celia was frowning at Michael. He'd been working at the restaurant for almost a week now and he was still treating her like she'd offended him in some way. She didn't get it and she was tired of it.

"Did I say something to upset you?" she asked. "Did I do something?"

"Wh-what?" he stammered. He didn't even look her in the face. His gaze was focused somewhere over her head.

She narrowed her eyes. "Did Carson say something to you? Because he's a pubic hair, okay?"

He looked down slowly, and it was like he had seen her for the first time. He stared at her a minute, examining her. She could almost feel his gaze, as if he was physically touching her. She knew her cheeks were reddening. It was an awkward moment, leaving her speechless.

Michael's brows furrowed in uncertainty. "I'm sorry," he said softly. "I . . ." He broke off with a shake of his head. "I guess I've been an asshole."

"I'll say." She smiled, to soften the words. An unspoken armistice was declared, even if the "battle" had been one-sided. He grinned a little, and the dimple appeared in his left cheek. He visibly relaxed. Even the tension in the air dissipated.

"What did I do? So I'll know for next time."

"It was nothing. I . . . I thought something . . ." He shook his head again. "I'm sorry."

She cocked an eyebrow.

He pointed over his shoulder. "I better get back."

She watched him leave through the swinging door. She stayed in the kitchen another ten minutes before heading back out to the bar, where she was greeted with an order for a large party that showed up without a reservation. Bobby had to rush off to set their tables. The bar had been unmanned for a few minutes. She didn't mind the large order; at least it kept her occupied. The fact that there was not a blonde in the bunch was a relief.

After helping Tina load up the last tray with glasses, Celia pulled the next slip. It was almost too simple after that round of gins and Cosmos and martinis. This couple just wanted sodas. Maria was still training Michael. She sent him to the bar to pick up the order.

Celia poured the second Coke and added limes. "Thanks, Celia," Michael said, placing the glasses on his round tray.

"No problem."

A genuine smile appeared on his face before he rushed back to the floor. It was at that moment she realized how calm she felt. Ever since she came back from her break, she was at ease, body and mind. She knew there were dangers out there but that was okay. In fact, she didn't even concern herself with anything outside of the bar.

Before she began to wonder from where this newfound serenity was coming, she pushed the questions away.

A huge smile spread across her face. She bounced over to the computer to learn her next round of orders. The last two hours flew by. At the end of the night, Bobby sent Michael over to help her clean the bar.

As her first task, Celia took up the black mats from the little ditch before the marble counter. They were used there as receptacles for spills while pouring drinks. She bent them over the sinks to empty the liquid that had collected during the night.

"Are you a student?" she asked him. That was usually the case for the part-timers. She secured the lid on the ice machine under the counter in the center of the bar.

"Yeah," Michael answered, while placing dirty glasses that had collected under the bar in the heavy-duty, plastic tray they used in the industrial dishwasher.

"At BU," he continued. "I'm a sophomore. I had taken two years off after high school," he told her, which explained why he was close to Celia's age. "To help my father out. He's a mechanic, you know. It's kinda weird being older than the other students. They're so immature sometimes because it's all a big party; at least some of the ones I've come across."

"Are you from Boston?"

"No, Baltimore, though originally from San Diego."

"Baltimore has such nicer weather. Even San Diego. Why would you come here?"

He looked at her, ready to laugh, except she was quite serious. He chuckled anyway. "To be some place new."

She shrugged, figuring that was a good enough reason. She showed him how to restack the shakers while she replenished the napkins and stirrers. She used disinfecting spray and a towel to wipe down the sinks after laying the mats flat on the well to dry.

Celia continued to quiz him while rushing back and forth between the bar and kitchen.

"What are you studying?"

"A combo of physical therapy and athletic training."

She paused to gape at him. "Really?"

She didn't know why that was so fascinating. Maybe because all of the college students she'd met, either fellow employees or people at the bar, had always stated the usual: pre-law, pre-med, English.

He found her reaction amusing. "Yeah," he said, wiping down the back bar. "So if you know anybody who works for the Red Sox, lemme know."

Celia shook her head in awe as she moved on to check the fridges under the bar for what needed to be restocked. Bobby had a clipboard with a checklist where she had to inventory what was used during the shift. Each brand had a total number already typed on the sheet as a starting point. The same was true of the bottles of liquor, which, from her quick scan, would last at least until the weekend.

"Do you live on campus?" She wrote "15" next to Bud Light.

"Near campus. Which is the only thing about working the dinner shift," he said with a chuckle. It was nearly midnight already. There had been a few late diners.

"Well, if you ever need a ride, let me know."

She paused. The words had tumbled out before she could think about what she was offering.

When he smiled, his hazel eyes seemed to brighten. Any misgivings that had begun to rise died away in an instant.

"Hey, thanks. That's really nice of you."

She nodded slowly, confused by her generosity. She placed the clipboard back on its hook. Carson had the morning shift. She left the restocking to him since he had left her in a lurch. It wasn't too much; most of the drinkers had wanted draft beers or wine. She hadn't inventoried the wine since there was a delivery scheduled for the morning.

Celia lifted the tray of dirty glasses from the counter.

It was too heavy and nearly tipped her forward. Michael reached for it before she lost her balance. He took the tray from her, hefted it onto his shoulder and carried it to the kitchen like it weighed no more than a bag of cotton. She followed him with wide eyes.

That was . . . interesting.

She quickly swept and mopped the floor. She then wiped down the countertop, and she was done. She grabbed her bag from Bobby's office and clocked out. Michael waved to her at the front door as she approached.

"Can I take you up on that ride? If it's no trouble," he added quickly. His expression was mildly sheepish. "I can take a cab or something. Or the train, it's not too late—"

She raised a hand to stop him. "It's fine."

He beamed again. They walked in silence to the parking lot. The wind was definitely kicking up now. The weathermen were predicting thunderstorms as soon as tomorrow night. It was a good thing she was going to be inside.

"I always like these cars," Michael commented as they climbed into her Honda Accord. He had to adjust his seat to accommodate his long legs.

"Oh?" she said a little dubiously. She loved her car but it wasn't glamorous or anything.

"Yeah, they're easy to customize. If you want, I can get you some speakers, a nice sub. Oh, and the lights. You should get purple headlights."

She laughed. "Um, I think I'm all set."

"Or you could get some street glows in blue."

"Street glows?"

"Underbody lights."

She rolled her eyes. "Boys and their toys."

"I'm just saying."

The drive to campus was about ten minutes once she turned onto Commonwealth Avenue. His apartment building was on St. Paul Street, a few blocks from Boston University's Admissions building. The edifice was brick with stone trimmings. Two lights shone over the glass door.

Three guys took up space on the stairs. They were all big and strong and laughing about something. She frowned as she pulled up front.

"Um," she said cautiously, peering around him to the group. "Do they live here?"

Michael looked to see what was making her anxious. He laughed. The sound filled the space and she found herself relaxing.

"Yeah. Thanks, Celia. I owe you."

He got out the car and strolled to the group. The guy sitting on the top stair nodded to the car, his mouth moving as he said something to Michael. Michael gave him the finger in response. The others laughed. Michael looked back to her. He waved over his shoulder, basically telling her to drive off.

As she made her way back to Comm Ave, Celia noticed that peculiar feeling of comfort and calm was slowly receding. Suddenly, the shadows danced ominously in the corners of her vision. Car horns and tire screeches made her jump. She was too afraid to press down harder on the gas lest her burgeoning fear made her run off the road. She took a page from Victor's book and visualized her living room. The exercise calmed her just enough to make it to the safety of her home.

***

At Ramsey's, Bryce was in an uproar. Annie had been visiting the Monte Carlos in Maine for the weekend but had not returned home. She had been expected back Tuesday. The Monte Carlos said that she left early last night.

No one knew what to say to reassure him. He had already punched two holes in the wall—funnily enough just to the left of where he had thrown that armchair a few weeks ago. Corinna repaired that with her mojo.

"Have you tried her cell again?" Elizabeth asked.

"I've been calling all fucking night!" he exclaimed. Elizabeth looked away at his harsh tone. He didn't mean it, of course, but it still stung to be yelled at.

Bryce was brooding by the window now, glowering out into the night. Victor glanced to Ramsey. He was very still, his eyes closed. No doubt he was doing his mental communication thing.

Well, trying anyway. He opened his eyes with a disappointed sigh.

"She's there," Ramsey said. "She's just not answering."

"She might be unconscious," Elizabeth offered in her professional tone she used with patients. Bryce spun around, his entire body trembling. He made a course toward the door, knocking over an ottoman in his way.

Okay, maybe she should've kept that to herself until later.

Victor called after him but the door slammed. He teleported right away. As soon as the vampires had left that night two weeks ago, Snipe made sure that their invitation into his home was rescinded. Therefore, Victor knocked on the door.

It was eleven. A light glowed behind the curtains in the front room. He could hear the television going, the sound of leather squishing as the person stood. The door opened. Jay stood in the threshold, leaning to the side. A dark red bruise had appeared under his left eye.

"What?" he asked unceremoniously.

"It seems that one of ours has been abducted. Bryce is on his way here because he thinks you all had a hand in that."

Jay snorted. "We don't abduct bloodsuckers. We kill 'em."

Victor held in his groan. "I just thought I'd check it out first."

"Well, thanks for the heads-up." He stepped back to shut the door. The Camaro skidded around the corner.

"Shit," Victor said. Bryce had gotten there extra fast. The car screeched to a stop. Bryce jumped out, leaving the engine going.

"Where is she?" he demanded. "Huh? Where'd you stash her?"

He bounded up the stairs but had to stop short at the front door. He stood toe-to-toe with Jay, who had stepped closer with his chest thrust forward as if he didn't have an injured leg.

"Like I was telling your buddy here," Jay said through clenched teeth. "We ain't in the hostage business."

"You're lying. He's lying!" he shouted to Victor.

"Well, you could look around, except—oh, that's right." He put a hand to his mouth in mock dismay. "You can't come in."

In a burst of rage, Bryce reached for Jay's neck. Halfway to their destination, his fingers bent downward in mid-air, like he'd hit an invisible wall. If the impact hurt, it didn't show. Jay's smirk was the last thing they saw before he slammed the door.

Bryce punched the barrier. When he pulled his hand back, there was a small dent in the wooden door from his knuckle. He jerked back for another hit. Victor grabbed his arm.

"Bryce, stop. They wouldn't have her."

"Then where is she?" he cried out. His anger had flipped into desperation in a blink of an eye. It was hard to look at. They stared at each other for a moment, neither knowing the answer.

Bryce yanked his arm free. He stalked down the stairs to his waiting car. Victor watched him whip the car into a U-turn and zoom down the street.

Five

JAY STEPPED OUT of the bathroom the next morning feeling grumpy. As he was toweling off from his shower, he halted at his left thigh. To his immense dismay, the skin and hair was back to normal. There wasn't even a scar from the sutures. He looked into the bottom of the tub.

There, hanging on for dear life to the silver drain, were the blue stitches Lauren had used to seal his skin together four days ago. He hadn't noticed they were gone when he was soaping up. You wouldn't have noticed either, however for different reasons entirely . . .

Jay glared at his leg, looking very much like he wanted to punch it. Angrily, he pulled on his clothes and stormed out into the living room. It was nine-thirty. Lauren and the girls were already gone. Jessa was at daycare and Morgan had orientation.

Snipe sat at the kitchen table in his pajamas, drinking coffee with Harold, who was wearing khakis and a blue-checkered shirt.

He worked in a cubicle in some building downtown entering information into a database for a textbook company. Perhaps, he had the morning free seeing as how he was at Snipe's table instead of behind his desk.

"Harold." Snipe sounded irritated. "We've already discussed this."

Harold sighed. "But Snipe, I think I've perfected the serum. It'll work," he insisted. So it appeared he was still trying to use vampires as weapons.

Snipe glared at him. "I said, no."

Harold's lips thinned. He looked like a child on the verge of a tantrum. Instead of arguing further, he stood slowly and left the kitchen. He didn't even look at Jay.

Jay made himself a bowl of Cinnamon Toast Crunch and plopped down in the seat Harold had just occupied. Snipe noticed his unhindered movements.

"Feeling better?"

Jay groaned. "I don't wanna fuckin' talk about it."

Snipe looked down at the newspaper before him.

Jay blew out a long breath. "I have to go back to Dallas," he announced. Snipe glanced up. "Some dickhead ran into my parents' living room. He was drunk. I have to go settle things, get the house fixed, all that shit."

He had received the phone call from Dallas police last night, after the vampires' interruption.

Snipe nodded before finishing his coffee. He needed to get ready for work. After rinsing his mug in the sink, Snipe lumbered off to his bedroom. The cool weather was making his leg hurt, worsening his limp.

Jay considered his next move. The drive back to Dallas was long. He hadn't intended on coming to Boston when he set off after that vamp; the city was where he had ended up. He was not down for sitting in his car for twenty-seven plus hours. So, he hopped on the computer to buy a plane ticket. The flight was to leave in an hour, unless he wanted to wait until the next morning.

Since he had practically moved into Snipe's living room, packing was an easy task. The cab he called for arrived in ten minutes. When Jay settled in the backseat, a ripple of sadness passed through him. He didn't know how long he would be away. He wished he had more time, just to stop by Cage's even for a minute.

He pulled out his cellphone and left a brief message letting her know he would be out of town. Celia stayed on his mind as the cab drove off.

***

Thursday night was busy as usual. Michael stuck around after his shift. He was decked out in nice jeans and a button-down shirt. He had to be in street clothes to sit at the bar. Whenever Celia came near, he'd ask her about the drinks she was making or her opinion on movies or other generally trivial things.

"Don't you have boys to hang out with?" Celia asked through a laugh.

He shrugged. "They're all unpacking. I don't want anything to do with that."

"Some friend you are."

They grinned at each other. Tina was short and Korean, her straight black hair up in a bun. She was playing cocktail waitress tonight. She fell against the bar beside Michael with a vexed groan.

"Ugh, there are these two assholes in the corner booth. They want Long Island Iced Teas, Celia. Maybe you can add some love with their lemons."

Celia chuckled and then set about making the drinks. Her bit of "love" was skimping on the alcohol. Since there wasn't a real feasible way of diluting Long Islands, she had to skip that route.

"Why are they assholes?" Michael asked.

"They were arguing with each other and I was just gonna move on, but then one of them grabbed my arm. I thought he was trying to break it." She winced as she rubbed her right wrist. "He was really rude when he was asking what we have that's strong. His friend was the one who ordered."

Celia placed the completed drinks on the bar. On the list of difficulty, Long Islands were somewhere near the bottom. Her eyes scanned the back booths, trying to find the culprits who had managed to rile the always cheerful Tina.

Two men were tucked into the corner booth, looking angry with the world. A single bulb covered by a burnt orange and brown Tiffany-style shade hung over the table.

The light was dim, to set an ambiance.

Even with the low lighting, she could see that both of the men were tanned, with short-cropped hair—maybe Native American, maybe some mixture of other races. Whatever it was, their nationalities gave them a deep, ruddy complexion. Muscles wrapped their arms and chest; the neck of one of them was like a tree trunk. Their dark eyes stayed at the table as they alternated glares with each other and the wooden surface.

The tension between the two was nearly tangible. The people around them seemed to sense it as well. No one lingered in front of their booth.

Tina took the large glasses, gave Celia one last look saying pray for me, then slid through the crowd to the angry men. Tina set the drinks down in front of them. Tree Trunk guy handed her some bills and she hurried away. Celia watched as the men downed the drinks so quickly, you would think it was actual iced tea.

There was something strange about the two men. She couldn't put her finger on it except to say that they seemed to give off an odd scent. It was a sharp aroma that pricked her nose. The only thing was they were a good ten yards away. Who was to say the scent was coming from them?

Somehow, she knew they were the source.

Suddenly, both men became very alert. They looked around like someone had called to them. Their heads shifted to the bar in unison and Celia froze. Had they felt her watching them? Heat inched up her neck.

She realized after a moment it wasn't she that they were staring at. She looked at Michael. Ever since Tina pointed out the booth, Michael had been studying the men, enraptured.

Now, Celia frowned. It wasn't sexual or anything of that nature, but he was completely captivated by the two strangers.

"Michael?"

He didn't snap out of it. She reached across the bar and shook his shoulder. Michael blinked a few times then glanced over to Celia. His hazel eyes were troubled. The atmosphere shifted a moment and a sense of confusion settled over Celia. But she didn't know what she would be confused about except for the strange confusion she was experiencing right now. It was all very . . . confusing.

Before she could figure out the change, it was gone. Just like that. Michael shook his head as if he were trying to clear it. When he looked at her again, the clouds were gone from his expression.

"I'm . . . gonna head out," he told her as he was sliding from his stool. He moved toward the exit. Celia kept an eye on him until he slipped out the main door.

She took a cautious glance back to the booth. The men had been tracking his exit as well. The smaller guy, with the normal-sized neck, turned his head back to the bar until his eyes landed on Celia. His dark gaze assessed her, sending waves of fear through her.

She averted her eyes immediately. After a moment, she went to the kitchen in the guise of getting water. When she returned five minutes later, the booth was empty.

***

Michael seemed fine the next day. Celia wanted to ask what that was all about; she just didn't know how to broach the subject. They had only known each other for a week, after all, and though they were on much friendlier terms right now, it didn't seem like her place to ask questions. And she had plenty of them. Like, did he know those guys? Why were they so pissed off? And why had they captured Michael's attention so fully?

Celia was working the lunch shift behind the bar. Every few minutes or so, she found herself spying on Michael.

At two, when the place was slowly emptying of the lunch crowd, he dropped his tray on the bar.

"Okay," he said. "What is it?"

"Huh?"

"Why are you watching me? I mean, I know I'm cute and all, but damn. You're being way too obvious."

He grinned, presenting her with his adorable dimple, and she couldn't help but smile. "I was just making sure you were okay."

"What do you mean?"

She surveyed him for a moment. Should she bring up last night? Was he trying to forget it had happened?

After a few moments of silent debating, she finally said, "Well, you left kinda suddenly yesterday."

His eyes shifted to the counter as embarrassment reddened his nose. Thinly, he replied, "I had something to do."

Celia nodded, deciding to leave it at that. Michael didn't owe her any explanations. She had just been concerned. Her lips pulled into a smile to lighten the mood. "You remembered you had a date?" she joked.

Instead of a chuckle or quip as she had anticipated, he looked even more uncomfortable. "No, nothing like that." His voice was low and he wasn't looking at her. She put her hands up, palms out.

"Hey, not my business," she said. "Are you working tonight?" She wanted to change the subject quickly.

"No, I have a game."

"Oh?"

"I'm in this league." Suddenly, he brightened. "Hey, you should come. It's at five. You'll have plenty of time to get back here."

"Maybe I will."

Terry was a graying, pear-shaped man in his forties. He leaned against the bar, offering Michael an unwavering stare. Michael smiled, and gave him a hearty pat on the shoulder.

"Terry! I was just looking for you."

"Yeah, I'm sure," Terry said without malice. "We have a table."

"Right."

Celia went to the Dorchester YMCA right after clocking out where she met up with Trixie. They sat with Maria and her oldest son and cheered Michael on. His team won by six points.

The rain the weathermen had been predicting soaked the city as soon as Celia went inside Cage's. She just hoped it wouldn't be too bad when she was leaving later; in her haste, she'd forgotten her umbrella in the car. Her hair was curly today so the bad weather wasn't a huge deal.

She was a little late going inside after dropping off Trixie, prompting a stern look from Bobby. She shrugged sheepishly and hurried to his office to clock in. The music was going and people were already lining up when she situated herself behind the bar. She was quickly wrapped up into the night.

It was around midnight when she saw him. Through the semi-darkness of the club, through the many faces mixing and blending together, she saw the white-blonde hair first. The woman standing in front of her was confused. She repeated her order for a Bud Light. Celia continued to stare into the crowd.

Milo's unctuous grin stood out on his pale face. She lost him for a second among the humans. Her eyes darted around frantically, searching him out.

He was gone.

Poof.

She bit her bottom lip.

"Hello?" the woman called, sounding concerned. Celia turned to her. The woman raised her eyebrows questioningly. Celia reached in the fridge behind her.

Subconsciously, she had heard the woman's order, which was why she pulled out a Bud Light. She turned back to the bar.

She was no longer facing the woman. The bottle nearly slipped from her fingers.

Milo leaned over the counter. His hair was brushed forward into his face in a pretty boy, sweeping bang style. His dark green t-shirt announced "I don't bite . . . hard."

"Hello, Celia. I've missed you."

His hand darted out and the bottle was no longer in her grasp. Milo popped the top without a bottle opener and took a long gulp. He placed the beer on the counter.

It took her a moment to find her voice. And when she did, she made sure her fury was front and center.

"What the fuck do you want?"

He made a regretful face. "Damn. I would love to feel that anger. You're always so furious. It's awesome."

He reached out so fast that he grabbed her wrist before she realized what was happening. She wanted to look around, to see if anyone saw what he was doing, but she couldn't tear her eyes from him. That itchy rope reached out for her, starting in her arm that he was holding captive. It encircled her, twisting its way around her body. She didn't want this to happen and just that affirmation pushed the rope back a little. She was panicking because she couldn't fully resist his magic, which only made it harder to fight him.

"Take your damn hands off her."

Milo glanced to his right. Celia was surprised to see Michael. He was wearing casual clothes, jeans and a gray sweater. His shoulders and chest were pelted with raindrops. He was probably celebrating his win, though you couldn't tell by the hostile expression.

His eyes were narrowed to tiny slits. The rope receded though Milo didn't release her wrist. She tried to pull it away but a vampire's grip was like an iron vise.

Michael took a step closer. "It's okay," Celia said quickly. "He was just leaving." She didn't want Michael to get hurt stepping into her mess.

Pitbull's "I Know You Want Me" pulsed from the speakers. Trixie wiggled her hips in her cage across the way. The green and red strobe lights sliced through the crowd. People stretched their arms above their heads, pumping their fists in the air, oblivious to the scene at the bar.

Milo's grin never left his face. He finally let her go. She jerked her arm away, tucking her hands under the bar to put more distance between them. Without realizing, she started snapping the elastic that was still around her wrist.

Michael stared Milo down. He was a good four inches taller than the vampire, who was only an inch taller than Celia's five-five frame. His glare was very intimidating, at least to a normal person. Milo kept up his Cheshire cat routine as he turned slowly on his heel. Michael followed behind him to make sure he left. He also pointed him out to Meat, one of the bouncers on tonight.

Not that that really mattered for a vamp with the power to enthrall humans . . .

Celia slid from behind the bar and hurried into the kitchen.

It was empty, thankfully. She sank into a chair off to the side, weighed down by her anger with Milo and her anger at being scared because of Milo. She wanted to throw something but there was nothing in reach that would do a satisfying enough job.

Deflated and defeated, she leaned forward, putting her head in her hands. A few seconds later, the kitchen door swung forward. She didn't have to look up to know who it was. Victor's cool fingers touched her thighs.

"Seal, what's wrong?" His voice was on level with her head. He must've been kneeling in front of her.

She sighed, relieved that he had come so quickly when he sensed her agitation. "Milo was here."

Victor's hands stiffened. Anticipating what he would do, she tried to grab him. He disappeared too quickly. Her fingers only grasped air and with him went the comfort.

She looked up just as the kitchen door opened. Michael's face was etched with worry. When he saw her in the chair, relief washed that all away.

"Who was that?" he asked as he crossed to her. "Why was he bothering—?"

He broke off abruptly, halting as well. His nose flared slightly and that same dark look he had turned on Milo returned. Celia's brows knitted in confusion.

"What is it?"

"Did . . ." He paused, contemplating. "Did he come back?"

Her frown deepened. "No. Why do you ask that?"

His head swiveled slowly as he searched the area. There weren't many corners or hiding places in the kitchen.

"Michael?"

He stood a few feet away, in the middle of the kitchen, like he wanted space between them. His gaze finally came back to her. She was surprised to find distrust in his eyes. He still appeared to be struggling with something.

"Are you okay?" His tone wasn't nearly as comforting as the words warranted.

"Yeah, I guess so," she said vaguely, still puzzled by his change. He hesitated a moment before nodding curtly and leaving her alone in the kitchen.

What was up with Michael's mood swings?

Celia knew she couldn't hide out for much longer. She pushed it aside for now, pulled herself from the chair and returned to work.

***

Victor didn't find Milo. His trail led him through The Public Garden, then the Boston Commons, then Downtown Crossing, then down Tremont Street through the Theatre District—basically a giant ass circle, which was probably intentional. The trail went dead at New England Medical Center, the hospital on the next street over from the theaters. He must've had a car or caught a cab. It was harder for Victor to track a car.

Celia said she was fine, plus she had two more hours of work, so Victor went to Ramsey's. He wouldn't let himself believe that Milo would be cocky or reckless enough to return to Cage's. He'd already accomplished what he had set out to do: scare the shit out of Celia.

Victor appeared in the front hallway a little off-balanced given that he hadn't fed since waking and that had only been a little taste. When he woke, he didn't have the peculiar sensation in his extremities. He hadn't drunk from Celia in a few days; it was the only way he could explain it. He wanted to, that was for sure. Her blood called out to him now. He had always been aware of her . . . liveliness. How could he not? A few times lately he caught himself staring at her neck in a daze, remembering her warmth. She hadn't noticed, thankfully. Her beckoning pulse had led him into the kitchen tonight where she was huddled forward as if in pain. His gums had tingled involuntarily when he stooped next to her.

He hadn't brought up the subject of drinking from her again because she had been busy and tired with work, which he greatly preferred to her finding numbness in a bottle.

Therefore, he was dizzy from teleporting. The Zen master within him was working overtime.

He was forced to recover quickly when he heard a loud bang.

Victor rushed to the spare bedroom. The room was a mess. The bed was overturned, the dresser on its side with its drawers hanging open. The female vamp was crouched in the corner, snarling at Ramsey, Elizabeth, and Bryce, who stood around her. They were all hunched forward, their fangs bared in defense. Their sharp eyes watched her every move.

"What do you want with me?" she demanded.

"To help," Ramsey said gently.

"Fuck you! That's what they always say."

Ramsey's voice remained calm. "What who always says?"

Her lips pressed together in response, like she'd just sucked on something sour.

"What's your name?"

"Let me the hell out of here!"

"Do you remember what happened to you?" Ramsey continued. "Do you know who did this to you?"

Her forehead wrinkled as she gazed sideways, visibly thinking. "I . . . It's not clear," she said after a moment. "They grabbed me from behind and tied me up. The chains burned . . ." She lifted her hands, saw what was left of the marks along her wrists and winced.

"Silver," Ramsey informed her. "It debilitates us."

Her gaze was still on the marks. "They hit me and cut me and licked my blood and took turns . . ."

She trailed off again as her face softened with a different emotion. Was she embarrassed? Humiliated?

She looked like she was going to cry except vampires lost that ability when they were reborn. She blinked around the room.

"It's okay," Ramsey coaxed. "You're okay now."

"Where am I?"

Sensing she was on the verge of relaxing, he straightened, his fangs retracted. "I'm Ramsey. This is my home."

"How did I get here?"

Ramsey nodded to Victor. It wasn't surprising that he knew he was there. "Victor and his girlfriend found you. They brought you here. It was close to sunrise. You were very lucky."

Her eyes scanned Victor. Now that she was standing and healing on her own he saw her more clearly. Elizabeth had cleaned her up. Her dark mane was a deep chestnut color that fanned over her shoulders. She was wearing a gray t-shirt and black yoga pants, her feet bare. Her eyes were a cobalt blue, set behind round cheeks. The same blue eyes and full cheeks he'd seen before. She was still incredibly pale but that couldn't be helped. At least the bruises were fading. The one on her cheek was more of a rosy hue.

Victor stood perfectly still. His nonthreatening stance helped her to relax even more. She limped to a chair next to the nightstand. Elizabeth flitted from the room and was back a minute later with a tall glass filled with blood. The woman sipped cautiously, still watching everyone.

"I'm Elizabeth," she introduced. "I'm sorry it isn't warm." She scrunched her nose up in commiseration with the vamp. Blood must've been gross at room temperature. "And this is Bryce."

Bryce's cellphone rang. He snatched it from his pocket. "Yeah?"

"Bryce, it is Andres." Andres wasn't yelling; the vampires could hear the other line. Andres was the patriarch of the Monte Carlos—the "vegetarian" bunch. His Spanish accent was thick.

His words rolled off his tongue fluidly, as if he were actually speaking Spanish.

"Have you found her?" Bryce asked immediately.

Andres sighed. "No, my friend. Ernesto followed her trail. He lost her around Portsmouth. He thinks she made it into Massachusetts."

Bryce's hand tightened around the phone. "What do you mean he lost her trail?"

"She was going on a straight path. Then it alternated. He thinks she believed she was being followed. She was moving around, making circles. Then her trail began to fade. She must have gone to ground for the day. He says she made it into Massachusetts, but he is not completely certain if she stayed there."

The other vamps exchanged concerned looks. "Thank you," Bryce forced out through clenched teeth.

"I am truly sorry, my friend. Nothing like this has ever happened before—"

"It's not your fault," Bryce said. The words sounded sincere, though going by this face, he was only saying it to be cordial. The Monte Carlo bunch was friends and allies, after all. Annie was a grown woman taking a routine trip home.

Andres sounded disappointed when he said, "Ernesto will be there soon."

Bryce hung up with the elder Monte Carlo. He didn't look at anyone as he slowly left the room. He was so tense, there was no way he could walk any faster than human, melancholy speed. A minute later, the front door opened and closed. Elizabeth placed a hand on Ramsey, who nodded in silent agreement. Ramsey flashed from the room after him. Bryce's temper was a higher priority at the moment.

Victor turned back to the houseguest. The glass in her hand was nearly empty. She stared at the red liquid coating the sides.

The pinkish hue on her cheek melted into the whiteness of the rest of her skin. She chuckled to herself.

"I always thought blood tasted like metal. Ever since, you know—" she rolled her wrist in front of her, indicating her new status in life "—it's the best thing in the world. I still crave my mom's German chocolate cake but it probably won't taste the same anymore." She had been directing her words to the glass.

"When were you turned?" Elizabeth asked.

The vamp's chin jutted out. "Three weeks ago, I think." Her eyes glazed over as she was seeing inward now. While she spoke, Elizabeth and Victor straightened the room.

"I was hiking, I remember. It was late and we were making our way back to our campsite. I told Frank way before sunset that we needed to get back but he wanted so badly to finish the stupid trail.

"We came to a bluff and were looking out over the trees when we heard this growling. I was confused because I didn't think there were big animals on the mountain. Then this . . . man was attacking Frank. He just—" she shook her head "—jumped from a tall tree on top of Frank. I picked up a branch and hit him. He knocked me away."

Her fingers grazed her temple absentmindedly. "I must've hit my head because everything went black. Then I remembered pain. Just . . . pain. I thought it would last forever but then it faded away. I woke up in a room with that man watching me.

"He smiled and I was scared. Then I heard a heartbeat, as clear as day, and I wasn't scared anymore. I was hungry and desperate. I didn't know for what. I saw the woman's face but I didn't really see her. I just saw . . . food."

She touched her lips. "My teeth . . . I was biting her. She tried to push me away. I was too strong. He had to pull me off, he said before I got sick, and I realized there were no more heartbeats in the room, not even mine."

Her eyes dropped to the glass again. The last vestiges of blood lined the bottom. She placed the glass on the nightstand. Elizabeth sat on the edge of the bed. She reached out slowly, so as not to startle her, and took hold of her wrist. The welts crisscrossing her forearms were a lighter shade than the rest of her skin. The wounds on her inner wrists weren't as wide as previously.

"I still see her face sometimes. Charlie said that vampires don't dream. But I do. She died. And it was because of me."

"It happens," Victor replied. "We've all made mistakes. The important thing is how you handle it. Do you carry on that way, taking more than you need? Or do you keep your humanity close?"

"But . . ." Her voice trembled. "I didn't know."

He shook his head gently. "I'm not trying to make you feel bad."

Elizabeth's expression was grim. "It's tough when you're turned like that," she said softly. "Such a violent end . . . It never leaves you."

The vamp stared at her. "How were you turned?"

Elizabeth didn't take her eyes from her work. "That's . . . a story for another time."

"Where is that man?" Victor interjected before she could ask any more questions of Elizabeth. "Your maker."

She rubbed her temple with her free hand, frustrated. "I don't know. We went to Boston because he was meeting with someone. He didn't tell me who. We went to a store and he told me to wait outside. That he would only be a minute. That's when I was attacked. They used a chain, around my neck. And handcuffs."

"Do you remember when you were taken?" She shook her head. "Or how many there were?"

"Three. There were three of them. I don't know where they

took me. I was so hungry and in pain that I could barely think straight. But I don't think it was more than one night. They messed with me for a while before I must've passed out. And they all took their turn . . . Even the girl." Her face pulled together again in that about-to-cry fashion. "It was probably my fault. He was always telling me to breathe, to blink."

She groaned and pounded her fist against her temple.

Elizabeth clasped both her wrists to stop her. Her breathing was coming in quicker now, like she was hyperventilating.

"Shh, shh, shh," Elizabeth tried to comfort. The vamp was getting herself worked up again.

"I never listen!" she screamed. She yanked her hands free from Elizabeth. She was already strong being a newbie but her frustration packed a punch. In two seconds, she was on her feet and throwing the chair she'd been sitting on across the room. Victor stepped out of the path. It smashed to pieces upon impact with the wall.

High-pitched screeching noises escaped her as she knocked the dresser over again, as she punched a hole in the wall. She was going for the bed when Victor jumped in front of her. He grabbed her shoulders hard, holding her in place. He was pretty strong himself.

"Ashleigh," he roared. "Stop this!"

She had been growling and trying to scratch at his face. When he said her name, her hands froze in mid-swipe. Her blue eyes seemed brighter as she stared at him.

"How did you know my name?" she asked, taken aback.

He waited until he was sure she wasn't going to throw anything else before releasing her. "Your sister hired me to find you. She didn't think you were dead."

"Courtney?"

Victor nodded once. Yet again, that mournful look crossed her eyes. Without warning, she stepped forward and pressed her face to his chest. Her hands gripped his back. She moved her head from side to side, silently crying with no tears.

Victor found it awkward being this close to another woman. She lacked Celia's heat he always found so soothing, and her human scent. Ashleigh smelled like Elizabeth's ointment and whatever flowery soap Elizabeth used to clean her. Even so, she was a female with all those . . . female assets. Her firm breasts pushed into his chest. Her fingers pressed gently into the small of his back. Uncontrollable urges and whatnot tried to occupy him.

Victor glanced over to Elizabeth, who was frowning in concern. He patted Ashleigh's upper back, to keep it casual. He then grasped her arms, took a step back, and directed her to the bed. She followed obediently. She spread out on the mattress, looking exhausted. Elizabeth fixed the covers over her.

"You should rest a little," she said. "I'll bring you more blood in a bit."

Ashleigh managed to nod. She looked so sad, so weak staring at her toes. Elizabeth motioned for Victor to leave. When he reached the door, Ashleigh called out to him. He peered at her over his shoulder.

She wasn't looking at him, nor did she blink or breathe.

"Don't tell Courtney about me." Her whispered request rang with hollowness.

Victor surveyed her a moment longer. Elizabeth shut the door behind them. She must've seen Victor's troubled expression because she rubbed his shoulder before disappearing upstairs.

Celia's shift was finishing soon. It wasn't the best idea but he teleported anyway. He appeared at the foot of the alley behind Cage's since he only had to worry about encountering the occasional bar back dropping off trash or empties.

Once, he'd appeared right behind one of the cooks, who had been finishing a cigarette. Victor was going to just step into the shadows until he went back inside, except the guy turned suddenly and yelped in fear. Just to fuck with him, Victor disappeared and reappeared a few feet away. His back was to the cook. He walked like nothing had happened.

At the mouth of the alley, he glanced back, shrugging his shoulder up to conceal his mouth in a dramatic fashion. The cook dropped his smoking cigarette before dashing into the building.

That cook left Cage's a week later. That was because he had been offered a job in a restaurant in the Park Plaza Hotel, not because Victor had scared the bejeezus out of him. He had never told anyone of that encounter. He was afraid of the ribbing he would no doubt receive from his coworkers.

Tonight, Victor needed a minute to regain his balance. He was still a bit shaky as he walked down the alley. It was after two. The club was closed. Meat and Rick were busing the crowd, making sure they got into cars and cabs and off the premises. Three uniformed officers stood back a respectable distance, observing.

Victor was at the corner. The smell of humans surrounded him like a thick cloud. He almost wandered behind a few people. He could probably get a little taste before Celia emerged from the restaurant.

Celia strolled outside at quarter to three. She was so late getting out because the computer system had gone down two minutes before the lights came on. The malfunction caused some confusion with closing out tabs, slowing the night to almost a standstill.

She went to Victor's side, zipping her jacket to her neck. Vampires didn't feel the temperature changes. He was wearing a black dress shirt, the sleeves rolled up to his elbows, and gray slacks. He should've had a light coat to withstand the cool. Oh, well.

He leaned down to kiss her lips. She seemed fine. Her heartbeat was steady, her pace calm. Her emotions were in check.

And she didn't want to walk the city tonight.

Victor put an arm around her shoulders as they ambled to her car. He appeared casual. He was a guy, walking his girl to her car, except he was keeping watch for anything out of the ordinary. She had washed up and changed. He couldn't smell Milo on her, of which he was grateful. Instead, colognes and perfumes, cigarettes, garbage, and vomit floated to him on the night air. He could hear televisions and rowdy sex in the hotel across the street and heartbeats throbbing at their backs from the departing crowd. You had to love heightened senses in a major city after let-out.

They climbed into her car, sealing the city scents and sounds outside. His thirst had risen to a consuming level. His senses were sharper than usual, his body ready to feed. Now that it was just the two of them in a closed-off space, Celia captured his complete attention. Her blood pulsed in her neck, a melodious drum for his ears only. Her curly, auburn hair was held back from her face by silver clips. She was still using the strawberry shampoo and he inhaled the aroma along with the smell of her skin, enjoying the combination as if it were a fine wine.

She smiled over at him as she started the car. He couldn't smile back because his fangs were sliding out. He fixed her with a long stare. Her smile slowly disappeared, the same longing in his eyes filling her own. Keeping his magic to himself had become second nature by now. He knew the lust was hers.

She put the car in drive to get to her house as quickly as possible. He kept his hands to himself because he thought he might force her off the road, which would lead to uncomfortable sex in a car, which could lead to being spotted by a cop, which would mean a ticket . . . It was too much to risk and just enough to ponder to keep him occupied until they made it home.

Inside, they ripped each other's clothes off. He literally tore the hem of her new tank top. She pushed him on the bed. Her eyes locked with his. She sank to her knees, a devilish smirk on her gorgeous face. He helped her out by holding her hair. She took him in her mouth while caressing his thighs, his stomach. She did this thing, this flick of her tongue at the tip of the head that sent shivers all through him.

Celia climbed onto the bed, straddling his hips. She easily coaxed him inside. He gripped her ass as she chewed his ear. Pretty soon, she was moaning in his neck. Her teeth went to his shoulder. He waited until her breath came in little bursts, indicating she was close to climax. That's when he lifted her hair and bit into the flesh of her neck.

Her gasp was a sough in his ear. Her hands twisted in his hair, holding him in place—not that he was moving away. Victor grunted as he dragged from her. Her glorious, glorious warmth filled him up, so much so that it began to cloud his head. When he was hungry like this, he tended to lose himself as the animal inside fought its way forward. That animal wanted it all, demanded he not stop, and he gripped the back of her neck a little too roughly to keep her head tilted.

The otherness about her was fucking marvelous.

Through the bliss, he realized her fingers were slipping from his hair. She felt heavy on top of him. The warning bells sounded; he was taking too much. Her moans were softer. He dug deep, fighting through the fog, to find the strength to stop himself. He had to pull away from the intoxicating warmth.

His moans turned into a snarl when he forced himself to release her neck. His chest heaved from the effort as his face distorted with greed.

Get a hold of yourself, he demanded.

He felt his body relax. There would be more time. Celia was his.

Her face was still buried in his shoulder. With his tongue, he traced the two holes he had created, coating the wounds with his saliva while capturing the last droplets of blood. He sat back and cut his wrist. She took it eagerly.

Celia moved drunkenly. She crawled off of Victor to the head of the bed where she collapsed on a pillow with a sigh.

Victor licked his lips. Her sweet blood flowed through him, pumping in his chest with her rhythm. His fingers and toes prickled. He stared down at his hands in awe. Her blood tingled beneath his skin. His body seemed so alive! The closest he had every come to experiencing this strange, wondrous sensation was back when he was first turned. He and his maker would go on hunts through the dreary London streets like deadly apparitions. Taking more than his fill of human blood united him with his former human self as his body quivered like strings of a violin. He loved it then, when he could be alive and powerful at once. Before he realized he could be a killer no more.

Currently, he possessed a piece of her that would normally only last one night. However, this was the third time they had shared blood. That meant they now had a bond. They would both have a line to the other, the ability to sense each other's presence and feelings. The stronger the bond, the easier it would be for Victor to locate her.

The next common step in this sort of connection was the complete devotion of the human to the vampire. Depending on the vampire, this could mean a variety of things. The human could stay with the vamp at all times for nourishment. The vamp could have full control, and the human would be compelled to oblige, no matter the demand.

Ramsey's groupies didn't have to fear outrageous demands. Most of them were even allowed inside the house without being enthralled. Once they were "called," the magic wore off when they stepped through the threshold.

Victor glanced over to make sure she was okay. Celia's hair covered her eyes, her chest rising and falling evenly. He sensed her bliss, though he was certain she did not fully recognize what ecstasy was. Losing the ability to feel human and gaining it back in one evening was indescribable.

Victor's warm hand circled her ankle. Could she feel him, he wondered. He thought maybe the warmth she had bestowed on him exuded through his pores. She murmured softly in response to his touch. She stretched her leg and rubbed her foot along his thigh.

He shifted on the bed to lie beside her. He watched her, how flushed her cheeks and nose were, how the light from the lamp danced in the hollow of her throat, how her brown nipples stood at attention. Heat radiated from her body, like on particularly steamy days when you could see the waves of baked-in sun rising from the concrete. Or, at least how he remembered it did.

Slowly, a beatific smile spread across her face, lighting her even more than the after-glow she was displaying. Her soft lips parted.

"You're thinking about me."

He frowned because it wasn't a question and kind of an odd thing to say. "What?"

"I saw it. You were thinking about me."

"What do you mean?"

"I saw me, lying here, and could tell what you were thinking."

Victor was quiet, bemused. His mind had been on her, but how could she know that? She must've detected his confusion, or maybe she "saw" it, because she opened her eyes.

"What's wrong?" she asked.

He paused a moment, trying to situate the fragments of thoughts. "I've never experienced this before. A human seeing into our minds," he added to clarify. "You should only be able to sense me and even then it is faint."

She propped herself up on an elbow and pushed her hair

aside so she could look at him. Her face was serious now. "What does this mean?"

He sat up, too. "Can you do it at will? Here," he said. "What am I thinking?"

Victor chose a memory, back in February, when they had slow-danced in her living room to a beautiful song about love. It was the first thing that popped in his head, even if it was gag-worthy.

Celia chewed her bottom lip while staring into his gray eyes. Then she smiled again. "I loved that song."

"Huh," he said excitedly. "That's amazing."

He visualized Celia's thighs. She had a beauty mark on her left one, just below her— "Hey!" she called, slapping his arm playfully. "Keep it clean, mister."

As he was rolling through his memories, trying to come up with another dirty thought, a different idea crept through.

"Celia," he started. His voice was pensive. He stopped. Tactfulness was the key. "Do you think you can see into Milo's mind?"

He waited for her reaction. Her jaw dropped slightly, her mouth forming a small "o." She didn't blink; she just stared at him. Her right hand went to the elastic around her left wrist.

Anxiety fluttered from her through their bond. He was going to take it back because he didn't want to be the cause of her apprehension. He wasn't given the chance.

"How do I do that?" she finally asked.

Victor shook his head. "This is all new territory for me. How did you do it with me?"

"I don't know. These visions just sort of popped in my head. That's what happened the last time. I got flashes from Milo. I couldn't control it."

He mulled it over for a moment. "Try thinking about him. I know, I know," he said quickly at the perturbed expression frozen on her face. "Just try it, okay?"

She sighed and closed her eyes. He watched her face for any signs of distress. Her snapping went into overdrive. After a minute, he placed his hand on hers, stopping her persistent habit with that damned elastic. She shook her head, unaware of what she had been doing.

"Nothing," she reported. She sounded more relieved if anything. "It probably only works if I share blood and that ain't gonna happen." Her breasts quivered when she flopped back against the pillow.

"Yes, I know." Disappointment tinted his words. He wondered, not for the first time, if Elizabeth or Ramsey knew anything about this sort of situation. Maybe there was a way to tap into Milo's mind. They could find where he was hiding.

Though, if sharing blood was the way to go, he was not thrilled. There had to be another approach, he told himself.

Celia's small fingers caressed his chin, bringing him back to the present. She had been watching him. If she'd seen what he was thinking, she didn't mention it. Instead, she tugged him forward for a kiss. He ran a hand over her naked stomach before pressing his body against hers. They melted into each other again. Only this time, he refrained from drinking from her. She had to work tomorrow and needed a clear head.

The next night, Celia had a peculiar surprise. Though Victor hadn't come to her as soon as he woke, she felt him, just under her skin. His presence helped relax her. And she hadn't received a shock when he did appear suddenly in her bedroom. She had known he was there before she felt his arms around her waist. This new sensation was comforting and bizarre and creepy all at once.

Six

MEG FINALLY GOT around to buying the paint for the shed in her backyard. She commissioned Celia's help Saturday afternoon. The sun was shining, warming the air to a nice seventy-five degrees. When she arrived at the cozy home in Lower Mills at three, the shed was already sanded, the primer already applied. Winston had taken care of that. He was covered in white shavings.

Meg poured a sunny yellow paint into silver trays. Celia whistled as she approached and Meg smiled at the tune. Winston rolled his eyes. He wisely kept his snide remarks to himself. Both of them would be all over him for treading on their tradition.

The blue tarp crunched under Celia's feet. They had laid it around the tiny shed to keep paint from the grass and pathway. The shed was just large enough for gardening tools, the lawn mower, and a few boxes. It wouldn't take too long to paint. Plus, the hard work was already done.

"Okay, I think we're ready," Meg said. "Oh, wait! I forgot the water. I don't want paint tracked into the house." She rushed off, up the back porch and into the house.

Celia peeked over at Winston. An awkward silence settled between them. It had been a couple of days since he stormed out on her. Seeing her cousin again brought up the issue of that gym bag. She put her hands in the pockets of her old jeans.

The silence was deafening. Well, minus the birds playing in the nearby bushes and the cars passing on the street. Celia could clearly hear her aunt moving around in the kitchen through the open door. Winston glanced at her. After a pause, he reached over to muss with her hair. It was his annoying way of breaking up the tension. He gave that toothy smile before picking up a paint roller. She eyed him while fixing her ponytail. He was focusing on his work a little too intensely. He knew she was looking at him.

Celia grabbed a brush to start on the trimming. "So, why are you in town?" she asked again. She was not ready to let this go.

He rolled paint onto the door in even strokes. "None of your business," he said simply.

"Are you on vacation?" she pressed.

"Celia."

"How long are you staying?"

His head jerked to her. The roller was stopped in mid-stroke. "What's it to you, huh?" he asked forcefully, officially dropping the unruffled act. "Why are you so fucking concerned?"

"I was just asking," she shot back.

"I'm not getting the third degree from my own damn parents. I don't have to answer to anyone, especially not my nosy-ass cousin!"

Her jaw slacked at his anger. He glowered at her a moment longer before slowly turning back to the shed. Miffed, Celia flicked her brush at him. Yellow paint splattered his face, hair, and shoulder.

"Hey!" he shouted, ducking too late.

In retaliation, Winston rolled his brush across her chest. She gasped in surprise. Good thing it was an old shirt with hair dye stains on it. She was about to swipe her brush across his face when Meg called out from the porch.

"How old are you two?" she said as she approached. Her face was stern because they were wasting her paint being childish.

She stomped onto the tarp with three bottled waters in hand. "Are we going to do this, or what?"

Meg looked from each of them. They glared at each other before grumbling something to the effect of agreement. It took an hour to apply the first coat.

They sat on the back porch, eating roast beef sandwiches on onion rolls and barbeque chips while they waited. Winston was staring purposefully at his plate. Celia peeked over at him a few times while chewing her sandwich. She was still curious about what he was up to, and he wasn't helping his case being so fucking secretive. He probably could've stymied this from the beginning had he just said he was on vacation. And hadn't left his bag of goodies in the living room . . . Okay, so maybe she would still be suspicious.

Celia offered to throw the trash away, also making an excuse of needing the bathroom. Inside the house, she went to the second floor. There were three bedrooms in the house. Her aunt and uncle's room was at the end of the carpeted hall. When she lived there, Celia had taken over Lyle's room on the left. She assumed Winston was staying in his old room.

She checked the stairs to make sure the coast was clear before pushing open the door on the right. She was greeted with a flowery scent, like fabric softener. Was Aunt Meg doing his laundry? Celia gagged at the thought.

The room was simple, having taken on the role of spare

bedroom after Winston moved to Brooklyn. A full-sized bed sat under the window, the plain brown comforter bunched up at the foot. A brown- and green-checkered rug poked out from under the bed; the rest of the floor was unadorned, highlighting the hardwood. There was a mahogany desk and dresser and lightweight brown curtains on the two windows. Celia heard Meg and Winston's voices from the yard though the windows were closed. Winston's black suitcase lay open by the closet. Jeans and t-shirts were pulled out.

She scanned the room from the threshold but didn't see the blue gym bag. A sudden noise at the bottom of the stairs frightened her. Celia jumped inside the room. She closed the door silently and pressed her ear against it.

Footsteps thumped on the stairs. Her eyes widened because they sounded heavy. It couldn't be her aunt. On the other side of the window, she only heard a bird singing in a nearby tree. The person reached the landing. She waited with bated breath, expecting Winston to burst through the door she was leaning on at any second. Of course, that would mean a door to the face but she couldn't make herself move away.

The footsteps continued down the hall. A door opened then closed. She blew out the breath she'd been holding. It was Max, coming home from work. Celia faced the room. She hadn't spotted the gym bag but there had to be something amongst his things that could let her in on what he was doing in Boston.

She went to the suitcase and gingerly picked up articles of clothes. She hoped against hope that she didn't come across any dirty underwear or vibrators or lube. Even condoms would creep her out. She couldn't afford the images. She finished her search, finding nothing out of place about the suitcase.

She moved on to the dresser, where he had laid out some of his toiletries. All she saw were hygiene essentials. The drawers were empty. At the desk, she rifled through the papers and books, careful to place them back how she found them.

A glossy, black three-by-five flyer caught her eye. She pulled it from beneath a sheet of paper advertising a motorcycle for sale—she took a second to snort in amusement at the visual of Winston on a Harley. Hopefully the helmet would cover his marked-up forehead when he was trying to impress the ladies.

In the upper, left-hand corner of the flyer was a picture of an inky-black hawk on the face of a full, white moon. Beneath, in Broadway script, was September 23rd—the upcoming Wednesday's date—ten-thirty pm as the time, and an address in South Boston. She flipped it over. The back was blank. Not a ton of information and just ominous enough to send a chill up her arms.

While contemplating the flyer, Celia tucked it where she found it before slipping out the door and back downstairs.

***

Ramsey, Bryce, and Elizabeth were in the living room when Victor appeared Saturday night. He eased down onto the sofa next to Bryce, who stared morosely at the television. A movie played—*Fast and Furious* it appeared since Vin Diesel was on the screen.

Ramsey was sitting on the opposite sofa, with his arm on the back of the seat. Elizabeth was nestled next to him, her legs tucked beside her. She wore another stunning maxi dress, her feet bare. She had the most interest in the movie.

"I hate to interrupt," Victor replied. "I just needed some insight."

"What's up?" Ramsey asked.

He took a deep breath. "Celia has been able to see into my head. She knew what I was thinking. She could even see what I saw. It happened before, with Milo, when he'd given her his blood. That's how we were able to find the hunters' house."

Elizabeth glanced over, intrigued. "Does it only happen just after exchanging blood or can she do it at other times?" After years and years of being a vamp—plus she was a doc—she obviously didn't feel the need to toe around intimacies.

"I don't know. It's only happened right after we shared." Apparently he wasn't too squeamish either. "Have you encountered this before?"

Her pretty face scrunched together for a moment as she pondered. She looked up at Ramsey. "Do you remember that witch, Claudia?

"She gave me the potion to defeat Nathan."

"There was another, in her coven. I heard she could locate vampires."

"She wasn't in a coven," Ramsey corrected.

Elizabeth frowned. "She was."

"No, she was never a part of that group. She would do rituals with them but that was it."

"No, I'm certain she had to join in order to—"

"This witch," Victor interrupted before they got on a roll. "How did she do it?"

Elizabeth shook her head. "I'm not sure. All I know is the other witches looked to her to find vamps." She shrugged. "They were trying to kill all the vamps in this area. That was before we moved here. I was staying with a friend when I heard about the hunt."

"Who?" Ramsey asked. His brow was touching his hairline in reprove.

Elizabeth poked him. "Oh, hush. It was Cooper's nest. You know I have nothing to offer that he wants. Something happened though," she said, getting back to the conversation, "because they disappeared. The whole coven. Well, except Claudia. I don't know how she was spared. I'm not even sure she still lives in the state."

Victor sighed because though it was an interesting story, it didn't really help his situation. The witch was dead and this

Claudia's location was unknown. She'd helped Ramsey fifty years ago; she might've been dead as well. He didn't bother asking Bryce, who was off in his own world of grief and worry.

"She tried to tap into Milo's head since she's had his blood, but she said it didn't work."

"You don't believe her?" Ramsey asked. Maybe he picked up something in his tone.

Victor shrugged. "Of course I believe her. I'm just wondering if she tried hard enough."

"Whatever they're using to block me may be affecting her as well," Ramsey replied. Victor had been wondering about Ramsey's connection with Milo and Clarice for a little while.

"We could do some tests, if you'd like?" Ramsey went on. He had a playful smirk. Elizabeth pinched his thigh. "What?" he cried, looking over at her. "I'm not talking about sex, love. We could test how well she reads vampire minds after a certain time."

"You mean, after having others' blood," Elizabeth added dryly.

He shrugged. "Sure. If she can still see into Victor's head after having you and me, that's amazing. It'll show whether there's a chance she can find Milo. I can partake without sex, I'll have you know."

She glared at him but playfulness was beneath it. Victor just rubbed his face. He didn't like the idea of her having others' blood, not at all. Even if it was an interesting idea, and he hated to admit that he was intrigued. What other abilities did she have? Were they only at their strongest right after exchanging blood? Or would they be able to surface even when she had been without?

Ramsey had been watching Victor during his little internal debating. He had a strange expression that was both cautious and optimistic. He was probably hoping he'd go for it. Victor just didn't understand why he seemed on guard all of a sudden. Elizabeth was studying him as well.

Victor shook his head to clear it. "I'll have to think about this," he said. "And talk with Celia."

"You do that."

He looked at Ramsey. His black hair had fallen into his face. "Do you think she's a witch?"

Ramsey shrugged. "In my experience, you can't tell just by looking at 'em."

"Are you still in contact with Claudia?"

He shook his head. "Elizabeth is right. She moved out of the city some thirty years ago. That's why I've had to use others, like Corinna."

"She didn't like us anyway," Elizabeth added.

Victor only nodded.

***

Michael was being weird again that night. His desultory behavior was like a hard jab to the gut. He had been telling some anecdote to two other servers and they were laughing it up. Celia smiled as she walked by, wondering what was so funny. As soon as she was in the vicinity, Michael immediately clammed up. He looked away from her, his chin in the air.

The servers didn't notice though, thank goodness. Celia didn't want others thinking there was a problem. Of course, there was a problem. She just didn't know what about.

Michael's shift ended at ten, when the nightclub was beginning its upswing. Celia spied him heading toward the hallway that led to the kitchen and Bobby's office.

"I'll be right back," she called over "Party in the U.S.A." to Carson.

"What?" he cried. His head snapped from the large group before them to gawk at Celia. "We're just starting. Deal with your period later."

"I'll only be a second, dickhead."

She hurried away from his scowl. Michael was stepping out of Bobby's office when she made it to the hallway. As usual, he froze when he saw her. His tall, broad frame seemed to take up the entire corridor.

He held her gaze, almost reluctantly, as if by obligation. She remembered Tina commenting once about how difficult it was to maintain eye contact with him most of the time. Celia didn't feel that way but she could see how his steady stare could be intimidating.

After a few seconds, Michael moved to go around her. She grabbed his arm and shoved him farther down the hall for a little privacy. She normally would've struggled with pushing someone as strong as him but her anger and Victor's blood did the trick.

Once they'd come to a stop, she shouted in a whisper, "I don't get it! What the hell is it now?"

"What're you talking about?" he asked in a strained voice that she guessed was supposed to sound indifferent.

"Why are you treating me like I ran over your goddamn puppy?"

Michael's nose flared slightly. She waited. The music thumped at her back. He groaned at the impatient insistence in her face. "I... I can't tell you," he said softly.

She shook her head. "That's bullshit. Either you want to be my fucking friend or you don't. And I must say, right now, I could go for the latter. I don't need this fucking headache."

She spun on her heels to storm off but he grabbed her elbow. His hand was warm, even through her shirt. She glared back at him.

His voice was a low growl. "Wait."

His hand dropped to his side. She faced him again, folding her arms at the chest. His expression was troubled, like he was fighting with something—which, come to think of it, seemed to be his usual expression when regarding Celia. At the same time, she noticed he wouldn't drop his gaze. As the seconds of silence stretched on, Celia's irritation rose. Why was she trying to figure out his problem, she asked herself. Why was she wasting her fucking time?

She rolled her eyes, annoyed beyond goddamn belief, and turned to leave. He took hold of her arm again and pulled her into the kitchen. She had to skip to keep up with him.

The chefs were cleaning for the night. Dishes banged, water ran in the sinks. The radio was on, and they were singing merrily to "Knock You Down." None of them noticed when they entered. Michael opened the back door and tugged Celia into the alley. The night air was comfortable tonight.

Michael used a loose brick to prop the door open to prevent it from locking them out. The door was normally locked at ten on club nights for security reasons, when business had concluded in the kitchen.

He didn't immediately look at her. Instead, he put his hands in his pockets and stared off to his right. A few cars sped by the mouth of the alley. After a long minute, he took out a crumpled pack of Newport's. He brought the pack to his lips. When he pulled it away, a white cigarette was clenched between his teeth.

Celia opened her mouth to object but he had already whipped out his lighter. He took a deep drag and released it with a soft groan. It helped him to relax, she noticed. Of course, she remembered those times and how a good ol' smoke could ease her anxieties. She could use a smoke dealing with all this bullshit.

After another puff, Michael still hadn't spoken. Tired of this waiting game, and the unexpected cravings his cigarette was bringing to the surface, Celia blew out a breath.

"Look, I have to get back to work."

She reached for the door.

"Okay!" he called. "Listen, this is gonna be hard to believe."

She frowned, intrigued and puzzled. If only he understood all the implausible shit she knew and, therefore, had to believe.

He finally faced her, shifting from foot to foot.

"You . . . smell."

She gaped at him. Involuntary tears actually welled in her eyes as embarrassment reddened her cheeks. She'd never heard complaints about her hygiene. She thought she was conscientious.

"I smell?" She was wondering if it was her breath. Armpits? She couldn't bring herself to think of other areas.

He waved his hands in front of him, frustrated by whatever he was struggling to convey. "Not like that."

"Then like what?" Her voice trembled slightly, which was fucking annoying.

"You, uh . . ." He broke off. With a shake of his head, he changed tracks. "What do you know about . . . vampires?"

Celia froze. Her eyes searched his as she tried to gauge how she should answer. He didn't give her a chance.

"That guy the other night, the one who grabbed your arm? He was a vampire."

"How do you know that?" she asked in a tiny voice.

He paused again with more internal debating and another drag. Her eyes were drawn to his lips as he sucked on the cancer stick. It looked so good.

"I'm a shifter," he finally blurted. His words came out in white smoke.

She didn't respond right away because she was certain she had heard wrong. After all, she'd been distracted by his cigarette.

She blinked up at him. "A shifter?"

"I change into an animal," he said hastily. "So, I can tell things. Smell things—" He tapped his nose. "He was a vampire. I smelled vampire again in the kitchen, after he left."

Huh.

"And you," he said. "You don't completely smell like one and I know you're not one but it's there."

Now it was her turn to fidget. Michael was being very upfront and she had a million questions but she didn't know what she could tell him. She wasn't about to out her boyfriend to a virtual stranger. Although Michael did know about vamps, which was something as far as trust went.

He looked at the ground for a moment, then back up at her. His expression shifted, making him appear uneasy.

"My friend says that means you had vampire blood."

"There are others like you?" Celia asked because that was the first question to tumble out and the easiest with which to deal.

"Yes."

Michael was eyeing her expectantly. She figured he wanted to know if she was drinking vamp blood. Oh, how to answer that?

"I don't know what to say," she admitted.

That seemed to be confirmation enough for him. His brows pulled together, his nose flared. He threw the cigarette to the ground.

"How could you do that, Celia? Don't you know how dangerous it is around vampires?"

"It's really none of your business," she retorted, her anger rising to match his. Who the hell did he think he was? He obviously didn't know Victor or Ramsey's bunch, or else he wouldn't be so fucking high-strung about vampires.

"Why would you drink blood? That shit's addictive and fucking disgusting. And what if the vampire goes too far, huh? You think about that shit? You could die and then where will you be? You think that vampire would care? That he couldn't find another sheep?" He had stepped up to her and taken hold of her shoulders. By the end, he was shaking her.

"Get off!" she cried, yanking his arms down. "You don't know anything about me."

"I know you're fucking nuts if you hang with vampires," Michael exploded.

She stepped up to him, pointing a furious finger at his chest. That same sharp smell she remembered from the other night filled her nose. It was the scent coming from the strange, angry men.

She was too distracted to process that. "You know what's fucking nuts? Trying to reason with someone who thinks you're disgusting."

His mouth slacked open. He was surprised she'd taken his words that way. She barely noticed. The fury in her eyes could melt iron.

"You leave me the fuck alone."

Celia swung the door open and stormed back to the bar. If Michael had tried to follow, he wouldn't be able to talk to her if she was working. Not that he'd try to have this particular conversation in a crowded lounge.

Five minutes later, she spotted him heading toward the door. Michael glanced over to her as he went. She couldn't decipher his expression but she told herself she didn't care. She dropped her head to break the contact as she prepared three Captain and Cokes.

At the end of the night, Celia and Trixie went to the parking lot. Trixie was aware of Celia's sour mood, and after trying four times to prompt a conversation, she sank into her seat, surrendering. Celia waited for her to go inside her apartment before peeling off. She was too angry to let her fear of being out at night alone distress her.

Victor was waiting for her when she got home. He was on the sofa, watching TV. His eyes were on her when she entered. Obviously he knew she was approaching. He didn't greet her with a smile; he could feel her anger.

"What's wrong?"

In response, she slammed the front door, jerked the lock into place, and then stomped to her room. She was snatching off her coat when Victor placed his hand on her shoulder. She shrugged him off.

"Don't," she said tightly, not looking at him. Michael's words were still in her head. He'd called her a sheep, like she followed behind Victor, waiting for the next chance to supply him with nourishment. She didn't know much about the humans vampires kept on hand but she was certain she wasn't one of them. Victor was her boyfriend. He didn't bespell her. He didn't force her to do anything.

Or did he? She knew the feel of vampire magic, his included, and she had never fully experienced it with him because she was able to stop him. But wasn't the point for her not to realize?

She groaned to herself, furious that she was considering Victor untrustworthy and saddened that Michael thought she was a piece of meat for him.

"Seal, what happened?" He sounded a little wounded that she was shunning him.

"Nothing, okay?" she snapped. She moved across the room to kick off her shoes and remove her clothes. She didn't want to discuss it with him, especially since she wasn't sure of how a discussion would flow. She enjoyed what they had and didn't want to think too deeply about it. That's how it always worked. Now, Michael was bringing another element into their relationship. She didn't like that one bit.

Celia noticed Victor watching her, which only made her angrier.

"Look," she said. "I'm home. Milo can't get me here. Why don't you go do . . . whatever the hell you do while I'm sleeping?"

Victor's expression went blank; he didn't even blink. She

knew she'd hurt him. She felt it through their bond. She closed her eyes a second to calm down.

"I'm sorry. I'm being an asshole."

When Celia opened her eyes, she saw that she was speaking to an empty room.

"Shit."

***

Victor eyed the runner as she passed him. He was seated on a bench at Jamaica Pond, attempting to keep his animal in check. He hadn't fed tonight although Celia's blood cursed quietly beneath his skin.

The runner wore black Lycra pants and a baby blue t-shirt. Victor trailed behind her. Though he wasn't running, he was able to catch up with her in a matter of seconds.

Headphones covered her ears. Of course, she would only have heard him if he wanted her to. Her heart raced at a steady rhythm from her stupid, late-night jog. Once they came around a more secluded bend, shielded from the cars on the road, he pounced. The woman didn't have time to gasp. His teeth were in her flesh before he'd fully concealed their bodies in a patch of spiky bushes along the path.

After a while, her puling became unbearable. Her tears were bringing Victor's conscious to the forefront. He jolted away with a snarl. The animal side of him was satisfied, leaving it up to his sensible side to clean up this mess.

The woman was okay. Maybe a few scrapes from falling into the bushes. A continuous stream of her blood pumped from her neck, coating the dead leaves under her. She trembled beneath him, her eyes wide in terror, her hands clenched together at her chest.

"Please," she whispered. "Please . . ."

Victor leaned down again. She whimpered and flinched, but he only laved her throat. When he straightened, he stared into her eyes. The fear receded. She stared back blankly. He fed her a story about tripping on a branch and falling into the brush.

He got to his feet. She was still looking up to where he had been on top of her. Disappointed with himself, Victor vanished.

Bryce was in Ramsey's living room, alone. He glanced up when Victor stopped in the doorway. His shirt was wrinkled and jeans stained with dirt along the cuffs.

"Has Ernesto arrived?" Victor asked.

"Last night. He's out now, trying to track her." A white pillow rested under his arm. He was twisting a corner, dangerously close to ripping it. "Ramsey made me come back here, like I was in the way or some shit."

Victor didn't say anything about that.

"She's been asking for you," Bryce said dourly.

"Who?" Victor asked.

"Ashleigh."

Victor went to the spare bedroom. Ashleigh sat on the bed, a glass in her hand. Elizabeth was at her feet, checking her ankles. Ramsey stood in the corner, one arm crossed at the chest, his other hand clutching his chin. He had the same dirt at the bottom of his khakis. He was the first to notice Victor.

Victor nodded to Ramsey before knocking on the open door. The women looked up. Ashleigh's face brightened from within.

"Victor," she said. She looked like she wanted to go to him. The only reason she couldn't was Elizabeth had her feet.

"How are you feeling?" Victor asked.

"Better, I think. Elizabeth's been helping me with breathing. I can't believe I have to think about it."

"It'll become natural again after a while," Victor replied.

She smiled. "I don't know how to thank you. I would've died if you hadn't come across me."

"I'm glad you're okay. Elizabeth's a wonderful caretaker. Believe me."

Elizabeth gave him a little smile in appreciation. She threw away the bandages that had been around Ashleigh's ankles. Her legs were pale and smooth. The only remainders were small bumps on her ankles and wrists, the last of the awful welts.

"You're doing well," Elizabeth told her.

Ashleigh's forehead crinkled in concern. Softly, she said, "I guess I'll have to go back to Charlie then. He's probably looking for me."

"He hasn't called you?" Ramsey asked. Sires were always able to call their progeny, no matter how much time had passed. She shook her head. He and Elizabeth exchanged glances.

Ashleigh caught the looks. "What?"

"Well," Ramsey began slowly. "That could mean anything."

"But you were thinking something. What is it?" she pressed.

He looked at her directly. "He might not have survived your attack."

Ashleigh's eyes widened in surprise. "Oh." She frowned down at her hands in her lap. She was quiet for a moment.

"He wasn't very nice," she said. "He liked to fight. He would bring people back to the house bleeding, sometimes unconscious. He liked to watch me . . ." She trailed off as embarrassment colored her cheeks. Well, as best as vampire skin could color when dehydrated.

Elizabeth stood. "You should rest." She and Ramsey headed to the door. Victor turned to leave as well. Her hand touched his wrist.

"Please," Ashleigh said. "I don't want to be alone."

Her face wore the same despondent mask. It probably wasn't the best idea, but he nodded anyway. Celia was in a mood. He wasn't looking to step in the line of fire again, especially when he didn't understand the reasons behind it. She had been doing fine. Her panic attacks were at a minimal and he thought he had been part of the solution. Once again, though, he'd gotten upset and lost control.

Not that he should blame her, he told himself.

He pushed that aside as he settled in the replacement chair for a while.

Two hours had flown by of them discussing Boston and New York and television shows. Ashleigh laughed often, which really made her seem younger. She told him about how clumsy she used to be. Since becoming a vampire, however, she found she was a lot more graceful. Victor made sure never to relax as much as he felt he wanted to. He consciously ensured that there was always space between them.

At five-thirty, he checked that she was comfortable. He was throwing away the last bags of blood into the garbage can.

"What's your girlfriend's name?" Ashleigh asked softly.

Victor tensed. This was the first time either of them had brought her up. "Celia," he said cautiously.

"And she's human?"

"Yes."

Ashleigh nodded. Her eyes dropped to her lap where she was smoothing down the comforter.

"And . . . that works for you?"

He straightened and looked her in the eye. "Yes."

"I would think that'd be a distraction." She shrugged. "Frank . . . Frank was an idiot. He didn't deserve to die but he was always making the wrong decisions. I hope your girlfriend treats you better."

Victor turned, and left the room.

Seven

JAY CALLED AS soon as Celia entered her house Sunday evening.

"Celia!" he cried in exasperation. "Where the hell have you been?"

She closed her eyes with a sigh. "I've been kinda busy." There was a pause, the silence so loud and accusatory that guilt made her gulp.

"I'm sorry," she said. It had been three days since he'd left the voice message saying he was leaving town. It seemed more like a lifetime ago. "I should've called you back."

"What's going on?" he asked quietly. She could tell he was trying to contain his irritation.

"Nothing." She didn't sound convincing at all. She winced, waiting to see if he would let it drop though knowing full well he wouldn't.

"Celia."

"So, you're back in Dallas, huh?" She crossed the room to turn on the lamp. "How's the house?"

"It's fine. Gonna cost a pretty penny but there's insurance. Now, what the fuck's going on over there?"

"It was your parents' house?" she went on. She didn't want to tell him, not yet. She didn't want him to worry. Her evasion wasn't helping. "Why do you keep it?"

"Dammit, Celia. I'm coming back."

"Jay, you don't have to do that."

"Something's obviously wrong. Was it that goddamn bloodsucker? Did he attack you?"

Giving up, she sank into the sofa. She told him about Milo in the bar and how Michael came to her rescue. She also told him about Ashleigh and her cousin's return and her suspicions, especially after finding the silver chain in his gym bag.

Jay was quiet through her rambling, injecting the occasional hmm or uh-huh.

"I don't think he was the one to hurt that woman but it's still so sketchy."

"Don't go to that meeting," he said firmly.

"Why not?"

"It could be dangerous."

"I just want to know what it's about."

"Don't do it. I'm gonna call Snipe and see if he knows of this group."

"You do that," she said snippily. She was not happy with his controlling behavior, even from thousands of miles away.

"Celia," Jay said warningly. "You might get hurt."

"Thanks for your concern but I can handle myself."

"Do I need to remind you of the last month?"

She rolled her eyes but had nothing to dispute that. "What do you know about shifters?" she asked suddenly.

"Shifters? Shape-shifters? There's no such thing."

"How do you know?"

"Never came across one."

"How do you know?" she insisted.

"I just do," he said definitively.

Great. She wasn't going to tell him about Michael. She had been hoping Jay knew something on the subject. She didn't think he was holding out on her. He also didn't seem too willing to discuss the possibility of other types of supernatural beings.

This coming from the guy who identified vamps because they glowed.

She hung up with Jay after a minute. She then called Victor, who didn't answer. She felt him, that strange sensation that he was with her even though he wasn't in the room. She sighed as she listened to his silky voice telling her to leave a message.

"It's me," she said softly. "I'm sorry."

She hopped in the shower then pulled on shorts and a t-shirt. Victor hadn't shown up nor called her back. He was probably still upset about her snapping at him, which she understood. He had had no idea why she was so cranky last night. She didn't even know how to explain.

Convinced that Victor wasn't coming, she went to her room. She was getting used to the floating feel of vampire blood. When she climbed into bed, she knew she'd get to sleep.

She settled in under her covers and turned off her bedside lamp. The half-moon was bright outside, shining through the lilac curtains. She closed her eyes to the shimmering light. The sensation of hovering above her mattress was more soothing now instead of disconcerting, and sleep began to wash over her.

Just as she was sinking into the pleasant blackness of unconsciousness, a peculiar noise broke the silence of her room. With some effort, her eyes fluttered open. She tried to decipher what had woken her. When her sleepy brain thought about it, it could've been the whine of a dog. There weren't many dogs on her block, so it was strange to hear one.

She shut her eyes again. The whine was a little louder the second time. It actually sounded persistent. Curious, she pushed the covers aside, went to the window and opened the curtains. Her mouth fell open in shock.

Down on the street stood the biggest, fluffiest dog Celia had ever seen in her life. Its fur was a sepia color, with a black underbelly. Its paws were massive, the snout long, the pointy ears perked. It was sitting, and had to be at least four feet tall. The tail swept the ground behind it.

Its tall stature reminded her of when she was in high school. A man in leather came on the Red Line train headed downtown with his bullmastiff. The man had been at least six-four. His dog came to his elbow, sitting. She'd been mesmerized, and had to suppress the sudden urge to mount the dog like a pony.

She frowned down at the creature, who stared right back with intelligent, golden eyes. Something told her it was a male. Images of wolves she'd seen on the Internet or in movies rose in her mind. This animal could definitely qualify, though it was larger than she thought wolves normally were. Even so, a wolf? In Boston? It didn't make any sense.

His left ear twitched backward. The head turned to the side. He looked back up at Celia before getting to his feet. She watched as he trotted off down the sidewalk. He disappeared around the corner just as a car glided down the street.

The wolf/dog took up most of the space in her head when she slowly returned to bed. She wondered if maybe she was dreaming. Could the vampire blood cause hallucinations such as this?

She shook her head firmly. As she drifted off, those golden eyes blazed behind her eyelids, peering at her, ensuring she slept.

***

Monday night, Ashleigh was allowed out of her room on

good behavior. She crept through the house, looking over everything, including Ramsey and Elizabeth's room, which was unlocked. She even went to the basement, following Cillian's rich baritone down the stairs.

Victor and Elizabeth were in the living room. He had ESPN on but he heard her descending the stairs.

Cillian's song flowed into a conversation. "You are the new one," he said through his door.

"Yes," Ashleigh answered, sounding curious. "Who are you?"

"I am Cillian ó Dubhghaill. Warrior of Dublin, Kildare, and Wicklow. Slayer and lover of many. The militia thought they had me in New Ross, but no, how I escaped the flame. Yes, the others were hanged and torched but their weapons had no effect on Cillian ó Dubhghaill."

"Why are you locked up?"

He chuckled, an airy sound that flowed mellifluously through his barrier. "Because, my child, we wouldn't want anything to happen to you. The thirst haunts me constantly, as I am certain it does to you."

Ashleigh didn't respond out loud.

"You will learn to master it."

"How did you know—?"

"I know many things, young one, including what astounds you as a new member of this wondrous sect. I can smell the last of your mortality on your breath. It is quite beautiful. The lady, with her golden locks flowing in the night breeze . . . She was the one I loved. Yes, if one in my state could still feel love that is what I felt for her."

"Who was she?" Ashleigh sounded eager. "What was her name?"

He sighed. "There are many things in this world to fear. Being vampire is not one of them." In classic Cillian fashion, the ancient vampire switched gears like a fussy transmission.

There was a pause as Ashleigh no doubt contemplated his words. "I like your voice. Can you sing to me?"

"Certainly." And he was singing again, a mournful song about crying in flawless Spanish despite his Irish brogue.

After a while, Ashleigh wandered into the living room. Victor turned the volume down when she entered.

Her hair was brushed and neat. She still wore the clothes Elizabeth had used to dress her. She sat next to Victor on the sofa where he was lounging. She was close enough that their thighs touched.

"It's so weird," she said. "I've been thinking about Charlie and I've noticed there's something . . . different. I can't . . . sense him. I guess that's the right word."

She peeked up at Victor. A small smile played at the corner of her lips. "Can we go somewhere tonight? I need some fresh air."

Victor looked to Elizabeth. "I have to go to work," she said. "It might not be a good idea. You're still so new—"

"I'll be okay, I swear," Ashleigh said quickly. "Besides, Victor will be with me. Right, Victor?"

She turned those big blue eyes on him again. He could understand her desperation, her need to get out in the world. She hadn't had any incidents since last Friday, when she first woke to the unfamiliar room. Plus, she would need fresh blood, not the pre-packaged and treated kind. Going outside would be the only way to learn self-control.

He didn't say anything though, because he knew Elizabeth would argue. She left around ten to head to the hospital. Ten minutes after that, Victor went to Ashleigh's room, where she had retreated soon after Elizabeth said it wouldn't be ideal for her to leave the house.

"Why don't we go out for a little?" he asked at the door. Her head snapped up. Her smile literally broke her face.

She hopped up from the bed and ran over to throw her arms around him. "Oh, thank you, thank you!" She stepped back and frowned down at her outfit. "I can't go out like this."

He shook his head in amusement. Girls!

"We're just taking a walk."

She pouted a little at that, obviously expecting something more. She didn't protest, though. The night was warm for the humans. Anyone out would only need a sweater for warmth.

Ashleigh stopped at the base of the stairs and took a deep breath. "It's so beautiful."

"What is?"

She smiled and her round cheeks swelled. "Everything." And then she shrugged, growing shy all of a sudden. "I love being outside. It's like I can feel everything around me."

They walked a steady pace down Ramsey's street; a cozy, tree-lined road with stunning homes that caught the sun no matter on which side of the street they lay. The lights were still shining in most of the windows. It was a school night, so the kids in the neighborhood would be indoors, puzzling through math equations and reading passages.

They were a few feet from the beginning of the street when Victor heard the woman approach. He stiffened. In only a few seconds Ashleigh would register the human. The woman, middle-aged in a dark blue jogging suit, was walking her brown Shar-Pei. He heard the clink of the dog's tags, the rush of ragged air through her nose—she was fighting a cold.

A breeze picked up. Ashleigh took a deep breath. She glanced around as she tried to find what had captured her attention.

The woman rounded the corner on the opposite side. A growl ripped through Ashleigh's chest. At the sound, a squirrel scampered from its hiding place among the branches of a nearby tree to the refuge of higher ground.

Her fangs slid out. Victor grabbed her arm tight in his hand.

"Easy," he said in a low, commanding voice.

She was inching forward, her eyes set on the oblivious woman. The dog found a tree that smelled good and took a moment to sniff. Ashleigh, for the most part, controlled herself. She was growling and had that intense, hungry look. However, she wasn't fighting to free herself.

"I want her," Ashleigh hissed. "Let me have her."

"Not like this," Victor warned.

The dog did its business and the woman moved on. They walked past two houses before climbing the wooden stairs of a purple house. Once they disappeared inside, Ashleigh came back to herself. Her fangs went away, her muscles relaxed.

She blinked up at Victor. "When can I have the real thing?" she asked.

Victor rubbed her shoulder. "We'll see."

He continued down the street. He didn't see her smile at his touch. She hurried forward to catch up with him. When she looped her arm in his, he wavered. Could he remove her hand without offending her?

He looked down at her. Ashleigh's face was soft and serene as they strolled. You'd never think she'd been the survivor of such a vicious attack. He couldn't bring himself to break the contact.

Her fingers suddenly tightened on his arm. He knew why; there was another person. They had already turned onto the main road, where the street was wider and the houses set farther apart. A man had pulled to the curb up ahead. He stood at the back door, taking a bundle from the seat. A tiny, demanding heartbeat sang from the blanket in the man's arms.

Ashleigh struggled with her control. She moved forward purposefully, her nails digging into his arm. Victor stopped and took her hand firmly in his so that she would halt as well. She didn't seem to notice that she was standing still.

Her growl was louder this time. The man glanced up. He

frowned at them, cautiously tightening his grip on his little baby he had outside so late. Wisely, the man picked up on the danger. He closed the car door and hurried inside the house, accidentally leaving a black canvas baby bag by the back tire.

Ashleigh groaned in frustration.

"In time," Victor told her, releasing her hand. "You'll need to learn how to compel them, as well."

She nodded. "Charlie used to do that all the time. He liked to be a mystery, he said. He didn't want people remembering him even in passing." Whether she agreed with his behavior or not, Victor couldn't tell. He couldn't really judge since he believed a vamp's prerogative was his own—and she didn't know differently anyway.

"Did you go out often with him?"

"No, not really. The only time he did, I kind of made a scene." She looked away from Victor sheepishly. "He laughed about it but I felt bad. I hurt three people in Central Park. He made them forget." Her chin trembled slightly but she kept the quiver from her voice. "Coming to Boston was the first time since then."

"And he left you by yourself?" This time his disapproval was evident in his tone.

She shrugged modestly. "I was doing fine, you know, when he brought them to the house."

They lapsed into quiet. He was thinking of Courtney. He'd been avoiding her calls, putting her off whenever he actually answered. He knew it wouldn't satisfy her to hear Ashleigh was dead.

Victor's phone rang. He pulled it from his pocket. Courtney's name flashed across the display, as if she had been beckoned. Ashleigh peeked down in curiosity, and then gasped.

"Don't," she said, placing her hand over his. "Please, I don't want her to know."

"What am I to do? She doesn't believe you're dead."

"It's a twin thing," she grumbled, though she didn't sound annoyed. "There has to be something. She can't know about me. I don't want her to know what I've done."

They stood like this for a moment: Victor holding out his phone, Ashleigh's hand on his while pleading with her eyes. The phone went silent for half a minute before it started ringing again. Victor pressed Talk.

"Courtney," he said.

"Hi." Her voice was flat with dejection. "I'm sorry if I'm calling too much. I just . . ." She trailed off into a sigh. "I don't know anymore," she finished softly.

Victor looked at Ashleigh. Her face seemed paler in the moonlight, giving the effect of a porcelain doll. She was very pretty, he admitted, even as she was squeezing his arm in a death grip. He didn't want her in pain, and this seemed to be a way of easing it, at least in part. She still had other issues to deal with— her new life as a vampire, surviving alone in an unknown city. Everything was new and unfamiliar to her, making her a newborn in more ways than one.

"I've found her," he finally said, his eyes on Ashleigh. Ashleigh's face fell. He injected sympathy into his voice. "She's dead, Courtney. I'm sorry."

Courtney's breathing grew spasmodic at this news. "Where? Where is she?" he made out through her gasps.

"I buried her near the mountain."

"What?" she cried in shock. "But I didn't get to see her."

He sighed. "You wouldn't want to remember her like that."

She didn't speak because she had started to cry. He waited, watching Ashleigh. She could hear her sister mourning her. Her eyes dropped to Victor's chest though she was lost somewhere in her head.

"Th-thank you, Victor," Courtney said when she found her

voice. "I'll have to thank Geoff as well."

They hung up. Victor tucked the phone away.

"She sounded so sad," Ashleigh whispered. She then shook her head, resolute. "It's for the best."

Victor rubbed her shoulder again before they continued their walk. Her hand laced with his. He gave her a gentle squeeze.

***

Celia was happily surprised when she stepped out of the bathroom in her robe at eleven-thirty. Victor was sitting on the sofa. He wore black pants and a royal purple shirt under a black leather coat. His dark hair was brushed away from his face and his eyes were as black as night. He looked grim.

She climbed into his lap and wrapped her arms around his neck. If he were a normal person, she would've been smothering him.

"I'm sorry," Celia murmured into his neck. "I was upset about something at work. I shouldn't have taken it out on you."

He didn't say anything, which made her nervous. Just when tears of disappointment began to well in her eyes, Victor's hand caressed her back. She took that as acceptance. She stood, grasped his hand, and led him to her bedroom.

Eight

CELIA HAD WEDNESDAY off. She didn't inform Victor of Winston's meeting. She figured he'd tell her she couldn't go, just like Jay. Either that or he'd want to go with her. The gym bag and ominous flyer made her scared but more so for Victor. She had a distinct feeling that he should be nowhere near that address in Southie. The location alone should've also warned her against going but she just had to know what Winston was up to.

At nine-thirty, she pulled on jeans and a plain, navy blue fleece. She braided her hair back to keep her appearance inconspicuous. After shoving her feet in her sneakers, she made sure she had her ID and some cash, and then headed out. She had to consult the directions she printed out since she didn't visit South Boston, well, ever. Southie wasn't known to be very . . . welcoming to people of color, even in this day and age. Luckily, she wasn't delving into the heart of the neighborhood.

The address turned out to be a bar off Dorchester Street, a

few minutes from Andrew Station. It was a small building at the corner of the block, with a black façade and neon green trimmings. The name of the bar—Olde Nessie's—was written in the same green color in an old-timey font above the door. She purposely parked a block away and hurried to the entrance.

The streets were slick from rain. The shiny surface reflected the lamps overhead and the headlights of passing cars. The light shower had left a chill in the air. The man standing at the door peeked down at her with a cigarette dangling from his lips. He wore baggy light-colored jeans and a Bruins jersey with Bergeron's name on the back. A sign behind him informed that "No One Under 21 Allowed Inside."

He held out his hand to her and jerked his fingers brusquely. She gave him her ID. He scanned it, checked her face, and gave it back.

Celia ducked under his cloud of smoke and went inside. The main room was badly lit and stuffy. The floors were grimy, and her sneakers stuck in places. Only three of the five fans hanging from the ceiling were working. Instead of cooling the place down, they only managed to swirl around the hot air trapped inside.

Celia made out about fifteen people, drinking beer and looking dismal. Like, all of them. This had to be where that saying came from: drowning your worries in beer. Or whatever the hell it was. It didn't seem to be working out so well for this bunch.

Booths lined the walls, two of them occupied. In the center of the room, illuminated by three hanging lights of various wattages, was the medium-sized bar. Lopsided stools topped by worn-out cushions surrounded it.

The female bartender leaned over the counter, flirting with a man who appeared to be three sheets to the wind already. Her peach thong peeked from her low rise jeans. The jeans were cute even if she wasn't very classy.

The male bartender was drying a highball glass. He looked

up when she entered.

Celia peeked around as she slowly approached the bar. The few people inside were all scattered. No way was there a meeting going on in the bar proper.

"What can I get you?" the man asked. He had a thick beard, sharp eyes, and a nose that hadn't been set properly, leaving it off-center up near his eyes. His voice was deep, tinged with some kind of Southern accent Celia didn't recognize.

"Uh, just a Coke, please." She actually would've preferred a rum and Coke—minus the Coke. Victor's blood was nearly gone from her system, sapping her fortitude. Her left wrist was bright red beneath the elastic.

The bartender scooped ice into the highball glass he had just been drying. He pointed the gun and filled it with soda, all the while surveying her with distant interest.

Just then, two men came into the bar. One wore green commando pants and a black shirt. His heavy black boots were laced halfway up his shins. The other man was more casual with jeans and a sweater. A few people looked up at their entrance. Their eyes soon sank back to their beers, their despair preventing them from even feigning interest.

The two men strolled across the room, nodding to the bartender as they passed, before pushing through an unmarked door next to the restrooms. So, maybe this secretive meeting was in a back room.

"Is that the way to the meeting?" she asked the bartender in a low voice. She indicated the door. He was still eyeing her but he nodded.

"How'd you hear about the Night Hawks?" he asked.

"A friend," she lied smoothly. She'd come up with a cover as she was driving. It was flimsy as all fuck but it was better than staring blankly at him with her mouth hanging open. "He couldn't come tonight. He's making me sit in for him. He thought

I'd learn something new."

She pulled out some cash and placed it in front of the doubtful man. She then headed to the door, keeping her pace unhurried when most of her wanted to run out into the night. Gingerly, she opened the unmarked door. There was a short hallway before her, covered with a gray Berber carpet. Three closed doors were on either side. Up ahead, a staircase dropped down to a lower level.

The door she had entered through closed behind her with a loud click that made her jump. A bit of the Coke splashed on her fingers. She shook it off. She took a deep breath before descending the stairs, telling herself to calm the fuck down. She didn't want to alert Victor. At the bottom, she came into a room that was about half the size of the bar upstairs—and better lit.

White folding chairs lined the floor in rows, facing a thin, wooden podium. Battered boxes and file cabinets were packed in corners. Two oscillating fans, positioned in opposite corners, kept the mugginess away. What was with this bar? Did they seriously check IDs before you entered Hell?

Men and women of varying ages filled the room. Some were sitting, talking amongst themselves while fanning away the heat with sheets of paper. Four of them stood by a table to the side, including commando man, pouring coffee and snagging chocolate chip cookies that looked homemade.

Celia spotted Winston. He was seated in the second row, in deep conversation with two other men his age. The one on his left was white, his brown hair spiked, probably on purpose to match the spiked bracelets on his wrists. The other was Asian, wearing a maroon hat and black-rimmed glasses.

When Celia saw her cousin, she immediately found a seat near the back. She slunk down in her chair and placed the soda on the floor. Winston hadn't seen her since he was so engrossed in whatever the hell they were discussing. No one else seemed to notice her either, which was just fine. Her fingers sought the golden heart at her neck. Now that she was sitting, she felt her anxiety ease a tad. She had made it inside; she had infiltrated. Now, to reconnoiter.

Two minutes later, a short, round man stepped up to the podium. He had red cheeks and eyes that didn't seem to widen more than a squint, making it tough to determine what color they were. His shoulders barely rose above the lectern. Like a cue, everyone settled into seats with his appearance. Silence fell over the room.

A woman in her late twenties with a dirty-blonde shaggy hairstyle that fell past her ears sat two seats over from Celia. She wore a tie-dyed t-shirt, no bra, and tight jeans with holes in the knees. Other than her, Celia's row was empty. The woman smiled over to Celia but she was too nervous to make her return smile genial.

"Let's get started," the man replied. He dropped the *r* on that last word; a born and bred Bostonian. He probably said things like *you's* and *pocketbook*.

"Thank you's for coming tonight. We appreciate your continued support of the Night Hawks and our mission to rid the world of the vermin infesting it."

Heads nodded, a few murmurs went up. The stumpy man looked to someone sitting in the front, giving an unspoken signal. A bone-thin woman with radiant skin and shiny brown hair rose from her seat. Her presence was sudden and seemed to alter the atmosphere in the room. Celia couldn't tell what it was that had changed. The people around her were either both extremely and swiftly nervous or in complete awe.

At the podium, the significantly taller woman leaned down to kiss the man's cheek before taking up his place.

"Thank you, Herb." She spoke in a smooth voice. Celia caught a hint of a Heidi Klum-esque German accent. It twisted its way through her words, and was light enough to make you pause in deciding where exactly she was from.

She didn't seem bothered at all by the heat sucking up the spare oxygen. Sweat trickled down temples but her makeup was flawless, as was her tailored black suit and the string of pearls around her neck. She was dressed more for a business meeting among high-powered CEOs or bankers than a clandestine gathering of a motley crew in the basement of a bar.

The woman's dark eyes scanned the crowd, as if she were trying to catch the gaze of all twenty-five or so people in the room. Celia shifted to the side, concealing herself slightly behind the curly-haired man in front of her.

"As most of you know, I'm Gayle," she introduced, placing a manicured hand delicately to her chest. Celia didn't think she had spoken that loudly yet her voice carried throughout the room. "As Herb mentioned, we are very grateful for your investment in the Night Hawks."

Enough already, Celia thought impatiently. What the hell are Night Hawks?

Gayle didn't answer her as she went on about expanding into Cambridge and Brookline because of the growth near the city. Celia assumed "the city" meant Boston; though she couldn't work out what growth she was talking about.

There'd certainly been an influx of smelly men at Cage's but she was sure the Night Hawks weren't renegades against bad hygiene. After all, Winston could put a-hurting on deodorant when he wanted to.

"Now," Gayle said, clasping her hands together ten minutes later. She scanned the crowd once again. "Shall we hear reports?"

The woman sitting in Celia's row hopped to her feet, waving her hand enthusiastically. Celia ducked her head as people turned to watch her approach the front. She seemed to enjoy that very much, adding a little swish to her hips as she walked.

At the podium, she ran a hand over her hair and tugged at her shirt. Those motions appeared to be nervous habits, except she was beaming proudly at the group. She had a wide mouth and a gap between her two front teeth. Her eyebrows were straight lines across her forehead, which was weird, but you could only see them when her hair moved. They were also very dark, compared to her light hair.

"So, I was in Cambridge—"

Gayle cleared her throat, cutting her off. The woman looked stunned.

"Your name?" Gayle prompted. Though her interruption was a little crisp, her tone was encouraging. "For any newcomers."

Something about the way she said that made Celia feel like a spotlight had just shone down on her. She cursed to herself and hoped people wouldn't start searching for the new faces in the crowd.

The woman at the podium smiled. "Oh, right! I'm Tilly."

"And where are you from?" Gayle asked.

"5th Street. Cambridge," she added with a laugh when she realized she didn't need her address. "It was me and Kyle and Leo and we were having dinner at this Brazilian place in Porter Square. We saw this guy hanging around outside and I immediately thought, something's up with this kid.

"So, when we left, I guess he recognized something about us—"

"Well, I was wearing my Night Hawk pin," a guy piped in. Celia guessed he was either Kyle or Leo. He stood, clasping the lapel of his brown, canvas coat. A small, round pin about the size of a dime rested just above his thumb. He swiveled around to show everyone. The same hawk-and-moon design as the flyer from Winston's room decorated the pin.

Tilly laughed and gestured to him. "There you go. Maybe they know us now. Anyway, he walked away and we followed. But he made the stupid mistake of turning off Mass Ave. We jumped him on a side street. Kyle tied him up and I went to get the car and we took him to my place."

Her voice deepened in pride as she came to the next part of her little story. "I got to use this silver knife I just bought. It was amazing!" Her eyes rolled to the ceiling in excitement. "It went through his stomach so easily; it was like I was slicing pie."

Celia's jaw dropped. She took a peek around to see if anyone else was horrified by this sickening twist of her tale. Of course, she was being stupid. The others were grinning and nodding. A murderous hunger clouded their faces. Celia was instantly scared shitless. She wanted to leave but she knew she couldn't. If she made a break for the door, she'd give up her cover and the entire room would be at her heels.

Her cellphone vibrated in her pocket. She'd forgotten it was there. A man in the row in front of her glanced back at the sound. She quickly flipped the phone open. There was a text from Victor asking if she was alright.

"Yes," she messaged back. "Big spider."

"We took turns," Tilly continued. She was really playing this up. Her hands gripped the podium. She peered around the room, speaking in a dramatic fashion, like she was telling a scary story at a bonfire. Well, it was a damn scary story.

"Cutting and hitting him. He was getting turned on by his own blood, the perv. Of course I didn't let that go to waste." She wiggled her eyebrows to ensure everyone got her meaning. A couple of chuckles rose from the group.

"And then I had the honors of driving the stake through his chest." She puffed her own chest out as she exchanged smiles with her comrade who had stood. A few people applauded.

Celia was so utterly confused that she didn't know what to do with herself.

A fucking vampire?

As she rolled this information around a few times, she actually felt a small twinge of relief that the poor man hadn't been a human or, more specifically, part of a particular ethnic group or religion. It was terrible to think that way about a vamp and she kicked herself.

"They should really bottle that smell," Tilly added. Laughter filled the room.

"Thank you, Tilly," Gayle replied. Tilly did a little curtsey before returning to her seat. She waggled her eyebrows at Celia. Celia couldn't even try to pretend, she was so mortified. She had hidden her shock as best she could but you could tell she was still shaken. Tilly didn't seem to take offense. She turned her attention to the man who had taken her place at the podium to relay his exploits.

The next round of stories was along the same lines as Tilly's: abducting vampires; tying them up; beating and torturing them; sometimes draining them. One man was happy to report he still had one prone to his basement floor.

"I got that sucker held in place with silver chains," he announced happily. "You know, you wrap 'em around their ankles and wrists so they can't move. You don't even have to tie the chains or nothing. They can't move when it's on them. It, like, melts into their skin. I don't know what I'm gonna do with him yet but I'll think of something juicy."

Celia put a hand to her mouth. She was battered with unwanted images of vampires being tortured to the last seconds of their lives and it was horrifying. The draining stories were the worst. How they'd cut along major arteries, keeping an eye on the wounds to make sure they didn't close up. That obviously wasn't enough to kill the vamps, because many of the stories ended with the Night Hawks leaving them outside in places where the sun would shine brightly.

Her eyes went to Winston. All she could see was the back of

his head. His leg was propped up on the opposite knee, his arm rested on the back of his Asian companion's seat. He seemed totally at ease. She wanted to throw something hard at his fucking head.

They hadn't shared any stories, which was good because Celia might've done something foolish that would have certainly called for unwanted attention.

The meeting came to an end shortly after that last story. Gayle spoke a little more; giving what Celia assumed was a pep talk. Keep up the killing, y'all!

As soon as Herb delivered his parting words, Celia rushed from the room. Needing fresh air to hopefully clear the images from her mind, she continued on outside. The bouncer was there, still smoking. She walked farther up the sidewalk for some distance from that despicable place. The porch light of the house she was standing in front of was off, leaving her in semi-darkness.

She paced back and forth. Her revulsion from those accounts dissolved into fury. She regarded each person in that room with such odium that she was shaking. Now she paced to keep from finding a rock and lobbing it through one of Olde Nessie's windows.

A half an hour passed before the Night Hawks began to emerge from the bar. They had probably wanted more time to discuss strategies and swap war stories. Celia folded her arms at the chest while she waited.

Aside from commando man, the people who called themselves Night Hawks were unremarkable. They could've been schoolteachers, accountants, and librarians.

Or youth advocates.

Winston finally stepped out with his two buddies. Huge smiles stretched across their faces. Winston said something and they both nodded. They shook hands. He waved to some others then walked in Celia's direction. She'd seen her uncle's car when she first arrived. Stationed in front of it now, she wondered if Uncle Max knew for what Winston was using his car.

Winston's steps faltered when he noticed someone leaning on his car. She faced him fully and his confusion melted into shock.

"Celia? What the hell are you doing here?"

When he stood only a few inches from her, she punched him hard in the arm. He grabbed his bicep with a pained expression that she took great pleasure in seeing.

"What the hell are you doing here?" she hissed. It was late and she didn't want to draw the attention of the Night Hawks. "You torture vampires?"

His eyes widened. Many emotions crisscrossed his face at once. Surprise clashed with guilt and anger. Anger won. He pushed her shoulder so roughly that she stumbled into her uncle's white Lincoln.

"You following me or something?" Winston demanded.

"You don't do that shit, right?" She was snatching at a slim bit of hope that he didn't. That he was just a bystander—which was just as bad in some respects. She didn't allow herself to ruminate in that.

Torture. Murders. Her own flesh and blood couldn't be that . . . that . . . inhumane.

"Do you kidnap people?"

"They aren't people," he grunted darkly. "They're monsters. They don't belong here."

Gee, she'd heard that before.

"What the hell's the matter with you?" she said. "And if you knew about vampires why were you being an asshole to Aunt Meg?"

"She doesn't need to think about people drained of their blood. She's already a basket case about crazy shit in the news.

And anyway, you just proved my point by bringing up those deaths. They don't give a damn about who finds their handiwork." His eyes narrowed menacingly. "What do you know about bloodsuckers?"

Celia's mouth flapped shut. She hadn't thought about that question, she had only made plans to throttle him. Her mind was a complete blank. Winston took a step closer. She saw his hand tightening into a fist. He'd never seriously hit her before. It looked like he was going to do it tonight.

"Winston?"

They looked to the smooth voice. Gayle floated to them with an unreadable expression. In her hand, she held a small stack of those glossy flyers that she stretched out to Winston.

"Herb said you wanted some of these, to take to New York."

She smelled faintly of Chanel, though below that was something earthy, like dirt. Her dark eyes landed on Celia. Her head tilted as she considered her.

"Is this a new recruit?" she asked Winston, though she was still looking at Celia.

"No," he said immediately. "I just saw her out here."

"No," Gayle said softly. Her eyes were slits as she tried to recall something. Even though she was frowning, Celia didn't spot one line in her forehead. "I saw you inside next to Tilly." Celia gulped. "Did you enjoy our meeting?"

Celia blinked a few times as she floundered for the right words. Winston was no help. He glowered at her so fiercely that she was sure Gayle could feel the heat. "Um," she managed. "I've never been to anything like that before." And that was the honest truth.

Gayle smiled, revealing a dentist's wet dream of straight, white teeth. There was something off about the smile, though. She couldn't tell if it was forced or rehearsed. It didn't add any warmth to her eyes either.

"We're a little unorthodox but we get the job done. Have you staked a vampire?" she asked so casually that you'd think she'd just inquired about Celia's preference of oranges.

Celia's mouth had gone dry. She only shook her head. Gayle patted her shoulder. There was no affection in the movement; she barely curved her hand to fit her shoulder. You'd think she was petting an insufferable animal.

"In due time, I'm sure. It is exhilarating."

Gayle nodded to Winston before floating back to the bar. As soon as the door closed, Winston grabbed Celia's elbow.

"Ow!"

"Shut up!" he barked. He dragged her farther down the street. "Now, you listen to me, you nosy little shit. You forget what you saw and heard here. I don't know how you found out about this or what you know about bloodsuckers but you better not come here ever again."

He released her with a shove. She nearly tripped on the pavement. She was glad she hadn't fallen on her face because she didn't want him carrying that image with him. She spun around with an indignant glare.

"And you better not tell my parents!" he added.

Winston turned from her and got in the Lincoln. The engine revved. He peeled out of the spot, spraying water from the rain and leaving tire marks on the road. Uncle Max would be very upset. Celia didn't know what to think—though she was extra miffed that he hadn't made sure she got to her car safely.

She looked at Olde Nessie's once again. The bouncer was there, staring at her under a thick cloud of white smoke.

She shivered then rushed to the shelter of her car.

Tina roused her from a deep sleep. Celia groaned as she searched blindly for the cellphone screaming at her from the nightstand.

"Yeah?" she grumbled into the phone.

"Hey, Celia!"

"Dammit." Tina was beyond cheerful this morning. Celia rolled onto her back to glower at the ceiling since her coworker couldn't physically receive it.

"Please, please, please swap with me today? Please? I have a study group I really need to go to. Please?"

She glanced to the alarm clock. Eight o'clock in the fucking morning.

"Ugh, fine."

Celia tossed the phone aside, and then forced herself to leave the comfy cavern of her bed. She stepped in the shower to wake herself up. She then checked the weather channel and saw it wasn't going to rain but the sky would be overcast. She decided on pants and a blouse for work.

Bobby didn't raise an eyebrow when Celia walked into Cage's, which was surprising since she was late. She dropped her purse in a locker, clocked in, and retrieved an apron from the kitchen. Day shifts were a different pace when she was serving. It was busy, but she tended to have more breaks to catch her breath.

Michael was on his own today. He kept looking at Celia. She held her eyes on her tasks to let him know she was ignoring him. At noon, he tried to approach her while she waited for the entrees for table twenty. The chef had placed the two plates on the counter just as he neared her. She picked them up and swerved around him to head to the table.

Michael was allowed to leave first. He'd only had two tables in his section and they were cleared out by two-thirty. After one last glance to Celia, he ducked out of the restaurant.

Celia told herself she didn't care. She told herself that this was better for her. Annoyingly enough, something still tugged at her. She was just starting to like Michael. Plus, she wanted to know more about him, especially with the bombshell—that wasn't quite a bombshell since she knew vampires existed and therefore wasn't that shocked other supernatural things did as well—he had dropped on her.

She wasn't ready to bite the bullet yet. She still recalled the revulsion in his face that night in the alley. How could they have an open and frank conversation if she disgusted him so much?

And what reason did he have to be repulsed? He didn't even know her!

She hurled the dirty napkin she'd had in her hand. It landed on the little server's station near the window that housed extra silverware, coffee cups, and two computers for entering orders. Maria frowned over to her as she moved her fingers across the touch screen monitor.

"What's wrong, Celia? They didn't leave you short, did they?"

"No," she grumbled. "I just can't wait to get out of here."

After finishing up with her tables, Celia found Bobby at the hostess' stand with Lynn. He consented to her leaving so she hurried through cleaning her station and tossing her used apron in the clear trash bag next to the pantry.

When she slid into her car, she sat there for a minute, contemplating her next move. It was only four. Victor wouldn't be up for a few hours. She didn't have any errands, nor did she have money for killing time at the mall or in Downtown Crossing.

Her mind shifted to Michael again, which she found maddening. Maybe he was at his apartment. Maybe she could get some answers out of him.

She drove over to BU and found a spot in front of his building. At the top of the stairs, she hesitated at the buzzers. Of the few apartments with names listed, none of them had first names and she didn't know Michael's last name. She chewed her bottom lip. The way she was staring at the buttons, you'd think she was willing the right one to call out to her.

Giving up, Celia turned to go back down the stairs. Two men stood at the bottom, their eyes on her. She gasped, and her hand clutched her heart from the fright. She hadn't heard them approach. When she got a hold of herself, she looked at them closer. They were both dark-skinned and muscular; one had a neck so thick it looked like he'd been birthed with a column to support his head.

She frowned, wondering what the two men were doing here. She realized suddenly that she was still hovering on the edge of the stairs. The men made no moves to come upstairs or continue down the street. Their sharp gazes held her captive with their intensity. She felt a shiver of fear.

The one with the thick neck tilted his head to the side with interest. The heat of his gaze intensified. She didn't understand. Was he trying to make her look away?

Cautiously, Celia took a step, then another, until she was at the base between them. That sharp scent from Cage's was magnified. She still couldn't identify it. The best she could come up with was how hand sanitizer smelled after it had been on your skin.

When Thick Neck spoke, his voice was a deep rumble from his diaphragm. "Why is it that you do not look away?"

"I'm sorry?"

He didn't answer.

She kept her eyes on her car as she went around to the driver's side. She hazarded a glance before she sped off. The men were still watching her.

Victor arrived at seven, ringing the doorbell instead of just... appearing like he normally did. He frowned when he saw she wasn't getting ready for work.

"Come on," Celia said. She'd already dressed in brown cargo pants and a white, long-sleeved shirt. She grabbed her purse and khaki jacket. "Let's get something to eat."

Victor raised a hand, stopping her. He smirked with a lick of his lips. "Me first."

He snatched her in his arms and pinned her to the bed in less than a second. She reached up and moved his hair out of his face. He kissed her pendent, kissed her neck.

His marks were gone by the time they picked their way to the main street. Victor halted at an ATM. She looked up at him curiously, especially when he produced a check from his wallet.

"What's that?" she asked of the sheet of paper.

"A check."

"No, duh. What's it for?"

He looked down at the paper. "I helped someone out and she paid me for my services. I didn't want to take this but she insisted. I didn't want to insult her."

He stared at the slip for a moment. The machine beeped. A message popped up asking if he needed more time.

Celia contemplated as he pressed away at buttons on the screen. "Are you an escort?"

Victor rolled his eyes instead of addressing that.

"You have a bank account?"

"Several."

She had never thought about it before. She knew he had money. He had to keep it somewhere, right?

Celia shook her head when he finished up. "Such a man of mystery."

She looped her arm in his as they continued on to their destination. They sat in a booth by the window of a burger joint on Dorchester Avenue. It was far enough to seem inconvenient to walk but too close to drive, especially if she found a parking spot on her street. At least she got to walk the burgers off afterwards.

The place was set up like any other small restaurant, with booths along the walls and windows, square tables in the middle, and a counter next to the door for takeout. They played hip music and served the best damn daiquiris in the neighborhood.

Celia and Trixie frequented the hole in the wall so often that most of the staff knew their names. Their server tonight was Jane. Jane always wore her brown hair up in two juvenile ponytails that swished around her head whenever she moved.

Celia ordered a bacon double cheeseburger, fries, and a raspberry daiquiri. Victor just asked for a Sprite. Celia used to have qualms about eating in front of him—in front of anyone really. She always thought it was rude when the other person wasn't eating as well. She knew he didn't particularly enjoy going out for food with her, but hey, she had to eat. It was one of those pesky human mores, like breathing and pooping. Over time, those reservations lessened and now it didn't bother her so much.

"So what were these services?" she asked, picking up a fry. He explained about Ashleigh and Courtney and how Courtney now thought her twin was dead.

"That's so sad," Celia said.

Victor eyed her for a moment as she chomped on her burger. It was delicious, so it had a good chunk of her attention.

"Where were you yesterday?" he asked. She paused in mid-chew. "Spiders don't usually upset you like that."

Damn that fucking blood bond thingy.

"I would've found you, however you settled down. Did you kill it?"

She swallowed the lump of burger, which hurt her throat. She sipped some of her drink before buckling in for her own little tale. Victor sat in silence as she explained her cousin's mysterious return and the Night Hawks' extreme measures.

"That would explain Ashleigh's wounds." His voice was low and menacing when he finally spoke. Celia's eyes widened. She hadn't made that connection.

She needed a moment. Propping her elbows on the table, she

kneaded her temples with her knuckles. Tears sprang to her eyes as she remembered the terrifying stories. She'd seen the result firsthand.

"Oh, fuck," she whispered. "I hope Winston didn't do that."

The silver chain flashed in her head, along with the Night Hawk's proclamation of how well silver incapacitated.

Victor didn't say anything about that. He reached over to rub her arm.

"Why didn't you tell me about the meeting?"

"You wouldn't have let me go."

He held her gaze. "You and I both know you have a mind and will of your own. Now, what else do you know about this group?"

She cleared the lump from her throat. "There's about thirty of them. I think they work independently, and then meet up to swap stories."

Victor nodded tightly. He was seething at this news. He'd only known about Snipe's crew. He solely associated with Ramsey's nest, and a few others. He hadn't noticed any disappearances.

A light tapping made them both look up. Ashleigh stood outside, framed by the window. The streetlight fell on her, making her dark hair shine. Her eyes sparkled as she beamed at Victor.

"Do you know her?" Celia asked in an undertone, though she wouldn't have heard her through the glass.

"Yes."

When Celia looked to the window again, she was gone.

"Hi, Victor."

Celia jumped at the sudden voice. Ashleigh stood in front of their booth now.

Victor glanced around cautiously. The people sitting along the aisle were puzzled by the sudden wind stirred up by her speedy entrance.

"Ashleigh, what are you doing here? Where's Ramsey?"

She cupped a hand to her mouth and in a mock whisper said, "I snuck out. I followed your scent after you got in the cab."

Celia scrunched up her nose at that. Victor didn't look too happy either. While she was talking about her trip,

Celia gave her a once-over. If Victor hadn't mentioned Ashleigh's name, Celia would not have guessed this was the same woman from the alleyway.

She was wearing a denim mini that stopped just below her cooch and a cute red top with lace along the collar and sheer sleeves. A thin, gold necklace hung from her neck down to her stomach. It appeared she had hit up the mall. She was very pretty, with cheekbones to die for. And she was eyeing her boyfriend with a little too much eagerness.

Celia's eyes narrowed.

Ashleigh laughed about something Celia hadn't heard. Then she touched Victor's shoulder in an intimate way. A flick of anger lashed at Celia's stomach, making her pulse pick up. Those feelings of sympathy she was experiencing earlier at hearing her story? Yeah, they were quickly disappearing.

Her anger caught Ashleigh's attention. She'd been ignoring Celia pretty good from the start. Ashleigh's arms grew taut. She slowly turned her head to Celia. Her pink lips parted. Celia could see her fangs were out.

It was crazy but Celia maintained eye contact. Fuck vampire etiquette. She did not want her to think she was intimidating and she definitely didn't want her to think she could basically flirt with her fucking boyfriend right in front of her. Good thing Ashleigh hadn't mastered that vampy coercion because that would've been a stupid move alright.

Victor's hand darted out and clasped Ashleigh's wrist, catching the hand that had been presumably reaching for Celia's neck. He'd seen her intentions before Celia had. She saw that

Victor's knuckles bulged against his skin. She was straining against him. Ashleigh actually had the balls to try and attack her in a public space, in front of her boyfriend.

Victor was out of his seat in a second.

"Excuse us," he said tightly. He had a firm hold on Ashleigh's shoulders as he dragged her out of the restaurant. Celia didn't even have time to protest. She just watched them go, her jaw hanging to the floor.

***

Victor never released his grip on Ashleigh. She growled and hissed at him but he continued down the street. They passed two women on their way to a fancy party, judging by their swanky, glittery dresses. Ashleigh attempted to lunge at them. Victor grasped her at the waist. The women gasped, and hurried along.

Victor pulled her around a corner, slamming her against the brick wall. The impact didn't hurt her, of course. She squeezed her hands into tight fists. Her lips were pursed in an angry line like a child in the throes of a tantrum.

Victor waited her out. His hands were planted on either side of her shoulders, ensuring she didn't try to run away. After a minute, she began to breathe, her hands relaxed.

"Celia is my girlfriend. You do not touch her. She is mine."

Ashleigh cringed at his intensity. His dark eyes bored into her with razor sharp precision.

"I'm sorry, okay?" she sulked, cowed. Her fangs were still out. "She made me mad."

"You have to learn to control yourself. You cannot go around attacking people."

"I know, Victor! Shit, it was a slip-up. I wasn't going to actually do anything to her. You thought I was going to rip her throat out? Tear her limb from limb? Give me a fucking break. You were there, right?"

"I won't always be there." He shook his head angrily. "You

need to figure out what you want to do. If living amongst the humans is something you just don't want to adapt to, then you'll need to find someplace else to go."

Her eyes widened; her mouth fell open. Her fangs slid back into place and the petulant monster left her.

"You . . ." She could barely form the words. "You want me to leave?"

"It's not about what I want. It's what you want."

"What do *you* want?"

Victor stared at her a moment. "I think you should stay. Ramsey and Elizabeth can teach you the proper way to blend in. It's the only way to establish a peaceful life."

She looked down. "That's not what I meant," she whispered.

He knew exactly what she meant. He was beginning to regret their talks, taking her outside—except she needed to learn. Ramsey was preoccupied with Annie's disappearance. Elizabeth had her new job. Someone needed to step in so that Ashleigh didn't slip through the cracks and become one of those reckless newborns that needed to be put down.

Her expression hardened at his silence. She didn't say more. Victor, assuming she would be fine, moved aside.

"I'll take you back to Ramsey's. I need to finish up with Celia first."

Ashleigh grounded her teeth then started the walk back to the restaurant.

***

Celia's food was cold by the time the vampires came back in, five long minutes later.

Victor held out his hand stiffly, indicating for her to sit. Ashleigh slid into the booth. He sat beside her to keep her contained. Celia couldn't believe it. She thought he had found her a cab and sent her ass back to where she'd come from.

She stared at Victor, wanting an explanation but far too

stunned to voice the question.

Ashleigh looked glum. Her blue eyes scanned Celia in a calculating manner. Celia wondered if she was trying to figure out how to get across the table and sink her teeth in her neck before Victor could stop her.

Probably.

"Celia," Victor began. Her lips tightened into a thin line while she waited to hear this. "Ashleigh is very new. And she's been deprived for almost two weeks. Please pardon her for that."

Celia would've preferred hearing that from Ashleigh so she could give her the finger. Instead, she crossed her arms at the chest with a huff. She didn't really have an argument.

"Whatever," she muttered, glancing out at the rest of the room.

Jane came around to clear the dishes. She looked them over, and immediately sensed the tension clouding the table.

"Would you all like anything else?" she asked politely.

"Just the check, please," Victor replied.

After Victor paid, the three of them stood awkwardly on the sidewalk. "So, I guess I'm walking home alone?" Celia asked crossly. She threw an icy glare at Ashleigh. Ashleigh snarled back.

Victor stepped in front of her. "I'm sorry, Seal." He did truly look apologetic.

I want to make sure she goes home without hurting anyone.

Hmm. She heard that clearly.

"Call me as soon as you get inside," Victor said aloud. He kissed her lips. Celia sighed. She figured it was no use arguing. She wanted to be in her house quick after what just happened.

Celia slowly turned to start the trip home, her doggie bag dangling from her hand. She glanced over her shoulder a few times. Victor was watching her go. She did notice his grip on Ashleigh's elbow. Ashleigh glowered at Celia with the disappointment of a predator that just lost track of their quarry.

Before turning off Dorchester Avenue, Celia looked back again. The sidewalk was empty.

She hurried on. As she made her way through the side streets, she became aware of another presence. Panic seized her as she imagined Ashleigh getting the slip on Victor and coming after her.

Surreptitiously, she glanced around. And then she came to a full halt.

Padding along across the street was the massive dog from the other night. He stopped when she stopped. Those gold eyes meant she hadn't been hallucinating. He seemed even bigger on level.

Celia turned her head from side to side, searching for a possible owner. The street was deserted. There were no open gates that he may have used to escape from a yard. When her gaze drifted back to the dog, he was crossing the street toward her. Something told her to run, but her legs didn't listen.

The dog stopped in front of her. Sitting on his hind legs, his fluffy head came to her navel. He cocked his head to the side. He didn't seem so bad. He probably just had a bad rap for looking so big and intimidating.

Slowly, she reached out and placed her hand on the top of his head. His fur was wiry but soft. She ran her hand along the side of his head until she was scratching behind his ear. In response, his tail swept the sidewalk clean. She smiled. He nuzzled his nose in her hand.

"Well, I don't know who you belong to," she replied, pulling her hand back. "But I'm sure they'll know you're missing. You should probably go home. That's what I'm doing."

She waited. The dog just blinked. "Okay," she said to herself. She turned to continue down the street. The dog got to his feet and strolled along beside her.

Suddenly, a wave of warmth flowed through her that she'd

never felt before. It was kind of like when you drank a mug of hot chocolate. Except that delicious drink only warmed your belly. This feeling encompassed her entire body. It would probably be unbearable if it was the middle of August but it was a cool September night.

"Whoa!"

Celia looked around for the voice, momentarily distracted from the strange heat that had been cursing through her. A man about her age walked toward them. His mouth was wide open as he took in the brown dog.

"Is that a dog?" he asked, pulling the headphones from his ears.

She shrugged. "Yeah."

"He's huge! What's that, a Siberian Husky or something?"

She examined him but she didn't know what a Siberian Husky looked like. He definitely wasn't it. First, those types of Huskies had way more white, especially around the face and neck. Not to mention he was twice their size.

"I don't know. Probably a whole mix of stuff."

"I'll say."

The man slid by them, keeping a distance between himself and the dog. She thought he was going to trip on his feet from the way he kept looking back. She carried on home with her new companion, pleased with the company.

At the foot of her stairs, she pulled out her keys.

"Um, well, this is me," she said.

Celia wasn't sure if he was going to follow her up. The dog took some steps forward, and she thought he was going to continue to wherever the hell he came from. Instead, he lay on the pavement, off to the side. He crossed his front paws for a headrest.

She sighed. "Suit yourself."

She was walking up the stairs, staring at her feet, when

suddenly she was viewing something completely different. Before her was a hallway with grand paintings. A wide staircase was up ahead.

There were arms around her waist; she felt them squeezing her tight. Warm lips pressed against her cheek. Deep in the pit of her stomach, she was turned on. The blood left her brain, leaving her slightly lightheaded as a hardness pressed against her pants.

The arms released her and she was staring into Ashleigh's blue eyes. The vision dissipated soon after that. Not before she glimpsed the sadness and, not to mention, longing in her striking face.

Well, that was unsettling. What the hell was Victor doing? And, gross, did she just get a boner?

Celia went to her apartment to settle in for the night. She called Victor but he didn't answer. After changing her clothes and flicking on the television to wait for Victor to explain himself, she peeked out the window. Amazingly, the dog was still lying there. She saw his sides expand and contract evenly.

"Looks like I've got myself a guardian," she said to the room before going to the sofa.

***

Victor headed back to Ramsey's with Ashleigh. They had to hail a cab since he hadn't fed enough and couldn't teleport, which would have been ideal for guaranteeing Celia made her way home safely. It was only an eight-minute walk. He hadn't wanted Ashleigh to know where Celia lived. Of course, if she was as good of a tracker as she seemed, there was the chance she already knew . . .

Ashleigh sat beside him on the cracked leather seat, eyeing the cabbie. He was an older man with thin graying hair, a chin hidden in the folds of his neck, and silver glasses.

His pulse echoed over the soft music playing in the front, even to Victor. He felt his gums tingle as the sound of blood flowing through his veins called to him. Victor checked out the window to see where they were.

The cab was rolling down a quiet street. Victor looked over the bridge, where he could make out the smokestack-shaped building that used to be a chocolate factory back in the late seventeen hundreds. The factory became defunct in the nineteen sixties and had been transformed into luxury condos in nineteen ninety. The Shaw's supermarket sat across a parking lot down below.

The cabbie glanced back through the rearview mirror. Victor reached out with his mind when they made eye contact. He was able to grab hold of the cabbie quickly.

"Pull over here," Victor commanded.

The cab drove into the parking lot of a barren building up for lease. The area was pretty secluded. No other cars had passed them. No one was on the street. Victor got out of the car.

"Come here."

The cabbie obeyed, climbing out of the driver's seat and walking around to stand in front of Victor. His eyes were filled with admiration.

"Get in," Victor instructed. The cabbie slid in the backseat, with Victor after him. "Now, listen," Victor told Ashleigh, who was staring longingly at the cabbie's turkey neck. "Go slow, okay? It's too easy to lose control and kill him."

His mind flashed back to the runner at Jamaica Pond. He let the incident go before he began to feel guilty. He may not have been as gentle as he usually was, but he hadn't killed her and she wouldn't remember the attack. There was no need harping on it.

"Stop yourself after a minute," he added.

Ashleigh came out of her trance to frown at Victor. "I've never had to stop myself before," she said quite seriously. She looked a little scared. Victor reached across the man to pat her hand.

"I'm here."

Her lips pulled into a happy smile. Her fangs pressed against her pink lip.

"I'll show you."

Victor tilted the cabbie's head away from him, exposing his neck. He bit gently and took a few deep drags. When he finished, he licked the wound clean.

"Use your tongue to heal them."

"My tongue?" she asked with a frown. She touched her lips.

"Yes."

He was new at this teaching thing. He'd always been a loner until he came to Boston. He had never turned anyone during his century of being undead. He never had to take on the role of a sire—also known as a maker.

Ashleigh moved slowly at first, calculating each second. When she was only a few inches away, she could no longer resist. She was on his throat in a split second, groaning hungrily. How they were able to find the man's carotid through the flabby skin was a mystery. Victor watched in consternation while keeping count in his head.

After a minute, he noticed her jaw working back and forth. She was gnawing on the man's throat. Victor tugged on her shoulder. She didn't release him. Instead, Victor saw her hand tighten on the cabbie's forearm. There was a snapping sound. The man grimaced but didn't pull away.

"Ashleigh!" Victor shouted. She didn't respond.

Victor leaned over the man and snaked his arm around Ashleigh's neck. It was going to be bad. He had no other choice. He pushed back. Ashleigh was shoved against the door. She snarled at Victor. A tiny chunk of the man's flesh was caught in her teeth. Her nose and chin and mouth were coated in deep red blood. She'd gotten it on her blouse and skirt as well.

Crimson blood spurted from the man's neck against the back

window, across Ashleigh's lap, on Victor's arm and over the seat. Victor jumped on the spray. He ran his tongue along the puncture marks and sealed off the mini-geyser. The man slumped to the side. His heartbeat was faint.

Victor looked at Ashleigh, whose chest rose and fell heavily against his arm holding her back. She was staring at the blood that was . . . everywhere.

"Shit," Victor said, and then shook his head. He'd been a fool. She hadn't attacked the humans that night they walked down Ramsey's street. He had thought she was ready.

"Get out," he said. Her eyes went to him a moment. She seemed shocked by his brusqueness. "Now."

She yanked the door open and stepped outside. Through the blood spatter staining the rear window, he saw her standing a few feet away. Her arms were crossed tightly, a long pout on her face.

Victor looked at the state of the cabbie again. His glasses had slipped down his nose. His yellow shirt was soaked through. Victor's saliva had stopped the blood, but on closer inspection, he saw that the ragged hole created by Ashleigh's teeth still remained.

His heart pumped feebly. It was too late; the man was at the crossing over point. He couldn't risk giving his blood.

The nail on Victor's right index finger sharpened to a point. He used it to make a U-shaped gash just under the place where his chin should've been. His nail sliced deeply. The blood poured from the wound like an overfilled bucket. There was a muffled splashing sound as it hit the faux leather seat. Victor's intention was to make it seem like Ashleigh's hole was the point of entry for a large knife. He thought he was successful.

Victor climbed out of the cab and slammed the door behind him. Ashleigh immediately opened her mouth but he held up a hand to silence her. He didn't want to hear her voice just yet. His eyes went to her clothes. She was covered in blood. So was he.

They couldn't walk the rest of the way.

He took hold of her elbow and teleported to Ramsey's. They appeared in Ashleigh's dark room. Victor quickly went to her door. Opening it a crack, he peeked outside. The hallway was clear. He waved her forward and they went to the bathroom across the hall.

He pointed to the shower.

"What's the—?"

Victor covered her wet mouth with his hand, cutting her off. He put a finger to his own lips. If she were paying attention, she would've noticed that Elizabeth was downstairs.

She was asking Bryce where Ashleigh would've gone.

"How the fuck should I know?" Bryce grumbled.

"Bryce! You're not going to help?"

Bryce mumbled something in reply.

Ashleigh nodded once she comprehended. Victor teleported to his own place to clean up. After showering and changing, he went back to Ramsey's. He was a bit lightheaded from the third trip but it passed quickly.

He appeared in the hallway outside the bathroom. Elizabeth was there with her hands on her hips.

"Ashleigh? I said is that you?"

"It's her."

Elizabeth spun around. "What's going on?"

The shower stopped. "She found me in Dorchester."

Elizabeth blew out a breath of relief. It would not look good to have the vampire leader's guest wreaking havoc around town.

The bathroom door opened. Ashleigh stepped into the hallway with a white towel wrapped around her body. The steam escaped behind her. Water dripped from her hair, making tiny rivers over her shoulders, down toward the curve of her breasts.

Victor glanced around her. Her stained clothes were nowhere to be found and the floor was clean.

"You can't just leave like that," Elizabeth said. "You had me worried out of my mind."

"I'm sorry," she said softly. She peeked at Victor.

"Where were you?"

"I followed Victor."

"Followed?"

Ashleigh shrugged. "It was easy."

So she was a tracker. Victor hadn't fed earlier and had taken a cab to Celia's. That meant she definitely knew where Celia lived. He'd have to be more careful.

Elizabeth shook her head. "I wish you had said something."

"I'm sorry. I won't do it again. It's just that I hate being confined to this house! I feel like an animal."

Elizabeth looked into her wide eyes. She nodded. "You're right. We'll have to work out a schedule so that someone is always with you. That way you can get some fresh air."

Ashleigh groaned softly. That was not what she had hoped. Elizabeth put an arm around her shoulder.

"Go get dressed."

Ashleigh looked at Victor. "Are you leaving?"

"Yes," he said. "I need to go to Celia."

She grabbed his arm. "Can you wait, just for a minute?" He hesitated. He really needed to make sure Celia was fine. She hadn't called yet. "Please?" Ashleigh pleaded.

He gave in. "I'll be downstairs."

A smile lit her face. She sprinted to her room. By the time he and Elizabeth made it downstairs, Ashleigh was running down behind them in that rapid vamp speed.

"Come here," she said. She took his hand and pulled him outside. "We're just on the porch," she called to Elizabeth when she started to protest.

Ashleigh closed the door after them. Victor pinched his sinuses. "Look," he said softly. "It's up to you but I think it's best that you don't tell Ramsey or Elizabeth about what happened tonight."

Ashleigh nodded quickly. "I wouldn't. I didn't mean to. Honest. I just . . . I've never had to stop before."

"I understand that. It was my fault. I should've made sure you were actually ready first."

"But I was! Or . . . I thought I was." She shook her head as if confused. Her wet hair was pasted to her back. Her t-shirt clung to her damp chest. She wasn't wearing a bra.

"How do you make yourself stop?"

He tore his eyes away from her tits. "You don't need all of it for nourishment," he answered smoothly. "Just a few minutes. It takes practice."

"Can I practice again?"

He hesitated once more. "Maybe with Elizabeth or Ramsey."

"No, with you." She stepped up to him. Her voice dropped an octave. "I like when you teach me. I know you can show me a lot."

He didn't respond to that.

"What does vampire blood taste like?" Ashleigh asked suddenly.

He shrugged. "I don't really know how to explain it. It's like how wines have different flavors and scents. Animal blood tastes different from human blood. Most prefer humans because their blood is full-bodied and we receive more nourishment."

"Are you one of those?"

He paused a second. "Yes, I suppose so."

"You can have my blood whenever you want."

Her cheeks were flushed from the cabbie's blood, or perhaps it had something to do with the inviting look in her eyes. Victor turned away without answering. It was bad enough she was able to track him; if they shared blood they would be just as connected as a vampire-human bond. The major difference was it would last a shorter period of time.

He'd heard stories of vampires going crazy if they were connected to another vampire for too long. Only partaking of each other's blood wasn't healthy. The mating of vamps only worked if blood came from other sources as well.

He didn't consider the notion further. Celia was his and he was Celia's.

They were quiet for a moment. He faced her again. "Ashleigh." She looked up eagerly. "You know what happened tonight was wrong. Right?"

Her eyebrows furrowed. "Sure."

That wasn't very comforting.

"I have to go," he said. He opened the door for her. Elizabeth stepped into the hallway. Ashleigh sighed and turned toward the light of the foyer. Then she spun around and rushed to Victor, wrapping her arms around his waist for a tight squeeze. Her lips brushed his cheek before she stepped back. Elizabeth's face was appropriately blank, thank goodness. The situation was awkward enough.

Victor closed the door between them. When he arrived at Celia's, she was knocked out on the sofa. A little trail of drool escaped her lips. He smiled down on her.

Gently, he lifted her in his arms and carried her to her bed. He lay beside her, watching her dream. She slept through the night.

Nine

CELIA INVITED TRIXIE over for an early dinner the next night. She hadn't spent time with her friend in a week. She made grilled salmon, rice pilaf, and asparagus. Trixie brought the wine.

They were laughing on the sofa about a table of rowdy patrons Trixie had on Wednesday. They had been drunk and were spilling drinks. One guy tripped out of the booth, falling on his face.

"Dumb ass," Celia laughed.

"I had to fix my face before going over but I don't think I did a good job."

Celia shook her head then took another drink of the white wine. She noticed Trixie surveying her.

"You haven't had any more trouble, have you?"

Celia slowly lowered her glass. The last thing she wanted was to think about Milo. "No," she fibbed. Trixie didn't need to know he'd been in the lounge. She was already a scaredy cat. If Celia told her, she'd be a nervous wreck, which didn't bode well with dancers or Celia's sanity.

Trixie nodded as relief came over her face. "Good."

"How's it going with Lee?" Celia asked to change the subject.

Trixie shrugged despondently. "Okay, I guess."

"What's wrong?"

She sighed. "I don't know. He's being distant. I was trying to make plans with him this weekend but he kept coming up with excuses. I guess I'll call him tonight and see what happens."

Celia squeezed her knee. She wanted to tell her not to chase behind some asshole, that if he couldn't see what a catch she was then forget him. She didn't get it. Trixie had mentioned Lee more than a few times since they grabbed drinks together so often. She never made it seem like more than coworkers hanging out but obviously something changed. So why was he being a dick to her friend?

Whatever the case, Celia didn't know the whole story and the last thing she needed was for Trixie to get serious with this guy and have things become awkward because Celia had mouthed off way back when.

Trixie wasn't working tonight. She helped Celia pick out an outfit. They chose black, low rise skinny jeans and a black polo with yellow along the placket and underside of the collar. It was just a little color but not enough to cause Bobby to make her change.

Trixie was going through Celia's nail polishes, trying to decide between a deep red or dark blue.

"Go for the red."

She shrieked at the smooth voice that materialized out of nowhere. Celia jumped too, but from Trixie screaming.

Trixie spun around to face Victor, who was standing right behind her. "Stop doing that!" she cried. She clutched her heart, the red polish still in her hand.

"I'm sorry," he said, though he looked more amused if anything.

He crossed to give Celia a kiss. She eyed him a moment. She had fallen asleep last night and hadn't asked about what she had seen. What she had felt.

"What's wrong?" Victor asked, rubbing her cheek.

She glanced to Trixie, who had turned back to the dresser, shaking her head irritably. She couldn't discuss this with her around. Celia went back to getting dressed since she was only in her jeans and pink bra.

There was a knock on the front door. Trixie hurried to answer it. She was probably thankful for a reason to get away from Victor, who was unfazed. He couldn't really get upset anyway. He enjoyed provoking her.

Celia was adjusting her shirt in the mirror when Trixie returned. She came to the bedroom door with a frown.

"There's a Winston here for you," she said questioningly. "Is that your cousin?"

Celia stiffened. She had no idea why he would be here. She definitely knew it wasn't for anything good. She hurried out to the front door where Winston was waiting with a stern look.

"What're you doing here?" she asked. "And how did you get inside?"

"A woman was leaving. I need to talk to you." He glanced over her shoulder at Trixie and Victor. Victor's expression was blank, as he looked him over. Through their bond, she knew he was curious. He'd met Winston several times. His urgency and his connection to the Night Hawks piqued his interest.

"In private," Winston added.

Fighting the instinct to tell him to shove his needs up his ass, Celia pushed past him and stepped into the hallway. She closed the door behind him. After a second, she decided to move farther down the hall, just in case Victor's sharp ears could pick up on what they were saying.

They stood in a corner, next to her neighbor Carrie's door. Her kids would hide their discussion if it carried.

"What?" Celia asked. She folded her arms at the chest. She was not going to like what he had to say, that was for sure.

He dove right in. "I need your help."

She was stunned into momentary silence. "Why would you need my help?"

"You seem to know something about bloodsuckers and I need to find some."

Her mouth flapped open. "Are you crazy?" she cried in a hushed whisper. She glanced over her shoulder, half-expecting Victor to burst through the door.

"So, tell me what you know," Winston demanded. She laughed out loud at his gall.

"You are crazy! I have to get to work."

She turned back to her apartment. He seized her upper arm.

"I'm not playing around," he hissed.

With a heated glower, Celia pushed his hand away. "You know, I'm getting real sick and tired of you grabbing me all the time."

He ignored her. "Look, I need this, okay? Tilly's already staked four bloodsuckers in the past month! I gotta catch up."

Celia wanted to call him crazy again; however, she knew saying it a third time wouldn't necessarily mean the words would stick. Instead, she went the indignant route, rolling her neck and all.

"Fuck Tilly. Fuck your little group. And fuck you for thinking I'd help you kill people."

She spun on her heel and stomped to her apartment before he could grab her again. He called after her but she kept going. Inside, she slammed the door.

"Is everything okay?" Trixie asked.

"Sure," Celia grumbled without stopping. She went to her room to put on her sneakers. Trying to apply makeup while you were pissed was no easy feat. She poked herself in the eye with her liner and her mascara wand.

Victor came to the door to watch her, which she ignored.

Her anger with her stupid cousin was piggybacking her anger and confusion from Victor hugging some girl and liking it.

She didn't look at him as she stormed out into the living room. Her purse was on the sofa. Trixie gave her a surprised look when she snatched it from underneath her.

"I'm late now," Celia snapped, searching through her purse to make sure she had everything. "So, Trixie either you take the bus home or Victor can drive you after I go to Cage's."

Victor didn't say anything about her offering up his services, which was good because there was a reasonable chance she would've exploded.

Trixie peeked over to Victor. Celia caught her shiver. She rolled her eyes to the ceiling in exasperation.

"He's not going to bite you!" she exclaimed.

Trixie stared at her in shock. "What is the matter with you?" she demanded.

Celia shook her head. "I don't have time for this. If you're coming, come on."

She stalked out the apartment. The cool night air reminded her that she'd forgotten her jacket. Her car was parked across the street. By the time she plopped down into the driver's seat and pulled her seatbelt across her body, Trixie then Victor emerged from the front door.

They got into the car silently. Fifteen minutes later, Celia pulled to the curb in front of Cage's. She was seizing her purse from beside Victor's feet when he took her wrist.

She tried to pull away but he wasn't allowing that.

There was a tug, and she found her eyes moving to seek his. She didn't want to look at him. If she did, she would undoubtedly yell or worse: burst into tears. So, she fought him and kept her eyes on her purse.

"Seal," he said softly.

"I have to go inside."

She had a flash of herself as she was: sitting in the driver's seat, staring at her purse on the floor, Victor grasping her arm. On top of her own heated state, she felt Victor's confusion. He was wondering if he did something wrong. How could he not know?

Actually, he was wondering what the hell he did this time. He knew to tread lightly because of her recent traumas but he couldn't make amends if he didn't know why she was upset.

She pulled away from him with a groan—well, he released her. It was strange to have received the flash when she hadn't had his blood in over a day. The flashes came immediately after ingestion. She got out, leaving the door open for him to go around. Victor stepped out of the car as she went to the sidewalk. She felt his eyes on her. She continued inside.

Needless to say, the night was long. Friday nights meant busy, busy, busy but Celia was in a terrible mood. Every little thing served to annoy her. And tonight it didn't help that Victor was under her skin. With a little concentration, she was able to push him to the background.

She was wiping up a spilled drink, and cursing to herself, when someone called her name.

Celia looked up to find Winston's chickenpox marks pulled together in a deep frown. She squeezed her eyes shut, praying that this was some kind of fucked-up dream.

"What the fuck, Winston?" she cried, not caring that others could hear her. "Go away."

"Not until you answer my questions."

"I'm at work, you idiot. I can't talk to you."

"You can't take five minutes?"

"Okay, let me rephrase. I don't want to talk to you."

She wrung the towel in an empty sink and hung it on a hook to dry. She then hastily washed her hands, using a cocktail napkin to dry them. She pointed to a short guy next to Winston, who called out for a Midori Sour. She stared at the guy for a moment, fighting the laugh that was trying to burst from her at his girly drink order.

Celia turned her back to the bar to prepare the drink—something she never did since it wasn't good customer service. People liked to see what you were doing when making their drinks. But she turned her back. She just didn't want to look at Winston anymore.

She mixed the drink, and then slid it across the bar. After giving the guy his change, Celia looked around for other orders. Unfortunately, everyone in her area was facing the dance floor or talking amongst themselves. All of their glasses or bottles were full. So, you could say she was at least productive in her irritation. Unless she wanted to barge into Joni's field, she had no customers at the moment.

Winston seemed to sense that she was trapped. "Celia, help me out. We're family."

She put a hand on her hip. "Don't give me that 'family' bullshit. It doesn't work on me."

"What do you want? What do I have to do to get information? Is it money?"

Now, she was insulted. "Winston, get the hell outta here before I punch you in the face."

Instead of listening to her, he leaned across the bar to keep their conversation somewhat private. That, of course, put him more at risk of said punching.

"You do know what a vampire is, right?" he said hurriedly.

"Sharp teeth. Harbingers of the night. Thirsty, like, all the time."

He disregarded her sarcasm. "Then you know they're dangerous. You know they kill and deceive and manipulate."

"So do you, apparently," she spat. That brought him up short. His eyes went a little wide, and she thought she saw him gulp. But just like that, his face clouded with fury.

"I'm no killer," Winston said darkly. "I stop killers."

"So, you're a hunter. No big whoop."

The muscle in his jaw jumped ominously. His hands gripped the marble of the bar. He actually looked like he wanted to lunge over the counter at her. Was tonight going to be the night he hit her?

Celia held tight to her stance though she was trembling a little on the inside because, hell, who liked the thought of someone hitting them?

"You're just so damn smart, huh?" he asked. "You know everything about everything. Fine." He pushed off the bar, his eyes still fixed on her. "I've never needed your help before; I can do without it now."

Winston stepped back. He bumped into a girl who had been trying to squeeze behind him. She gave him an irritated look as she shoved past. He threw Celia one last glare dripping with contempt before he disappeared into the crowd and, she hoped, out the door.

"Celia," Joni called. "Take a break."

Pleased with that sentiment, Celia went to the kitchen. She snagged a bottle of water and sat at the prep station with a Metro newspaper. She tried to read the front page. All she saw was Winston's face. She flipped the pages so roughly that she ripped one. Groaning, she tossed the Metro on the table.

The back door swung outward. She hadn't noticed it was propped open. Michael stepped inside, smelling like cigarette smoke.

Celia scrunched her nose. "Smoking's so bad for you," she said before she could stop herself.

Michael glanced at her in surprise. After all, she was supposed to be mad at him.

"Yeah, I know. I need to quit."

"Especially since you play basketball."

She kicked herself to stop speaking. She turned a glare on him so he'd know she was still upset. That's when she noticed he was still in his work clothes. Black slacks with pressed creases clung to his long, muscular legs, matching his long-sleeved black dress shirt.

He reached behind his back to untie the apron around his waist. Balling it up, he tossed it into the clear bag. He then went about adjusting his outfit, which really didn't need any adjusting. He was stalling for some reason. She picked up the newspaper again.

He finally stepped up to her. "Celia? Can I get a ride home tonight? I stayed longer than I had planned."

Celia glanced at her watch. It was just after midnight. If he hustled, he could catch the train. The Boylston station was just down the street, where he could take the Green Line that ran through BU's city campus. But if the trains had stopped running, he would probably have to take a cab. Though she was feeling real vindictive at the moment, she knew guilt would plague her if he were stranded.

She sighed. "You know I'm not off until two-thirty, right?"

"I don't mind waiting."

She looked up at him. He was so tall that the motion strained her neck. There was a small, hopeful smile on his lips and his hazel eyes were soft. She relented.

"Fine."

Michael squeezed her shoulder as if she had surrendered

enthusiastically. Curiously, her own tension relaxed slightly with the contact. When he pulled away, the sense of ease remained, even after he left the kitchen. It was amazing. When Celia thought of her insensitive cousin or the vampire who may or may not have been pushing up on her boyfriend, she didn't feel the need to break something. She was still upset, of course. It just wasn't affecting her so wholeheartedly at the moment.

She decided it would be best to return to work while she was feeling better. Happily, the sensation lasted through the rest of the night.

After getting her cut of the tips from Joni and clocking out, Celia went outside. Michael was waiting for her by the door, smoking a cigarette. She grinned a little when she realized that ten months ago she would've bummed one from him. Every once in a blue moon, when a sporadic craving would hit, she'd make herself busy with something, like baking, reading, or chewing gum.

Michael quickly snuffed the cigarette in the nearby ashtray— one of those smokeless apparatuses that looked like I Dream of Jeannie's bottle. He beamed at her and she relaxed even more, as if his smile had a direct line to her tense muscles.

"I will quit."

As he spoke, he waved his hand in front of him to rid the air of that smoky smell. Now that she did not miss about smoking.

They walked together to the lot. Victor had parked her car toward the back, near the big green dumpster. She faltered a moment because she had left her keys in the ignition and the doors would be locked. Michael looked at her quizzically.

"Is something wrong?"

"I, um . . ."

For whatever reason, she opened her purse. Her keys were in the side pocket, nestled beside her cellphone. She smiled briefly as she pulled the keys out and unlocked the door. Michael fiddled with the radio, switching back and forth between the only two stations that played some semblance of hip-hop.

"The radio's so shitty up here," he complained. "You should get satellite."

"Let me guess, you can hook it up," she said dryly.

"You joke, but I can."

Celia laughed, genuinely amused after such a long night.

She navigated to Commonwealth Avenue. Halfway to his street, he told her to go right. She hesitantly turned off the main road. Michael directed her down Bay State Road and told her to pull over at the first empty parking spot.

He opened his door, nodding his head outside. "Come on."

Confused, she followed him out of the car and down the street. For some unknown reason, she felt safe with him. Though she didn't know where they were going, she remained calm. Normally she was a lot more cautious about walking at night with a guy she had just met. And of course, Milo was close to mind. She'd moved past her fear, though. Slightly. It had been only directed at Milo. She knew he was dangerous. That he was targeting her because he was an asshole. He was the only real threat at the moment.

Celia realized suddenly that though they had their ups and downs, she trusted Michael. His presence was comforting and familiar.

There were a few benches along the grassy knoll but he sat on the ground. She followed suit. Storrow Drive, an expressway that crossed Boston, allowing motorist access downtown and into Cambridge, lay ahead. The road wasn't busy tonight because of the late hour. Past the road was the Charles River. Sparkling lights of the Cambridge skyline reflected in the choppy water.

Celia shivered. "Lie back," Michael said. She gave him a look that clearly asked *you're kidding, right?* He chuckled and she felt a rush of warmth eerily similar to the "hot chocolate" sensation from the other night.

"Seriously. Lie back."

So, she did. He stretched out next to her.

"Now, close your eyes," he said.

She peeked over at him. His eyes were already shut, his expression serene. She stifled a giggle then closed her eyes.

Just then, a few cars zoomed down Storrow Drive. Instead of tires on pavement, the wind whipping past the cars created a comforting whoosh. It sounded just like the ocean.

"That's incredible!" Celia cried.

Michael's chuckle rumbled in his chest. "They call it the BU Beach."

More cars drove by in both directions. The effect was magnified. She laughed.

"I've lived in Boston all my life. I didn't even know this existed."

"Well, now you do."

She glanced over to him. The half-moon was bright tonight. It shone down on them like it was made for them alone, for this moment. Michael's lungs expanded and contracted, pulling in the night air in deep gulps. From the look on his face, you'd think he was listening to the most beautiful sonata. It was a wonder if the music captivating him was coming from the faux waves or . . . the moon.

He must've sensed her watching him. His eyes fluttered open. He turned his head to meet her gaze. In the moonlight, Michael's eyes looked golden. Waves of serenity washed over her. It was so powerful, she could only gasp.

"What is that?" she asked breathlessly. She wasn't sure if he'd know what she was talking about but she couldn't find the words to describe the feeling.

Tranquility erased all lines from his face. "I guess you're one of the few who can feel my emotions. I wonder why that is."

She wanted to frown because she was confused except she was too relaxed to do so.

"That's . . . interesting," she sighed. She closed her eyes, breathing his serenity into her body. "Is it because of the moon?" That was the first thought to pop in her head.

"Partly. When it's a full moon, I'm most open so you'd get more of what I'm feeling. It's not always a good thing for me, but what can I do?"

"I don't know. This is pleasant."

Michael laughed. "I'm not always this calm."

She smiled. "Why is this happening? Why can I feel what you're feeling?"

"I don't know, really. I've only had other shifters experience this."

She paused. "Does that mean I'm gonna get hairy at night?"

His laugh was deep, carrying over the car-ocean. "I don't know, Celia."

She sighed away any normal misgivings at that statement. "This all has to do with the moon, right?"

"I'm sure it does. The moon dictates a lot of what we do. We shifters can change pretty much whenever we want. The moon makes it easier since the change is so draining—at least, for me it is."

"Why does the moon help?"

"Magic, I guess."

"What do you change into?"

He chuckled again. "I thought you knew."

Celia had to think through this strange, unfamiliar bliss; a task that was the equivalent of navigating through a thick fog with a penlight. His golden eyes flashed in her mind.

"Oh! The dog."

"Wolf, you mean."

She pried her eyes open with some effort. This thing he was

doing was like a strong drug. She didn't think she'd be able to get up. Her head lolled to the side to look at him. He was still smiling up at the moon, his eyes closed.

"But if you turn into a wolf, doesn't that make you a werewolf?"

Michael shrugged. "I've never met anyone else like me. I'm just a shifter." His tone was casual, yet just below the surface she could tell he was troubled. Plus, the blanket of tranquility wavered slightly, giving him away.

"I thought you said there were others?"

"My roommates. They change into dogs. And one fox."

Yes, he was definitely troubled. His drug was rescinding, which was disappointing. She thought she should stop with this line of questioning in order to experience it a little longer, except she wanted to know more. Either direction seemed selfish on her part.

"Why are you upset?" she asked.

He sighed. The blanket seeped away until it was gone. She could still hear the car-made ocean, feel the breeze the vehicles were making, but it wasn't the same. She was just laying on the ground now, shuddering from the cold, the moon a white, partially deflated ball in the sky.

Michael sat up and tucked his knees to his chest. He stared out at the river. She sat up, too, surveying him. His jaw was tense from clenching. She reached out and touched his arm. He flinched a little, like he'd forgotten she was there.

He turned his sad eyes on her.

"I don't know," he said. "I've been feeling kind of . . . I don't know what the word is. Restless, maybe? My friends have noticed. I've been picking at them, they say." He shook his head. "I can't help it. Sometimes I feel like I don't belong here. Because I'm the only one."

"What about your parents?"

"I've tried to ask my father about it. I could never come right out with it. What if he doesn't know? I don't want him to think I'm a freak."

"You're not a freak, Michael," she said firmly.

He looked down at her, and his eyes briefly blazed golden. He smirked and turned back to the water.

"Your mom?"

"My father doesn't talk about her. She died having me."

She knew that pain very well. Only, she had been able to spend time with her mother before she died.

"My mom passed away when I was younger. It's not easy."

"No, it's not."

Celia chewed her lip. "So, your dad isn't a shifter?"

"As far as I know, no. Like I said, I'm the only one." He paused for a second. "I wish I could figure this all out. Figure out where I'm supposed to be. But what would I do? Where would I go?"

Her hand was still on his arm. She rubbed it gently. His muscles were taut under his shirt.

"You sound like a college student," she said lightly. Of course, her only real experience with college students was in books, but his restlessness and indecision fit the formula.

His gaze drifted to the grass by his feet in a dejected way, like he was silently wishing it were that simple. "Not the same."

Celia didn't know what to say. This was all new territory for her. She tried recalling what little knowledge she had of werewolves. All she came up with were horror movies from the Sci-Fi channel. That didn't help at all. Michael in wolf form was nothing like the scary beasts in those movies.

Instead of words, which she couldn't find, she leaned into him. His body was so warm, almost feverish. He wasn't clammy or coughing. She reached up to place the back of her hand on his forehead.

"Are you sick?" she asked.

The question brought him out of his funk, if only slightly. He chuckled with a shake of his head. "No. It's a shifter thing. We're always hot."

They watched the light traffic. Five minutes later, Michael stood. He held out his hand to help her to her feet. She noticed his eyes were back to normal. They strolled to her car and she drove to his apartment.

"Do you wanna come up for a bit?" he asked.

She was tired but she didn't mind being in his company. She didn't try to decipher if it was because of his magic. They went up the stairs to the heavy door of his building.

In the long hallway, a wide staircase was to the right. Seven doors lined the left side of the corridor. Their feet sounded extra heavy on the thinly-carpeted floor. She followed him to the last apartment on the left. Raucous laughter filtered through the door.

Michael groaned. "I thought they were asleep."

Nope. She and Michael were greeted with the smell of pizza and something spicy when he opened the door. Perhaps buffalo wings. Well, it was more like a slap to the face. The spicy wings were making her nose run and Celia wasn't even eating the damn things.

A short hallway sat just beyond the door. The kitchen was to the right, a closet to the left. The hallway spilled into the deceptively large living room. It housed a big, projection-style TV, chocolate sofa and matching loveseat, and the largest collection of DVDs and video games she'd ever seen outside of Blockbuster.

There were two doorways on either wall. From what she could see, each hallway held three doors. They must've been the bedrooms.

Her attention went to the scene in front of her, where the

three guys Celia had seen that first night she'd dropped Michael off were scattered on the large sofa and the floor. There was a fourth guy with them. He wasn't dark or as brawny as the others. They were all laughing and eating. Three of them fiddled with wireless Xbox controllers. Four pizza boxes and five wing containers stained the coffee table. Three bottles of two-liter sodas sat beside them, sweating onto napkins and envelopes on the table. A box fan in the window behind the sofa exchanged cool air outside with all of the testosterone inside.

"Shit, man, he's kicking your ass!" the one not playing cried. He was stuffing pizza in his mouth at the same time.

"Shut up! I got this!"

"You ain't got shit!"

"Shoot 'im! Right there!"

"Shut up!"

They didn't notice Michael and Celia's entrance. Michael took her hand and led her to the doorway on the right. She didn't know if she was comfortable with this. If the guys weren't so enraptured with their game, she would've pulled her hand away. She liked Michael, just not in that way. Since they were heading to his bedroom, she grudgingly told herself she'd have to set him straight. There was a conversation she hated to have.

Through the entryway, he went to the door on the left. The one in the middle was ajar. She saw that it was a bathroom. A messy bathroom going by the towels and gym shorts lying on the floor. Oh, wait. Those were boxers. Michael closed the bedroom door halfway to muffle the guys' noise.

His room was small. The full-sized bed took up most of the space. It sat in the center of the room, neatly made with a black jersey sheet set. It was raised from the floor with those Bed Lifters. She could see clear storage containers underneath since he didn't have a bed skirt. She had similar containers under her own bed, since storage was limited in her apartment.

Squeezed to the left side was a tiny desk holding his laptop and speakers; the right, a dresser and a three-drawer unit were stuffed with clothes. A small television rested on the dresser among his toiletries. His closet was open and she saw his collection of fitted hats hanging from hooks on the door.

Michael sat at the desk. With one finger, he woke up his computer. Celia stood by the door, feeling a little uneasy in such an intimate space. Michael directed his grin at the computer.

"You can sit, you know," he replied.

She glanced around but the only place to sit was the bed. Trying not to seem prudish, she perched on the edge, facing him. He was checking his email. He put both hands on the computer to reply to a lengthy message.

"It's a little warm in here," she said. "Are you trying to remember the good times in California?"

He chuckled. "Nah. That's just the way it is here."

"What do you mean? You can't control the heat?"

"The heat's not on."

She frowned. "That must suck in the summertime."

"Believe it."

"Do you all live here?"

"Yup."

She frowned as she counted that in her head. "So, someone shares a room?"

"Tommy and Puddles do. They got the short sticks."

"Puddles?" she asked with a raised eyebrow. "That's not a very manly nickname."

He chuckled, eyes still on the computer. "Yeah, he hates it."

"Where did it come from?"

Michael's fingers paused over the keys. He glanced over his shoulder at her. From his look, she could tell he was debating.

"He has a nervous bladder," he said haltingly, considering how much to say. "He gets kinda jumpy sometimes and he . . ."

He trailed off. Celia got the picture. Her nose scrunched. "That's pretty gross."

One look at her face and Michael doubled over in laughter. It went on for such a while that she started to get annoyed. She didn't see what was so damn funny.

"I'm talking about when he's a German Shepard," he said through his mirth.

Her face loosened. "Oh."

He shook his head in amusement and went back to his typing. Her cellphone rang.

"Where are you?" Victor asked. "I've been waiting. Is everything okay?"

"I'm sorry, honey, I guess I lost track of time." She peeked up at Michael through her lashes. He was still scanning his emails but it didn't have his full attention anymore.

"Should I go?" Victor asked. She could hear the edge of disappointment in his voice. He'd be upset if she said yes. It was late though and she was tired. Except, now that she was in a better mood, she felt she could deal with him more appropriately. She didn't want to put it off any longer.

"No, no," she said hurriedly to cover her pause. "I'll be home soon."

They hung up and she put the phone away.

"Boyfriend?" Michael asked. He wasn't looking at her, his tone hollow.

"Yeah." She hopped to her feet. "I should get going anyway."

Michael stood as well. His back and shoulders were rigid. He wanted to say something, she knew. If he wasn't going to spit it out, she wasn't going to concern herself with whatever issues he may have had.

He led her to the door, and nearly walked into one of his roommates. He was the one with pale skin, messy black hair, and green eyes. He looked to be their age, if not a year or two younger. The rings of acne on his cheeks were an indicator of his youth as well.

He frowned at Michael. His mouth twisted into what Celia assumed would be a masculine insult but then he caught sight of her. Instead, his mouth formed a knowing smirk. He patted Michael's shoulder approvingly, who shoved him into the bathroom, where he had been originally headed. The guy burst into laughter as he closed the door.

Michael rolled his eyes to Celia, telling her to forget about him. She didn't say anything; she just wanted out. The others had settled down in the living room. Three sets of eyes turned as they emerged from the suite. And they all regarded her curiously, wondering what this unknown girl was doing in their personal space.

Her steps faltered under the scrutiny. These three looked like Michael: tall, dark, strapping, crew cuts.

Michael placed a hand on her shoulder. "Celia, this is Tommy, Elliot, and Kane."

She distinguished them by small features. Tommy was black, with a cut across his left eyebrow where the hair never grew back. Elliot looked to be of Hispanic descent, maybe Dominican based on his curly, dark hair. He wore a black bandana under a black baseball cap with a black "B." She couldn't determine where Kane was from. His sharp, high cheekbones could've been Native American attributes. His eyes were pale blue, like Trixie's. They looked unnatural in contrast with his tanned skin.

She mused briefly about what kinds of dogs they changed into and who was the fox. She would've guessed Chuckles in the bathroom was the fox because his appearance differed from the others. Since none of these fellas was named Puddles, she'd have to rethink that notion.

Celia waved meekly after the introductions. Only Elliot and Tommy gave little nods in response. Kane, she noticed, was not thrilled by her presence. It was minuscule, but his top lip curled slightly from his teeth in a silent snarl. The tension in the room was making her uncomfortable. Not to mention that sharp sanitizer scent was steadily rising. Now, she really wanted to leave.

She nudged Michael as discreetly as she could. He got the hint and continued on outside. He held the main door for her.

"Well, thanks for the ride." He sounded the teensiest crestfallen. That hadn't gone as swimmingly as he had expected, she assumed. She hoped he was upset about the unreceptive introduction with his roommates and nothing more.

"Thanks for taking me to the ocean," she said.

"Don't worry about the guys," he blurted. "They get like that sometimes."

There wasn't much to say to that. She patted his arm then slid past toward the stairs.

Michael took hold of her shoulder, making her halt. "Do you really drink vampire blood?"

"Michael . . ." She moved away from him. "You make it sound like I'm taking it as my meals or something. It's not like that." She patted her stomach. "This is proof I get my daily burgers."

He just looked at her. She raised her hands, asking *what the fuck else do you want?*

"I'm sorry Celia, but I just don't get it."

She stared at him directly. "Have you ever tried it?"

"No."

"Have you ever been committed to another person? Been in a place where nothing comes between you? Where you want to be as close to them as physically possible?"

"It's your boyfriend then?"

She couldn't read his expression. Disgust. Fury. Envy. His nose flared angrily. Whatever was bouncing around in his head never became words.

Celia turned slowly and went down the stairs. At her car, she glanced back. Michael was still by the door. Sadness appeared to win out in the battle for his face. Celia didn't know what to say; how to make him understand.

She got in the car. At the end of the street, she looked back through the mirror. Michael turned from the door. The light on the stoop hit his eyes at a slight angle. The beam reflected on his pupils and bounced back as a yellow shine, like dog eyes.

The first thing Victor asked after she gave him a kiss hello was, "Why do you smell like wolf?"

She frowned down at herself, even lifted her arm to her nose. She only seemed able to detect that strange sanitizer scent in the presence of a shifter.

"I don't smell anything."

"You wouldn't." His gaze narrowed. "You know a wolf now?"

She shrugged. "What can I say? The supernatural just seem to find me."

Celia moved around him to go to her room. There, she pulled out her pajamas from the dresser.

"Who is it?" Victor asked. He had sat on her bed to watch her change.

"Someone I work with," she said as vaguely as she could. She didn't want to lie to him. "You don't know him."

"Vampires and werewolves aren't known to be, well, friendly." There was a laugh in his tone.

"Why not?"

"They think they're as strong as us, and don't get me wrong, they can be a challenge. In the end, we've always defeated them. Wolves don't like that we have the upper hand."

"Well, that's too bad. He said that he's the only one. Wouldn't that be something hereditary?"

"Unless they are bitten, yes, it is passed through families.

Female werewolves can't carry their offspring to term because they have to change every month with the full moon. It's up to the male, but like every other genetic characteristic, it's not always passed on."

She paused in undressing. "He said his father isn't a shifter."

"The father has to be."

Celia wondered if Michael was aware of that. "What about other kinds of shifters? Is it the father?"

He shook his head. "They are able to change whenever they want. The females aren't affected in the same way. I don't know why it is different for wolves. It has to have something to do with the magic in their bloodline. Some argue that other shifters evolved from werewolves. That they were the original."

Celia had changed into her pajamas and disappeared into the bathroom for a moment to do her nightly routine. When she came back to the room, Victor was under the covers waiting for her in his boxers. The light from her lamp played in the crevices of his toned torso. His sumptuous gray eyes watched her every move. She glanced to her alarm clock as she settled in beside him and saw that it was nearly four.

She sighed. Though all she wanted to do was snuggle up next to Victor and drift off to Never-Never Land, she needed to talk.

Victor rubbed her thigh. He was waiting for her to speak.

She clutched the gold pendent at her throat. "I saw you with Ashleigh," she said at last.

He frowned. "When?"

"The other night, after dinner. She was hugging you."

His face was blank as he absorbed her words. She couldn't tell what he was thinking. He really could pull a "vampire" when he wanted. She found it irksome and unfair. Their bond was useless tonight. She couldn't distinguish what he was thinking through that route. It was still too new and she didn't know all of the mechanisms. Plus, she was above blatantly searching his head, not that she knew how to manipulate that course either.

"Is that why you were upset earlier?" he asked with an even voice. No emotions there.

"Yes, partly."

"I'm sorry you witnessed that and got the wrong idea. Nothing unseemly happened, if you're worried. She gave me a hug goodnight and I left her with Elizabeth."

Celia squeezed her eyes shut. She knew nothing happened because she trusted Victor. It was just frustrating knowing he was turned on by another woman. She probably wouldn't have taken it so hard if she were dating a human man. Guys were so easily aroused. The fact that she had seen and felt it from his point of view was killing her.

It appeared the downsides of sharing blood were poking through the veil. Yes, she had received a boost of confidence, a little extra strength, some amazing orgasms, and was able to call Victor if she was ever in need, though she could've done that before. Except what was the cost?

She realized at that moment she didn't want to see into his head. His thoughts and feelings should be his own. That's the way it was supposed to be.

"What are you thinking about?" he asked with a curious tilt of his head. He'd been watching her since she had fallen silent for so long.

She shook her head and opened her eyes. "I don't know. Life."

"That's a lot to ponder."

"Ugh, I'm such a shithead, getting mad like that. I just didn't like what I had seen. And then my fucking cousin was annoying me."

"That's all understandable."

"Of course nothing inappropriate had happened."

"She did want to try my blood."

Celia's jaw dropped. "You said no, right?"

"Of course."

Celia put her hands on her hips. Her brows were pulled low over her eyes. "How could she ask you that? Did she just come out of the blue with it?"

Victor paused, as if surprised by her possessiveness. "I was showing her how to properly feed. She asked about the taste of vampire blood."

Celia stared at him for a really long time. So many different thoughts passed through her head. They were drinking blood from some unsuspecting fool. He was getting close to another woman. Ashleigh was experiencing things Celia never would. She was seeing parts of him that Celia wouldn't.

He was drinking from someone else.

Victor reached out and used his thumb to smooth the lines in her forehead.

"What the fuck, Victor."

"I'm sorry, Seal. She has to learn. We can give her the proper training to ensure she doesn't hurt anyone in the process. *I'm* learning things, too."

"Well, what the hell am I supposed to say to that shit?"

He squeezed her arm, like that helped at all. She was quiet for another moment.

"Why can I see into your head?" she asked suddenly. "Why am I different? I don't feel different." She looked down at her hands as if they held the answers.

"There's someone I want you to talk to. Perhaps she'll have some insight on this. You're free Sunday? I'll arrange a meeting."

He grinned and her worries lifted knowing he would help her. She cupped his cheek and kissed his lips. She then turned off the bedside lamp and climbed on top of him. She wasn't too tired to remind him of what he had in his possession.

He was warm tonight. That impulse of anger or jealousy or

whatever it was that always licked at her when he fed was trying to emerge. She didn't know it was because of her blood that he wasn't as cold to the touch. Her mind couldn't help imagining him with Ashleigh.

She fought it down, though, deciding instead to close her eyes and enjoy the feel of him taking up space inside her— physically and mystically.

***

Celia was asleep ten minutes after she fell against the pillow, sweaty and panting. He figured he had about an hour and a half before sunrise. Victor disentangled himself from Celia, whose arms and legs held him hostage. He pulled his clothes back on and materialized on Ramsey's front stoop, which was different. Perhaps he was trying to gauge Ashleigh before entering.

After collecting himself from the trip, Victor listened closely at the door. He felt ridiculous.

"No one's home."

He turned at the voice. Ramsey's back was to him from his seat on the top stair. Victor went over and sat beside him. He found Ramsey had his eyes closed. He waited him out. He didn't really have a choice.

A minute passed before Ramsey sighed. He shook his head. "I should be better than this," he drawled in that Georgian accent of his. The older lady with the Shar-Pei emerged from her house in a bright pink track suit. The tiny dog sniffed the air and then barked a few times in their direction. Both vampires locked in on the woman as she tugged his leash toward the opposite direction.

Victor waited for him to explain. Ramsey's sea-green eyes turned on him and he saw that he was disappointed.

"I can't find Annie. She's not gone—no, I'd be able to tell. But she isn't . . . there."

Victor nodded distantly.

"Milo and Clarice," he went on, "are probably in cahoots with a witch from Corinna's coven."

Victor raised a brow. "Not her?"

"Nah. I would've known if she was lying."

"May I borrow Corinna? I need to ask her a few things."

Ramsey shrugged. He then shook his head again in that same discontent way. "If I could find them, then maybe I'd feel like I'm doing my job."

Victor thought it wise to change the subject. "How's Ashleigh coming along?"

A small smile touched his face. "Pretty well, actually. I took her out earlier and she handled herself with Mallory. I think she was nervous. She only drank a little."

Victor nodded. He didn't mention that she had had some practice.

"Looks like we've got a tracker on our hands," Ramsey said, confirming Victor's conclusion. "I haven't brought up the issue of her staying here or going back to New York. I got the sense there was no one there for her. Elizabeth likes her. Cillian's taken a shine to her. She visits with him often.

"The strange thing is I don't believe that her maker is gone. She doesn't appear to be resisting his call and he would've found her by now. He may be incapacitated."

"Like Annie?" His gaze snapped to Ramsey's as a bulb lit in his head. "Do you think that group Celia was talking about has them?" he asked   urgently.

Ramsey frowned. "Perhaps. It does make sense."

"But I thought they only staked. I wouldn't think they'd hold anyone captive for so long."

Ramsey sighed wearily. "From what I've found out, they are a pretty large group. Much larger than your Celia's friends."

Victor resisted the urge to roll his eyes at the mention of Jay & Co. At least Ramsey's sense of humor was still there somewhere.

"They enjoy torture," Ramsey continued. "I wouldn't put it past them to hold captives."

Victor frowned down at the stairs. "I wonder if Celia could get information . . ." He trailed off. He didn't like that idea one bit. Anything involving danger to her was not something he welcomed. Plus, her cousin had been a cause of her agitation earlier that night.

Ramsey was silent beside him. Victor was certain he would be up for having Celia's aid. Proof of that was when he had gone behind Victor's back two months ago to inquire of her help.

"Is everything alright with you and Celia?"

Victor looked up. "Why do you ask?"

"I'm only concerned, buddy. You don't smile anymore when you speak of her."

Victor hadn't realized.

"It's as if you're guarding her from us. You know we aren't a threat—"

"Of course not," he said fiercely.

"When I mentioned testing Celia's ability, you sort of snarled at us."

Had he? That would explain why Ramsey and Elizabeth both seemed so wary.

"I guess I am a bit more possessive as of late," Victor admitted. "She's special to me."

Ramsey squeezed his thigh. "I understand."

Victor didn't like this turn in the conversation. Just hearing her name come from his mouth had started a burning fury in his chest that he had to consciously control. He changed the subject once again.

"It appears we have a wolf in our midst."

Ramsey cocked an eyebrow. "Oh?" He sounded interested.

"This is the first you've heard?"

"Yeah. He must be the only one. We would've known if there was a pack in the area."

Victor nodded mutely, knowing he was right. Packs announced themselves by way of their group magic. All other predators in the vicinity would feel it as a warning, like a prickle along the back of your neck. Vampires hardly ever yielded to it, unless they were severely outnumbered.

"He'll probably move on soon," Ramsey said.

Just then, the red sedan glided down the street. It didn't stop its trek up the driveway to the three-car garage around back. Victor saw that Elizabeth was driving with Bryce beside her and Ashleigh in the back. Thankfully, she didn't notice him; she appeared to be reading something in her lap. That meant he could leave without incident.

"I should go," Victor said.

Ramsey clasped his hand. "Take care."

Victor disappeared.

Ten

C ELIA MADE IT through Saturday night without much issue. She collected her purse from the locker, said goodnight to Bobby and her coworkers, and then headed out into the night. She was distracted as she rummaged through her purse. It was a strange sound, the scuffing of a shoe followed by complete silence that eventually crept through, catching her attention.

Someone was following her.

She glanced around casually as all of the hairs on her body stood on end. She didn't see anything out of place. The corner that concealed the parking lot loomed just ahead. She calculated mentally how quickly she could get around the building and into her car.

Naturally, Celia knew who was watching her. No matter how fast her legs went she'd never make it. Instead of giving her pursuer more pleasure by panicking, she forced herself to continue at an even pace.

She took two steps into the parking lot when the first blow came. Two hands smacked into the middle of her back, sending her pitching forward. Her hands flew out in front of her to break her fall. The concrete dug into her cheek and palms.

Celia didn't have time to think about the pain. Scrambling to her feet, she rushed toward her car. Clarice ran so fast it seemed she just appeared out of nowhere in front of her. Celia stumbled to a halt. She was still a good distance from her car, not that it would be easy to get around her.

Clarice was smiling, of course. And her fangs were out, of course. Her long hair was pulled into a neat bun. She wore dark jeans and a flowered top that Celia would've thought was cute in a different circumstance.

The vampire had a friend with her. This woman was in her thirties, also wearing dark jeans that struggled to contain her sizable thighs and a feminine plaid top in turquoise and black that was very stylish as well. Her hair was light brown around her shoulders. Deep dimples punched her cheeks. She leered at Celia, a ravenous glint in her eyes. She wanted Celia. More evidence, her pointy fangs.

"Hello, sweet-*haht*," Clarice replied. She sniffed the air, probably picking up on her fear and anger. Whatever it was, she was satisfied.

Cool hands wrapped around Celia's neck. She was too startled to scream. Her breath caught in her throat in a loud gasp. He could've crushed her larynx or, hell, snapped her neck. Instead, he only held her in place. His tongue ran up her cheek. His body was pressed against her and she was swamped with memories so suddenly that she couldn't breathe.

In a fit of anger, she swung her fist out without making contact. She jerked her face from him. Belatedly, she realized that he was licking her wound. She hoped he choked on the gravel bits caught in her skin.

Without further preamble, Milo wrenched her head to the side and bit her neck. "No!" Celia cried but he was already sucking away. She fought it though, fought the blissful shivers starting in her stomach.

He lifted his head a moment to lick his lips. She twisted in his grasp and elbowed him in the side. It didn't have too much effect, which she knew. He did loosen his hold slightly. Milo was about her height, so when she wheeled around, she was pretty much eye-to-eye with him. She gathered all her strength and kneed him in the nuts.

Surprisingly, it worked. Probably because he had a hard-on that she crushed with her knee.

Milo stumbled away, groaning. He was bent over, clutching his crotch. Clarice giggled. Milo found the energy somewhere to give her the finger.

Celia only had a second to feel triumphant before the unknown woman barreled into her with all the force of a Mack truck. She was on her back, holding her arm up to shield her face and neck from the snapping teeth. The other arm trembled with the effort of keeping her at a distance. The vamp did connect with her forearm a few times, making Celia cry out.

"Hmm, she likes you."

That was Clarice, who hovered off to the side, watching the show. Clarice reached over, not to pull her away, but to rub the vamp's head affectionately. Milo collected himself and bounded over. He yanked the vamp off Celia. She flew somewhere Celia couldn't see, landing with a grunt. She was back in an instant. She used her hands to transfer what little blood was on her face to her mouth.

That wasn't Celia's main concern. No, her main concern was Milo, who kicked her hard in the side with his black-and-white Skater Boi sneaker. Sharp jolts throbbed in her side and back. She bit back her scream of pain as tears stung her eyes. She wanted to call for Victor. His face flashed before her eyelids. A wave of alarm flooded her insides and she knew he could tell something was wrong.

She was about to call him when Milo kicked her again in precisely the same spot. Through the curtain of tears, she saw he was extremely angry. She'd only seen him this furious once; the night he broke away from Ramsey. His expressions mostly encompassed arrogant and cocky.

A vicious growl ripped through the night. It was low to the ground and from a distance. Clarice glanced around at the sound. Milo, too preoccupied with making Celia cry, swung his leg back for another kick. Something snapped behind him. A long, wooden object whizzed through the air, striking him in the shoulder. Celia only saw it after it had made contact.

Milo yelped as he fell to his knee. He was leaning over her. His injured shoulder bled profusely onto her chest, chin, and mouth. She didn't allow it purposely, but some of his blood found its way past her lips. She didn't notice. Her whole body shuddered in fright as she fought to keep track of what was happening.

"What the fuck!" Milo bellowed. He tugged at the stake that protruded from his shoulder and tossed it aside. When he jumped up, Celia had a clearer view of what was going on around her.

Three men had joined them in the lot. Clarice flashed closer, kicked one in the chest and he was on his ass. The female vamp screamed like there was no tomorrow. Celia followed the sound. The vamp was covered with a mesh net made of sterling silver, judging by all the white smoke escaping from her skin. Clarice looked at her; she even took a step to help. The two other men pounced on the vamp before she had a chance.

Celia watched as one of the men held the screaming vamp down to the ground. The second man rammed a stake through her chest with all his might.

"You missed!" one of them said. The vampire was still screaming.

"I didn't!"

"Then what the hell? Why's she not dead?"

He extracted the stake and tried again. The wailing that had been permeating the air ceased with a strangled cough. The noxious burning smell that replaced it could gag a pig.

Clarice's opponent got to his feet and stared her down. Celia finally identified the wavy hair, the marked-up forehead.

Winston.

His two companions were the men from the Night Hawks' meeting.

Victor stirred in her mind again. His presence was fainter than before.

Stay away, she warned him. She hoped that he would hear it. It had been five days since she'd had his blood, though he had had hers. Her side of the bond was running on E.

Milo had been watching the Night Hawks' curious attempt at destroying their tag-along. He looked to Clarice questioningly before glancing to Celia. Something shifted in his eyes as he seemed to come to a conclusion. He snarled at her and then attacked the closest hunter. A brown hat topped the Asian guy's head tonight. He fell to the ground when Milo punched him three times in the stomach. His hat stayed put as he staggered to his feet.

Celia's eyes darted between the fighting. During one sweep, she paused.

A set of eyes peered out at her from the bushes surrounding the far side of the lot. She nearly shrieked but contained herself at the last moment when she recognized the golden color. She used her eyes to convey the same warning to Michael: stay away.

Clarice flitted past. Winston swung his stake at her but she was quick. She played with him a little, waiting for the second when his weapon was close before zipping out of reach. She finally ended the game by slapping him across the face. She cackled when he dropped to his knees. It was a horribly grating sound, her laugh.

Stooping down, Clarice snatched up the dead vamp's turquoise peep-toe platform pumps. She smirked at Celia before running off at lightning vampire speed, trailing black ash along the way.

Milo gave the Asian guy one last uppercut before taking his leave. He, too, offered Celia a last look. He was furious they had been interrupted. His expression told her this wouldn't be the last time they'd meet.

Well, she figured that much.

Celia groaned as she struggled to her feet. Her side ached with her breath. She looked to the bushes but Wolf Michael was gone. She hoped he hadn't gotten it in his head to follow Milo and Clarice. She didn't think a two-on-one fight would bode well for her furry friend.

Winston tended to his companions, who were considerably worse off than him. They clutched their sides, bleeding from noses and cuts. The Asian man had bite marks on his neck.

Winston was ignoring her. She could tell because he purposely gave his full attention to his friends, though there was really nothing he could do for them at the moment. The Asian guy picked up what looked like a modified crossbow from the ground. It was old, with chips in the wood. That must've been what he used to shoot the stake. Too bad his aim had been off.

Celia limped over to Winston and pinched his arm.

"Ow!" he barked, turning to her.

She was outraged. "You were following me?"

"We just saved your stupid ass," he said coldly.

"How long have you been following me?" she demanded.

"Since last night? Since that meeting?"

At the mention of that, she turned her glower on his two companions. Neither of them seemed concerned or intimidated. In fact, the white guy had made his way over to the pile of ash and clothes and was snapping a few pictures with his phone. Disgust roiled through her. Her hands tightened into angry fists. Even if the bitch had been trying to kill her what he was doing was repugnant.

Winston didn't answer her questions. She needed to get out of there so that Victor wouldn't worry. She was in pain, she was filthy, and she wanted to pound her cousin. Celia turned from the men and stalked to her car as best she could. He didn't stop her. She peeled out of the lot, narrowly missing the Asian one, and tore down the street.

Victor swung the door open as soon as she mounted the stairs of the second floor. His face was pulled together in worry. It dropped when he got a good look at her. All the blood. The dirt.

"What happened?" he demanded.

She went past him and straight to the bathroom. A sob had been building in her chest since she turned down Washington Street—the Dorchester one. She hated this so much. Being scared and feeling useless. She couldn't protect herself and now here she was, a victim all over again. She had allowed herself to relax and they'd taken advantage. Granted, it could've been worse; a lot worse. A few bites and a bruised side still meant she was alive.

She sighed miserably and turned the water on in the sink. She pulled an orange washcloth from the hook next to her toothbrush and soaked it under the stream. She looked at herself in the mirror and froze. Yes, there was blood and dirt staining her face and neck, but the scrape from kissing the pavement was gone from her cheek.

Celia glanced down at her hands. Those scrapes were gone, as well as the bite marks from the vamp. That sob that had been tightening her chest exploded from her. She began to sink to the floor. Victor's arms captured her. She fell into him, crying and crying. He brought her to the floor, which was good. She didn't know if her legs would give out.

She clutched his shirt, vaguely aware of the washcloth caressing her cheek and neck. She needed to stop crying because it was aggravating her side. The more it throbbed, though, the more she cried. She finally got it together, after a few minutes, until she was only whimpering. That's when she noticed her side wasn't aching from injury.

Victor was stroking her hair and squeezing her tight. He was scared; it had to be why he was forgetting his strength.

"Victor," she gasped. "I can't breathe."

"What?" He looked down in concern, realized what she meant and loosened his grip.

She wiped her face with her hand. Now that she was calm, the warmth in her belly registered. So did the heightened hearing and sharper vision. She could see the cracks in the tile of the floor. She could hear her neighbor playing Rock Band solo. He was pretty awful.

She'd had Milo's blood. And he'd had hers. She was going to cry for a second time because that meant he had a hold on her again and she had no control over these fucking emotions. What if he called her again? She couldn't fight it before, what were the chances she could withstand his call now?

Just as she was building up for another crying jag, she remembered her uncanny ability. She could feel Milo with her, now that she was aware of the change. Taking over the space inside her, under her skin, where Victor had occupied these last four weeks. It was the third time she had Milo's blood. They shared a connection now like she had with Victor.

She stopped her nervous habit of snapping the elastic still on her wrist. That was Victor's space. The affirmation was just the boost she needed to push her sniveling away. She wanted this over—needed it over.

Celia closed her eyes because that just seemed like it would help. She never knew what she was doing but she conjured Milo's face in her mind.

Where are you, you son-of-a-bitch?

At first, nothing happened. She was staring at the inside of her lids, with Victor cradling her and the neighbor jacking up "Black Hole Sun." She blocked that out and tried again.

A spark, a flash of light broke through the darkness before it was consumed and she was left with the obscurity provided by her eyelids. She concentrated harder. Okay, now she was seeing a living room. The vision was blurry and it took a moment to adjust, like she was fiddling with the lens of a camera.

The background noise of her apartment melted away. She heard a truck rattle on the street. Somehow, she knew it wasn't outside her building. The living room before her was crowded with gaudy furniture: a gray, plaid sofa, a black coffee table low to the ground with bright golden legs, two wingback chairs in powder blue with some kind of gold design.

Clarice was sitting in one of the chairs, resting her hands delicately on the arms, her legs crossed at the knee. She had the posture of a queen looking down on her peasants. She was eyeing Milo, who sat on the sofa based on the angle of the vision. It was like she was looking directly at Celia.

"I actually liked that one," she replied. Celia figured she was referring to the dead vamp. "Oh, well," she sighed, examining her nails. That was as close to mourning she would get.

Milo wasn't speaking. From his emotions, he was still pissed, too pissed to realize their infuriating connection. She tried to keep her anxiety at bay. Any drastic emotion might put her on his radar. Only, she didn't know how long the vision would last and she couldn't tell anything from this vantage.

A door opened. Arturo came into view. He swung the front door open with a shit-eating grin lodged under his sharp cheeks. The space where his missing incisor used to sit gaped in his smile. Through the threshold, Celia saw across the street a small park was surrounded by a tall, silver chain-linked fence. There was a basketball court, and past that, a playground almost engulfed by weeds. She got all of that in the few seconds when Arturo stepped back outside.

Two young females were pushed inside. One of them tripped over a hill in the carpet and landed on her knees with a grunt. Both were crying.

"What're you so happy about?" Milo asked irritably.

"Life, my friend." He indicated his treats.

Celia didn't get to hear more because the vision faded to black. She opened her eyes to Victor surveying her with interest. Her pulse had picked up when she saw the park. Now, Victor looked concerned. Celia was smiling brightly.

"I know where they are," she said excitedly. Victor's brows furrowed at first. His face quickly cleared with understanding. She described the park in Dorchester. It was across from an Army National Guard recruitment center over on Victory Road. To the right of the basketball court sat a row of houses all connected as one.

Victor's face was stern though his kiss was gentle. "Will you be okay?" he asked.

She nodded. "I'm getting my butt in bed."

He kissed her again, a deep kiss letting her know how much she meant to him. She was a bit breathless. His eyes were black as pitch when he looked at her again.

"I love you," he said.

Celia blinked. She hadn't expected that at all. She thought when this moment came she would need a minute to think it over. Assess her feelings and calculate the future. Instead, "I love you, too," slipped out easily.

Aw.

She smiled warmly and so did he. Victor helped her to her feet, made sure she was fine, and then vanished. She actually felt a million times better now, though she hoped Victor and Ramsey got there before Milo, Clarice, and Arturo did any major harm to those two women.

First thing she did was strip off her dirty clothes. She then put her hair up using the elastic on her wrist before climbing into the shower. Her stomach growled while she dressed in her pajamas. As she was pulling on her shirt, she lost her breath. She clutched her side in surprise. It felt like someone had just punched her.

The sharp pain disappeared as suddenly as it came. Celia was pleased but at the same time knew she'd get annoyed very quickly if she experienced all of Milo's beating.

Celia went to the kitchen to make a sandwich then settled on the sofa with the remote. There was another pain, this time in her neck. Her hand flew there reflexively. It was a wrenching pain, like when you had a crick and you turned your head the wrong way too fast.

She ate her sandwich absently, the TV watching her. Ten minutes later, a wave of magic pulsed throughout the room. She glanced around, startled. She didn't understand what was going on. The magic sucked up the oxygen. Her breathing became shallow, as if she were at the top of Mt. Everest.

Victor appeared suddenly in front of the coffee table with a muffled pop. The magic reverberated, pressing painfully against her eardrums. She covered her ears with her hands while squeezing her eyes shut. It took a moment for the wave to recede. Her eyes opened slowly. She peeked around before removing her hands.

That was a first. The only magic she'd ever had experience

with always felt more like a shiver. At most was the constricted feeling of Milo's power. It had never been this physically painful. It frightened her to know magic could be harmful.

He had been crouching on the floor, growling softly like a hurt animal. Now that he was stable, Victor fell to his side. Alarmed, Celia pushed the coffee table aside and rushed over. She looked at him more closely.

His sleeveless argyle sweater was ripped, so was the white shirt beneath. His khakis were stained with dirt and what looked like tire tracks. He was going preppy tonight, apparently. Cuts— some bleeding, others just red—littered his forehead, lip, and neck. She saw three bleeding scratches through the three slashes along his chest.

Clutched tightly in his hand was a human arm. It was a slender arm, the fingers curled into a fist. Blood oozed out in thick drops from the upper section, the part that was supposed to be attached to a shoulder. She could clearly see the white bone and pink muscles at the top.

She gulped as vomit burned the back of her throat.

Victor's injuries would've normally been on their way to healing. Celia looked away from the dismembered arm in his possession and immediately held her wrist out to his mouth. His free hand darted out so quickly she didn't realize he had her in his grip until she felt the crushing tightness around her wrist. He couldn't lift his head. Instead, he pulled her to him. She lost her balance and fell into his chest. A muffled cry made its way from her mouth when she touched the arm. It was pale and cold.

His fangs cut into her flesh. She tried not to watch or listen to his savage grunts. She'd seen her boyfriend's hidden nature (true nature) a few times in the past and it always scared the shit out of her. She focused instead on his shoulder while stroking his hair.

After a few minutes, Celia's hand stopped rubbing his hair.

Weakness was making her eyes close. She attempted to extract her wrist. His nails dug into her skin, making her whimper. The sound seemed to clear his head. His fingers relaxed, his fangs retracted. He still held her wrist to his mouth but she felt his wet tongue cleaning her wound.

Victor held her hand in his and slowly stretched out on the floor. She was sitting with her legs tucked beneath her. His eyes were closed, his face soft. The cuts sealed themselves, leaving his skin flawless again. His cheeks and lips were pink now.

"I apologize," he whispered.

"It's okay." She whispered, too, because she was lightheaded. Maybe he heard a tremor in her voice. His eyes popped open.

"Shit, Seal."

He went to make a cut on his own wrist but the extra arm was in the way. He laid it on the floor beside him then offered his wrist to her. She only needed a minute and she was flying high. Her wrist was good as new and Victor was there again, under her skin. They lay side-by-side on the dirty shag carpet with their fingers entwined.

"What happened over there?" Celia asked, breaking the companionable silence.

"Arturo was taken care of. Milo and Clarice got away."

She groaned. She was not irritated with Victor, rather with whatever pact the rogue vamps had made with the devil or whoever kept saving their hides.

"They had moved too close to Morrissey Boulevard." The busy street ran through Dorchester, connecting with the town of Quincy. "Ramsey didn't want an audience."

"Or police," she chimed in. The staties often patrolled that stretch of road, especially near the entrance to UMass Boston. It was a trap for people speeding around the bend toward the bridge.

"Right. So they fled. They won't be causing trouble for a little while," he added, sounding pleased. She assumed that meant they had sustained enough damage to constitute bed rest. He held up the arm as proof. The fist flopped from side-to-side. Judging by how small it was and the perfectly rounded nails, it was Milo's. She was certain.

Good, Celia thought callously. Sensing her flaring fury, Victor squeezed her hand.

"You should probably get to bed," he said. There was a thread of ardor in his tone.

"Sure," she replied, feeling joyful again. "Although, I hope you aren't suggesting sleep."

"Not at all."

The hot water and Celia's lemon-scented shower gel washed away the last of the caked-on blood. Celia was facing Victor's chest and giggling while he shampooed her hair. He had piled it all on top her head and his long fingers scratched gloriously at her scalp.

"You know this means I'm gonna have to spend an hour drying my hair now," she replied with a raised brow.

"I like doing this."

She peeked up at him. A tiny smile played at his lips while he worked.

"I like you."

He met her eyes. "I love you."

Celia gave a silly squeal. "Oh, baby!"

She jumped up, wrapping her legs around his waist. His hands gripped her slippery thighs. He was inside of her so quickly that her moans started up without her knowledge. She leaned back until her shoulders rested against the tiled shower wall. She held his forearms for support. Victor planted his feet. His hips moved in a circular motion, his pelvis rubbing her clit until it swelled. Little shockwaves erupted from her center and she shuddered against the wall.

"Shiiiiiiit," she blew out as the last quake left her system.

Victor stepped forward until he had her sandwiched between him and the wall. Her breath was hot and rapid against his face.

He moved her soapy hair off her shoulder. His nose grazed the skin of her neck first, before his teeth punctured. She was moaning again. After only a few draws, however, Victor pulled back. He made a face.

"What?" she asked. She ran her hand over her neck.

"I should've washed the shampoo out first."

She laughed. "I thought you said my blood was too sweet to pass up."

"Don't worry," he replied, his gray eyes dancing wickedly. "I'll get some."

He lowered her to her feet. She shook her head in amusement as she stepped under the water to rinse her hair. Victor was frowning at her.

"What?" She swiped the water out of her eyes.

"You are okay with this, right?"

She tilted her head to the side. "With shower sex? Of course."

He didn't crack a smile. "I mean with my taking from you. Are you fine with that?"

Now she frowned. Where had that come from? "Yeah. Why?"

"Are you sure?"

She dropped her hands to her hips. "I don't understand. Why are you asking me that?"

"For a while, you weren't interested."

"Yeah, and now I am."

He was quiet for a second. "I just want to be certain that you don't have any reservations. I know you aren't particularly comfortable with the fact that I have to feed."

She stiffened. Why was he bringing this up? Why was he ruining their evening?

"That was with unsuspecting people who didn't remember it

happening. I'm consenting, okay? I know you need this. I don't like some of the . . . side effects sometimes," she added, remembering Ashleigh's hug, "but I like helping you."

She spun from him to rinse the last of the soap from her skin. She then turned off the water and stepped out onto the bathmat. They toweled off in silence. Celia shrugged on her kimono robe.

"I'm going to Ramsey's," Victor said. Celia looked up at him through the mirror. She had just rubbed in conditioner and now held her blow dryer in hand.

He kissed her temple.

"Okay," she said softly. He must've changed his mind about drinking from her. "Night."

"Good night, Seal."

He melted away. Celia's eyes slowly met her reflection. Her brows were furrowed, her lips puckered slightly in distaste. *What?* she asked her. *Do you have a fucking problem, too?*

Her reflection remained impassive.

***

The closest graveyard to Celia's was bordered by Adams Street and the Neponset River Reservation, called Cedar Grove Cemetery. Victor found a shovel in a shed at the far northeast corner. He picked a grave under a tree with a simple headstone dated in the sixties and began to dig. Once he was about four feet deep, he dropped Milo's arm inside and then covered it with the loose dirt. It would deteriorate over time since it was no longer attached. It wouldn't be completely destroyed until Milo was destroyed.

Victor checked in at Ramsey's before sunrise. The mansion looked like a scene from a gruesome massacre. Bloody handprints stamped the off-white walls, providing a smeared pathway to the stairs. Someone had knocked one of the paintings askew, marring the golden frame with red. Blood spattered the hardwood floors as if someone had been struggling with the task of carrying a bucket of it, and managed to spill half of the contents on the way to their destination.

He paused when Bryce's door opened suddenly.

"Get out," the vampire growled from the depths of the dark room. A woman stumbled into the hallway. She fell into the opposite wall with a grunt. Bryce slammed the door with enough force to rattle the walls.

Victor went over. The smell of her blood filled his nose. She clutched her neck where she was still bleeding and blinked up at him. It was Mallory, one of their groupies. Her dark brown braid had come undone. Tears streamed down her cheeks. Black mascara pooled under her eyes, her eyelashes clumped together like spider legs. Her arms were bare, and he could see red rings on her biceps where Bryce had grabbed and held her in place.

Victor's mouth pursed at the sight. Ramsey would not be pleased with this treatment. But Bryce had been injured, taking a tree branch through his side courtesy of Arturo, before Ramsey stabbed the Italian through the heart with an iron pole. Clarice had latched onto Bryce's neck when he was down.

"He's so mean now," Mallory cried. "I want Annie back!" She pushed past Victor. Her feet slipped in the wet blood on the floor and she almost lost her balance. She sobbed harder as she raced up the stairs. Victor went upstairs as well. Mallory rushed into the first room at the top of the landing. Ramsey's door was open at the end of the hall.

Victor heard Elizabeth calling out commands before he reached the room. He rolled his eyes, as he was unable to contain his grin. She was lying on the bed, holding her dislocated shoulder in its socket, and still giving out instructions.

"In the basement, Ashleigh," she said through gritted teeth. "There's a box on the back wall."

Ashleigh nodded determinedly and flashed out of the room.

Ramsey clucked his teeth. "Elizabeth, you need real blood."

She shook her head, and then fell back against the pillows. Victor moved closer. She'd taken the most hits, an effort to rattle Ramsey. A deep gash cut across her left cheek and nose. A clump of her hair was absent near her ear. A chunk of her dislodged shoulder was missing and she was bleeding from an injury under her blouse. The light blue material was steadily turning red. Her left leg was broken, her foot twisted at an impossible angle on the bed. Her clothes were still covered in sand.

Clarice had managed to separate Elizabeth from the rest of the group and overtook her on the sands of Malibu Beach. Elizabeth wasn't a fighter, but when she was determined enough, she was a reliable ally. By the time Victor came to her rescue, Clarice was spitting out the meat of her shoulder onto the sand. The damage had been done.

Victor helped Ramsey with mopping up the blood from her wounds. Ashleigh was back in the room with three blood bags in her hand. She ripped one open and handed it to Elizabeth. She finished it in a few gulps, and then eyed the other two bags.

"Is that all?" she asked with a grimace.

"Yeah, I didn't see anything else down there."

"Damn," she muttered. Ashleigh handed her the next bag. By the time she finished off the third, everyone in the room knew it wasn't nearly enough.

"I'm getting Mallory," Ramsey said firmly.

"She's with Bryce," Victor interjected. He would make sure to heal her before he left.

"Cindy's here," Ashleigh said. "And Matt and that other one."

"Get Matt," Ramsey demanded. Ashleigh was only gone for a minute. She led Matt over to the bed.

Elizabeth watched him approach, her eyes filled with fear. She looked to Ramsey and shook her head.

"Don't be silly, love." He stooped down next to her. "You'll be fine. I'm right here."

She didn't respond. Victor saw his own fear reflected in her, from when he needed blood to heal. She knew how easy it was to lose control, to kill in order to survive. She was afraid she would go too far.

When she didn't protest, Ramsey placed a hand on Matt's neck, rubbing his skin gently. He wasn't applying his vamp magic because Matt enjoyed the sting of fangs. Ramsey lowered him to the bed. Matt had to lean over Elizabeth, he was so tall. Her fangs sharpened and she bit him, hard. Matt's groan was a mixture of pleasure and pain. After a few pulls, her hand gripped his hair, craning his head to the side for the best access to the carotid artery.

Her hungry grunts filled the room. Ashleigh hissed, and when Victor glanced to her, he saw her fangs were out. They'd all been too preoccupied with Elizabeth's condition to notice anything off about Ashleigh being in the same room as a human. She flexed her hands a few times, making tight fists.

He anticipated her intention a second too late. Ashleigh lunged at the bed. She had Matt's arm stretched out behind him at a painful angle. Her teeth were in the crook of his elbow before Victor reached her.

Victor had to pry her mouth loose. She snarled at him, thick blood and saliva drenching her mouth. Victor got his arm around her neck in a half nelson and jetted out of the room. He didn't stop until they were in the kitchen.

"What the hell's your problem?" she shouted at him. She wrestled herself free, and then shoved him in the chest. The counter jabbed him in the lower back when he slammed into it. She was in front of him, her hands on his neck, her fangs bared. She moved in close and smelled his skin. Matt's blood dripped from her lips onto his collar.

Victor pushed her back. "It's the blood," he told her. "This is what I meant about control. You could've killed that man."

She threw her hands up. "Oh, who gives a shit, Victor?" she cried. "That's all you ever say to me anymore." She raised her voice in a mimic. "'You have to control yourself, Ashleigh.' 'You're going to kill someone, Ashleigh.' Get a new fucking record already!"

Victor pinched his sinuses. Cillian strolled into the kitchen, whistling softly.

"What are you doing out?" Victor demanded.

"I was talking to him before they came home," Ashleigh said.

"With his door open? When there are humans in the house?" She knew the rules.

Ashleigh's bottom lip quivered when he yelled. She clapped her hands over her face and rushed to Cillian.

Cillian rubbed her head. "Shh, my pet," he whispered.

Ashleigh was making these gasping sounds; it was the only way for her to sob. "I can't do anything right!"

"Death is a good thing," Cillian replied. "It frees us of pain. Of fear. Only through death can we rise to a greater plane."

Victor pointed at Cillian. "Is this the kind of bullshit he's telling you?"

Ashleigh's head jerked up. Her face was flushed in anger thanks to Matt's donation. "Don't talk about Cillian like that!"

She stroked his chest as if to mollify him. Cillian couldn't care less. Something on the fridge had caught his attention. He released Ashleigh and wandered over. His hand reached out and lifted a picture of Ramsey with Annie, Bryce, Clarice, and Josiah. He began to hum and left as suddenly as he entered while stroking Annie's photographed face.

Ashleigh used the back of her hand to clean her mouth, which only made her chin and cheek bright red. She returned Victor's glare then rushed after Cillian.

Victor didn't like their friendship. He made a note to speak with Ramsey.

Eleven

THE SKY WAS gray and bleak. But Victor loved her and Celia was on Cloud Nine. When she gave Trixie the news this morning, her best friend squealed in her ear.

Celia parked her Honda in front of the house and let herself in. Max sat in the living room, watching football highlights.

She tiptoed over to kiss his cheek then left quickly so as not to disturb him. Meg was hard at work chopping veggies in the kitchen.

"Hey," Celia greeted.

"Hi, dear."

She smiled warmly. She was pleased her niece was visiting more. "I just started. Dinner won't be ready for a little bit."

"No problem," she replied cheerfully.

The dryer buzzed. Celia skipped to the pantry before her aunt could stand. She placed the plastic basket in front of the dryer and tipped the wonderfully-scented linens inside. She carried the basket to the living room and plopped down on the loveseat.

She didn't really care for sports. Her mind wandered as she folded towels. Her uncle *tsked* at something a commentator said. He looked around for someone to agree with him. That's when Celia realized Winston wasn't there. She frowned over at the empty spot on the sofa where her cousin surely would've occupied. Daytime precluded him from stalking vamps, which she thought he'd put aside if a Pats game were on the tube.

She glanced at the television and waited for a commercial.

"Where's Winston?" she asked. Her uncle had just begun to pull himself from the cushions. Apparently he'd been waiting for commercials as well.

"He went home," he told her, then shuffled out to the hallway. He was walking slower than normal. His back must've been acting up. Meg was always getting on him about lifting heavy boxes at the shop.

She thought Winston's absence was strange. After seeing there were still vamps in the area, she figured Winston would stick around for the action. She didn't know whether to be pleased that Boston was now one poacher short or troubled. What if he was going for reinforcements? Or maybe the Night Hawks made him leave? Or maybe something happened to him and he told Meg and Max that he was home in Brooklyn when he was actually hiding out while he was recuperating . . .

She shook her head. There were too many possibilities to ponder. You'd think an easy answer would be to call him up but Celia was not her cousin's favorite person right now. He'd just as much tell her to fuck off.

She decided happiness was the way to go. Winston was an adult who could take care of himself. She hummed softly as she placed a royal blue towel with the others. That joy carried her through dinner and out the door at eight-thirty. Victor was waiting for her in the apartment. She saw the vase of fresh flowers sitting on the coffee table. Purple orchids blended with cream and white roses. A card peeked from the bunch, and she recognized Max's emblem along the top: black swirls on cream cardstock, Apple of Meg's Eye written in pretty cursive.

"Hey, honey," she said, crossing to give him a kiss. He rubbed her arm while studying her. No doubt he was assessing her after last night. She didn't mention it.

"Listen," he said. "Ramsey's having company tonight. He has invited us over."

She raised her eyebrows, surprised. "Really? Is it a party or something?"

"Sure."

"'Sure?' What kind of answer is that?" She went to her bedroom to search her closet. "Is this dressy?"

"A little, but not formal."

She scanned his outfit. He had donned a pressed black suit, dark purple shirt and a purple and blue tie to bring it all together. He looked good.

"Hmm," she murmured, moving things around. She found a strapless black dress that stopped at the knee. It was form fitting with a slit up the side to mid-thigh. She'd only worn it once, for a dinner party Trixie had dragged her to a little over a year ago. She figured it still fit.

While she dressed, Victor told her about this group of vampires traveling through Boston to Maine to visit with the Monte Carlos. He didn't go into too much detail about the Monte Carlos, just that they enjoyed hunting and were always inviting others to join. Ramsey and the leader of this traveling crew were old friends.

Celia was surprised and touched that he had invited her. And just the tiniest bit nervous about what to expect. She hoped that her presence wouldn't upset anyone's self-control.

Cautiously, she asked, "Will there be other, uh, humans there?"

"I'm not sure."

She stood in front of her dresser, peering at herself in the mirror she hung on the wall. There, she applied mousse to her hair that she had wet in the sink. She then set about sweeping on a smoky silver shadow, black eyeliner, and lots of mascara. She dabbed on Chap Stick since she hardly ever wore lip gloss and was even less likely to wear lipstick.

Using Victor's shoulder as a prop, she pulled on her leopard print shoes with the stacked heels. In her heels, she came to his chin. She turned around for him a few times.

"Do I look okay?"

"Baby," he said tenderly. The lust in his eyes was plenty answer. She flushed in appreciation. It was nice to see she could still turn him on. As they headed to the door, his hand gripped her waist in a way that proved he didn't want to leave.

Victor held open the passenger's side door for her. She pulled her seatbelt across her body and laid her dark red clutch in her lap. She noticed he hadn't started the car. She glanced over at him, her expression quizzical.

He tried to smile. "I have to do this," he said reluctantly.

She knew what he meant. She groaned. "That's not necessary."

"They are Ramsey's rules. I have to oblige."

She understood but she did not want to be put under. She'd lost enough free will under vampire mind-control.

"How about this . . ." She reached in the back and moved some things around on the seat. There was a gym bag—though she didn't go to a gym—an umbrella, and a pair of backup black sneakers. Her hand closed on a yellow scarf resting under a murder mystery book. As if she didn't have enough mystery in her real life.

She folded the scarf three times to make sure it was no longer sheer. She carefully tied it around her eyes, minding her makeup and hair. She turned her head in his direction.

"There," she said victoriously. She heard him chuckle before the engine roared.

The ride was about ten minutes. Celia wondered what people thought when they saw her sitting beside him with a bright blindfold. They were dressed nicely so maybe they imagined them heading off to a romantic dinner or a five-star hotel.

Victor had been distracting her with small talk about an action movie that was coming out the following weekend. He'd only just recently gotten into going to the cinema. Action movies were a little tougher to endure. All the explosions and ass kicking usually amounted to many pounding hearts. A good storyline was what he loved.

He came to a final stop and cut the engine. Celia removed the scarf and tossed it on the backseat. She then primped her hair to make sure it hadn't gone flat. Victor got out first to open her door. They were in the garage but she didn't recognize it. The last time she was in this section of the house she had been enthralled by Ramsey. The red sedan and Ramsey's convertible were in a line beside her car. Other than that, the garage was bare.

Victor's hand was on the small of her back, guiding her through a door to the left. It opened into the modern kitchen with its gleaming appliances and unused flatware. She noticed the dozen or so wine glasses sitting out on the counter. The overhead light twinkled on the rims, all of which seemed thicker than crystal.

Elizabeth came in just then, looking amazing in a gown that crisscrossed her chest and flowed behind her like she had her own personal wind machine. The yellow material went beautifully with her dark chocolate skin.

Ashleigh trailed in after her. She wore a simple, sleeveless red dress that stopped mid-thigh, showing off her toned legs and teeny waist. Around her neck was a pretty white choker made with feathery beading. A matching bracelet wrapped her left wrist.

Elizabeth's smile widened when she saw them. Ashleigh, who had begun to smile until she saw Celia, now looked grim.

"Everyone's in the living room," Elizabeth announced. She was fully healed and in bright spirits. "Celia, would you like wine?"

"Yes, thank you."

"I'll bring it to you. Go ahead inside." She opened the microwave door, which made Celia frown.

Victor and Celia went through to the living room. A saxophone crooned from a record player in the corner. Ramsey and Bryce were there, clad in dark suits. Ramsey's had thin pinstripes while Bryce's was a solid steel gray. The other four vamps in the room turned to the door as they entered.

The man had been talking with Ramsey. He was older, maybe late fifties, with salt and pepper hair and a round belly. His nose was broad and his chin cleft. The others were all females. All thin females, wearing fashionable dresses with sequins and broaches, and draped with gold jewelry. They had dark hair and similar features—the same small faces, sharp collarbones, thin hands.

"Victor, Celia," Ramsey said formally. "Thank you for coming."

Victor inclined his head and they approached the group. Ramsey introduced the visitors as the Pérezes. The women were beautiful. Celia wondered if the leader, named Rafael, had changed a family. Was it his family? Did he do it all at once since they seemed to be of varying ages? She shuddered and pushed the thoughts away. She only hoped they had a choice in the matter.

Elizabeth and Ashleigh entered carrying gold trays laden with glasses. Ashleigh stood next to Celia so that she was the one to hand Victor a glass. She was trying to catch his eye. Victor only spared her a glance.

Ashleigh's tray tipped. Purely on instinct, Celia reached out to help her. Subconsciously, she knew the vampire would have better control than she was showing. Even if the tray had actually been slipping, she would've caught it way before Celia could.

She didn't notice the glint of amusement in Ashleigh's eye. Celia's fingers grazed the nearest glass to make sure it didn't spill. She gasped in surprise, twitching her hand away. The drink was hot. She looked at Ashleigh for explanation and saw her barely containing a laugh.

"Oh, Celia, dear," Elizabeth replied, appearing in front of her with a lone drink on her tray. "This one's for you. I hope red's okay. It's Chateau de Sancerre Rouge, two thousand-five."

Celia didn't understand any of those words. She hesitated a moment before taking the glass Elizabeth held out to her. This one was room temperature, and she could smell the wine. She glowered icily at Ashleigh, who turned her back on her.

Victor rubbed the base of Celia's neck. It took a moment, but she began to relax. She peered over to his glass. The crimson liquid was thick, leaving a coat along the sides when he took a sip. A sudden impulse to step away, to run from the house nearly overwhelmed her. Would he have stopped her? Where did they get the blood, she wondered. Was it volunteered?

She'd never freaked out this much about his vampiness before and she didn't like this unexpected fear. Though she still wanted to leave, she forced herself to stand there. She gulped her drink.

It was only a minute before the wine took effect. There. Now that she was a little more at ease, her mind returned to the room. Avoiding their glasses helped. Rafael was telling a story about skiing, of all things.

"What a wonderful invention!" he said merrily. "Esperanza goes with me all the time."

The one wearing satin black gloves that stopped at her elbows nodded modestly. "Father's quite good at it now."

"Maybe I'll enter the Olympics," he proclaimed to quiet chuckles. Celia smiled but probably for a different reason. Could you imagine? He'd step out to the start line, wave robustly to the crowd . . . then promptly burst into flames. Everyone would be screaming. It would be a mess.

As she glanced at the others around Rafael, she noticed two new people had joined the crowd. Two women, wearing similarly stunning dresses as the Pérez women, stood at Rafael's right elbow. She didn't know where they had come from or when they joined the room.

They held wine glasses, whispering to each other. Both women had long hair—one with black tresses, the other deep red—that cascaded past their shoulders. They knew how to accessorize, that was for sure. Celia was in love with the giant black ring on the red head's middle finger, and the dangly red chandelier earrings the other was wearing. The red was a nice contrast to her black dress.

There was something about the two that captivated Celia. The dark-haired one watched everyone around her. The red head was cool and confident. Her back was a straight line, coincidentally (or not) showcasing her large tits pushing against the corset-like bodice of her dress. She had a hand on the curve of her lower back, the other holding her glass. You'd think there were men galore in the room going by her look-at-me stance.

She was also the only one of the out-of-town group with color in her dress. It was a soft gray with shimmering beads on the front of the bodice. The hem stopped high on her thighs, flowing around her as she moved. Now Celia understood the whole "she had legs for days" sentiment.

Celia wasn't all that shy, but she was definitely wishing she had a pinch of this woman's self-confidence.

The women looked at her. The red head smiled invitingly.

Celia glanced to Victor, who was talking to Esperanza about Barcelona. Celia patted his hand on her waist. He released her almost reluctantly. Celia accounted that to protecting her from the strangers in the room.

She eased around the crowd to the women. They met her halfway. The three stepped aside, giving them distance from the rest of the group.

Now that she was closer, Celia saw that the red head had full, pouty lips, a round nose and brown eyes that were set a tad too close. But she used makeup perfectly, utilizing dark liner on the outer edges of her eyes to make them appear wider.

The black-haired woman's makeup was very minimal, just shadow and gloss. Her eyes were shaped like almonds and a collection of tattoos decorated her arms. Groups of butterflies flying through shaded stars. Two black bands about a half an inch apart wrapped her left wrist. Two more bands, made of vines, were on her right wrist. There was a Gothic cross on the anterior side of her right ankle. When she turned her head, Celia noted a tiny infinity symbol behind her left ear. She had a thin, red headband across her forehead that was tied off at the back of her head.

"Hi," the red head said. "You're human."

"Yes," Celia said cautiously. She had really been drawn to the women. Now that she was thinking about it, she wondered if she had been bespelled without even realizing.

"I told you," she said to Black Hair with a huge smile.

Black Hair rolled her eyes, uninterested. "I didn't say she wasn't," she replied snippily. Red Hair kept on smiling as she sipped from her glass.

"Are you two . . .?" Celia trailed off because she was unsure of which way to go with that question.

"We're humans. I'm Serena," Red Hair answered. She nodded to Black Hair. "This is Grace."

"I'm Celia."

"Nice to meet you, Celia."

Serena leaned forward and kissed Celia's cheek. When she stepped back, she left a light cloud of peony and amber in her wake. Serena was just as happy as punch, it seemed. There was a slight twang to her voice, almost Puerto Rican, Jersey-ish. Her cheerfulness made Celia smile. She was glad to find other humans. She wasn't sure of what to say if one of the vamps had decided to strike up a conversation with her. As it were, she felt multiple eyes on her everywhere she moved.

"How long are you all in Boston?" Celia asked.

"'til tomorrow."

Celia frowned. "What will happen during the day?"

She shrugged. "They've made arrangements. There's someone who houses vamps for a fee."

Celia raised an eyebrow at that. She wondered how exactly one went about advertising such services. Were there code words in a Classified ad? Did they use coffins? Were they lined up in their basement? Were there assurances if anything happened?

"He keeps them in his basement," Serena said, as if she'd heard her musing. "It's all sealed off and he uses these steel container things. Rafael trusts him but the girls don't. We'll check on them during the day."

"I'll be sleeping," Grace replied, and took a long gulp of wine. At least, it looked like wine.

Serena chuckled. "Yeah, sure, Gracie."

Grace's eyes narrowed at her. "Don't call me that," she said tightly. Celia got the feeling Serena used that nickname as often as she could.

Serena turned back to Celia. "Are you dating that guy?" She nodded to Victor, who could probably hear every word, as all the other vamps could.

"Yes."

"He's real cute."

"He's alright," Celia said offhandedly.

She peeked to Victor and though he was staring intently at Esperanza, she saw the small smile tugging at the side of his lips.

"Oh, he's more than alright," Serena replied. "He has a nice butt. I want to bite it. Rafael's great, too." She was twirling a lock of her hair around her finger and staring up at the ceiling with a faraway look.

Celia was confused. Had she heard correctly? Serena had spoken of Victor's assets so airily how could Celia be offended?

A matching infinity symbol was etched on Serena's inner wrist. "I've only been with him for three months but he takes us everywhere. Have you been to the Greek Isles?"

She looked eagerly at Celia.

Celia shook her head.

"Aw, that's too bad. It's absolutely beautiful there!"

"I'll have to take your word for it."

"Your vampire doesn't take you places?" Grace asked outright. She sounded bored and pitying at once. Celia cocked an eyebrow at her but kept her attitude in check. Just as Serena seemed to say whatever popped in her head, Grace seemed to be a direct kind of person.

"We do, but I work and it's hard to get time off."

"This is our job," Serena said. She waved her glass around the room, indicating the Pérezes. Celia glanced at Rafael. Victor had drifted over and was in a deep conversation with him and Ramsey. They seemed distracted. Celia took the moment to indulge her curiosity.

"What does that job entail?" she asked.

Serena tilted her head to the side, pondering her job description. "Well, we stay with them, go to parties and on trips. I guess you can say we're their 'people.' If they need things done during the day, we take care of it."

"Shopping, dry cleaner runs," Grace chimed in dully. "Fun shit like that."

Grace didn't sound like she enjoyed her job too much. Serena just rolled her eyes and patted Grace's hair.

"Gracie loves it. Don't listen to her. Otherwise, how else could we wear these fun dresses and travel the world? I got out of Jersey. What more could I ask for?"

"What does Rafael do?" She was wondering how he could afford so much traveling and partying, although she'd never come across a vampire bum as far as she knew.

"He's a writer. You've probably read his books. They're—"

"Popular," Grace cut it, giving Serena a severe look.

Serena slapped a hand to her mouth in surprise. "I almost spilled the beans, huh?" She removed her hand and laughed. "He writes under pennames," she explained. "All kinds of stuff. He's rolling in it."

Celia was fascinated. She looked at Rafael again. She noticed simple things: the cut of his suit, the diamond-encrusted cuff links, and the shiny Italian shoes. The deep blue of his shirt went well with his eyes, but other than those superficial aspects, she didn't see the appeal. He didn't seem very . . . creative. But there was no standard formula of what a writer should look like, was there?

"Wow," she said, facing Serena again. "But what about when he has to meet with agents and publicists and fans?"

"Others step in," she said simply. "They all think he's this really eccentric artist, who coops himself up in his house, writing around the clock, when actually all he needs is, like, an hour or two a night and he can finish a novel in a month. His agent doesn't care about the secrecy and stuff because he's making him money."

"Makes sense," Celia agreed.

"I think he does other things, too, but the writing's all I know about."

"Do you go to many parties?"

"Sure! Rafael even lets us mingle on our own. Some vamps don't allow that of their humans. They have to stay in the house all night so the vamps can eat and have sex."

"That's what it was like with her last master," Grace replied while picking at her nails. "Your vampire doesn't keep you inside, though."

"He's my boyfriend," Celia corrected. Grace ignored her.

Serena laughed. "Hawthorne was not a boyfriend, that's for sure. He was no fun. It gets boring staying in one spot. That's why I love Rafael." She wrapped an arm around Grace's shoulders. Grace winced since she had her hair caught in her embrace.

"Hawthorne didn't want to let me go at first." She shrugged. "I met Gracie in the mall. She was buying this gorgeous dress. She's the one who introduced me to Rafael. He must've seen something he liked because he bartered for me that same night. I was free."

She stretched luxuriously and Celia tried hard to hide her disgust. Bartered? She glanced over to Rafael. He laughed heartily at something Ramsey had just said.

"I've tried lots of different types of food," Serena continued, unaware. "I've shopped in Milan and Paris and Madrid. I've met so many people." Undead people but that was semantics. "You name a city, and I've got a place to crash."

She grinned proudly. Celia managed a polite smile. She did feel a twinge of envy at her jetsetter's life. She'd never seen any of those sights outside of a movie screen. Although, she was stuck at mingle on our own. What did these women do to get in the good graces of vampires?

And what was that bit about her last vampire? Her master, Grace called him. Michael's words in the alley hit her abruptly.

"You could die and then where will you be? You think that vampire would care? That he couldn't find another sheep?"

Sheep. It had sounded so demeaning, so filthy coming from his mouth. Grace had lumped Celia into that category just as Michael had done. Except these women seemed healthy and of their own will. According to them, the Pérezes treated them like assistants with perks. With whom they shared their fortunes. Was this the life of sheep?

Serena interrupted her reverie. "There was this guy," she said in a tenor indicating she was launching into an anecdote. "It was in Tokyo, like, three years ago. He was hosting this posh party in his hotel for New Year's. There were so many celebrities. I went with this vamp from Houston—this was before Hawthorne—and I met Ivan.

"We hit it off right away. Ivan was telling me about his chain of hotels and how the Tokyo one was the newest and had been making him so much loot! I mean, I was interested in that or whatever but what I really wanted was to be alone with him. I think he could read minds—you know mostly all vamps have some kind of talent. Isabel can read minds, which I think is fun but Gracie says is annoying.

"Anyway," she barreled on before Celia could ask which one was Isabel. "He showed me the penthouse suite. It was amazing!" She squeezed Celia's forearm excitedly. Her eyes twinkled as she recalled the view. "All the lights of the city, the tall buildings . . . It was such a turn-on!"

Celia hid her smile behind her glass. This girl was something. Celia could never be that brazen about her sex life.

Serena wasn't done.

"Oh, he came up behind me—he wouldn't let me turn

around—and then he was inside me—he was thick, you know—
and we did it right there, right up against the window. I mean,
backward, frontward, wheelbarrow, you name it. We were too
high up but I'm sure someone would've enjoyed that view."

She giggled mischievously then finished her wine. That
faraway look returned to her face.

"He was so loud, too."

Celia tried to keep her expression neutral. She thought that
had been the end of this little saga. She just hoped she didn't go
into detail about his girth because then she would have to stop
her. She didn't know the man but the images Serena had
implanted were more than enough.

"Serena, are you sure it wasn't you?" Grace said pointedly.
"You do like to wake the neighbors."

Serena ran a hand through Grace's hair. "Well, if the loving's
good, then I can't help expressing myself. You know that."

She shrugged like she was trying to be modest. Yeah, like she
had a modest bone in her body that wasn't put there by a modest
man.

"He was putting me to shame in that department."

That made Celia pause. She could only assume that Serena
gave blood during her little trysts. She knew taking blood during
sex was something vampires normally did. She didn't think she
was shameless enough to ask what was of concern to her: if they
hadn't been sharing blood, was the guy making noises anyway?

Before she could think too much and chicken out—and after
glancing over to make sure Victor was still in conversation—she
took a step closer to Serena and lowered her voice.

"Are, uh, are the vampires you've been with always . . .
noisy?"

Serena frowned, confused. "Noisy? You mean, do they moan
and stuff?" Celia nodded, feeling incredibly stupid and
inexperienced for asking. "Sure, I guess. All the vamps I've been

with let you know they're enjoying it. Maybe because it's something warm on them, I don't know. But regular guys are like that, too, huh?"

Okay, gross. She did not need to hear all that. Serena looked to Grace for confirmation. She only shrugged and gulped her wine.

The light sparkled in Serena's wide eyes. "Do you think guy vampires can only have sex after they eat? I mean, how else can they get it up?"

Grace's glass now empty, she glanced around.

"I'm getting more wine," she reported, and then headed off. Serena was right behind her, her hands on Grace's shoulders, her thumbs moving in small, massaging circles. Celia didn't follow since her glass was half full. Plus, she was afraid that Serena would take one look at the kitchen and remember a time she was in Africa and had randy sex with a Kenyan vampire who owned a villa.

She took a deep breath and did a scan of the room. The three men had opened their conversation to Esperanza and the youngest Pérez. Celia went to Victor's side. He automatically wrapped his arm around her waist; he hadn't even needed to look to know she was approaching. His lips brushed her temple. She sighed in relief at the comfort. Serena and Grace seemed okay but she was thankful for the break.

She took another sip and became acutely aware of Ashleigh, whom she had almost all but forgotten. She'd sat in an armchair a while ago, her legs crossed. She was nearly finished with her drink. And she was alternating heated looks between her and Victor.

Her indigent gaze shifted to Celia again. Celia felt her brows pulling together in anger.

Victor's hand became insistent on her waist. She turned her gaze to him. There was a warning in his eyes. She obeyed and twisted so that she no longer had contact with Ashleigh. He smiled in appreciation.

If she had been a lesser woman, she'd probably have kissed him or pinched his butt. She decided to take a higher road. Then she leaned forward to peck his cheek. Okay, so maybe the road wasn't much higher.

A glass slammed on a table, interrupting the quiet camaraderie in the room. She jerked her head around but Ashleigh was already gone from the room. Elizabeth glanced to Celia, her expression unreadable. Everyone else exchanged their own glances, mixtures of disguised intrigue and curiosity.

Ashleigh didn't return to the party. Serena and Grace were back at Rafael's elbow. He absently caressed Serena's thigh with his finger while speaking with Bryce. She leaned on his shoulder, sipping more wine.

Celia spoke to Esperanza for a little bit while Victor conferred with Bryce and Rafael about something going on in California. She didn't catch what it was. Through Esperanza, she found out the brood was from Florida.

"Are you all related?" she asked gently, hoping she wasn't being tactless.

Esperanza's lips pulled back, revealing crowded teeth. The canines weren't aligned properly with the rest, giving her a snaggletooth smile. It was actually cute, though Celia wondered if she had trouble when her fangs wanted to come out and play.

"Yes, these are my sisters." Esperanza's words were spiked with an accent derived from Northern Spain.

Celia nodded now that that was confirmed. She wanted to ask more questions. Decorum made her pause. Victor never shared his "coming over" story. Was it in bad taste to ask, especially as a complete stranger?

Her eyes landed on the third Pérez sister, with whom she hadn't interacted. She was just as lovely as the rest. Maybe sensing Celia's interest, she met her gaze. She had those small features—tiny nose, small, thin lips—that reminded Celia of a pretty bird. A shadow darkened the woman's face as she surveyed Celia. After a moment, the vampire smiled briefly before turning back to Ramsey.

"What is it?" Esperanza asked and Celia faced her again.

"Hmm?"

"You want to ask something."

How did she know? Didn't Serena say Isabel was telepathic? Esperanza waited patiently.

"May I ask what happened to your family?"

Esperanza's smile wavered. She looked down at the floor, pushing her hair off her shoulder. Her eyes didn't meet Celia's as she spoke.

"Our father was attacked on his way to the market. We didn't know what happened; we only heard about a band of gypsies passing through. He came home a week later and killed us. He didn't want to be alone. Mother was the only one not to survive. She was with child."

Celia looked to where Esperanza had been staring. Rafael was engrossed in his conversation. Celia studied him for a moment, before facing Esperanza.

"I'm sorry."

She smiled at Celia. "You're empty."

Celia looked down. She had finished her wine. She turned to seek out Elizabeth for a refill. Before she could search, she nearly bumped into the youngest Pérez. The vampire was uncomfortably close and staring at Celia's neck. Suddenly, she leaned into Celia's hair.

Celia stepped back. At the same time, Esperanza's hand clasped the vamp's thin shoulder. Celia realized that she only sniffed her. The young girl, who was maybe sixteen, wore entirely too much makeup. She'd overstepped smoky and careened straight to billowing cloud in a backdraft. It would have looked atrocious on a normal woman but on her it was only a brow-raiser. That vampire appeal had its uses.

"Isabel. No." Esperanza said the command firmly, as if disciplining a dog. Isabel poked her bottom lip out, pouting. Esperanza shoved her half-full glass into her hands. She moseyed away, drinking it up eagerly.

Esperanza's roll of the eye was playful. Celia gripped her glass to her chest.

"You're very appealing," Esperanza explained. "I don't know what it is, but believe me. Everyone wants to be near you. She's just the only one bold enough to do so." She flashed a comely smile. For a brief moment, Celia glimpsed her other side, hungry and dangerous.

Gulp.

Celia managed to nod and let her gaze drop to her chin since it wasn't a good idea to look a vampire in the eye too long. She held her glass up.

"I'm going to scrounge up some more wine," she said.

Esperanza watched her as she left for the kitchen. Celia noticed Rafael, Bryce, and Isabel surveying her retreat.

They all had the same barely disguised predatory gleam. Elizabeth and Victor glanced her way as well.

In the hallway, she did a mental shake to rid herself of the heebie-jeebies. When she came to the doorway of the kitchen, she paused. Ashleigh was there, leaning over the counter in front of the microwave. The yellow glow bounced off her necklace, casting rainbow lights all around. A beige mug twirled on the glass plate inside the microwave.

"What the hell do you want?" she grumbled without looking up.

"Nothing in here."

Celia turned to leave. When she faced the hallway, Ashleigh

was right there in front of her. She jerked her head back in surprise. Ashleigh looked her up and down with enough hostility that proved she obviously wanted to hit her. If that happened, Celia swore that she would find something sharp real quick.

"Maybe we should have a talk," Celia said steadily. Her hand clenched around the stem of her glass.

"I don't have anything to say to you."

"Then why do you keep watching me?"

Ashleigh took a step closer. Celia came to her nose. Her cobalt eyes dug into her.

"Maybe," Ashleigh hissed menacingly, "I want to rip into your neck and play with your blood until there's no more left." She smirked. "You know that's what we do, right? We kill. It always comes back to that. Just ask Victor."

Celia froze. "What are you talking about?" she asked in spite of herself.

Ashleigh's smirk transformed into a full smile. Her fangs were down. "Looks like somebody's been keeping secrets," she said in a sing-songy crone. "I wonder what else about us he's been hiding from you."

Suddenly, Victor was behind Ashleigh. "Celia," he said tightly, though that tone was directed at Ashleigh. "There you are."

Celia didn't take her eyes off Ashleigh. Her heartbeat had picked up. That was probably what had alerted Victor. "I was trying to get some wine," Celia said. "I think I'll pass."

She placed her glass on the counter. She brushed by Ashleigh on her route to the living room only because she took up the entire threshold. Ashleigh had a chunk of her hair, pulling her back into the kitchen in a matter of seconds. Celia's heels scraped on the tiled floor when she fell into the counter. On impact with the edge, Celia's elbow sent her wine glass crashing into the wall.

Victor grabbed Ashleigh's arm, wrenching it behind her

back. Ashleigh spun around and shoved him aside. She flashed in front of Celia. Her brows were pulled down low over her manic blue eyes. Her hand clutched her neck, squeezing tight. Celia tried to step back but the cabinets held her hostage. Victor took hold of Ashleigh's hair in his fist.

"Let her go," he growled into her ear. He didn't want to notify the others. But Ashleigh didn't let go. It was like Victor wasn't there. There was only one objective in her mind.

Celia's fingers grazed a shard of the broken wine glass. She snatched it up and lashed out at her. Victor stepped out of the way as Ashleigh hissed and stumbled backward, cupping her cheek. Celia held the shard out, ready for her.

Ashleigh removed her hand. The deep scratch was already healing. She wiped the blood away then took a step toward her. Victor appeared in front with his back to Celia.

"Go in the other room, Celia."

She dropped the shard on the counter then stalked to the hallway. Outside of the living room, she breathed deeply. Her trembling hand went to her left wrist but the elastic was no longer there. She looked down and saw the red line from where the glass dug into her palm. She closed her eyes, concentrating on the dark space her lids offered. Soon, her heart stopped banging against her chest. She was still shaking a bit when she went to Elizabeth's side.

Elizabeth patted her hand absently. She was preoccupied by the conversation going on in front of her. There was a new vamp in the mix now. He was Celia's height without her heels. He wore black pants and a red shirt with the sleeves rolled up under a black vest. His dark hair was tucked behind his ears. Two other vampires, both taller and broader than him, flanked the unexpected visitor.

Celia was able to take all of this in since he was speaking in Italian and therefore she had no idea what was being said. The three vamps had looked at Celia with curiosity when she approached. After surveying her briefly, they turned back to Ramsey.

Celia figured her beating heart was what captivated them, as was the case with all the other vamps. She was still trying to control her breathing.

Ramsey looked somber. He nodded a few times, responded every once in a while in Italian. Elizabeth looked anxious and confused. Celia figured she didn't know the language either.

The smaller man tucked his hands in his pockets, his eyes going to the floor for a moment. The silence stretched on. Then he laughed sharply and slapped Ramsey's shoulder. He motioned to his buddies. One of them stepped ahead of him, the other behind. Ramsey walked them to the door.

"I'm sorry for the interruption," Ramsey told the room when he returned. "Does anyone need a refill?"

The room buzzed with conversation again. Ramsey made his way back to Elizabeth. She rubbed his arm in an intimate way, which surprised Celia. She didn't know they were a couple. Then again, why would she know? It's not like they hung out. She didn't even remember meeting her before she and Victor crashed their house with an unconscious Ashleigh.

"Is everything okay?" Elizabeth murmured, concerned. She spoke softly. Celia's sharper hearing was the only reason she caught the words.

He smiled but his eyes were troubled. "Sure. He wants reparations for Arturo."

"What does he want?"

Aware of their company—mainly Celia who was staring at them in open interest—he caressed her cheek. "We'll discuss it later."

Victor came up beside her. "We should go," he told Ramsey. "It's getting late for Celia."

It was only ten-thirty but she wasn't complaining. Her skin was prickling from the eyes tracing her every move. Plus, she wanted far away from Ashleigh.

"Ah, Victor. I wanted a word with your human friend."

Rafael stepped up to the group, his eyes on Celia. Serena gave her a knowing smile, which Celia thought was strange. Grace was more interested in her drink than what was going on around her.

Victor took her hand. She noticed him step forward so that she was slightly behind him.

Rafael grinned. "Don't you worry, Victor. These girls are handful enough. *Mi plato esta lleno*, as they say." He chuckled at his own joke.

Even as he said it, he took her in fully. She felt like a piece of meat, and maybe she was to him.

"You are very beautiful, as I am sure Victor agrees."

There was a snort of disagreement from someone, and when she risked a glance around, Celia saw the third Pérez, whose name she couldn't recall, hiding her mouth with her glass. She didn't look at Celia, but she knew the derision had come from her. She didn't have time to think about it too much.

"'Celia,' derived from *cielo*," Rafael replied, recapturing her attention. "A wonderful comparison, no?"

"What does that mean?"

"'Heaven.' Tell me, heavenly one," he said, "are you looking to join this life?"

Though she wanted to snap at him for asking such a personal question, something told Celia to mind her words with this one. He killed his own family to avoid loneliness, for fuck's sake. And he scarcely masked his hunger. As he spoke, she caught glimpses of his pearly fangs. She didn't think he'd attack her, especially in a room full of vamps she was certain would step in to protect her.

"No." She kept her gaze on the space between his eyes.

Rafael shook his head remorsefully. "That's too bad, really. Although, your scent is very pleasurable. I see why Victor keeps you around. You must taste wonderful."

"He doesn't keep me around," she snapped.

"What do you want, Rafael?" Victor barked.

Rafael grinned. "I will be attending a lecture in Switzerland. I would very much enjoy her company. Will you come with me?"

Celia stiffened in shock. Well, that was . . . random. Victor pulled away from her, taking a step closer to Rafael.

"Thank you for the offer," she said quickly, before Victor did something he might regret. "But I'll have to decline."

She glimpsed Serena looking away with a disappointed shake of her head, like Celia was giving up the opportunity of a lifetime. Of course, from her point of view, perhaps that was true. Celia imagined getting dressed up and mingling with celebrities would be fun, but how soon would the novelty wear off? What were the other requirements that Serena hadn't mentioned? And what would happen when Rafael found someone whose scent was even more irresistible? Was the current blood supply tossed aside?

It was all too complicated for her. *No thanks*, Celia told them mentally.

"No thanks."

Celia jumped at hearing her words spoken aloud. Isabel had sidled up beside her. Her dark eyes seemed to see through her. Her voice had been a whisper that only Celia heard.

"We're leaving now," Victor said. "Enjoy your trip. Andres is a gracious host."

Rafael bent forward in a bow but it was an empty gesture. His reproachful glare was directed at Victor.

Victor wrapped his arm around Celia's shoulder and practically hustled her to the garage. She didn't even have a chance to say goodnight, he was in such a rush.

In the car she let him know that. "They didn't take offense,"

Victor said.

"Well, I did!" Celia cried. "That was so rude. I didn't get to say thank you to Ramsey for inviting me."

He rolled his eyes like she didn't get it. She was convinced that Rafael and the Pérezes wouldn't have done anything, especially with Victor there. Didn't he tell her that once a vampire staked a claim (no pun intended) on a human that no other was supposed to touch them?

Which reminded her. "What happened with Ashleigh?"

He gripped the steering wheel. "You don't have to worry about her."

She would have been comforted if that meant she was currently staining the linoleum floor.

"She said that you killed someone."

Victor looked at her. His face was expressionless but she could feel that he was surprised. She so loved when this fucking bond worked in her favor!

"Is it true?"

He sighed. "I thought she was ready." He shook his head solemnly. "She wasn't."

Celia waited. He didn't elaborate. "What does that mean?"

"You don't want the gory details, Seal."

"I do want the gory details. That's why the fuck I'm asking."

Victor squeezed her shoulder. "Believe me," he said in a low voice. "You don't." She knocked his hand off in irritation. "Just know," he continued, unfazed, "that it hasn't happened again since. I've learned my lesson."

She stared at him. "Why didn't you tell me?"

He folded his arms at the chest. His scowl was severe. "Why would I? Why would I put those images in your head?"

"It's not that," she protested. "It's the fact that you lied to me."

"I did not. I said that we are trying to ensure that she learns how to feed properly. There will be mistakes."

Celia was quiet. Maybe Jay was right. How many people died because of vampire "mistakes?"

Victor started the car. When he didn't move, she saw that he was staring at her expectantly. She finally realized why he was waiting. She found the scarf and put it back on. She didn't say anything during the ride home or upstairs. He made himself busy with something in the living room while she changed out of her clothes.

Celia went to the bathroom to take off her makeup. Victor was peering out the window as she passed. Something must've had his attention completely because his shoulders and back were tense. Even though he wasn't facing her, she was sure he was following her movements as well. Their connection gave her that little insight. She allowed herself a quick moment of being creeped out, and then carried on as usual.

She washed her face, brushed her teeth, and braided her hair back. Victor came up behind her. They stared at each other through the reflective glass. She couldn't tell what he was pondering. She was thinking how handsome he was, even when he was so incredibly infuriating.

He stepped closer to wrap his arms around her. He nuzzled her neck, grasped her hips. She moaned because his kisses were nice. She wondered the meaning behind this sudden passion.

He massaged her neck, kissed along her jaw. Her heart pumped faster, rushing blood to the important spots. This was one of those times where she was going to have to push aside her uneasiness. She didn't like that Victor had lied, omitted the truth, whatever. She understood, though, that he had been trying to protect her.

Celia watched him suckle her shoulder through the mirror. His hair fell forward, shrouding his face. He scraped his fingers across her scalp. When he looked up, their eyes met again.

She turned to face him. He greeted her with his lips.

They didn't make it out of the bathroom.

**

After Celia laid in bed, Victor went outside using the front door. Standing on the quiet street, he glanced around. The wolf was gone, which was disappointing. He had wanted a word.

With a sniff of discontent, Victor melted into the darkness.

Twelve

C ELIA'S PHONE RANG when she turned off the shower. She pulled on her robe out of pure habit, since living alone meant she could stanky leg in the buff if she so chose.

"Hey," she answered in her room. "I don't have much time. I'm getting ready for work."

"Damn," Jay replied. "I was hoping I woke you up. Your voice gets all husky. It gives me tingles."

"Is that the only reason why you called?"

"No." His voice grew serious. "I've found some info on those Night Hawks."

She perked instantly. Late last night, Victor had told her about Annie's disappearance. She'd come to the same conclusion as he and Ramsey; that the Night Hawks or some faction of theirs was involved.

"They're more popular than I thought. This was the first I've heard of them."

"Maybe you're getting rusty," she joked.

"Ha ha. Anyway, they've set up shop in some of the major cities—L.A. for the west coast, Chicago for the middle, and Miami for the south. But it looks like they originated there in Boston."

"Great," she muttered. "Boston: Inventers of Baked Beans, Tea, and Vampire Slayers. They should put that on a fucking shirt."

"Uh, tea wasn't invented in Boston. And I don't think baked beans started there either."

Celia rolled her eyes. "Was there anything else?"

"The leaders of the Boston group, a man and a woman, they're lethal."

"Well, I've heard some pretty despicable stories from their members."

There was a pause. She heard him sigh. "What the fuck, Celia? Do my words sound like Chinese when I speak to you?"

Shit, she thought. She'd misspoken. "It's too late, Jay, I already went. You can't yell at me."

"See, this is why you're always in trouble. You don't fuckin' listen."

"Fuck you, I am not always in trouble! My cousin was being too damn sketchy. Victor didn't get upset," she added with a huff.

"Your boyfriend's a fool."

She grounded her teeth. This was so not the conversation she wanted to have with him.

"Sorry," Jay muttered at her silence.

She knew him enough to know he was only apologizing for speaking out of turn, not the words.

"The leaders are supposedly worse," he continued. "I know if I tell you to stay away, you won't listen. Be careful, Celia. Fuck."

She'd soaked through her robe. Boy, would Jay enjoy that view. "Look," Celia said, glancing down. "I need to dry off and get dressed."

"Oh?" She could hear the sauciness. "Put me on speaker phone and describe everything you do. Don't leave anything out, dammit."

"Goodbye, Jay."

She clicked the phone shut and hurried to get ready. At Cage's, after the morning meeting, she tied an apron around her waist and sat across from Michael in a booth to fold napkins. The other servers were huddled over the plates of food.

Michael glanced up when she sat. She smiled but it froze on her face before it could fully form once she saw his expression. He stared at her, unblinking. His lips were pursed together, as if he were trying to contain something attempting to burst from him.

His anger washed over her. That, he couldn't control.

She knew immediately he smelled Victor. She flashed back to her bathroom floor. She had been on her hands and knees, and struggling with keeping a grip on the tiled floor. Victor had finally laid her on her back on the bathmat to complete the job. He had better traction that way and was able to slide in and out of her with ease. She'd nearly ripped down her shower curtain when she came.

Embarrassment flushed her face now. Jeez, why couldn't she keep those intimacies from him? Damn his sensitive nose.

Suddenly, she was furious. She thought they were past this. He was surveying her like she was stealing to feed a habit. He didn't know the situation. What right did he have to be upset?

"What the hell is your problem?" Michael only shook his head. "Spit it out!"

"You already know!" he bellowed back. He lowered his voice because Tina and Maria glanced over at their outbursts. "It makes me fucking crazy to think how you're putting yourself in danger."

"I am not."

Michael looked disappointed, very much like a parent confronted with a misguided teen.

Her eyes narrowed. "Why do I need to explain anything to you?"

She hated this back and forth. She moved to get up. He grabbed her wrist. His hand warmed her skin.

"Just . . . why?" he asked. "Why do you do it? I don't buy that 'closer' bullshit. There are other, normal ways of doing that."

"It's none of your goddamn business," she replied hotly.

"Do you even know why? Is it out of obligation? Because mind your beeswax can't always be the answer."

She faltered. He was searching her eyes. She could see a hint of satisfaction that he had stumped her. Mostly, though, he was angry. She could still feel it, hovering over her like a sheet.

Celia's voice was even. He'd already seen her hesitate. She wanted to make this clear. "He's my boyfriend and I love him and would do anything to keep him safe,"

"Even if keeping him safe means *you* getting hurt?"

"I'm not fucking hurt. See." She wiggled her fingers, twisted her head from side to side. He wasn't convinced but she didn't care.

"You wouldn't know if he was controlling you," he said darkly.

She used her free hand to pry his hold. Then she slid out of the booth, snatched up her pile of white napkins, and stomped to the kitchen.

Michael glanced over to her often during the day but he kept a distance. She was off her game with him surveying her. She was so incredibly incensed that she couldn't even make herself smile to her tables, who all noticed her sour mood. She paid the price for that in tips.

Bobby let her go at four, after a little tongue-lashing about her attitude. She hightailed out of there. Meg called as she got in her car, asking her to go to the house to wait for the cable guy. Great. She was pissed and wouldn't have television to distract her. She tried thumbing through some of the books on the shelves in the living room. Nothing piqued her interest.

On the bottom shelf, Celia found three photo albums. She sat on the floor and pulled them into her lap. She flipped through the pages in silence. Inside the first two, she found photos of Meg and Max with Winston and Lyle during holidays, birthdays, and celebrations. She saw herself, running along with her cousins, playing tag or catch.

Before her mother died and Lyle went off to college, the family held flag football tourneys every Thanksgiving before dinner. Her mother Daphne held the ball in the air triumphantly in one photo. Celia smiled as her eyes watered.

When she made it to the last album, her fingers turned the pages slowly. She'd never seen these pictures. Meg and Daphne were spitting images when they were younger. They couldn't have been more than six and eight. The same curly hair worn in two long plaits rested on their backs. In most of the photos, they were dressed the same: pleated skirts; bellbottom jeans; fluffy sweaters; cowboy boots. They both presented the camera with wide, face-breaking smiles.

As the pages turned, their lives progressed. Elementary school, summer camp, softball, volleyball games, and swim meets were all displayed. Celia noticed the subtle changes happening between the girls. In middle school, they no longer dressed alike. By the time high school came along, it appeared they'd had separate lives. Meg had dyed her hair a light brown and begun to wear it straight. They didn't even do activities together anymore.

Celia turned a page. This sheet was incomplete. Several of the photos were missing, leaving only light patches where they used to rest on the sticky sheet. The ones that remained showed Meg in random, candid moments: horseback riding in Vermont;

kayaking in Maine. She wasn't smiling in these photos. In fact, she didn't smile much in any of the photos as a teenager.

Celia stopped on the last page. There was only one picture. It was affixed to the center of the sheet. Meg's light hair was bone straight. She wore bellbottom jeans with a white blouse and a fur vest. She was sitting on the porch of their erstwhile home in Brockton. Celia had never been to the house. It had been sold right around the time she was born, from what she was told.

Daphne stood on the bottom step, leaning against the railing. Celia saw herself in the teenager, with her jeans and her dark brown hair up in a ponytail. Daphne's lips were pulled into a small smile but it wasn't genuine. Celia could tell. The strain in her mother's eyes was evident.

Her gaze went back to Meg. She was staring intensely at her younger sister. She gripped something in her hand so tightly Celia saw her knuckles poking against her skin. She brought the book close to her nose. She couldn't make out what was in her grasp. Some kind of necklace, she guessed. A blurry pendent hung below her fists. It was round and a dark color. Maybe made of wood.

Celia placed the open album back in her lap, puzzled. This was the only photo that remained of Daphne together with her sister during their teenage years and it appeared Meg was angry with her. From what she remembered, Meg and her mother got along just fine. What had caused such a rift between them? What happened to the missing photos?

Without thinking too much about it, her fingers found her phone in her purse. Winston answered after four rings.

"What?"

"Have you ever met our grandmother?" she asked.

"What? Yeah, I've met Nana." He said it like she was the biggest idiot in the state. "You did, too. You were, like, five when she stopped visiting."

"Why?"

"She had an argument with your mother. I think it was around the time Granddad died."

Celia's face fell. "An argument? About what?"

"I don't fucking remember," he huffed. "Anything else, Celia?"

She was too distracted by this new information to be concerned with her cousin's attitude. "Why would she stop visiting? Was it that bad? How could you stop seeing your own family, especially if our grandfather had died?"

"Who the hell knows?" His voice softened a fraction. "A few days pass without a call, then a week, then a month. That's how it goes."

She was quiet as she thought about that.

There was a soft buzzing in the background. "My Chinese is here," he said.

Takeout? Meg would have a fit. "Why did you go back to Brooklyn?"

He groaned. "Oh, what the fuck? Now you care? Why do you have to know everything? I heard this bloodsucker came back to town, okay? I'm looking for her."

"Well, I'll let you get back to that," she snapped. She closed her phone.

Celia flipped through the albums two more times, deep in thought. Her mother's smiling face flashed in front of her. She was reminded of that calming air that always surrounded her. And the way she would help her style her hair. How she would let her try on her clothes and jewelry.

Celia paused. Daphne only owned a few pieces of actual value. Most of them were pretty, but inexpensive necklaces and rings from Macy's and Filene's Basement. The more valuable ones were a pair of diamond earrings she received as a graduation gift when she finished nursing school, and three 24-

karat gold bangles she wore all the time. They clinked together with her every movement.

And the ring.

Celia hadn't thought about her mother's ring. It was a medium-sized ruby set on a simple gold band. Her mother always had it on her right ring finger. Celia had asked her once where she got it. Daphne couldn't recall. They'd been sitting at the table, wrestling with her science homework.

Daphne had stared at the ring on her finger for a full minute as if it were having a conversation with her. Celia'd watched her captivation without interrupting.

Celia slowly placed the albums back where she found them. When she stood, she had to shake out her legs to get the circulation going again. Upstairs, she went straight to the room at the end of the hall.

Her aunt and uncle had the largest room. Their king-sized bed sat against the wall, neatly made with blue and white zebra print bedding. Blue curtains hung from the windows on the right wall. A large, abstract painting was on display above the bed.

Celia crossed to the vanity on the left side, next to the master bathroom. She sat on the bench and turned on the light above the mirror. She scanned the makeup and hair accessories. Meg used a jewelry tree for her necklaces and bracelets. The rest were in a large ivory box. She lifted the top. A few rings were there but none of them contained a ruby.

She checked in the drawers. It wasn't until she opened the bottom drawer that she hit pay dirt. A small black box slid forward. Her fingers closed around it. She held it in her hand a moment, running her thumb along the felt material. It popped open with a creak.

The ruby sparkled in the light. She took it from the slot. She held it a moment, and then slid it on her right ring finger. She let out a breath she hadn't realized she was holding. The ring fit perfectly.

Celia closed the drawer, adjusted whatever she touched on the vanity, slipped the ring box in her pocket and rushed downstairs. The cable man rang the bell just as she reached the foyer. By the time he was finished replacing their DVR box, the sun was already set.

Celia drove home. She gathered her leftovers of chicken farfalle and focaccia bread and climbed out. She was glad to have them; she was starving. A light yet frigid breeze blew across her face. Her purse hung from her shoulder, her to-go bag with Cage's new logo from the crook of her elbow.

She had her head down, seeking out the key to the front door. The street was empty. That was something she noticed. Thanks to Milo, she'd started becoming more aware of her surroundings, especially when she was alone.

That's why when she looked up, the person standing on her stoop made her gasp. Where had he come from?

He stared at the front door as if confounded by its purpose. Her steps began to slow as she got a better look at his olive green suit that hung perfectly on his frame, the dark hair carefully brushed back. She had come to a complete stop two seconds before he turned. She hadn't needed to see the freaky milk-white eyes to realize Cillian was waiting for her.

His smile was pleasant, warm. "You are a gift for me."

Celia took off in the opposite direction. Her first thought was to get herself and her shit into her car. Except she didn't have keyless entry. Fumbling with the lock would cost her precious seconds. She continued on. At the end of the block, she hazarded a glance back. Cillian was frowning after her. He took a step down the first stair.

Celia tossed her purse and leftovers to the ground, even though a part of her hesitated. Her cellphone and wallet were in there. And she was still hungry! But they were becoming cumbersome and she was silly enough to try and outrun a vampire. She turned left at the next block and thanked her stars that she was wearing her New Balances.

The neighborhood was very quiet. After another two blocks, she came to the pathway that led to Shawmut train station. A black sign hung from a post at the curb. A white arrow along the bottom indicated the station. She didn't know why she headed there. Maybe she would find a security guard. Or an attendant who could help her.

She was only halfway down the path when two men rounded the corner, headed in her direction. "Please!" she called out breathlessly. "Help me!"

The men stopped short. She stumbled into them. They were both wearing baseball hats pulled over their faces.

"Whoa," the first guy said. "What's going on?"

She pointed behind her. "Someone's after me."

They looked over her head. "That guy?" the second man asked.

She turned. Cillian was at the beginning of the path. His presence, the fact that he had caught up so quickly dawned on Celia. This was a mistake.

She clutched the first guy's shirt. "Go!" she prodded. "Go now!"

It was too late. The men had already begun to puff themselves up to protect her. The first guy took hold of her arm and tried to maneuver her behind him. Celia looked back to Cillian. He was no longer a block away. He was there, in front of them.

The men gasped. That was the last sound they made. Cillian knocked the second guy aside with a swing of his arm. Before he hit the ground, Cillian punched the first guy square in the chest with that incredible vampire speed. The second guy fell to the ground. A small spatter of blood hit the pavement near his mouth.

Cillian's head jerked to the blood on the ground. He seemed to register the men finally as humans. He was a hawk honed in on fallen prey. He took a deep breath in, and then was on top of the man with his mouth on his throat. The man's head bobbed flaccidly.

The first man had staggered backward in the split second that Cillian latched onto his companion. The man stepped on Celia's foot but she managed to move from behind him before he tripped to the ground. His head bounced off the pavement on impact. His loose jersey sank into an unnatural curve in the spot where Cillian's fist had made contact. Spots of red were seeping through the tiny pores of the shirt. He groaned and grew quiet.

Celia stared down at him in horror. "Oh no," she whispered.

Cillian dropped the man with a grunt. With one hand, he smoothed his hair back. He followed the smell of the guy at Celia's feet and pressed his face onto the curve in his chest. Celia backed away, shaking her head. It didn't matter; she couldn't unsee what she saw.

She was running again. The instinct to survive drove her forward.

A few feet away, she tripped on the uneven ground. She lost her balance and landed on one knee. A rock dug through her pants and into her skin, causing her to wince. Suddenly, a hand gripped her bicep. Before she could scream, she was lifted up. He overestimated her height and her feet dangled in the air for a few seconds.

"Let me go!"

"Seal, it's me."

She instantly relaxed at the sound of his voice. "Victor," she panted, grabbing his shirt. "Cillian . . . He's after me. Those two guys . . . They're . . ."

"I know. This way."

They dashed to the right, leaving the pathway. As they ran, Celia wondered why they weren't teleporting. When they crossed under a streetlight, she understood why. Victor's skin was like ice, his face as white as paper. He must've felt her panic as soon as he woke. He hadn't drunk from her last night; he was probably wishing he hadn't refrained. Before that was following the fight with Milo and Clarice. What he had taken from Celia had only been sufficient for that night.

They had just made it to the end of Mather Street when

Cillian dropped down from the sky in front of them. They stopped short. Victor pushed her, causing her to stumble into a front yard. She fell onto her side on the damp grass. Before she could muster the choice words, she realized why he had done that.

Cillian was so fast, he was a blur. Victor was standing there, then suddenly on the ground ten feet away. Cillian rushed at him again. He lifted him into the air by his neck and tossed him back. Victor landed on his stomach with a groan. Cillian's feet lifted from the ground a few inches. He flew forward until he was on top of him.

Grasping his hair, Cillian jerked his head back. Victor growled, showing his fangs. There was a deep scrape on his chin. Cillian's fangs were already bared. His lips were still shiny with warm blood. He leaned down and sank his teeth in Victor's throat.

"Stop!" Celia screamed.

Victor tried to push him off but Cillian was stronger. She could plainly see him struggle against his hold. Cillian pulled back at the sound of Celia's voice, ripping the flesh of Victor's throat in the process. His blood hit the pavement with a wet splash. Victor cried out in pain, but managed to disappear. He materialized behind Cillian and kicked him in the side, right in the kidney. He punched him in the jaw repeatedly, before he could regain his balance.

Cillian's leg swept out, taking him off his feet. Victor's head hit off the side of a parked car. The alarm chirped for a second. Cillian grabbed Victor's calf and dragged him closer. He put his nose near the wound and sniffed. He was going to bite him again, and from the look of his other one, Celia understood that mutilating his victims was part of the package.

A branch lay at her foot. It wouldn't do shit but she couldn't sit there, watching Victor lose so much blood. She scrambled to her feet and snatched up the branch. It was splintered on the end, indicating it had been twisted and yanked from its trunk.

Celia rushed over to the two. Cillian bit into the other side of Victor's neck before she reached them. Celia wielded the branch like a bat, ready to bring it down on his head. She stopped. Jay's voice had popped in her head. Two months ago, he told her about when his family was attacked. How he had used a broken table leg to pierce the vamp's heart.

She surveyed Cillian's back. He lifted his head. He was pointing his blood-smeared face to the night sky. His eyes were closed, a content smile offered upward.

His mouth opened. "Let the blood of the fallen nourish my soul."

Celia raised the branch over her head with the traumatized end faced down. She aimed it at the center of his back where she hoped his heart lay. He lowered his head again. Celia brought the branch down with an exerted yelp.

Cillian's warm blood spurted back into her face. Vampires turned to ash immediately after a foreign object was introduced to their hearts. Cillian, however, began to rise. The branch protruded from his back. She had known on impact that she had only penetrated him shallowly. Celia staggered backward until she tripped on the grass behind her. Cillian stood before her, his head cocked to the side. The light blue eyes under the milky film took her in.

"Why?" he asked. He sounded confused. "Why did you do that?"

"Leave us alone," she hissed. She didn't know what someone would think at the sight of the three of them. She was certain someone had heard her shout before.

Cillian shook his head. "But you're my gift."

"I'm not."

"Don't lie to me!" When he screamed, his voice deepened a few octaves. The tremor of his voice was the stuff of nightmares. The white film coating his eyes blazed in the streetlight. Celia cringed.

"Cillian!"

Ramsey's shout was a loud whisper. He was jumping out of his convertible at the corner. Just then, the bulb came on above the porch behind Celia. The light fell across her shoulders. She heard the locks turning. Ramsey flitted forward in that vamp speed and got ahold of Cillian. They darted down the street.

Victor gurgled something. His hand rose to her. Celia lunged forward. He was already disappearing when she landed on his chest. It was like she had just dived headfirst into an artic wave. The coldness that went along with his teleporting was magnified by a hundred percent. It took longer for her apartment to appear. They seemed to be stuck between the street and her home.

A sidewalk and shadowy houses stood just behind her blurry sofa. She heard a door open, a person calling out. The voice sounded far away. She squinted as the cold enveloping her leached into her head. Her brain felt foggy. She clamped her mouth around her chattering teeth. The iciness turned sharp, like shards of glass piercing her veins. A ringing had begun in her ears.

Pieces of her furniture came into focus, one at a time. The beige sofa. The brown coffee table. The entertainment center. The trees and houses melted away. Her fingers grasped the carpet beneath her, though she felt nothing with her numb fingers. She buried her face in Victor's shirt, whimpering in agony. The fog lifted slowly. The ringing receded.

Celia laid there for what had to have been a half an hour. That's how long it took the painful numbness to ebb. She moved her left arm first, stretching it toward Victor. Her muscles protested, slowing her progress. Her fingers found his chin, inched over his lips, his nose, his closed eyelids.

She slowly, carefully lifted her head. Victor lay motionless underneath her. His hands that had held her to his body had flopped to the rug. His name rose in her throat. But her mouth wasn't working. She clasped his wet collar and dragged her face closer.

His skin was so pale it was translucent. Celia could make out the shape of his skull beneath. His lips were the same clear color. His blood was everywhere and still pouring from both sides of his neck, soaking her rug, their clothes, her hair. The scrape on his jaw was too light for comfort as well.

She shook him lightly. It wasn't an attempt at being gentle; she couldn't muster as much force as she wanted. Something came from her mouth, something mumbled. She shook him some more, then lifted her hand and let her fist drop to his chest. She repeated that until she found her strength returning.

"Victor," she said hoarsely. He didn't rouse. Celia moved her feet to make sure they'd hold before struggling into a standing position. It took her a minute and she wobbled dangerously. She looked around, contemplating. She wanted to call Ramsey. He'd given her his number once but she never needed to use it. She had no idea where she put the notebook he'd scribbled on.

Then again, if she had Ramsey's ear she'd do more than ask for help with Victor. Wasn't he supposed to have a fucking reign on Cillian? Why was he waiting for her?

Celia stooped down next to Victor to search his pockets. They were empty. Her eyes went to the cable box. It was only a little after nine. She tried holding her arm out to him, hoping her pulse would pull him from this catatonic state. He continued to remain unconscious.

She went to the bathroom to freshen up. Just washing her face and brushing her teeth seemed to shake off the last of her disconcertedness. She placed a towel from the hamper on Victor's wounds. When she stepped onto the tiled floor of the kitchen, she remembered her purse. She grabbed a knife and rushed outside. Her purse and food were where she left them tossed to the ground beside a set of stairs.

Celia ate the cold, topsy-turvy pasta on the sofa while alternating glimpses from Victor's inert body and the television. She was checking for any special reports. At ten-thirty, she took a shower after running a hand through her hair and finding it tangled with Victor's dried blood. She returned to the sofa, biting her nails.

The evening news came and went with no stories of a mysterious, fanged psycho with a branch in his back. Midnight was creeping up. The adrenaline had completely left her body and exhaustion made her lids droop. She felt her body tilting to the side but couldn't summon the will to fight it.

When Celia stirred, the cable box said four-ten. A Dyson vacuum infomercial played on the television. Victor was still lying there. The light green towel around his neck was dark pink. Her eyes went to the windows. The curtains wouldn't be sufficient in blocking the sun that would surely filter inside. That was one of the draws to the building, plenty of sunshine. The same would be true with the bedroom.

She thought of her closet. And then she remembered all her clothes and shoes crowding the small space. That was not going to work. Her mind flicked to the bathroom. She jumped up and went to her room. On her knees, she pulled out one of the storage containers from under the bed where she retrieved a spare blanket. She also grabbed his pillow. She dropped them on the floor in the bathroom.

She studied Victor a moment before grabbing hold of his forearms. She strained as she dragged him the six feet to the bathroom. The pasta and rest had helped to invigorate her but he felt like a sack of bricks. Damn, if only she could employ her neighbor's help. He was currently fucking up "Livin' on the Edge" on *Guitar Hero*.

Of course, he would probably question why she was dragging an unconscious man into her bathroom.

At the threshold, Celia hooked her hands under Victor's armpits and hefted him forward then up over the edge of the tub. As soon as she got his torso in, the rest was easier. She straightened him out, put the pillow under his head, and then covered him with the comforter. She closed the shower curtain. She also shut the curtain covering the small window where the moon was shining through. The room was plunged into darkness. Celia breathed a sigh of relief. She closed the door then went to bed. She had to work in the morning.

Celia was behind the bar tapping her foot and trying not to bite her nails. She hadn't slept much during the night. The images of those two men . . . They wouldn't leave her. Luckily, not many people sat at the bar for lunch. When her shift was over, she slung her purse on her shoulder and made her way to the exit. As soon as she stepped into the foyer, the front door was pushed opened. The cold air washed over her.

A young girl stomped inside. She wore black leggings, black high-top Chucks, and an oversized yellow sweatshirt. Everything about her was petite, except her nose, which was too big for her thin face. She had short blond hair with a couple of light green streaks throughout. Her dark blue eyes landed on Celia.

"You," she spat.

Celia halted at once. Her head jerked back in offense. "May I help you?"

"You're Celia."

Her eyes narrowed. "Who are you?"

"Your vamp boyfriend stood me up," she said very loudly.

Celia looked around quickly to make sure they were alone, and then pulled her outside. "What the hell's the matter with you?" Celia demanded. "You don't say something like that where anyone could hear you."

Corinna yanked her arm free. "What're you getting mad for? I'm the one who was waiting around last night. He could've called."

"He was . . . indisposed. How did you find me?"

"With a Locating Spell."

Celia waved her hands in front of her because she thought her head might explode. "Who are you?"

"Corinna. He wanted me to meet you." She paused to look Celia up and down. "Yeah," she said. "Yeah, I see it, I guess."

Celia felt a little violated. She crossed her arms at the chest. "See what?"

"Every living thing gives off energy. The more power you have, the more visible your energy is." She sounded like she was reciting from a manual. "Sucks when you're trying to hide yourself but not everyone can see it anyway."

"*What* are you talking about?"

"He thinks you're a witch," she said matter-of-factly.

"He . . . he what?"

Corinna rolled her eyes. "This is boring. We don't meet 'til next month. You'll have to wait 'til then."

She turned to leave. "Hey, wait!" She continued down the

sidewalk. Celia rushed after her.

"Wait."

Corinna stopped short with a groan. "What?"

"Victor thinks I'm a witch? But why?"

"He didn't say. Shouldn't you know? Have you made things levitate? Or move? Or disappear?"

"No. Is that . . . possible?"

"Duh."

Celia scratched her head. Those all sounded like magical abilities. Her knack for seeing into a vamp's head wasn't very magical in her eyes.

"Who's 'we?'" Celia asked. "Who do you meet with?"

"My coven."

"And you want me to meet them?"

"I don't. Your boyfriend thinks it's a good idea." She shook her head as if she wasn't convinced. "I guess we'll see."

Corinna marched away. Celia stared after her as she wondered if teleporting had maybe knocked her into some kind of parallel universe.

Celia went straight home after meeting Corinna. She hesitated outside the bathroom door before pushing it open. She made sure the door was closed tight behind her. Holding the shower curtain aside, she gently lifted the comforter. Victor hadn't moved an inch. She covered him up quickly because seeing your boyfriend as a corpse was beyond creepy.

Trixie stopped by at six-thirty. "I just had a fight with Lee," she announced with a pout.

"Uh," was all Celia said. Trixie stomped inside and went to the kitchen where she retrieved a Corona from the bottom shelf.

"He doesn't even try to make time for me anymore. We both had tonight off and I said, let's get dinner. I even said we could go to Cheesecake since it's in the mall. But he said he had to meet his friends. He wouldn't even tell me what they were doing. Plus, he had these nasty bruises. He got into a fight and he didn't say anything!"

She chugged the beer. Celia tried to think of something reassuring. Her mind was too preoccupied by Victor and Cillian's attack and Corinna to be a decent friend. Maybe Trixie was too distracted herself. She went right past Celia and stepped on the bloodstained carpet. She continued across the smears on the wood from his shirt where the blood hadn't completely dried without noticing. Celia didn't realize Trixie was headed to the bathroom until she had already gone inside and closed the door behind herself.

"Trix, wait!"

It was too late. After a second, the toilet flushed. The water ran in the sink. The door opened and she gasped. Celia was standing there, her toes at the threshold.

"What're you doing?" Trixie exclaimed. She held up the pillow. "Why do you have this in your tub?"

Celia stared at the pillow with her mouth agape. She pushed by Trixie. The shower curtain was moved aside. The formally green towel lay on the floor beside the tub. Her comforter was bunched in a pile under the faucet.

Celia's eyes widened. She rushed to her purse on the sofa and pulled out her cellphone. The call went to Victor's voicemail.

"What's going on?" Trixie asked. She'd come up behind her, the pillow still in her hand. "Oh, my God, is this blood?"

Celia just gaped at the phone in her hand. That fucker better had been feeling the anxiety he was causing, she thought crossly.

***

Victor had awoken in a dark space. It took much longer than normal to materialize in Ramsey's hallway. When he did, it felt like all of his nerves were on fire. Still, he lumbered to the door that led to the basement. He took the stairs slowly, gripping the railing as he descended.

The black door was there, the gold locks staring back at him. Two of the locks were crossbars you had to slide open. The other was a deadbolt.

A new addition was at eye level. Unlike the other locks that discouraged Cillian from getting out, Victor saw this one needed a key to open.

Cillian was allowed to roam when there were no humans in the house. Ramsey only utilized the locks in those instances. Cillian usually stayed in his room anyway—a measly door with four locks meant nothing more than a warning.

"Cillian," Victor called in a raspy voice. "Answer me, dammit."

"Umami," Cillian whispered to himself. "Sweet Umami. Gift of mine."

Victor pounded on the door.

"Victor." Ramsey floated down the stairs. When he was near, he touched Victor's neck. His eyes scanned Cillian's wounds. They were salmon pink in color. Bits of fabric from the towel clung to his throat. The wounds had stopped bleeding before sunrise, when his body died for the day. The skin was ragged, giving the unexpected impression of gills. The rest of him not covered in dried blood was white, ghostly.

"How is Celia?"

"She managed to get me into the bathroom. I'm going to assume she is fine."

Ramsey's eyes were filled with sorrow. "I'm sorry." He caressed Victor's shoulder. "I wanted to come to you. It took me, Elizabeth, and Bryce to calm Cillian. He hasn't spoken to me about why he did this. He just seems distraught that she rejected him. His head's a mess right now. I can't even get through to him that way."

Ramsey was talking about his mental comms. It wasn't telepathy, more like a walkie-talkie. He could speak directly into the heads of the vampires in his nest—as they with him—but he couldn't hear or see what they were thinking. Cillian, when he was troubled, usually blocked Ramsey out. Cillian was so far-gone from humanity that when he was distressed, his thoughts and memories swarmed and overlapped, causing him to shut down.

Ramsey's compassion was lost on Victor. "You don't know how he got out?" he demanded. He was glowering at the new lock.

"No. Elizabeth said she was the only one home. She'd come down here to check her supplies when she saw his door was open."

The golden lock made Victor angry. It shielded Cillian from the fury he was barely containing. It was that white-hot ire alone that allowed him to remain on his feet at the moment.

Victor pounded on the door. "Come upstairs," Ramsey said gently. "Cindy and Matt are home tonight."

Victor continued to bang on Cillian's door. Ramsey watched him in silence. Then he turned and went upstairs.

Victor would wear himself out eventually.

***

Celia had stayed up as late as she could. Victor didn't call. Under the covers, her dreams were still plagued by the men. She got up a little after four and turned on her computer.

"'LaShawn Jackson and Miles Lubin,'" she read aloud. The men had been found twenty minutes after Celia and Victor left but there was nothing to be done to save them. LaShawn's heart had been destroyed, much like the injuries sustained in a head-on collision. Miles' neck was broken. He'd been paralyzed before he'd hit the hard ground. There was no mention of the loss of blood. Celia wondered why the police would withhold that information.

The men had been older than Celia by a few years. Miles was a paramedic and LaShawn worked in a restaurant in the South End.

Celia cried over her keyboard. It was her fault. If she hadn't stopped them. If she had only made them see the danger. Except, that was one of the perils of living in a city; you would always run into someone on the streets. She was lucky it hadn't been rush hour or that a train hadn't just pulled into the station, releasing twenty or thirty people on their way home from work. It would've been a bloodbath as Cillian fought to catch Celia.

She called Victor at least fifty times. Each call went to voicemail. She didn't want his voicemail. She wanted him right there with her, with his arms around her, telling her it would be okay.

She fingered her mother's ruby ring. She pondered what her mother would say about this situation. The best part was that she wouldn't need to speak. Just being next to Daphne would've been enough.

It was nearly six when Jay answered the phone. The sun was turning the sky a light shade of pink behind the white clouds.

"What's up?"

She couldn't muster the words. At the sound of his voice, Celia's tears blurred her vision and her throat closed up.

"Celia? Hey, what's going on?" His tone was urgent.

Somehow, she managed to tell him. There was silence on the other line. Her crying finally subsided to sniffles and a runny nose.

"I'm coming back," he said.

She pursed her lips. Most of her wanted him to return. She couldn't undermine Victor in that way, though, even if he was being a complete ass at the moment with his radio silence. His presence under her skin had already begun to fade with the rising sun.

"Don't do that," she said. "You have your own business to handle. I just needed to talk to someone who would understand." She rubbed her nose with her knuckle.

The article about the two men was still on the screen. The words swam in her watery vision.

"I'm the reason they're dead."

"Circumstance is the reason they are dead. Weren't you the one always mouthing off about how people are gonna die?"

"That was different," she muttered

"How so? They could've stepped off the curb two minutes later and been hit by a goddamn Mack truck. You just never know."

"But I did know!" she shouted. "A fucking vampire was after me. There was nothing they could've done to help me!" The tears returned. He quietly waited her out. She was a bit calmer when she told him, "I've never seen anyone die like that before."

Jay exhaled. "It's something that takes time to get used to."

Celia shook her head. "I don't want to get used to that. It's different with vampires, when they die. I guess because there's nothing left after but ash. I don't know." She fought the tears stinging her eyes. "I don't want to see any more death, Jay."

"Ditch your undead company then," he said gruffly.

Her jaw dropped in angry surprise. "Goddammit, Jay, why does it always come back to that?"

"Because it always fuckin' does, Celia. Think about it for a fuckin' second. If you weren't with a fuckin' vampire, then you wouldn't know about 'em. You'd go to work with your head in the fuckin' clouds and life would be chipper."

His voice rose with each successive *fuck* as his Southern twang took over his words.

"What kinda future you tryna have with this guy, Celia?"

She was too stunned to respond.

"Are you gonna just keep taking his blood? Sure, that'll slow the aging process somewhat but not enough to keep up with him. Is that what you want? To be his feedbag until you dry up?

"Or are you tryna be like him, Celia? You gonna die and come back? Live in the dark, feeding off humans? Is that the kind of fuckin' life you want?"

This time she refused to answer. How dare he. Jay had always pushed the limit with his strong opinions on her decisions but this was too much.

"I don't know how to make it any clearer for you than that," he finished.

Celia was trembling. She hung up the phone and threw it across the room with enough force to wrench her elbow. The cordless receiver hit the wall she shared with her neighbor Carrie with a loud thud. Celia stared at the mark it left on the wall.

"Shit," she muttered. She hoped she hadn't woken Kenny; his bed was against that wall.

The phone rang from the floor. She ignored it.

Celia worked behind the bar Friday afternoon rather than the night shift. There was nothing she could do during the day but she fretted just the same. At least being angry with Jay took her mind off the two men who had tried to come to her rescue.

Michael sauntered in at one to pick up his paycheck. When he caught sight of her, he marched past without a word. He left two minutes later. She went back to fretting. She guessed that Victor had gone to Ramsey's and hadn't wandered the streets, zonked out of his mind in bloodlust. She was certain that would have made the news.

A woman sat at the end of the bar. Celia automatically went over, carrying a newspaper with her since she was alone. She placed it on the counter beside her and a bar napkin in front.

The woman peeked at the paper. "Hmm," she said. "Another couple was murdered."

Celia looked to where she was pointing. A picture of a white colonial house took up most of the space on the front page of the Globe. Police cars were parked at the curb. Officials filed in and out of the front door.

The woman shook her head. "Same as the last one, husband was brutalized and the woman was tucked in her bed. Neither of them had blood." She clucked her teeth. "Some people are real sick, you know that?"

As the woman rattled off her order, Celia found herself staring at the curtain of her blonde hair. The memory was vague but she recalled Annie having long blonde hair. She hadn't inquired lately of the vamps' search.

Winston was still out of town as far as she knew. The vamps were convinced that Annie made it into Massachusetts. She didn't think Winston would've taken her to New York, and then come back to Boston. What would be the purpose? More captives? He seemed only concerned with killing vampires, with beating out Tilly and her crew for most slayings.

Tilly was the one who held vamps to draw out the torture.

"Oh," Celia said aloud, her brows rising. The woman frowned at her.

Her conversation with Jay about the Night Hawks resounded in her head. They were known for their extreme tactics. They didn't just want to kill vampires; they wanted to send a message. That was why they were organized. That was why they had flyers and little pins.

She chose to ignore the part where Jay said she was always in trouble. Determination pushed away her apprehension over Victor's wellbeing. Sitting around on her ass, worrying out of her mind wouldn't accomplish anything.

After her shift, Celia rushed home and went straight to her room to change. Nondescript jeans, black t-shirt and sneakers. Once again, she braided her hair back. The sun was low in the sky, surrounded by gray clouds. The effect was an eerie orange glow across the city. She made it to Olde Nessie's in twenty minutes.

The same bouncer from last week was outside with white smoke surrounding his head. He gestured for her ID. There was no indication that he recognized her. She was just another face in the crowd.

Inside, she hesitated. She stood off to the side of the entrance, scanning the room. She didn't really have a plan. Perhaps a neon sign would flash somewhere saying, *secret lair this'a way.*

As she looked around the booths, her eyes landed on a woman eating wings and reading a magazine. Tilly's shaggy hair was in her eyes. She wore an ill-fitting peach dress that looked more like a very long camisole if anything. The front had a deep scoop neck and Celia could see she wasn't wearing a bra. She did know it was October, right?

Celia ducked her head and made a beeline to the booth. She slid in quickly. Tilly looked up in surprise at the intrusion on her quiet time.

"Can I help you?" she asked severely. Her voice had been a little too loud. Two men sitting at the round table beside them glanced over.

"You're Tilly, right?" Celia kept her voice low in the hopes that she would follow suit. Tilly stared at her suspiciously. "I saw you at the meeting." She put enough emphasis on the word to let her know she wanted a discreet conversation.

Tilly's eyes narrowed at first. She then flashed that gap-toothed smile of hers. "Oh, right! I remember now. How's it going?"

"Good."

Okay, now what? She couldn't just blatantly ask her if she had Annie.

"This weather's pretty bad, huh?" Tilly said. "It's supposed to rain again tonight."

"I know, it sucks. Um, I was wondering if I could ask you a few questions."

"Like what?"

Celia shrugged and let her gaze drop to the tabletop to appear bashful.

"That was my first time at the meeting, so I'm kinda new to all of this." She leaned closer, lowering her voice even more. "How exactly does it work?"

She prayed that Tilly didn't ask her how she knew about vampires. She didn't have a story for that yet.

Tilly's eyes lit up. Apparently imparting knowledge was exciting to her. Both of her arms had been resting on the table. She waved her hands around now as she spoke to illustrate her point.

"Most of the Night Hawks work in groups. You have to be very watchful to catch a bloodsucker. They'll give themselves away sooner or later." She chuckled to herself, conjuring a memory perhaps. "Like, not breathing or blinking. Watching people a little too closely. Staring at their necks, as corny as that sounds."

She rolled her eyes. The sweet and tangy scent of Tilly's barbeque came at her across the table on her breath. The perpetual mugginess of Olde Nessie's shrouded them, pressing down on their skin.

"Mostly, we—me and Kyle and Leo, since we work together all the time—snatch them and bring them to my place. There," she said, her voice trembling with hungry pleasure. Her eyes were pretty scary in their intensity. "We have fun."

She picked up a wing and took a huge, satisfied bite. Celia shuddered. Tilly used the back of her hand to wipe the barbeque sauce from her mouth. She looked at Celia with something in her eyes that could've been best described as a mixture of hatred and exhilaration.

"Do you all keep them, like, for a while?"

She shrugged. "Depends."

Celia waited but she didn't elaborate. "On what?" she coaxed.

Tilly eyed her again with that quizzical look, like she was contemplating. "What they have to offer," she finally said.

Celia shook her head with a small laugh. "What could you possibly want from—from one of them?" she asked haltingly, stumbling at the end of the question. She just couldn't force herself to insert bloodsuckers, even if that would have impressed Tilly.

Tilly's stare was steely. "Plenty," she said, just as vaguely. She ran her tongue slowly over her lips, though no sauce coated them. Was she . . . flirting? Did that mean that along with torture they would . . .?

Celia couldn't finish the thought. It was too horrific to process and she didn't want a repeat of the nightmares after hearing the Night Hawks' stories. She told herself to concentrate on the matter at hand.

"Do you have anyone now?"

"Sure. Three of 'em, actually. Two guys and a girl." Tilly grinned. "Kyle loves her. Very pretty, nice body. She had this long blonde hair that was so shiny."

"Had long hair?" Celia asked, catching the past tense.

Tilly shrugged nonchalantly. "I may have gotten a little carried away with my scissors."

She reached into her brown hobo bag on the seat beside her. A small lock of blonde hair tied in a knot dangled from her fingers.

At that moment, Celia wanted nothing more than to escape from this stifling place, from this crazy woman with her maniacal gleam and hair souvenir. She'd been bombarded with too many disconcerting images lately and it was trying to eat at her. Her legs even twitched, ready to propel her from the booth and out the door.

Except, she needed to be sure it was Annie. She had to help Victor and Ramsey as best she could. It wasn't right what these people were doing. She wondered if she should wait around, follow her to her house? She lived on 5th Street; that she remembered. But who knew how long the street was? Celia wasn't too familiar with the residential areas of Cambridge, only the Galleria mall where Trixie worked and the squares: Harvard, Central, and Porter.

The other option was to secure a place in her crew. Ugh, she hated that possibility. Hated the things she would have to say to weasel in. She didn't want anything more to do with Tilly or the Night Hawks or—

"Tilly."

Celia's head snapped up at the familiar, smooth voice. Gayle and Herb were approaching their booth.

Shit!

While Herb lumbered from side to side like Frankenstein's monster as he walked, Gayle glided next to him with ease. It reminded her so much of how Ramsey walked and that was disturbing. Glancing over Gayle's stiff posture and smooth face, Celia realized just how alike she was to the things she hunted. She needed to work on her "human" nuances if she wanted to blend in more.

Tonight, Gayle wore another polished suit. This one was black with a lacy shirt or bodysuit or something in a cranberry color underneath the jacket. The cuffs of her pants were wide and flapped as she moved, revealing black, crocodile print heels with pointy toes. The shoes were square across her foot, showing off a little toe cleavage.

Well, vampire or not, Gayle knew how to dress.

Her sharp gaze slid from Tilly to Celia. "Ah, I see you have a friend," Gayle said.

"We were just talking a little," Tilly said, smiling up at her. Her entire posture shifted in the presence of her revered leaders. Her back straightened, showing nipple through the thin material. Her smile was so wide you could see all the teeth in her damn head.

"You know we like to meet with all new recruits," Gayle said gently.

Tilly's face wavered. She glanced to Celia and back. "I'm sorry. I didn't realize you hadn't met."

"We have, at least informally," Gayle replied. "You know Winston," she said to Celia. "We like to have a sit-down with any interested parties. I'm Gayle. And this is Herb."

She glanced to Herb as she introduced him but his eyes were glued to Tilly's chest. Well, shit, your eyes would've been there, too. Her nips were begging for attention.

Gayle cleared her throat sternly. Herb jumped, before receiving her disapproving look. Gayle was probably five-ten, while Herb's head came to her shoulder. He shifted slightly as his already red cheeks flamed. He turned to Celia, but after a few seconds, his eyes drifted to her chest, as if that was just an automatic response when he was in the presence of a female.

Celia wasn't too nervous to scowl at him. He met her eyes briefly then looked away. How this pervert could be the organizer of malevolent killers was beyond her.

Gayle looked to Celia expectantly. Her Chanel was stronger tonight, doing a much better job of disguising that earthy scent that seemed to radiate from her.

This was not good. Not good at all. She was supposed to just be in and out and here she was, in the company of the lethal leaders (borrowing Jay's words) of the Night Hawks.

A drop of sweat slid down the back of her neck. Her mouth

was suddenly dry. She managed to croak, "Renée. I'm Renée."

"It's nice to meet you, Renée." Gayle's smile didn't transform her face one bit. In fact, it was a tad icy. Celia hoped it wasn't because she didn't believe her. She could be a Renée dammit.

"Now, I hope you won't be too upset that I need to borrow Tilly for a little while," she went on. Tilly was stunned by the request. It was a pleasant surprise judging by the raisins she was currently smuggling under her dress.

"No problem," Celia said.

Tilly quickly scooted out of the booth with her purse, gave Celia a waggle of her dark brows, and then followed behind them through that unmarked door. Tilly must've been wearing a cami since it stopped just below her ass. She also had a pair of tan Uggs on that clopped across the floor. Her bag patted her butt as she hurried after the two.

Celia blew out a breath. She was glad they were gone but it appeared she'd have to go with Plan A and wait around to follow Tilly home.

She looked over the spot where she had occupied. Tilly had only eaten half the wings. The magazine sat open where she had left it. Celia flipped it over but there was no name or address printed on the front. It was Cosmo. She'd been reading an article on achieving the perfect orgasm. She did not want to imagine Tilly having orgasms, at all. Of course, now she was envisioning it. She was probably obnoxiously loud, to the chagrin of her neighbors. She probably shouted things like, "Oh, yes, baby, fuck me like that!" Or, "Slap it harder, daddy. Slap it across my face!"

Celia shuddered.

She placed her elbows on the table and leaned forward to run a hand over her hair. She was trying to figure out her next move. She didn't know how long Tilly would be. Should she hide herself outside until Tilly left the bar, and then follow? Hopefully she'd go straight home.

Celia groaned. She wasn't enjoying this one bit. She wished that Victor was there. He'd know what to do and then she wouldn't be alone, either. Or Jay. Only, if Jay was there, she would've punched him.

He probably liked when girls talked dirty like that. He seemed like he would enjoy the sound of his hand smacking someone's ass while he pounded away.

Celia shook her head hard to clear the image. What the fuck was wrong with her? She could only reason that her mind was too much of a jumble to control which path it chose to travel.

The stuffy air was making her breath come in shallow intervals. She looked to the empty seat across from her again. That's when she noticed the pink material tucked in the corner of the seat across from her. Gingerly, she stood to retrieve it. She ended up pulling out a gauzy, rayon scarf, with yellow tassels hanging from each end.

Now, what did Victor say about vampires who hunt? She couldn't quite recall but something told her this scarf was important. So, she held it lightly in her hand, making sure not to touch it too much, and hurried outside.

It was six-thirty and the sky was darkening with rain clouds. She sped home, calling Victor on the way.

***

Victor had been upset that Celia put herself in such danger going to that bar. She countered with the fact that he had disappeared without a word to her, leaving her worrying for a whole day. Telling her Ramsey had no explanation for Cillian's actions was not sufficient.

They called a stalemate. They were both equally angry yet equally impotent. Victor held her for a little while. She cried some more but through their bond he knew she felt immensely better with him there. He regretted leaving her the way he had, causing her such distress. He vowed to himself to make it up to her.

He told her not to leave the house and took the scarf to Milton.

Ramsey was in the living room with Elizabeth and Bryce. The three vamps glanced up when he appeared suddenly in the doorway.

"Where's Ashleigh?" he asked quickly.

"In her room," Ramsey answered. She'd been unofficially confined to her quarters after her assault on Matt. "What's going on?"

Victor held up the pink scarf. "She may be able to lead us to Annie."

Bryce stood slowly, his body rigid. He glared at Victor with such intensity that Victor thought he might lunge at him. He did propel forward. Instead of attacking, he ran right by. A second later, he was back in the room, gripping Ashleigh's arm. She tried to snatch herself loose but he held on tightly.

He faced her to Victor. She stared up at him with a strange blend of contempt and longing. Victor tried not to notice. After her little display at the party, he had spoken to her frankly.

Ashleigh's cold gaze was on Celia until she disappeared around the corner. The microwave beeped.

That seemed to snap her back to reality. Her face fell as she realized what she had done. She rushed to Victor, her eyes wide. Victor knocked her hands away before her fingers could touch him.

"I'm s—"

"I don't want to hear it," he said. He didn't curse; he didn't even raise his voice. "The only reason I'm not running a stake through your chest right now is because this is Ramsey's home."

Her jaw dropped slowly. He took a step closer, rising up to his full height. "Don't leave this place or I swear, Ashleigh. You're dead."

Her chin trembled. He left the kitchen. The sound of something crashing to the floor followed him into the hallway.

Now, Victor kept his voice and face expressionless. "Ashleigh, I know you're new to it. We need you to track the owner of this scarf."

She didn't move to take it. Bryce pushed her forward and she winced. Her hesitation was not helping matters.

Ashleigh took hold of the lightweight scarf with her free hand and brought it to her nose to inhale. She closed her eyes. After a second, she moved the scarf away and raised her face slightly, putting her nose in the air.

"Where did you get this?" she asked after a moment. "I can't follow it from here."

Ramsey, Bryce, Victor, and Ashleigh headed out to the red sedan while Victor called Celia to obtain the address to the bar. Elizabeth stayed behind in case of injuries. Ramsey found Olde Nessie's with relative ease. The men stood at the corner while Ashleigh went to the entrance. Her dark hair, pale skin, and pretty eyes instantly captivated the bouncer. He didn't even motion for her identification; he just held the door open.

Ashleigh didn't need to go inside. She glanced back to the guys and nodded once. She then turned and headed down the street. The bouncer stared after her, longingly. The guys walked behind her, keeping a distance. She paused in front of a convenience store. After a minute, she continued on. At the end of the street, she halted.

"She got in a car," she said when the guys caught up. Victor took the keys from Ramsey and vanished, not caring if anyone saw him. Luckily no one had. He whipped the car down the street and they piled in. Ashleigh had her window down, nose to the air.

When they came to the expressway, heading north, Victor began to grow nervous. They would have to go through the

Callahan Tunnel. That meant more cars. Conversely, Ashleigh didn't seem bothered in the least. She still had Tilly's tail. She sat in silence, only speaking when giving directions.

Fifteen minutes later, she told him to take Storrow Drive. They continued on, over the Longfellow Bridge toward the city of Cambridge. A Red Line train followed along with them. One of the cars was filled with teenagers jumping around merrily.

The skyline caught her attention. She gazed in wonder at the people jogging or ambling across the bridge in both directions, at the lights winking in the buildings. In the John Hancock building and the Prudential they were leaving behind. In the cluster of MIT buildings just ahead.

When the traffic light at the 3rd Street intersection turned green, Victor had to call her name to bring her attention back to the car. Bryce growled from the back.

"Sorry," Ashleigh whispered. "Turn right."

Five minutes and he turned right on 5th Street. He pulled the car to the curb at the first spot he found—though the street was reserved for Resident Permits only.

They climbed out and trailed behind Ashleigh for a few feet. Thunder rumbled above their heads. She stopped at a blue Impala and peered inside. She then looked up at the duplex behind her. She nodded to the men. Standing there, in front of the house, Victor recognized Tilly's scent from the scarf. This was her place. Bryce snarled angrily. Ramsey laid a restraining hand on his shoulder.

"I'll look around," Victor volunteered. He went toward the back, glancing in windows as he passed. The windows, unadorned by curtains or blinds, were low enough to frame his head and shoulders. He only had Celia's description of Tilly to go by but there was no one in the living room or kitchen.

As he neared the edge of the house, a glass shattering made his sharp ears perk. He stopped to listen more carefully.

"That was the last one, you fucking idiot!" a male cried.

"Go get sa'more," a second man slurred.

"Why don't you? You dropped it."

By Victor's ankles, a row of small, square windows were covered by dark curtains. The interior light seeped underneath. He stooped down next to the nearest one.

"Would you clean that up?" That was a woman.

Victor rounded the corner. The backyard was meager and unkempt. Tall weeds poked out from under the picket fence. Patches of dead, brown grass made the ground look like a polka dot blanket. Two tires sat in the back corner. There was a staircase leading to a tiny porch with a metal awning. The light was off, cloaking his presence.

The window before the stairs was less concealed. A crack in the curtain from someone not closing it properly allowed him a peek inside. Victor stooped down to investigate. He barely contained his snarl at the sight.

The only heartbeats came from the two men sitting on a ratty couch in front of the television at the far end of the basement. One of them tossed pieces of pizza crust at a nearby cot—those old-school cots they used in kindergarten, with metal legs and polyester upholstery. These were well used and sagged in the middle. They didn't look like they could support a blanket, let alone a full-grown person.

On this cot, tucked in the corner by the couch, was a vampire. Silver chains bound his wrists and ankles to the corners. His skin was gray and lifeless—you know, corpse lifeless—and he wasn't moving. There were nasty gashes on his bare chest and arms, along with the pizza crust. Apparently, the asshole was aiming for the cuts. His wounds lay open and raw since the vamp was dehydrated.

One piece of crust bounced on the vamp's chest, rolled and then settled into a ditch just under his sternum. The man cheered at his accomplishment. Three points.

A wooden chair sat in the center of the room. It was ancient, but looked sturdy. Silver chains were wrapped loosely around the arms and legs, waiting for their next victim. Dried blood and black ash stained the seat of the chair, the arms of the chair, the back of the chair, and the floor around the chair.

In the left-hand corner, another cot was stationed next to the door. The male vamp on this one writhed weakly against his constraints. White smoke rose from his blistered skin. He only wore black jeans and his gashes matched those of the other male.

And across from him, just below Victor, Annie lay motionless. She was dressed only in her dark blue bra and lime-and-blue boy shorts. She was bound to a cot as well. Her hair was cropped badly. Uneven and pointy in sections, the longest pieces probably only stopped at her ears. Her eyes were closed—otherwise Victor was certain she would've seen him—and she wasn't breathing. She didn't have as many cuts as the others, though there were bruises on her inner thighs and biceps. Since they were still visible, whatever assault she'd received was fairly recent.

The sky opened with a strike of lightning that lit up the backyard. Oversized round raindrops started up a percussion beat on the metal awning over the stoop. They pelted Victor's head and shoulders.

The female human entered the space holding a dingy cream towel. She was still wearing the cami dress though she had black slippers on her feet. She tossed the towel at one of the men, who shouted in surprised anger.

"Clean up your mess."

He grumbled something then pulled himself from the couch. He stumbled on his own feet as he went to the spot where a beer bottle had dropped, spilling the amber liquid on the concrete floor. Slowly, trying to keep his balance, he knelt down. He wasn't really mopping up the mess, just sort of swishing it around, glass included.

Tilly had crossed her arms and watched him in annoyance. "I tell you the greatest news we've ever received and this is how you act."

He rolled his eyes. "We're cel'bratin'."

"Yeah," the other guy said, tossing another bit of crust. This one bounced off the vamp's forehead. "Gayle and Herb want us to come with them to Chicago. To talk to the Midwest Night Hawks. That's pretty fucking awesome!"

"Fuck right!"

She sighed as if she couldn't argue with that. She sauntered over to Annie. Victor could no longer see her face from his angle but he saw Annie flinch when she neared her. Annie never flinched from humans.

Tilly ran a finger down Annie's stomach to her navel.

Victor darted to the front. Bryce hadn't calmed at all in the short time he'd been gone. The rain was already soaking their hair and clothes. Thunder trembled around them. Victor looked from each of them, his stern expression confirming that this was the place. Ramsey delegated Bryce and Ashleigh to the front, he and Victor around back.

It only took half a minute for the dripping vamps to break through the doors and enter the basement. The room stunk of death. The stench clung to everything.

The three humans jumped in fright. Ashleigh was on top of the male on the couch in an instant.

The second man, still kneeling, lunged for the wooden chair, seemingly to grab the chains. Ramsey flashed in front of him and stomped his arm. The bone broke through the skin and the man screamed. Ramsey kicked him in the face.

Bryce jumped on the man's back, and flipped him around to pound his face. Tilly pulled a knife from a table and ran at

Ramsey. She jammed the blade into his shoulder. Ramsey grimaced. He reached around and caught her wrist, then yanked, sending her flying across the room. The knife was silver, making it hard to extract. Once he did, he flung it aside. The sharp end hit the wall. The bloodied knife vibrated from the sudden stop.

While the others were taking care of the humans, Victor rushed to Annie. She'd been watching the action with tired eyes. She didn't seem to be following.

Gritting through the pain, Victor removed the chains snaked around her wrists and ankles. The silver peeled off, taking scraps of skin and leaving deep, pink crevices. She didn't have enough blood to cause her wounds to bleed. She let out a small sigh of relief when the chains were gone and closed her eyes.

Victor untied the others as well, though he picked up the towel from the floor to untie the last vamp since it was handy and his fingers were blistered. When he looked back to the room, he saw Ashleigh continued to drink noisily from the man. The bumps on the curve of her spine were visible through her wet shirt. Tilly had sunk to the floor after Ramsey tossed her into the wall. She was unconscious.

Bryce was still punching the man. Bits of flesh and bone scattered the floor near the man's head. Bryce was silent now, which was scarier than when he had been grunting and snarling.

Ramsey pulled him off. "Bryce!" he commanded as he tugged him to his feet. Bryce got in a few kicks before Ramsey managed to drag him completely away. He grasped Bryce's chin so that he was looking at him and not at the fool on the ground with his face caved in. Ramsey's gaze was direct, collected.

"Enough. Now go to Annie."

Bryce looked around. His entire body limped at the sight of her lying weakly on the cot. If he could cry, tears would've streamed over his lashes. Kneeling down beside her, he took her hand in his. His other hand stroked her cheek, inadvertently smearing traces of Night Hawk remnants across her skin. Her eyes were shut but she nuzzled closer to his touch.

Ashleigh emitted an *ahh* sound when she finally released the man. He dropped to the couch. His heart beat weakly. Ashleigh's face, flushed a rosy pink, relaxed. A tiny giggle burbled from her mouth. She looked around at the others. Her giggles erupted in intervals. She threw her head back.

"I feel so . . . nice," she hissed through her blood-drenched fangs. Her hands caressed her neck, down to her breasts.

Victor sighed. He'd forgotten the man was drunk.

Aware of the other, stronger heartbeat in the room, Ashleigh's giggles ceased at once. Her head jerked to Tilly, her eyes focused on the vein pressing invitingly against the flesh of the downed hunter's throat. She jumped at her with a growl.

Victor went to Ramsey. "I have an idea."

Thirteen

L IFE CARRIED ON for the next three days. Victor stayed by Celia's side. They went to dinner, had sex in her kitchen, and watched TV. He informed her that they found Annie. She was relieved. She didn't ask after Tilly and her friends, which was best.

On the second night, they went to dinner at Papa Razzi on Dartmouth Street near Copley Square. After, they walked up Newbury Street—a road filled with posh shops and restaurants—to J.P. Licks. The line for the ice cream store curved out the door. They took their spot in front of the chipping, eccentric mural painted on the wall beside the store.

Victor held Celia's doggie bag. He placed a hand on her shoulder. She knew she'd been quiet. Jay's angry words still bugged her.

She was currently fiddling with the ruby ring. He took her hand and studied the ring.

"What is this?"

"It was my mother's. She wore it all the time." She shrugged. "I kind of stole it from my aunt."

Victor squeezed her hand. He was probably grateful it was gold and not silver, which would've burned his skin like her old ring.

Celia sighed and looked across the street at the passing pedestrians. She was thinking about stopping at Newbury Comics for used CDs on the way back to the car when her eyes landed on a pale face.

Milo leaned against the brick façade of the So Good jewelry store. His skinny jeans were dark gray, black Chucks donned his feet, and his short-sleeved shirt was a black-and-white checkered design. She saw that his left arm was shorter than the other; it had only grown back as far as the elbow.

He was chewing gum slowly. He'd been looking at her hand of all places. When she spotted him, his eyes came to hers.

Milo pursed his lips. His blue gum stretched out into a giant bubble. He held it a second before it burst.

Celia nudged Victor. She turned back with her hand out, pointing. The wall was bare.

"It was Milo. He was over there."

Victor was instantly alert. He scanned the street, his head turning quicker than humanly possible. He even sniffed the air.

"Come on," he said firmly. He held her hand tight in his as they hurried back to where her car was parked next to the church on Boylston Street. He took another look around before sitting behind the wheel.

Thursday night, Victor waited patiently while she paced the floor of her living room. She had removed the destroyed rug. The soles of her Nikes clicked on the hardwood floor.

"Is he going to be there?"

"Yes," Victor said. "Locked in his room."

Celia crossed to the window.

"We don't have to do this. You've been through a lot. And Corinna will take you to her coven."

"Yeah, next month. One of my problems is still out there right now."

Her mind was churning with the latest incidents. Cillian was taken care of as far as she could see but what about Milo? He had been right there. What if she had been alone? Or if the street wasn't so crowded? She hadn't noticed him until he let her become aware of him. How often had he done that?

If she could help rid the world of the nuisance, she wanted to do whatever she could.

Celia paused in the middle of the room and looked at him. A new purpose lifted her chin. "Let's go."

Victor pulled her close. "Ready?"

She took a deep breath and they teleported. Celia opened her eyes to the white living room. Ramsey and Elizabeth were both there. Elizabeth was rubbing his arm.

"Was it enough?" she asked Ramsey.

"Yes, love. Stop worrying. He's satisfied. We don't have to mention Arturo ever again."

The vamps glanced their way. At the sight of the Southern vamp, Celia told herself to be calm. There was nothing Ramsey could do or say to change what had happened. Without anger, anxious butterflies plagued her stomach.

"Hi," Celia squeaked. She was feeling sheepish now, being in the same room as the other vamps. Suddenly aware of what they were going to do. How intimate—

She swallowed hard.

"Are you okay?" Victor whispered. He rubbed her back, obviously sensing her nervousness.

She nodded.

"Yeah."

She nodded again, just to be sure.

"Yes."

Celia looked around at all those white surfaces. "Are we going to do it here?"

"No," Elizabeth said. She glided from the room, followed by Ramsey. Celia looked up to Victor. He gave her a reassuring smile. The warmth in his eyes helped to ease her nerves. A bit.

They trailed behind the vamps to the staircase. The house was very still.

"Is there anyone else here?" she whispered to Victor.

"Annie and Bryce are in their room," Ramsey answered from the top of the stairs. "Ashleigh and Cillian are to remain in their quarters. And these rooms are occupied. Don't worry; no one will disturb us."

She figured she should be comforted. Elizabeth and Ramsey went to a room at the end of the hall. Celia rounded the corner after them. It was another sitting room, with a forty-two inch plasma television mounted on the wall above the fireplace, a chocolate brown leather sofa, and an overstuffed red armchair in the corner. This room was a lot homier than the living room on the first floor. The walls were painted a warm, buff color and mocha curtains covered the windows.

The wings of Celia's butterflies didn't hurt as much once she stepped into the cozy room. Victor closed the door behind them. Celia clasped his hand tightly when he returned to her side.

They sat on the sofa. Ramsey settled into the chair, Elizabeth perched on the arm. She smiled at Celia, trying to soothe her. She felt so awkward. Sharing blood had become a part of her and Victor's most intimate moments together. Opening that up to not just one, but two other people was very strange, indeed.

"Have you guys, um, ever done this before?"

"No," Elizabeth said. "This is a first for all of us."

"Well, as an experiment, anyway," Ramsey chipped in,

amused. "You know, where we're tryna find some answers and whatnot."

Celia decided not to touch on that. "So, uh, what do we do?"

Elizabeth and Ramsey exchanged nods. Elizabeth stood, crossed around the oak coffee table, and sat on Celia's other side. She wore high waist gray pants with flared bottoms and a mint green sleeveless top that fluttered when she moved. Her hair was bone straight with a green flower at her temple. Celia liked the wooden necklace that draped down to her stomach.

Elizabeth took her hand in hers. Her skin was chilly but the gentleness with which she handled her was pleasant. A shiver ran up Celia's arm, making the little hairs stand on end.

Elizabeth reached over and gently brushed Celia's hair from her neck. Her thumb massaged the spot under her jawline. Her touch made her relax, her muscles turning to goo, which was unexpected. She'd never been turned on by a female before.

Elizabeth smiled a little. "Let me know if you want to stop."

"Bananas," Celia said. It was the first word to pop in her head.

Elizabeth looked confused. She peeked over to Victor for explanation. He was just as clueless.

"That'll be my safe word," Celia explained. "When I want to stop," she further explained when they still stared at her.

"Oh!" Elizabeth said with a giggle.

She was still chuckling when she leaned in close. Her breath tickled Celia's neck. She smelled like a green apple. Elizabeth placed a hand on her back; the other moved her shoulder aside so that it was no longer poking her breast. The sting of her fangs made Celia clench Victor's hand harder. He squeezed back.

The pain from her bite quickly subsided, replaced by that pleasurable pulling. Elizabeth stroked her neck then ran her hand through her hair, caressing her scalp. Celia's eyes closed. A sigh of pleasure vibrated in her throat as she tightly gripped the firm muscles of Elizabeth's upper thigh. She couldn't help it. Those spastic shivers were starting in her lower back.

Elizabeth's grip tightened, starting a minor flare of concern somewhere beneath the yearning for her to keep going. Victor growled low beside her. Through their bond, Celia received a rush of emotion from him. He didn't like the vampire being so close. Faintly, so that she wasn't even sure she heard it, the single word "mine" whispered in her head.

Elizabeth must have taken his growl as a cue, because she pulled away after cleaning her wound. She hid her face by letting her hair fall forward. Celia saw the voracious, predatory hunger before she could fully conceal it.

"Wow," Elizabeth whispered, after she regained her composure. She looked over at Victor. There was a twinkle in her eyes, like she had just been let in on some big secret. She also seemed embarrassed by her loss of control since she wasn't meeting Celia's eye.

Celia touched her neck lightly. Two small bumps met her fingers. She was wondering whether Victor had ever had such a strong reaction to her blood. She couldn't recall.

Ramsey leaned forward and handed Elizabeth a pocketknife. She snapped it open and ran the blade along her inner wrist. She held it out to Celia, who distractedly brought her bleeding arm to her mouth.

Elizabeth's blood was a lot cooler than Victor and Milo's, which she thought was strange. Then again, what did she know about what vamp blood was supposed to taste like? She was not a connoisseur. Whatever the case, Elizabeth's blood ran slightly cooler than room temperature.

Celia leaned back into the smooth cushions of the sofa. Tiny bursts of light appeared before her eyes. She closed her lids on the sunbursts as she allowed the effects to settle in. Ramsey chuckled from his seat across the room, and she almost giggled, too. She felt light, light as air as all of her worries faded away. Milo; Cillian; the two men at Shawmut Station; Jay. They all floated away like wisps of smoke.

Suddenly, she was no longer looking at the inside of her lids. Instead, she saw Ramsey. Only he wasn't in the room. It was nighttime and the ground was wet from a recent shower. He was leaning against an old-fashioned iron lamppost. The golden glow glittered in his sandy-brown hair.

Celia looked down at the dark cobblestone street beneath her feet. She could feel her cheeks blushing. A single red rose was in her hands, the thick stem cool against her fingers. A swell of love filled her chest.

"Hey."

She peeked up. Ramsey was watching her, looking at her through his lashes. He grinned.

Not at her. Elizabeth.

"Oh," Celia breathed. She opened her eyes, blinked a few times. The vision faded away and she was back in the room. Elizabeth tilted her head to the side curiously.

"Did you see something?" Victor asked.

She described the scene. Ramsey and Elizabeth both went still. They managed to exchange stares that Celia couldn't decipher.

"Interesting," Elizabeth replied after a moment. "Victor. Think of something. Let's see if she can see it."

Victor nodded. He turned his gaze on Celia. Celia closed her eyes and concentrated. She got another flash from Elizabeth's head—the same scene as earlier, only this time Ramsey was holding her hand as they walked along the street. She felt the smoothness of his skin against her own palm. The sweet aroma of chocolate and pastries floated on the night air. A stranger's voice crooning in French followed behind them.

Elizabeth must've still been amazed, still thinking about the early days of their courtship.

Celia pushed that aside. She squeezed her eyes as she strained to reach out to Victor. She was still getting blackness. Elizabeth's memories were faint, just below the surface. She was about to give up when there was a flicker of something.

She focused on it, like a beacon through the darkness. She ignored Elizabeth and headed for that light. The picture slowly came into focus. He was remembering when they had first met. Celia's hair had been so short then; she could barely get it into a ponytail. In the vision, she smiled sheepishly at Victor, who held out a lighter for the cigarette she gripped between her fingers. Her nose and cheeks were bright pink from the cold.

Celia blew out a breath she didn't know she was holding. She felt dizzy.

"Are you okay?" Victor asked immediately.

She nodded. "Ugh, I can't believe I used to smoke."

Victor grinned. He looked at Elizabeth, silently informing her that Celia had seen into his head. She was exhausted, too exhausted to tell them how draining that had been. She leaned back in the seat, concentrating on breathing to ease the dizziness.

The vampires waited out the full twenty minutes it took. Of course, they were used to waiting, time being limitless for them and all.

When she looked around the room, she found three sets of eyes on her. Staring. Unblinking.

Creepy.

Celia sat up in the chair with a groan. The making of a headache was forming just behind her eyes. A wave of nausea hit her belly. But she had already agreed to go through with this. She needed to find out if she could help. She needed to find out if she had an ability.

Secretly, it was exciting. What if she did possess an ability? How fucking cool would that be?

Celia looked at Ramsey, gave him a determined nod. Elizabeth stood, and Ramsey replaced her. He rubbed her knee gently. They really were trying to put her at ease, which she appreciated. She did have to admit that she wasn't as nervous anymore. Elizabeth had broken the ice by going first. Celia wasn't sure she would've been able to go through with it if the muscly, handsome Ramsey had initiated this experiment.

He nuzzled her neck where Elizabeth's wound was nearly erased. His stubble prickled her skin. His scent reminded her of the beach. She suddenly remembered the feel of his magic, how warm and tingly it had been under his control. A smile tugged at her lips and she moaned. Where had that come from? She just felt so good at the moment that it had slipped out. Then she realized that Ramsey was drinking from her. He was pulling her into him, into his sun-drenched ocean.

His bite hadn't registered. She wondered if it hadn't been her recollection, if he had actually enthralled her. She didn't care enough to worry, too caught up in the moment.

When Ramsey pulled away, she found she was a twinge wistful. Ramsey smirked. Maybe he'd seen it in her face. He held his wrist out for her, bleeding and ready. His blood was rich, almost spicy.

When she finished, Celia was swimming. The high from the blood was making her lightheaded now. Her eyes landed on her hands that rested on her knees. The ruby seemed to blaze brightly. She didn't need to concentrate. She could see herself through Ramsey's eyes, sitting on the sofa in her jeans and Celtics' hoodie. Then she had a flash of Ramsey's nest, all scattered around the white room. They were looking at her (Ramsey), presumably waiting for instruction.

Next, she was watching television with Elizabeth tucked beside her. Her summery perfume teased her nose. Victor appeared out of thin air. Before he could speak, the vision changed. She was in bed with Elizabeth. Her skin was silky like polished mahogany from feeding and making love. She reached over. Her fingers grazed Celia's temple.

The vision melted into a new one. She stood over a hospital bed. Machines beeped and churned around the room. Shiny balloons and brightly-colored bouquets cluttered the windowsill beside the bed. The roses were particularly new. Their scent was a bit unbearable for her sensitive nose.

The vertical blinds were open, giving a full view of the crescent moon outside. Her hand stretched out and took hold of the young boy's wrist. This step was just for show since his pulse thumped clearly in her ears. The boy looked up at her. His round face was sad, full of pain. She caressed his cheek. The gesture seemed to soothe him.

Like a flick of a channel, Celia saw herself in her bedroom. She was getting dressed for Ramsey's party a week ago. She had just zipped up her dress and peeked over her shoulder, giving herself (Victor) a pretty smile.

The visions came faster. They overlapped until she could no longer tell them apart. The sounds, the colors, the smells shrouded her and she couldn't think. She clapped her hands against her temples, shaking her head hard. She knew it wouldn't do anything, and she was right.

"Gah!"

She jumped up from the sofa.

"Seal?"

Celia rushed from the room and down the stairs. Her feet missed a couple of the stairs when the flashes blinded her to what was currently around her. She had just made it to the door when Victor appeared in front of her. He held a hand out to stop her. He didn't want her to go outside, to see where she was.

She shook her head. She could barely see anything real, only the memories bombarding her. Her eyes were narrowed into a squint. That didn't clear the visions.

The ruby of her mother's ring pulsed like a heart. It warmed the skin of her finger. She stumbled into the living room. She sensed Victor following.

"Just . . . stay there, okay? I need . . . a second."

She crouched in the corner beside the bar, as far away as she could get. With a lot of deep breathing, she was able to push them out of the forefront of her mind. She had to relax her body in order to calm her mind and take somewhat control. The idea came from some magazine article on meditation, she was certain. The ring cooled as well. The vamps were still there, though they were only buzzing in the background. One of the flashes was of her, crouched in the corner, looking like a fool.

She sighed. "It's okay, I think. You can come in."

Victor's cool fingers touched her arm. "What's going on?"

"Overload."

"You all should go back upstairs," he said. Of course she couldn't hear the other vamps. Her eyes were closed but she sensed them moving away, giving her space.

"Seal?"

"What's wrong with me?"

"I don't know."

Well, that was reassuring.

"Can . . . can you take me home? Please?"

Victor's hand tightened around her bicep. She held her breath in anticipation of the icy tidal wave. Before that happened—perhaps she had relaxed too much—a barrier broke. All of their memories returned in full force. This was worse. The sounds and faces and smells churned her stomach. Her teeth clenched together. Her hand was on fire beneath the ring. She bent forward and put her head between her knees.

Suddenly, all was silent. Darkness slammed into her as if it had weight. Her nausea eased up and the ruby was no longer ablaze. She took a few deep breaths to make sure she was okay. The abrupt change was strange. Celia opened her eyes slowly.

She was in a bedroom now. The lights were dim, warm. The cream-colored curtains on the windows were drawn. White candles flickered from strategic places around the room. A silky, soft duvet covered the queen-sized bed. It was white with golden petals. The material was nice against her skin. That's when she realized she only wore her panties.

Celia frowned, confused. She didn't remember leaving Ramsey's. She certainly didn't remember taking off her clothes. The even stranger thing: she didn't mind being naked. And when she looked to her right and saw Victor nude beside her, instead of asking what was going on, she simply smiled.

He stroked her cheek with cool fingers, kissed her jaw with chilly lips. Her eyes closed as he traced the tip of his tongue along her neck. A trail of goose bumps followed. Someone else's mouth was on hers. She opened her eyes. Elizabeth sat back with a lovely smile. Her firm breasts were like teardrops, her nipples a darker shade than her own. Black lace lined the hem of her silver panties.

Elizabeth ran a hand down Celia's arm until she held her wrist. Her skin was just as icy, and she shivered. Victor's teeth pierced her neck. She gasped. Elizabeth brought her arm to her mouth and bit.

Ramsey was there, standing beside the bed in his entire splendor. A soft, blonde down crossed his chest, making a path downward. He pointed to her without his hands. His demanding, fervent gaze elicited a curl of lust just below her navel. She wanted him. Her return look asked why he was waiting.

Victor leaned back. He removed his hand from her breast and laid her down on the mattress. He trailed gentle kisses down her stomach, past her navel. His hands grasped her panties. The cotton material ripped like paper and he tossed them onto the floor.

His mouth was on her, sucking warmth from within as if her center, too, were a life source. Her knees were on his shoulders, her toes curling tightly. Her back arched up from the duvet. Elizabeth squeezed both of her breasts, her hands burning now thanks to Celia. Ramsey coaxed Celia's warm mouth open and slid inside.

She didn't need to see them to know where they were in the room but every time she opened her eyes a different vamp hovered above her. Elizabeth: nuzzling her neck, tickling her side. Ramsey: staring up at her from between her legs, his mouth on her thigh, drinking from the major artery. Victor: on top, thrusting deeply inside her. Elizabeth between them. Ramsey behind her.

They were everywhere, inside her and out. The four of them, their moans and cries of pleasure mingled into one sound. Celia's saccharine blood stained the white duvet, the cream-colored sheets beneath, and the skin of her partners. The vampires throbbed and pulsed around her until she could hardly see their features at all. She only felt their bodies, her rhythm magnified in them until she tingled with their scorching heat.

Her heat.

She did this. She was the source. Their searching fingers were in her hair, on her skin, between her thighs. Rubbing, stroking, flicking. Celia fell back against the down pillows, biting into her lower lip to contain the primal cries vying to escape her.

Just when she thought she might literally explode her eyes sprang open for the last time.

The dark ceiling was above her. Only a few of the stars held the faintest glow. The fridge hummed from the kitchen. She was still in her jeans and hoodie. Her heart thudded in her chest at half speed.

A page turned. Victor touched her thigh. From the corner of

her eye, she saw he was reading. He must've noticed she had stirred.

"You gave me quite the scare," he said softly. "Are you okay now?"

"I think so."

She rolled until she was on her side, her back to him, her hands tucked under her cheek. It had been a dream. A very, very vivid dream, but a dream all the same. She should've been relieved. Instead, embarrassment heated her neck. Could the vamps tell what her mind had played out for her, what she had felt?

Victor was quiet beside her. She could still feel the three of them inside her head, though she didn't receive any visions. At the moment, they weren't an overload like before. They were more of a low hum—like the sound of the refrigerator in the next room.

"What happened?" she finally asked, when she could take the quiet no longer.

"You kept saying 'bananas' over and over again. Bryce asked if you wanted ice cream. You climbed right into bed and fell asleep."

She breathed a small sigh. Unless he was holding out on her, at least she hadn't humiliated herself.

Her thumb moved to touch the ring and she found it was missing. She looked at her hand. "My ring," she gasped in surprise.

"Yes, you said it was burning you and for me to get it off. Elizabeth thinks it's enchanted. It wasn't hot to me but it was definitely glowing." So that hadn't been her imagination. "It's in your jewelry box."

Victor slid behind her and cupped his arm around her chest. "I have to go," he whispered in her ear. "I love you."

She nodded. Her brow was still furrowed when she felt him

disappear.

Celia awoke to glorious silence. Oh, she could hear the cars whizzing down the street, and the birds singing, and the clock ticking in the kitchen, and her neighbor moving around in his apartment next door. But she was alone in her head.

She had slept through the night without any visits from the two men. She didn't feel exhausted. She wasn't on the verge of crying.

The vampire blood made her feel light on her feet. She floated rather than walked over to her dresser, unaware that her feet were moving. She slowly opened her black jewelry box that sat beside her makeup case. It used to belong to her mother. She never realized she had inherited all of her mother's jewelry except the ring.

Celia gazed down on it in the center of the box. There was no glow. She picked it up. It wasn't warm to the touch. What was that all about? And why did her mother have an enchanted ring? She recalled again her mother's captivation when she asked from where it came.

She decided to leave it in the box for now, where it would be safe.

On the way to the door, she paused at her closet. When she looked at herself in the mirror, she had to do a double take.

Her skin was radiant, her hair was silky and shiny, and her eyes were bright and cheerful. She was . . . stunning!

Celia gaped at her reflection for a full minute. Not in a narcissistic way, not at all. She was actually quite horrified. Her very sudden, very overwhelming attractiveness didn't appear to be the result of a facial or new makeup. Not even a good night's sleep. She seemed to be quite literally glowing. She would definitely attract some stares.

Grumbling to herself, Celia picked out an outfit. After showering and dressing, she brushed her hair back into a low ponytail. She had hoped the low-key style would detract a little from the glow.

She was wrong.

"Whoa, Celia," Rick replied with a whistle. Celia gritted her teeth as she passed him at the front door. She ducked her head on the way to Bobby's office.

"Celia, we're low on pinot . . ." Bobby's voice trailed off so she had to look up. He stared at her, his mouth open, the unvoiced words stuck somewhere in his throat.

"Low on pinot," Celia said hurriedly. "I'll keep that in mind." She'd have to check for herself if he meant pinot noir or pinot grigio.

She quickly stowed her purse and clocked in before heading to the kitchen. Of course everyone was huddled there. She stopped short just inside the doorway. The door swung back and hit her ass. All four of the servers on duty this morning glanced her way and froze. Even the chefs looked up, as if she had rung a bell upon entering.

Celia managed a weak smile before retrieving an apron from the pantry. She wrapped it around her waist as she approached the prep table where the specials were laid out for the servers to examine. Tina stared at her in open astonishment.

"Did you . . ." she began. "Did . . . Wow."

"What did you do?" Maria asked from her other side.

"Oh, well, you know . . ." Celia rubbed her cheek. Two of the guys perked even more. One of them looked very much like he wanted to reach out to touch her. "It's this new face cream. From Malaysia. It exfoliates and cleanses and, um, tones and stuff."

"I want some!" Tina chirped.

"Not that you don't usually look beautiful," Maria added quickly. "It's just . . ." She trailed off when her jaw hung open.

Celia made her smile as sincere as possible. "Well, thanks, guys. I guess I'll have to buy stock in the stuff."

Thankfully, Bobby and Silvio entered the kitchen—she didn't have any more creative verbs in her repertoire. Bobby began the morning meeting, his eyes always coming back to Celia as if she were the only one there. Even sourpuss Silvio stared nakedly.

Once the lunch crowd filed in, her day took a smoother route. Her customers drooled whenever she came around. The attention made her uncomfortable but the upshot was huge tips. She couldn't feel too bad about that.

She crossed paths with Michael when she was clocking out a little after four. He was the only one not impressed by her glowing state. Instead, he looked furious. She knew what he was thinking, and she hoped he choked on it.

Victor smiled when he saw her that night. "Look at you."

"Shut up," she grumbled. "I've been stared at all day. It's not a nice feeling."

"People stare at you all the time," he said, quite seriously. "You're very beautiful."

She rolled her eyes, though the compliment was pleasant. "If it's all the same to you, I'd like to stay in tonight."

That smoldering look took over his expression. "That's just fine with me."

He started to kiss her, and she was beginning to relax into it. Just then, the hum of Elizabeth and Ramsey started up in the back of her head, depleting any sexy feelings that may have been aroused. They were discussing their plans for the night. It appeared Elizabeth wanted to go dancing on her night off.

Celia groaned. She stopped Victor from completely unbuttoning her shirt. "I can't do this. There are too many people in my head."

There was such a mixture of emotions going on inside her that she couldn't even decipher her own.

Victor tried kissing her cheek. She had to step away.

"Sorry, but it ain't gonna happen, bub."

She felt guilty—his eyes were jet black. She hurried to the bathroom to shower. The three of them stayed with her. She noted the three-day timeframe for vamp blood to leave the system. Two more days, she told herself. Two more fucking days.

Apparently, Ramsey was feeling a little frisky before heading out. Celia received the passion from both sides. She took a seat on the edge of the tub for a moment, as flashes of them undressing each other made it seem as if she was in the room with them. She recalled her vision or dream or whatever it was and shivered in unexpected pleasure.

She wished she had control over this. Most times, Victor was low in the back of her brain. A comforting shadow. But sometimes, like right now, it was as if she had turned up the volume. That was when the flashes occurred.

"Brown eyes?" she heard Ramsey say. "Is that you?"

Celia groaned. Ramsey's chuckle sounded in her ear. After a minute, however, the flashes stopped. She could still feel their lust for each other, making her own body temp rise, but they had ceased their fooling around. Elizabeth's decision, she was sure. Another few minutes and their presence died away to the background. Celia felt kind of bad. She hadn't meant to interrupt them.

Back in the living room, she and Victor sat on the sofa together. Celia concentrated on Milo. She tried really hard for forty minutes, alternating positions throughout the room.

"Ugh!" she exclaimed at last. She plopped back next to Victor on the sofa. "It's not working. I only see the three of you."

Victor stroked her hand. "It's okay. Don't think about him anymore."

"Then what was the point in all of this?" she groaned. She threw her hands in the air. "Do I really have to have his blood for the stupid fucking connection to work?"

"I don't know, Seal. We'll figure it out, okay? Don't worry."

"And that's another thing. I'm not worried."

He paused. "What do you mean?"

She rubbed her cheeks. "I've been dreaming about those two men for days but today . . . I've barely thought about them. What's wrong with me? How can I be so . . ." She shook her head as she thought of a word. "Cold. How can I be so fucking cold?"

"It must be a side effect of the blood. Most humans are ecstatic. It's euphoric."

"I'm not most humans," she grumped.

"True. There is something special about you and it must be reacting with the blood."

"Something special that makes me a heartless bitch?"

"Would you stop that?" he demanded. His eyes flashed angrily. "You're just at ease at the moment."

"But I don't want to be at ease if that's the cost. I want to remember them. I have to." His blank expression told her he didn't understand. "I'm the only one who saw what really happened to them," she explained. "Someone has to be responsible for that!"

"Cillian is responsible."

"Yeah, and he's so remorseful."

"Maybe not but that has to do with his age. Remorse and culpability don't always go hand-in-hand, Seal. Cillian is responsible. And by extension, so is Ramsey. He's stepped up to take on that burden. Allow him to do so."

She covered her face with her hands. That logic just didn't sit right with her. She knew Victor felt bad about deaths at his own hands. He always took responsibility. He also didn't let his remorse hinder his actions. It was the way of existing as a vampire. Yes, guilt tied one to their humanity but who could live off the blood of others for an eternity with such a burden? Even she had been able to forgive his slip-ups.

This time it was a little too personal.

She repeated the men's names in her head. She was able to see their faces, before Cillian arrived. When they were only filled with concern rather than terror. A small lump formed in her throat. When she noticed the lump, the men's faces disappeared, along with the feeling of remorse.

Before she went to bed, Celia printed out the article about LaShawn Jackson and Miles Lubin. She taped it next to the mirror on the wall above her dresser. She scanned it a few times once it was in place. Each time, the small piece of sadness returned. She held on to it until it swooped down beneath the cloud of the vampire blood, vanishing again.

***

On Friday, Victor met Celia after work, watched her dance around the living room in her underwear when her favorite song played over the radio, before lying with her under the sheets. She was drifting off since it was four in the morning. He held her right hand. She hadn't worn the ruby ring since the night at Ramsey's. Elizabeth was supposed to be asking around. Ramsey had . . . some knowledge of enchanted objects.

"Someone cast a spell on it," he said simply when Victor called that next night after their experiment.

"What kind of spell?"

"Hell if I know, buddy."

Victor wondered why she wasn't wearing it anymore. It had been a part of her mother. Ramsey didn't know of any connections Celia or her mother Daphne would have to the witchcraft world.

He ran his finger over the space it used to occupy. Celia had worn a silver one for a long time. It had a thin band with a tiny leaf and acorn. She put it away when Victor revealed what he was. He had been extremely relieved since she used to use that particular hand to hold his all the time. He'd have to adjust frequently—switching hands, putting his arm around her shoulder or waist—anything to avoid the burning flesh smell.

You could only imagine what happened when that hand roamed inside his boxer briefs. There was pleasurable pain and then there was painful pain.

"What do you do when you're not with me?" she asked suddenly. He had thought she was off in La-La land.

"Stuff," he answered.

Celia was quiet a moment and he waited to see if she was asleep. "Stuff?" she asked. "Stuff like what?"

"Okay, I wait in the dark living room until you come home, counting the seconds until I can see you again." She wasn't too sleepy to know he was joking.

"Ass," she muttered into his chest. She yawned. "I just can't imagine what vampires do when people are mostly sleeping."

"Well, Elizabeth works at Beth Israel."

He felt her eyebrows pull up. How she could breathe with her face buried in his side like that was a wonder. She must've been enjoying his scent.

"Really?" she asked. "Isn't that too much temptation?"

Victor shrugged. "She's had a long time to get it together. Although, I think her biggest hurdle is not giving her blood to save people. She believes in the power of medicine."

"And it would cause too much attention if she was healing people like that."

"True."

"How long has she been doing this?"

He chuckled. He was surprised she was able to keep up a conversation in her state. She probably wouldn't remember it all tomorrow.

"A hundred and ninety or so years."

"Hmm. Has she been with Ramsey all that time?"

"Pretty much. Her daughter had just turned six when she was taken from her and sold to a family in Tennessee for fifty dollars and two cows. Elizabeth was living in North Carolina then. That's where she had been sold when she turned ten.

"Two months after her daughter was sold, Elizabeth ran away to find her. Two men captured her before she could leave the state. She feared they were going to take her back. She would've faced working in the fields as punishment. Instead of sending her back, they turned her. She became their slave; that was all she knew. They treated her terribly. She might've been better off in the fields."

Celia's head turned, and he saw her brown eyes looking up at him sleepily. She was too stunned to speak.

"Bored with the choosing in North Carolina," Victor continued, "they moved on to Georgia. Ramsey came across them about two years after she was changed. They were terrorizing a home and drawing too much attention. He killed the vamps, and was about to stake Elizabeth. There was something that stopped him, though. He saw how damaged she was. It took a lot of coaxing for her to trust him. After all, he looked like her captors. But she did go with him. What else could she do? All her life, she was told what to do, what to wear, what to think.

"I believe it wasn't until Ramsey showed Elizabeth her daughter, when she saw that she was alive and learning to write and to read and being treated well, that was the last barrier.

"Elizabeth was happy for the stability of Ramsey. She had freedom and companionship. She's the only one to stay with him unconditionally even though he is not her sire. Mostly we drift off on our own after a while, sometimes coming back, sometimes starting our own nests." And because he figured this was the actual reason she had asked, he added, "They've been a couple for twenty years."

Celia made a sound that seemed agreeable. "What does

Ramsey do while she's working?"

"Ramsey watches a lot of television. And when he's not, he's out watching people. He likes to keep up with the times."

"That's in—"

He never heard the rest of that statement. "Celia," he whispered. She snuggled closer. Her warmth seeped into him. It had been three nights since last he'd tasted her but his body still felt alive. There were no injuries this week to sap her magic from his system; he was able to hold on to it.

Her pulse thumped at his ear, in his chest. He drew her nearer. Inhaling her bewitching perfume, he wished he could lie like this for eternity.

Ramsey's house was quiet when Victor appeared in the front hallway. He went upstairs where they had been holding them behind the two doors at the top of the landing. He knocked lightly before pushing open the first door. Ramsey stood over the bed, arms folded at the chest.

Tilly's pale body lay across the bed. Her peach cami was twisted and wrinkled from her writhing around on the bed. The hem had ridden up over her navel, revealing her black thong. Her left breast pointed to the ceiling from the top of the dress. Her head moved from side to side, like she was having a bad dream.

"Wake up," Ramsey commanded. Her eyes sprang open. They rolled around until they landed on Ramsey and Victor. This was the first time she was seeing with her new eyes. She seemed both amazed and frightened. Though a human's sight was much sharper when they ingested vampire blood, it was no match to actual vampire sight. She would be able to see everything in crystal clear, 1080i high-definition. She would be able to hear cars moving on the main road and smell the barbeque chicken Ramsey's neighbor was baking for supper.

She'd feel the air, the liveliness of everything around her. Her first rain shower would be heavenly as the earth swelled in welcome and she witnessed each drop fall from the sky.

"What's going on?" she asked. Her voice was raspy from non-use. Or perhaps from all the screaming she'd done the night before during the final stage.

Ramsey didn't answer her question. Instead, he glanced down at his watch and saw that it was after five.

"Up," he said.

Tilly moved cautiously, swinging her legs over the edge. She didn't want to get up but she was compelled to obey. She pulled herself into a sitting position, and then stood on wobbly feet. Clutching her forehead, she blinked at Ramsey through her shaggy hair.

"Who are you? What's going on?" Her memory was still a little groggy because of the change. It would take a couple days for her to sort through what was real. Then she would remember her family, her friends. Her life.

"Come with me. All will be explained momentarily."

He took hold of Tilly's elbow and led her out the room. As they stepped into the hallway, Bryce shoved the other hunter from his room. Bryce grinned excitedly. The hunter's expression was blank. His slumped shoulders were the only indication of his gloomy mood.

The five of them went downstairs to the kitchen where Elizabeth and Annie waited. Annie sat at the table, drinking from a tall cup. Her new hair was frizzy, casting a wild halo around her head. Her skin clung to her bones, her face gaunt. The gray sweater she wore seemed too big for her body and was buttoned to her neck.

She struggled as she stood. Bryce was at her side in an instant, taking her arm in support. Elizabeth held her hands out, too.

Tilly hesitated after catching sight of Annie. Her gaze immediately fell to the floor when Annie looked at her. She twisted her fingers in front of her, giving away her guilt.

So, her memory wasn't *too* foggy.

The group went through the door to the garage. Ramsey, Victor, Elizabeth and the two hunters slid into the red car. Bryce and Annie were in his Camaro. Ramsey seemed pleased that Bryce had his own car so he didn't have to share his convertible. He needed to stay close to the hunters, just in case.

The two cars were off. Tilly peered out the window from her spot in the middle of the backseat. They were zooming down the expressway, heading north.

"I feel weird," she said. "What happened to me?"

None of them answered. The other hunter was trembling now. He kept his eyes on the back of the seat in front of him.

"Where are we going?" Tilly asked. She smacked her lips a few times. "I'm thirsty. Can we make a stop?"

Ramsey drove over the bridge into Cambridge. She looked down on the choppy, gray water below. Her eyes went to Victor sitting beside her. The spell had been lifted with the change. When the vampires burst into their playpen, they all had a slight luminescence that made them seem flawless. Now, she could see the creases at the corners of his gray eyes, the laugh lines at his mouth. There was a round scar on his temple from when he was accidentally hit by a driving bit when one of his family's horses reared suddenly. He had been hitching them to the carriage to deliver his mother's blankets to their town.

Victor saw her from the corner of his eye. She lifted her hand, examining her own skin. She touched the spot in the center of her wrist.

"I . . ." She shook her head. "There was a sore here. From a . . . bite."

She quickly held both arms out, inspecting, searching for more missing wounds. She even looked to her companion.

Ramsey pulled up to the curb on 5th Street. The hunters

cautiously followed the vamps out onto the sidewalk. Tilly stared up at the building.

"My house," she said. She looked from each of them for explanation. Victor stared right back at her. She glanced away from his severe expression.

Ramsey went up the stairs first. The door was still broken. Well, shattered to pieces to be more precise. He stepped over planks and entered the foyer. The house was in shambles. Thieves had taken whatever of value that wasn't nailed down, leaving a mess behind.

Tilly's hand flew to her mouth as she surveyed the wreckage. She was too choked up to utter anything more than strangled gasps. As they came to the living room, she stooped down in the threshold to pick up a broken piece of porcelain. It used to be one of those commemorative plates—this one for the state of Mississippi. The piece of plate she held displayed the bottom half of the state.

"I never did sign the lease after my aunt died," she muttered in a bit of a daze.

Ramsey and the others continued on to a door at the end of the hall. He threw Tilly a stern look. She hadn't made eye contact with him but she placed the plate on the floor and went to him. His command was that strong.

They descended into the basement. A sickly odor greeted them. The bottom level had been left pretty much intact. The only thing missing was the television. Made you wonder what the vandals thought when they saw the little torture chamber. The slowly decaying body in the middle of the floor didn't seem to serve as a deterrent.

Tilly looked around at the place but her expression was unreadable. Only Ramsey knew that a tremor of fear was working its way up her spine, since he'd been the one to give her blood. He'd broken his own rule so that no one else would, even though

Bryce had offered enthusiastically. As a maker, he had control over Tilly and her buddy.

That fear must've ratcheted up a notch because Ramsey bounded over to Tilly just as she turned to sprint from the room. Towering over her, he gripped her shoulder so hard that she cried out. Victor stepped up to Tilly as well.

At the same time, Bryce shoved the male hunter—Kyle or Leo, who knew. He staggered forward. He didn't look at his dead companion or the flies buzzing noisily around his crushed skull. Bryce kept pushing him until he fell onto the cot on which Annie had been strapped. Elizabeth handed Bryce a pair of leather gloves. Kyle/Leo didn't fight as they bound his wrists and ankles. Like that Night Hawk had said: all you needed to do was lay the silver on their skin and the vamps would be incapacitated. A low hiss did escape his lips when the silver sank into his skin with a sizzle loud enough to rival thick-cut bacon. His fangs pressed into his bottom lip. Blood dribbled toward his chin.

Tilly's eyes widened as she watched this. Then she really tried to bolt out the room. She was unsuccessful; Ramsey still had her shoulder. She pushed him, scratched at him, even screamed for help. The main reason for the Night Hawks using her basement for their games was the soundproof quality of her sublevel.

Victor took her other arm. They lifted and carried her to the wooden chair as her legs kicked out. Her fangs slid down, momentarily stunning her with their appearance. She screeched some more and tried to bite Victor's hand. Since she already had gloves on, Elizabeth tied the silver chains. She added one around her neck for good measure.

Tilly's pained shrieks were deafening. Victor snatched up the old towel and shoved a good amount into her mouth, shutting her up. It smelled sour, and it probably tasted worse. Her eyes darted around the room, no longer hiding her terror.

Bryce stood on furniture, or whatever was near, to open the curtains on the side and back wall. That way, no one walking down the street could see inside the windows. He took up a space between Ramsey and Victor in front of Tilly.

The vampire leader folded his arms. "My name is Ramsey," he said evenly. "This is my family." He indicated the rest with a tilt of his head. "You'd been holding Annie captive for over a week."

Annie's eyes narrowed from her spot near the door. She hadn't stepped far into the room. She had one arm crossed in front of her, clasping her other elbow as if shielding herself from an upcoming assault.

"Victor and Bryce had suggested giving you a taste of your own medicine. To let you see what it's like to be abused and tormented. In your new state, you would heal and we could do it all over again. What am I saying?" He chuckled lightly. "You are well aware of that. Nonetheless, I turned them down. We won't stoop that far to your level."

He glanced to one of the windows. A tiny sparrow hopped past in search of food. "We don't have much time," Ramsey went on. "Your little activities have alerted us to things going on right beneath our noses. I thank you for that. And thought we'd return this favor."

Tilly's muffled cries followed them out the room.

"You watching *24* this season?" Bryce asked Victor. He was walking on a cloud. "I missed a lot of it last season but Ramsey has the DVDs. I love DVDs. And have you heard of the newest things, Blu-rays? They're pretty friggin' awesome."

The sky had turned a light shade of gray. Large, puffy clouds moved slowly in the light breeze. As they strolled down the stairs outside, Victor checked his watch. "It's supposed to be sunny skies today," he commented.

"The sun comes through," Annie muttered, her first words

since coming home. The vamps faced her. "Believe me."

Her expression was stormy. She was still weak, shuffling more than walking. "They cut us, kept us awake. Did other things." She paused. "They brought other vampires. They'd cut them and stake them in front of us. Sometimes they'd cut themselves and taunt us with it."

She shook her head. "I don't know why they held on to us. After a few days, the one in the corner started screaming for them to end it. They just laughed. What happened to the others?" she asked. Her words had been directed to the street.

"One didn't make it," Ramsey answered, referring to the screamer. "The other's named Charlie. He'll live but it'll take some time."

"I felt your call," Annie said to Ramsey. "But, I don't know, I just couldn't respond. I knew they were tracking me, when I was leaving Maine. I didn't want to lead them to the mansion. They got me near Lynn." Ramsey nodded tenderly. Annie clammed up after that. Bryce helped her to the car.

"You best get home," Ramsey told Victor. "Thank you for your help."

"And thank your Celia," Bryce added as he approached. "Give her a nice pounding from the both of us." He smiled and slapped Victor on the back. It was great to see him back in brighter spirits, even if he probably just left a handprint on Victor's spine.

The vampires piled into the cars and zipped down the street. Victor took one last look at the duplex before vanishing.

Victor went to the white house the next night. *Everybody Loves Raymond* played on the TV. Victor sat across from Ramsey on a loveseat.

"Is everything good?" Victor asked.

"They're dead. Bryce'll probably show you his keepsake," he

said with a shake of his head and a smile on his face.

Victor sat with him for a few minutes before wandering down the hall to Bryce and Annie's room, which was next to the kitchen. Bryce opened the door when he knocked.

His face was lively when he motioned for Victor to come inside.

Their room was one of the largest in the mini-mansion. A light purple color covered the walls. The queen-sized bed sat between two windows. They were concealed by large paintings of a sunny field bursting with yellow and white flowers. Butterflies fluttered around the buds. Annie had hung lightweight, sky blue curtains that mostly covered the frames, adding to the open window effect.

A long dresser was pushed up against the left wall. A rectangular mirror hung above the dresser. Front and center on top of the dark wood of the dresser was a small, decorative urn. It was white, adorned by flowers and vines. Bryce's souvenir, Victor guessed.

Annie was on the bed, under the plaid covers. She peeked down past her toes at Victor when he entered. She was still pretty pale. Well, paler than normal. You couldn't see her blonde eyebrows at all.

Bryce grinned merrily and nodded for Victor to follow. At the dresser, while watching Victor, he lifted the top of the urn. That nauseating death smell greeted their noses. A pile of black ash stained the interior.

Victor pinched his nose. "Close that. How can you keep that shit around?"

Bryce chuckled. "I think it's nice." He used his free hand to waft the smell to his nose, like he was reveling in bottled cologne.

Victor stared at him. "You're a strange man."

Bryce slapped his shoulder. Again. Victor tried not to grimace from the ache in his back as he went around the bed to

Annie's side.

"I just wanted to check on you."

A small smile tugged at her round mouth. "I'm better," she whispered.

"That's good. I'll leave you to rest."

His lips brushed her temple. When he stepped into the hallway, a glass shattered in the kitchen. Victor followed the noise. Ashleigh was on her knees near the fridge, picking up the broken cup. Victor lifted the trashcan and brought it to her.

She must have been preoccupied because she looked up in surprise. Her face softened when she saw who it was. She tossed the shards into the can and stood awkwardly in front of him.

Victor set the trashcan back where he'd gotten it and was going to continue out into the hallway.

"Victor?"

He licked his lips slowly, telling himself to stay calm before facing her. She looked from him to the floor, and then finally back. He waited.

"Um," she started with a nervous shrug. "Charlie's better. He's been in and out of consciousness. I'm sure as soon as he can move he'll want to go back to New York so he can recuperate at home." As she was speaking, he was conscious of her closing the distance between them. "I love New York but . . . I really like it here." Her tone was wistful. "I don't want to go but if Charlie says so, I think I have to."

She stood right in front of him now. "Please, Victor, why can't I stay?" she asked, stubbornly. "I've learned so much. Ramsey, Elizabeth, they've been amazing. And you . . ." She laid a hand on his chest. "You're a much better teacher than Charlie."

As he lifted his hand to remove hers, she grasped behind his ears and brought his face to hers. Her kiss was so sudden that he froze for half a second. And just in that half a second, a frisson of arousal ran through him.

Victor's hands went to her shoulders, shoving her into the fridge. She bounced off and landed on her hands and knees. Victor flitted over and lifted her to her feet by the hair. Ashleigh grimaced.

"I'm sorry, Victor. It won't happen again, I swear! Charlie can easily find others. I'm sure he'd be okay with letting me go, especially if you asked him—"

He released her. "Forget it."

Her mouth hung open for a moment as she tried to come up with another argument. "But . . . why not?" she asked meekly. "I said I was sorry. I couldn't help it."

"And how many more times will I hear 'sorry' from you?" Victor took a deep breath. "If you want to stay in Boston, that's something you'll have to discuss with Ramsey."

She looked like she was going to burst into tears. "I thought you understood what this is like. What I've been going through. I thought you cared. Why are you being like this?"

"Because," he began, then lowered his voice since he had practically shouted in frustration, "I have a girlfriend, who I love very much and we can't be friends because you put your hands on her. And after I told you not to."

He *had* understood what she was experiencing. After seeing that life could be different for vampires, different from Charlie's hapless teaching, she wanted desperately to hold on to it. He could comprehend the torment. His change hadn't been so easy either. He didn't have a Ramsey around to show him the way.

She shook her head. "Why are you wasting her time? You'll outlive her. She's going to grow old and die, Victor. Let her find someone who will die with her."

He wanted to slap her. More so because of how much truth rang in her words. He could release Celia and allow her a normal life. Was he selfish for not doing so?

Ashleigh inched closer with his silence. "We'll always be

young, Victor. Forever. Why are you setting yourself up for heartache? There's too much time in the world to throw away mending a broken heart. What kind of hold does she have on you?"

Victor felt his fangs sliding down in anger.

"I heard Ramsey and Elizabeth talking about her blood. How it's different. Is that it? Why not keep her—?"

"Stop."

She cringed slightly at the sight of his fangs, the fury building in his eyes.

"I don't have to justify anything to you. I *will* say that I am in love with Celia. She is my girlfriend, my equal. I loved her before I tasted her. She offers more than you ever will. Whether I am allowed to experience her for eighty years or only one, I wouldn't trade it for you."

Ashleigh's bottom lip trembled; her eyes were round with misery.

"Sharita?"

Both Victor and Ashleigh looked to the hallway. The gravelly voice floated down the stairs, barely higher than a whisper.

"Chris? Alan? Ashleigh?"

Ashleigh sighed heavily when her maker called her name. He sounded disoriented. She gave Victor another beseeching look but he stared back, steadfast. There was just no way he could interfere, even if that was what he actually wanted.

Her shoulders sagged as she shuffled past him and into the hallway. He heard her mount the stairs, then a door opened and closed.

"Who's there?" Charlie asked.

"It's Ashleigh," she responded, injecting a tiny bit of emotion into her otherwise hollow voice.

Victor thought of Celia as he vanished.

Fourteen

CELIA HAD DINNER with Trixie and bubbly Tina before heading to Cage's to face the Friday night crowd. Carson was being an ass tonight.

For instance, currently he was twirling bottles of vodka and rum simultaneously. It was a lame-ass attempt at impressing two women who'd ordered Long Island Iced Teas. They did look excited as they watched him go. However, the vodka bottle spit at Celia, who stood next to him. Luckily, the liquor was clear and her clothes were black. She was used to coming home from work smelling of booze, since drunken fools were clumsy.

"Carson, stop dicking around," she complained low enough that the patrons didn't hear. "Bobby's right over there, you idiot."

As if he'd heard his name, Bobby looked up from his post at the edge of the dance floor, where he'd been speaking to one of the security guards. Carson stopped his foolish twirling before he caught him and finished the drinks.

After giving them their change and accepting the tip, then trying and failing at getting their numbers, Carson turned to Celia.

"There's nothing wrong with adding a little *finesse* to the drinking experience."

She gave him a serious look. "You looked like a douche."

His jaw dropped in mock surprise. "Celia! Why do you always treat me with such hostility?"

She ignored him now that someone shouted for a Blue Kamikaze. She made a point of pouring the vodka and Blue Curacao as non-flamboyantly as she could, prompting a roll of the eye from Carson.

At midnight, she took a quick break. She noticed that Ramsey and Elizabeth were still with her. She found it very odd, and extremely annoying. It had been over a week since that night. She would talk with Victor but her only guess at the reason for this extended timeframe was the amount of blood she had consumed during their experiment. She still didn't drone on the two men, nor was she having nightmares.

When she emerged from the hallway to get back behind the bar, Celia's eyes landed on a familiar head of red hair. Colin and Harold stood a few feet from DJ Mickey's booth. Colin was without the sling tonight and he seemed to be fine. She wondered if she should go talk to them. Were they on speaking terms?

She took a step forward. They were glancing around casually but she noticed their attention kept returning to one particular man.

He wore all black with a gold chain and a diamond rock in his ear. Comb tracks were visible in his slicked-back hair.

Celia stopped moving toward them. They were working.

Harold nudged Colin. The two approached the man. She stood there, transfixed and intrigued. She wanted to know how they operated. She couldn't hear a damn thing over the music and she didn't dare approach lest she became a distraction.

Harold discreetly flashed a badge at the man then nodded toward the exit. The man became furious. He handed off his drink to the lady he'd been talking up and stomped off between them. Celia's brows rose as she watched. They worked fast, and had apparently adopted Jay's fake cop routine.

As she followed their progress, her eyes met Bobby's. He was frowning at her, probably wondering why he was paying her to stand around. She waved with a friendly smile then hurried back to the bar.

At two-thirty, she waited by the front door for Trixie. When she approached, Celia saw that she had changed out of her tight black shorts, sheer black tank that showed her lacy red bra, and funky knee-high socks with red lips. She now donned fashionably ripped jeans, a white shirt and a dark purple cardigan. Celia frowned at her despondent expression.

"Lee's picking me up," Trixie explained, though she didn't look or sound too thrilled.

Celia rubbed her shoulder. Rick held the door for them. Apparently it had rained at some point during the night. The ground was a darker shade than earlier. Water dripped from the awnings above doors.

Rick smirked at Celia, like he had done every single time he saw her these last couple of days. The lingering effects of their little experiment still showed in her clear skin and shiny hair. The nice part was it eliminated the need for makeup.

A gray Acura idled at the curb. The tinted windows didn't allow a view inside. Trixie waved then climbed into the passenger's side. Celia continued on to the parking lot. Carson's red Jeep Grand Cherokee sat a few spots over from her Accord. Other than that, the lot was deserted. Celia stuck her hand in her purse in search of her keys.

She heard the person approach, thanks to the vamp blood.

She attempted to jump out of the way but she was shoved to the ground, landing on her side this time. She saw Ashleigh a second before she snatched her up by the neck like she was nothing and hurled her across the lot.

The air left her when she hit the pavement. Perhaps it was time to find a new parking place. Ashleigh was there in an instant, straddling her and punching her in the face. Silver stars blinded her vision. She'd never been hit in the face before and it hurt like hell.

"I am not going back to New York because of you," Ashleigh hissed. She clutched the collar of Celia's jacket. "There's only a matter of time before Charlie is fully awake. He'll make me go back but I'm not fucking going back, you hear me, bitch? He can't control me anymore!"

She sounded like a madwoman. Celia didn't even know who Charlie was.

"What's so great about you?" Celia struggled as the vampire pinned her face to the side. Her cheek was squashed against the pavement. Ashleigh studied her exposed neck. The muscles contracted beneath her skin when she swallowed.

Ashleigh opened her mouth, exposing her sharp fangs.

"I guess there's one way to find out." She leaned down.

Instinctually, Celia reached up, tangled her hand in her hair and yanked. Ashleigh yelped, pausing in her assault. Celia pulled her hair until Ashleigh's head was nearly level with the ground, which lifted her off of her torso. She then pushed her hard and she was on the ground beside her.

When Celia pulled her hand way, it was full of dark chestnut hair. Freaked, she shook it loose. The locks were wet and clung to her hand. Ashleigh must have waited by her car for her to come out.

Her face throbbed and her back ached from being thrown. She rolled to get up but wasn't quick enough. Ashleigh pounced on her again. This time she wrapped her hands around her neck. Celia began to black out almost immediately.

Through the growing darkness, she heard claws on the pavement, moving quickly. Ashleigh's head jerked to the right just as a furry beast rammed into her, removing her from Celia's torso. Warm blood wet Celia's neck. It must've grabbed her with its jaws.

Air rushed into her chest. She wheezed as she sat up. A flood of worry and anger washed over her and she knew Victor was coming. She couldn't think about that just yet as she waited for her dizziness to clear.

To Celia's right, some fierce growling mixed with Ashleigh's screeching. Another bundle of fur zipped past her, then another. Ashleigh pushed one of the smaller wolves, sending him flying in the air until he hit the green dumpster. The dumpster squealed as it scraped the ground from the force of impact.

The other small one bit down on her outstretched arm. She let out a frustrated cry at the tag team. The wolf jerked his head, and her arm dislodged. He held it in his teeth like a grotesque plaything. She was about to swing at him with her still-attached arm when the larger wolf jumped and got a hold of her neck. He landed on his feet, bringing her to her knees. The wolf twisted and snapped her neck. Well, to be more accurate, he locked his jaw and her head popped off like a champagne cork. Instead of fizzy bubbly, a geyser painted the ground crimson.

Celia watched with eyes as wide as saucers. Ashleigh's head bumped across the pavement, leaving a gooey, red trail behind. It came to rest at her foot. The cobalt-blue eyes stared vacantly at her, the mouth open. Her pointy fangs glinted in the light. She shrieked and kicked the head away.

All of this happened in the span of a minute. Celia needed a moment to collect herself. Seeing someone beheaded was a little traumatizing.

When she finally brought herself to look over, she got a better view of the wolves. Michael was there. His sepia fur rustled slightly like stalks of wheat in the night breeze. The other two were smaller in height. The one with silvery fur and black paws was thicker. The other was entirely black.

The silver one put a paw on Ashleigh's stomach. Without a pause, he plunged his snout into her chest. Bones cracked and there was a sick squishy sound. When he lifted his head, he held a red, dripping mass crushed between his teeth. Ashleigh's body began to char and flake away. The wolf swallowed her heart whole.

Celia's stomach clenched. Saliva filled her mouth. She leaned over as the vomit forced its way up her throat. After a few retches, she scooted away; the acidic smell was twisting her stomach again.

The black one padded over to where Celia had kicked the head. It was lodged under Celia's muffler. Picking it up by its hair, he carried it back to the body. The head swung and bounced from his mouth like a yo-yo, sprinkling black ash around as it disintegrated.

Michael gazed at Celia a moment before strolling over to where she was still seated on the wet pavement. She could see the muscles of his legs and back work as he approached. They rippled and flexed with his movements. She couldn't take her eyes off of him. He was beautiful and scary all at once.

He halted a second to retrieve her purse. He placed the bag in front of her and leaned in, sniffing her or something. His breath warmed her neck and shoulder. The smell of the forest clung to him, rustic and invigorating. Under that, she detected the distinctive Shifter Smell. That's what she was going to call it. She ran her hand along the side of his head to let him know she was okay.

His tongue flicked at her collarbone. She couldn't help a

giggle because he was tickling her. His tongue, larger than any dog she knew, grazed her skin a few times, bumpy and rough. Suddenly, she realized he was cleaning Ashleigh's blood from her neck and she was no longer laughing. She had to assume this was normal behavior and tried not to be too weirded out. This was the equivalent of him handing her a towel if, you know, he was in his human form and . . . had a towel. She tried not to let herself wonder if he was enjoying the taste but her mind wasn't obeying. His wolfy exhalations weren't indicative.

"Hey!"

Celia twisted her torso to see Victor storming over, his face a deep frown. There was a snarl behind Michael. The silver wolf lunged at Victor, the fur around his snout soaked with Ashleigh's blood.

"No, wait!" Celia cried, reaching her hand out in a futile attempt to stop the silver blur.

The wolf sprang at him. Victor caught him at the shoulders and flung him away. He skidded across the pavement, kicking up dust and pebbles. He was on his feet quickly and barreling back.

Michael left Celia and ran at the wolf to block him. Victor stood at the ready for another attack. Ramsey and Bryce raced around the corner. They paused though, when they saw that Michael was controlling the wolf. The black wolf rushed over to cover his comrades. He growled at the vampires, warning them not to come any closer.

"You okay?" Ramsey called to Celia.

"Yeah," she croaked. Her throat still ached. "What are you doing here?"

"You were distressed. I almost missed it. Looks like you won't be getting my thoughts soon." He actually sounded disappointed. Obviously her ability to see in on his intimate moments had been amusing.

"I'm getting her out of here," Victor said.

Ramsey nodded. "Go. We'll clean up."

Victor went to Celia and placed a hand on her shoulder. She held her breath just as the iciness took over her. The hard floor in her dark apartment replaced the hard pavement under her butt. She coughed, which aggravated her throat. She could still feel the pressure from Ashleigh's hands on her neck, the bile in the back of her mouth.

Victor turned on the lamp and went to the kitchen. He returned shortly with a glass of water. She swished it around absently in her mouth before swallowing. She was staring at the dirt they had tracked on her floor. There was no way she could get another rug, unless it was black. That would hide future stains the best, right?

Victor sat beside her on the floor with one knee bent to support his elbow. He looked her over quickly, and when he was satisfied, he rubbed her thigh. Celia replayed the last few minutes over and over in her head, growing angrier and angrier.

"That . . . bitch!" Victor nodded modestly. She looked at him, astonishment in her eyes. "She tried to kill me, Victor."

"I know. I believe that's my fault."

She frowned now. "What happened?"

He took a breath. "She wanted to leave her maker and stay here. She thought I would be fine with that."

Celia rubbed her sore cheek. She shook her head in disbelief.

"I'm sorry," he said.

"You don't have anything to apologize for."

"I should've handled her better." He eyed her a second. "Was that your wolf friend back there?"

"Yeah."

Victor's face was motionless. "They'll want to watch themselves." She fixed her mouth to tell him off since they had just saved her life. He cut across her. "Ashleigh's maker is still at Ramsey's. He will look for retribution."

She frowned. "Is that like what Ramsey's going through? With that Italian guy?"

Victor paused a moment, probably wondering how she knew that, then nodded. She thought back to Ramsey's troubled expression.

"What kind of reparations do vampires demand exactly?"

He still looked like a statue. A statue with moving lips. "It varies, depending on how old the vampire was and how reasonable the sire wants to be."

"So, they could demand whatever the hell they want, really."

He didn't answer. From the way he was acting, she started to wonder if he'd had to deal with paying back someone for killing a vamp.

Victor came out of his trance and his face took on some emotion. His expression was grim, which was not exactly comforting. "They ask for anything, from money to property to services. And you have to pay."

"What happens if you don't?"

"You forfeit your existence. We gain many allies over time. It won't be easy to hide out and hope they forget about it. Your debt will follow you."

She thought that over for a minute. "But doesn't it become, like, a vicious cycle? I mean, you kill someone" — His face hardened at the use of second person but she didn't mean it like that — "whether on purpose or by accident, and then their maker comes calling. And if things don't work out and they kill you, then your maker comes calling. Doesn't that get repetitive?" she asked with a wave of her hand. She was exhausted just thinking about it.

"No. Once that initial conflict is settled—and that includes with a death—then it's the end of the confrontation."

"Vampire politics," she mumbled, making sure her tone wasn't condescending though it was all so perplexing.

"We don't have a court system, so to speak. This is our process." She had a feeling there was more to it but she didn't know where to begin with questions.

She tilted her head to the side as she considered. "This applies to Michael as well? He'd have to pay something or be hunted down?"

The question made Victor revert back to the blank slate. "It's not exactly the same. We know the procedure and don't apply the rules to others, be they humans or otherwise. That doesn't mean he won't go after them. It depends on how hard Charlie takes Ashleigh's loss." He ended with that.

Celia chewed her bottom lip as she stared at him. The request was right there on the tip of her tongue. For some reason, she struggled with asking it. Would Victor become entangled in this shit if she asked him to speak to Charlie? She knew he'd do it if she requested, but what were the consequences? She decided to go that route.

"What would happen if you asked Ashleigh's maker not to go after Michael? Since you're technically not involved?"

His gaze was so intense that she dropped her eyes to her lap. That's when she saw the road rash along her forearms.

He didn't seem surprised she had asked. His voice was low and cold when he finally spoke. "He could drop it. Or he could ask me to take up the debt."

She didn't like that. No, Victor shouldn't have to do that. She forced herself to look at him again, this time showing resolution.

"I'll talk to him," she said.

"Absolutely not."

"What?" she asked matter-of-factly. "I'm just a human. He can't demand anything of me. I have nothing of value. I'll explain the situation, that she was trying to kill me and that they came to my rescue."

To her amazement, Victor chuckled. The bastard actually

chuckled. She glared at him.

"You're so innocent."

Her cheek burned as blood rushed to her face. "I am not!" she exclaimed with as much contempt as if he'd just called her a wretched whore.

He squeezed her thigh but she pushed his hand away. "Don't get so upset. I think it's sweet."

He was not helping his case. Seriously. Celia got to her feet in a huff and stalked to her room. She flicked on the lamp and stripped off her clothes with so much animosity that she nearly stretched out her top. She pulled on her robe then stomped to the bathroom.

Victor let her shower in peace. The heat and steam did relax her stressed and aching body but it didn't melt her resolve. She was thinking of Michael here. She didn't want him hurt for stepping in to protect her. In her mind, Ashleigh was not worth anything more than a passing glance. Michael at least had promise.

She smirked as she recalled his tight expression the last time she spoke to him, when he'd smelled Victor on her, in her, whatever. An odd reaction to his revulsion but she smirked anyway. Everyone was entitled to their opinions. He was only concerned with her wellbeing. If he wasn't, tonight might have ended differently.

The water was growing cold. When she pulled back the shower curtain, Victor stood there, holding out an orange towel. She took it as she stepped onto the gray shower mat. He was quiet for a moment.

"I know why you're doing this," he said at last. She stared at the floor as she toweled off. "It's very admirable, as usual. I just can't have you in harm's way again."

She groaned. "Do you really think I like being in harm's way? It fucking sucks! But I can't let that run my life anymore. I hate being terrified whenever the sun goes down. Not knowing who might be waiting for me when I step out the door."

"Those were all situations you didn't have control over. By talking with Charlie, you're purposely opening yourself up to trouble. You're making yourself visible to a dangerous stranger."

"I have to do something, Victor. Don't you get that?"

Victor rubbed his face like he was exhausted, when in fact she was the one who should be exhausted. It was nearly four in the damn morning and she was wet and sore and adrenaline-laced. And she had to work tomorrow. And Ramsey and Elizabeth were buzzing in her head. She would scream if she thought that would accomplish anything.

"I'd probably be able to take you more seriously if you weren't standing in your full glory."

She snatched the towel around herself, closing it as tightly as she could. "Focus, dammit. I want to talk to Ashleigh's maker. I won't have Michael getting killed for coming to my aid."

Something crossed his face—was he hurt? Her brows furrowed. Did he feel guilty about not being there in time for her?

He looked away from her, his expression tense. She sighed, her own guilt finding a space on her already full plate of emotions. She hadn't meant to discount him or his efforts. She stepped up to him and wrapped her arms around his waist. His breathing was shallow. After a minute he hugged her back.

"Please let me do this," she said into his arm.

"I'll do it," he said tightly.

She shook her head. "No."

"I can afford whatever he may ask."

"No," she repeated.

Victor tried to move, so that he could see her face she guessed. She held on tight. "Why does it matter who does it as long as someone asks for the animal's mercy?"

She didn't like that term. She chose to deal with it later. "You know why. And I get that you're trying to protect me. But I'd have a better chance at asking for mercy without some inflated reparation as the cost."

This time he pulled away from her. He wanted her to see he was serious. "They don't always ask for money, Celia." His forceful tone caused several horrendous images to pop into her head of other . . . services to be performed. She shivered.

Okay, that didn't help her resolve. Celia looked away. Victor took hold of her chin, forcing her to keep up his gaze. His steely eyes were as black as the night sky.

"And you'd have to agree to his terms in order for your friend to be saved. If he sees how much it means to you, it may only serve to make him more vindictive."

"Okay, okay," she muttered. She tilted her head back so that he was no longer holding her face. "I get it. Vampires have mommy issues."

"This isn't just about making sure you aren't hurt. I'm trying to protect your life!"

She shook her head. "I have to at least try."

Was she even listening? He groaned at her persistence.

"Celia!"

"Victor!" she bellowed back in the same exasperated tone.

Now when he looked at her, his eyes were desperate, something she'd only seen once before. That time when she kind of, sort of broke up with him. He'd wiped her memory—a vampire thing he had promised to never do to her—and she kicked him out of her apartment.

Celia had gotten angry with the ever lovable Milo and threatened to tell the hunters where to find him. Of course she hadn't meant it. In order to safeguard the mansion, Victor had done the hoodoo.

He had looked so sad, so distraught then. He had been in a situation he couldn't control. But he had cared about her too much to make things worse by enthralling her that night, anything to take back what he had done, to take back the broken promise.

The memory nearly made her cry.

Victor's eyes may have been desperate but his voice was stolid. "Please. Is there anything I can do to change your mind?"

She didn't give herself time to think about it. She didn't allow his pain to make her crumble.

"No," she said firmly.

He sighed. His eyes dropped to her collarbone somewhere. When he leaned forward, his lips pressed against her forehead. She stayed in her spot as he left the bathroom. She was afraid to move because she might run after him and take it all back. They'd had enough problems. Why was she loading more weight onto the delicate teeter-totter that was their relationship?

She didn't hear his feet on the floor but the front door clicked closed.

Fifteen

W INSTON WAS BACK in Boston. Celia was not happy to see him when she dragged her laundry through the kitchen. He was eating a turkey sandwich and reading a magazine (*Slayings Weekly*, perhaps?), and didn't look up when she entered. The only indication of acknowledgment was his jaw clenching.

Celia thought it was just as well and continued her path to the washer. She only had one load this week so it wouldn't take too long. Soft music wafted in through an open window in the kitchen. She followed it outside where her aunt was on her knees in filthy jeans, one of Max's rejected "jazzy" shirts and a floppy hat. She was checking for weeds among her roses. The little radio beside her played Smokey Robinson.

"Hey, Celia." She hadn't even turned around to see who was approaching. "Are you here for dinner? You're a little early."

Celia sighed. No, dinner was not what brought her to Lower

Mills. Following her happy little talk with Victor the night before, Celia had been distracted all day. Something tugged at her as she waited tables and served drinks. She felt uneasy about pleading with an ailing vampire and that made her conscious of her family. Though it appeared that she didn't seem to listen to Victor, his words had stuck. She wasn't ready to die, not yet.

She needed to be near her loved ones, even her dreadful cousin—though she would keep a nice distance.

She stooped down next to her aunt to uproot weeds. Meg pointed to a thick stem peeking under a bush. Celia had to use both hands to pull the stubborn weed. When it came loose, she fell back onto her butt. She should've worn gloves; the stem had dug into her palms.

"Ow." She tossed the weed onto the pile. She was still sore. The sun must've hit her face at just the right angle because her aunt's hand was on her chin, turning her face to her. Celia knew why.

When she woke up this morning, her left eye and cheek were bruised red and yellow. Her new "attractiveness" had downplayed it slightly but her cheek was not pretty. She had piled on concealer and foundation—which hurt to the touch—and made it through work, she thought without being noticed. Maybe not. Her aunt was staring at her cheek with a stern expression.

"What happened to your face?"

"I was playing basketball with a friend and I was hit with a ball." Celia said it as steadily as she could and it sounded truthful for something she just came up with on the fly. She was imagining she had been playing with Michael, which helped keep her voice even.

"You know how much I suck at sports." That part was true.

Meg's frown lessened and she released her chin. Celia tugged at the ends of her long-sleeved shirt, which she'd worn to cover her scrapes. She was relieved, though she couldn't help wondering if she just gave her aunt the impression that Victor was in the habit of hitting her. Great. Now, she'd have to bring him over for dinner or coffee or something to remind Meg that he was a stand-up guy.

At five, she helped start dinner. Winston had disappeared into the living room with Max to watch football or whatever it was that made men whoop and holler at the television.

Celia paused in mixing the cornbread. She peeked over to Meg, who was inspecting the chicken in the oven. The open door released the fragrant smells of herbs and garlic.

"Do you think my mom would be proud of me?" she asked. She almost didn't recognize her own voice: high-pitched and strained.

Meg froze. Slowly, she straightened and closed the oven. Her cheeks and nose were flushed from the heat.

She frowned at Celia with concern. "Of course, honey. Why would you ask that?"

Celia shrugged, growing timid now. "What's there to be proud of?" she muttered. This question plagued her every once in a while. Would her mother be delighted to say her only daughter was a bartender?

Did Celia have other aspirations? Not really. Did she want to be rich and famous? Nope.

What would life have been like if her mother was still alive? Would she have encouraged her to go on to college or something? Become a schoolteacher or scientist? Or a nurse like her?

They were questions to which she would never have answers. She tortured herself anyway.

Meg crossed to her and placed a hand on her shoulder. "You're kidding, right?" Celia's look indicated that she was very much not kidding. "Celia, one of the best thing's my sister did in this world was bringing you into it. You're smart, resourceful, independent. That's plenty to be proud of."

That was supposed to make her smile. She couldn't muster it. Instead, she stared at the end of the spoon in her hand as she made tiny swirls in the cornbread batter.

"Not to mention, beautiful," Meg added with a smile. She ran her hand over her niece's hair and moved it off her shoulder so she could see her face. "What's the matter, sweetie?"

Celia forced herself to swallow this self-deprecation with which she was conflicting herself. She couldn't explain it all to herself, how could she voice it to her aunt? Besides, she had a lot for which to be thankful. Her family. Victor and Trixie. Her health. She had her own place, worked hard to make her own money to support herself. There was no need for this moment in the dumps and she needed to get it together. Her mother wouldn't have anticipated the kind of troubles she was dealing with but she would've been confident in her ability to handle any situation. She was always Celia's personal cheerleader.

A small smile appeared on Celia's face. She looked up at her aunt. "Nothing. I was just thinking about her. Thinking about family."

Meg nodded knowledgeably. "I do that, too, sometimes."

"I miss her."

Meg turned but not before Celia saw the pain in her face. She moved away to check the rice on the stove. Celia resumed stirring the cornbread mix. She was distracted as she poured the batter into the greased pan.

"What happened between my mother and grandmother?" Celia asked. "Did they have a fight?"

Meg tensed. "Yes, but I don't remember why," she answered too quickly.

"Can I call her?"

She stopped stirring for a second. "If you want, of course. I'll have to look for her number."

"I, um, found this album the other day," Celia said softly.

"There were some photos missing. Did you and mom get mad at each other or something?"

Meg laughed. Celia noticed it was a bit like how her voice had been: high-pitched, unnatural. "Those albums in the living room? We were kids, Celia. Kids get mad."

"There were pictures missing—"

Meg slammed the spoon on the stove. Specks of rice sprayed across the burners. Her back was to her. "Because I was angry and didn't want to see them. Believe it or not but your mother had a knack for making people angry. I didn't get rid of them, if that's what you're worried about. They're in a box somewhere."

Meg stalked over and took the pan from the table. She slid it in the oven alongside the chicken.

"Ten minutes until dinner," her aunt said tightly. Celia thought it wise to drop the subject now. Her aunt didn't get truly cross with her often. Sure she would snap at her about her language. Whenever it was something worse, the incident was always an unsettling shock.

Celia went to the living room to inform the fellas. She hung around on the threshold because it took another five minutes for the guys to turn off the TV. After Max passed her for the kitchen, Celia turned to follow. She stopped though, because Winston's hand was on her shoulder.

She looked at him, confused at first. She shrugged his hand off.

"Have you seen those bloodsuckers again?" he asked directly. He kept his voice down so the others wouldn't hear.

She gave a gasping sort of laugh. "Are you kidding me?"

"Shh!" he snapped, looking to the hallway. It was clear.

Celia glared at him. "Are you asking that because you're concerned for my safety, or just to add a few more notches to your tally?"

He rolled his eyes. "Why can't you just answer the question?"

What an asshole. Of course he was only thinking about his Night Hawk reputation. Suddenly, she no longer wanted to be near family. She punched him in the chest. He grunted and crumpled forward a little, which was satisfying. Her little fist probably felt like a rock.

"You suck," she grumbled.

He recovered enough to shove her shoulder, which made her stumble. "How you get that shiner, huh? Don't you want payback?"

"You're such a fucking idiot," she spat in a whisper. "I don't want anything to do with your kind of payback."

"You're the idiot," he shot back. "These bloodsuckers have been invading our cities, feeding off of us, and you think it's okay to just sit back and let them? Or maybe we should hold their hands and talk through our issues? Maybe they can even join our society." His face lit up with false enthusiasm, which pissed her off even more. "We could give them jobs. Give them services. We could date them, marry them. So what if they feed off blood? So what if they kill people? As long as they're treated with *care*."

Her hands were balled into tight fists at her sides. She wanted so badly to let him in on the fact that vampires were already doing those things. She wanted to tell him that his own cousin was actually dating one. That she kissed him and fucked him and let him drink from her. She would get as graphic as possible, too. His head would probably explode.

That in itself was enough to make the words spill from her mouth. But she clamped her lips because that course of action was unwise. Not only would she out her boyfriend and his friends, she'd open herself up to more scrutiny and surveillance by Winston, and maybe even the Night Hawks. Saying that would not be nice was the understatement of the year.

"People kill people, too," Celia said matter-of-factly.

"Yeah, and they get the death penalty," he snapped back.

Instead of responding to him, Celia stomped off to the kitchen.

Dinner was quiet. Meg and Max chatted about the roof; it needed some repair before the winter. Winston and Celia exchanged hostile glares between bites. Her aunt and uncle noticed, but decided not to get involved. Meg wasn't meeting Celia's eye anyway.

After eating, Celia stood at the dryer as she folded. Winston wouldn't have any plausible excuse to interrupt her there. She placed her clothes neatly in the gray bag and dragged it out into the kitchen.

"Take some cake, honey," Meg said. She was already cutting a huge slice of chocolate cake. She wrapped it in aluminum foil that she had shaped into a swan and handed it to her. Celia kissed her cheek and wrapped her arms around her. After a pause, the tension left her aunt's spine and she hugged her back.

Celia headed out. Her uncle was upstairs, leaving Winston alone in the living room. He called out to her as she passed. Damn, he was persistent. She gave him the finger and kept on trucking.

Victor didn't visit her that night, which was frustrating, especially after her exasperating evening. She called him a few times on the phone, only catching his voicemail. She felt him, but wasn't receiving any flashes. Thankfully, he was the only vampire under her skin.

She didn't know where he lived, not even the city. She had never really thought about it because she knew how vamps guarded where they rested. She was just fine with hanging out at her place. All of her shit was there and she had control of the remote.

The first three months they were dating, Victor had shown her a tidy, posh apartment downtown. She realized that he didn't actually rest there since it was on the tenth floor of his building with windows as walls and no curtains. Plus, he had stopped taking her there once she found out he was a vampire. It had served its purpose as a shiny front.

Now she regretted not asking for that little tidbit. She didn't know if he would actually tell her, but she should've at least asked.

She even racked her brain in an attempt to remember where Ramsey lived. That was a useless waste of energy.

She groaned to herself as she pulled out ingredients to make brownies. There was no chocolate but she had plenty of brown sugar. She set to work making blondies instead. She discovered a half-full bag of walnuts tucked away in the back of the fridge when she grabbed the baking soda. It took a moment to recall the quantities since she hadn't made blondies in years.

Eight years to be exact. She'd made her last batch for her mom when she had first become bedridden.

Mixing the sugar and flour and eggs distracted her from the current issue. Celia poured the beige goop into a pan and placed it in the oven. Satisfied, she stood back to stare at the white door.

The calm soon relapsed. The process had been over too quickly.

She needed more distractions. Without them, she was annoyed with Victor for not responding to her fucking calls, nervous and scared about talking to Charlie, and angry with Winston for his stupid beliefs and prejudices. The combination was bending her stomach into knots.

She marched to her room, snatched up her phone and dialed. It was close to nine in Texas when Jay answered. It had been a week since she'd spoken to him. The longest they had gone was that two-week stretch after the vampires and hunters settled on a pact in Snipe's kitchen.

Loud, metallic clanging sounded in the background.

"I'm not interrupting anything, am I?" She was taken aback

by all the noise. "Hunter team-building exercises?"

"I'm watching this guy make a sword."

She paused at that. She wasn't sure whether to be more confused by someone crafting a sword or by Jay possibly having one made.

"Say what now?"

He laughed. "Can't you just see me packing a sword?" he asked. "Chopping off bloodsucker heads as I go."

"Okay, stop, because I can't tell if you're joking or not."

"He's making it for someone. An anniversary gift, I think."

She raised a brow. "I always thought diamonds were suitable."

He chuckled. They both lapsed into silence. She chewed her bottom lip.

"So, what's up?" he asked after a minute.

She could've brought up their last conversation that had resulted in the dent in her wall. Instead, she said, "Nothing, I'm just bored."

"Hmm. Wishing I was there?"

"Sure, but not how you're insinuating. Are you living there now?" she asked to change the subject. "Or, back living there?" She frowned at her convoluted question.

"It's taking longer for the contractors to finish." His tone was as sharp as glass, letting her know he was very upset—probably more so since he couldn't just ram a stake through their chests like how he solved his other problems.

"Sorry," she said. She'd sat on the sofa with her legs tucked under her. Just hearing Jay's deep voice was making her feel better already. "I don't know anything about fixing houses but when my Aunt Meg remodeled the master bathroom, it took forever."

"Yeah, well, they need to fuckin' hurry up."

"Are you coming back here when it's done?"

"You want me to come back?" he asked slyly.

"Jay," she sighed. She didn't answer because he knew damn well would want to see him. She wasn't going to give him the satisfaction, though.

He was quiet and she didn't know how, but she knew he was smiling.

"Where have you been staying?"

"In the house. It's mostly closed up."

"But isn't that dangerous?" she asked, forgetting to who she was talking. "Is there even a front door?"

He chuckled. "I think I can protect myself."

"Oh," she said, feeling silly. "Right. So, why do you keep the house?"

Jay sighed. "I don't know; I just couldn't sell it. My grandfather's helping me clean."

"Your grandfather?"

"Yeah. The last time I saw Pops we were burying my sisters."

She lowered her eyes. He said it casually however Celia caught the strain beneath the words. "What were their names?" she asked gently.

"Colleen and Rebecca. Rebecca was the youngest." Celia felt a stab of sorrow for him. "Pops is kinda quiet. But my grandma's been telling me stuff about my family."

"What about?"

The clanging in the background turned into a sharp scraping. Jay's chuckle showed his disbelief. "She said Pops is a Seeker."

"A what?"

"Yeah, that's what I said. She actually called him a *Cautator*. It's a Romanian word. In American, it's a Seeker. She said Seekers are hunters of vampires. They're able to identify them, giving them an advantage."

Celia's jaw dropped slightly. "Like you."

"Oh, good. You're keeping up." She rolled her eyes. "It's

passed through the males but that was all she really knew on the subject. She said Pops knew he was a Seeker but he shunned his father. He concentrated on providing for his family. He only told my grandmother when he wanted to suddenly move. He had to. There was no fuckin' way she was gonna uproot their family just because he came home drunk.

"He finally explained the whole glow thing. He'd known about vampires and Seekers because his father made him go on hunts with him. But once he moved out of my great-grandparents' house, he stopped hunting. Pops never wanted to do it in the first place. He vowed to never put his own sons through that. So, he worked a nine-to-five. He went to recitals. Apple picking. Fuckin' bowling. He learned to ignore his ability.

"Until that night he got shit-faced. He told my grandma he'd seen a vampire and they had to move."

"Wow," Celia whispered. She found it incredibly cute that he called his grandfather Pops.

"You can fuckin' imagine how he took the news of his son's family dying at the hands of a vampire. He barely made it through the damn funeral. I obviously didn't know there was more to his mourning."

"Wow," she said again. "Wait, I thought you said you didn't have family?" She remembered his negative response when she asked at The Pit back in August.

His soft laugh was sardonic. "I guess I'm like my Pops in more ways than one. If I didn't mention it to them—if I didn't mention them—then I was protecting them, right? I didn't think he knew about vampires and I wasn't 'bout to be the one to tell 'im."

"How did the subject come up?"

"He was cleaning the living room and I was bringing him some water. He was just sitting there, in the middle of the floor, staring at a frame. The glass was cracked, and you could barely see the picture. It was of all of us one Christmas.

"There wasn't anything special 'bout it but he looked like he was gonna cry. That's when he told me about how he moved his family 'cause he saw a bloodsucker. He said, 'That's how they died, you know. Your family. My son.' I tried to ask him more about it but he just shut the fuck down. My grandma sat with me that night and explained."

"It must be tough on him." He probably made himself forget about vampires. What a tragic way to come full circle.

"I told her what I do. She said she figured as much. I didn't seem too surprised by this new information. She told me to be careful. And to call more," he added with a laugh. "I'm a dick, I know. I need to stay in touch. She said she would worry. She really knows how to lay on that Jewish guilt."

"You're Jewish?"

"She is. It stopped with her and Pops."

"Your family's not one for passing on traditions, huh?" she joked.

"We can be lazy, yes."

"What happened with your great-grandfather?"

"Jason Young the First was very disappointed in Pops. He basically disowned him. He died before I was born, in a nest raid. My grandma said that the heritage would've died with Jason the First, if it weren't for me."

"Because Jason the Second rejected him, and Jason the Third—your father—didn't know."

"Right. She said that I had to have seen a vampire. It was the only way to trigger my ability. That's the extent of what she knows on the subject. She wasn't able to ask Pops' dad. So, I think when my dad saw that vampire, like me, he didn't understand. Not until he saw him biting his children."

Jay had woken to find the vamp sucking away on his dad. He stabbed him in the heart.

Jay's first kill.

The second would be his mother.

"Wow," Celia said again. "I know a Seeker."

Jay chuckled. "That's worth about two nickels."

Celia smiled, though she disagreed.

"So, what's new up there?" Jay said. "Snipe only just started sending Colin and Harold out again. I think the morale's down or something. Their low numbers are taking a toll. The only reason he's letting them go on patrol is because of those goddamn couple murders."

"Oh, right. I've heard about those. I don't think there've been any lately."

"Yeah, two nights ago. A couple found in their bedroom by one of their children."

Celia groaned. "That's awful. What are you guys doing about it?"

"We have help from a cop. We're just trying to track the son-of-a-bitch but it's not like forensics is on our side. I really want to be there to help. Shit," he said softly, as if recalling something. "Colin's birthday is in four days. He's turning twenty-one. I'm thinking about getting him an escort."

Celia shook her head. "It's so nice to see you're a stereotype."

"Hey, he's about to be a man. The poor fuck hasn't had any real experience yet. He has to get his dick wet at some point."

"And if he catches syphilis in the process and his dick falls off?"

"That's really derogatory, Celia. Besides, I'll make sure he's got plenty of rubbers and lube."

"Ugh," she groaned. She decided to change the subject from Colin's dick. "How exactly do you recruit hunters?" she asked. "You know, the ones who can't see a glow. Is there, like, an audition process or something?"

"Do you hear yourself when you speak?" he asked and he was

lucky he wasn't in the room because she would've punched him.

"I was just asking. You don't have to be a jerk."

"Oh, right, 'cause asking about a fuckin' audition process isn't a jerk thing to say."

Touché. She didn't have a good retort so she grumbled, "Shut up."

He laughed. "I don't know if Snipe's gonna recruit more people. If he meets someone who would fit in, he might try to get him to join up."

"Or her," she interjected.

His pause told her he was rolling his eyes. "Sure. Or her. You didn't answer me, though. What's going on with you?"

"Well . . ." she began. She didn't know where to start. "The Night Hawks are down three hunters," she told him. Victor hadn't exactly spelled it out (no matter how much she pouted about not receiving all of the gory details, he knew she didn't truly want them). Even so, she knew they wouldn't have let them live after all they had done. She didn't know how disturbing it was that that didn't bother her.

"Oh, yeah?"

"Yup. I got the girl's scarf and Victor and Ramsey and them found her."

"Let me get this straight. You handed over a couple of hunters to a group of vampires?"

Celia paused. She hadn't thought about it like that. "It's not how it sounds. They were bad people."

"Bad in what respect?"

His voice was too calm for her liking.

"They tortured and kidnapped people," she said.

"Vampires," he corrected. "Not people."

"Why is there a difference?"

"Bloodsuckers have a huge fuckin' advantage over humans."

"They were holding one of theirs hostage! I only gave them

the scarf so they could find Annie."

His words were as flat as a board. "You tell yourself whatever you have to to sleep at night, Celia. You do know this breaks our pact, right?"

Celia's entire face fell to her toes. She managed to croak, "Jay—"

"No human deaths," he interrupted coldly.

"Jay, come on." She was flailing. He wasn't in front of her but she could clearly see the rage and implacable lust for a hunt burn in Jay's emerald eyes. It coursed through the line. Her brain searched around for anything to change his mind.

"This vampire tried to kill me last night!"

She waited, her heart thumping at a normal freaked out pace.

"See, now that's the kinda shit you start with." His voice was still perilously level. "What the fuck happened?"

She continued cautiously. "I told you how Victor and I found this vampire who was badly injured?"

"Yeah, Ashleigh or something."

"Well, she started to get feelings for Victor and wanted to leave her maker to stay with him but he turned her down."

"How admirable," Jay sniffed. She ignored him.

"So, she came after me."

"How did you get away?"

That's where she hesitated. She knew Jay didn't believe in shifters . . . except he would have to now, right? Especially with his newfound status as a Seeker?

"These, uh, werewolves saved me."

The line was quiet for a moment. She waited. He hadn't hung up since she could still hear the clanging in the background.

"Werewolves?" He sounded both dubious and angry.

"Yeah."

"How do you know they were werewolves?"

Again, hesitation. "Just take my word," she finally said, sounding more confident than she actually felt.

"Don't give me that shit, Celia. What do you know?"

"Look, I can't tell you, okay? Just—" The timer went off in the kitchen and she glanced over. "My blondies are going to burn."

"What?"

"I have to go. We'll talk again." She hoped that would ease him a little. She was being an idiot, of course.

"Fine," he said tightly.

"Don't do anything before we talk, okay?"

He grunted. "We'll see."

That would have to do. She hung up and rushed to the kitchen. Her dessert actually needed another five minutes or so but she was happy to be off the phone after the turn in conversation. She cut the blondies once they cooled and put them on a plate that she placed in her cake holder.

She then changed and climbed into bed though her brain was too wired. She couldn't decide if it was worthwhile to alert the vamps about the broken pact—or rather that the hunters now knew of the breach. She didn't fall asleep until one.

Celia was behind the bar the next day, Sunday. When Maria came around to collect her glasses of wine, Celia stopped her.

"Where's Michael?" she asked. His name had been on the table chart at the hostess stand but she hadn't seen him.

Maria shrugged. "I think he called out. He probably had homework to do." Celia didn't think so. She didn't voice this to Maria. She only hoped he wasn't injured. "Are you going to his game tonight?"

Well, that was news to her. She couldn't help feeling hurt, even if they were technically mad at each other. "No," she said simply. "I have plans."

Maria hurried off to serve her drinks. Bobby's rules were to greet patrons within a minute of them sitting, even if in passing, to show your face. Next, serve drinks within two minutes of taking the order. There were more timing rules after that but those were the most important.

Service was pretty slow today. Celia found herself with a lot of downtime. She blamed the rain for the lack of patrons. It was coming down in buckets outside. From her spot behind the bar, where the music wasn't as loud, she could hear it pelting on the roof. The only upside to that was the storm would wash away any remainders of Ashleigh and her vomit from Taco's parking lot.

"Excuse me, young lady."

She crossed to where the older gentleman was perched at the curve of the bar. After quickly assessing his plate and drink—all still plentiful—she smiled genially.

"How can I help you?"

He was a professor, she believed. He sometimes brought papers with him when he came for lunch and she had spotted folders with Emerson College's emblem among his things. Most of Emerson's buildings were a block away, including their radio station.

He was the corduroy-jacket-with-the-patches-on-the-elbow kind of guy. Under the jacket, he wore a dark green vest over a green- and blue-striped shirt. His thinning hair was mostly silver, as were his eyebrows and nose hair.

He nodded behind her. "Would you mind turning up the television? I would like to hear this story."

Celia found the remote near the register and increased the volume on the flat-paneled LCD TV hanging above the back bar.

". . . Her family is very worried," the anchorwoman was saying in a solemn voice. "If you've seen this woman, please contact your local precinct."

Celia's heart stopped when the picture flashed across the screen. Tilly was sitting on a bench in a park, wearing plaid shorts and a light blue tank top. The wind had blown her hair into her face. She used a hand to push it aside, all the while laughing at whoever had snapped the picture.

"She's been reportedly missing for over a week. She was last seen on the seventh at Olde Nessie's bar in South Boston."

Oh, no. Celia couldn't even breathe as she waited for the inevitable; for the woman to say she had been talking to a young, black girl with dark hair and dark clothes. Next, her mediocre driver's license picture would be displayed for the world to see because of course the fucking bouncer would remember her this time. Her hair was short then, no longer than a few curly inches and she looked like she was about to sneeze. She'd shorn her hair in a fit of anger after her mother died.

The anchorwoman moved on to a traffic accident on I-93 and Celia blew out the breath in relief. Bobby let her go at four. She went to his office to collect her purse and clock out. Carson was there, dressed in black, an apron around his waist. He was stuffing a small gym bag into an empty locker. He stiffened when he saw her, which was a weird reaction. She was used to a snide comment or borderline sexual harassment from him.

"What?" she grumbled as she opened her locker.

"I . . . I . . ." It seemed that was all he could manage.

She looked over to him with a frown. He was as white as a sheet, his blue eyes wide in terror. His brown hair was messy and she could see that he'd buttoned his shirt wrong.

"Carson?" she asked in actual concern. "What the hell?"

She took a step toward him, but he stumbled backward so she wouldn't come near. He pointed at her, his mouth flapping open and closed a few times.

"I saw . . . everything," he said in a hysterical whisper.

She still didn't understand. "What're you talking about?"

"That . . . that woman. She was fighting you. And . . . and then   those . . . dogs. They bit her and ate her—"

He broke off with that. Now it was her turn to pale.

She didn't know what to say. She ticked through different explanations of what had happened. She discarded them all as incredible. Not that what had actually happened wasn't incredible. But wait. Why did she have to explain? She could certainly plead ignorance. Say some batshit crazy girl jumped her and random dogs . . . attacked the woman . . . and spared Celia . . . Umm.

She was opening her mouth to say something along those lines. Carson stopped her with his next statement.

"And your boyfriend came and touched you and then you both   just . . . disappeared."

Uh-oh.

She'd forgotten that part. All she could do was stare in muted shock. He stared right back, maybe waiting for an explanation, maybe waiting to see if she would vanish right before his eyes. She had no explanation. She could tell the truth, just say, "Yeah, so, my boyfriend's a vampire. That's why he can teleport. And those dogs were actually werewolves." That would go over so well.

"I . . ." Celia said. She was saved by Bobby and Rick entering the office. She didn't know what was going to come out of her mouth. They weren't too surprised to find people in the office but from their postures, it appeared they wanted to talk shop. Celia snatched up her purse and neon green umbrella and flew out of there.

Outside, the rain had tapered off somewhat. She walked briskly to prevent from getting completely soaked. She'd have to deal with Carson later. No one would believe his story in a million years so he would keep. She decided not to worry herself about it—she had other issues at the moment.

She went straight home where she changed into a white baby

tee and pink sweats. She then grabbed the plate of blondies and carried them next door. Carrie's oldest son, who was twelve and went home after school, didn't answer when she knocked.

"Kenny, it's Celia," she called through the door. A shadow crossed the peephole, then the locks turned, the door opened a crack. Celia smiled at the skinny boy with his mop of blonde curls. He took his mother's instructions on security to heart. He didn't even answer the phone when it rang until his mom and siblings came home at six.

"Hi, Celia," he said cheerfully enough, though he looked troubled. She was going to ask what was going on when he caught sight of the goodies. His eyes instantly lit up. "You baked?"

She chuckled. The storm had passed apparently. "Yes. Save some for your sisters."

Kenny took the plate with glee. Celia waved and returned to her apartment. As soon as the sky was basically dark, she called Victor.

"I'm coming." He hung up on her ear.

She scowled at the phone for his abruptness. It was twenty minutes later but he did show. Celia jumped to her feet when he appeared next to the coffee table.

I have to tell you something, was what she should've said. She wrestled with it a second. She decided to trust that Jay wouldn't go after the vampires. He hadn't said it directly but he knew how upset she would be if he went ahead and confronted the vamps when she said she wanted to talk first.

"Are we going?" she asked instead. She had reverted back into a ball of anxiety. She hoped he couldn't hear it in her voice. Then she remembered he could sense her feelings, so her front was just that, a front. It didn't matter though, because she wasn't going to show her nerves on the outside.

"Yes," he said tightly. "Charlie is still recuperating. He had been resting."

And why couldn't you just tell *me that?* The words sat on the tip of her tongue. She held onto them. This wasn't the time to argue.

Victor took her hand in his. His skin was warm so she knew why he'd taken so long. Another rush of anger she struggled to contain licked at her. She wasn't able to hide the twitch of her lips. Victor remained quiet.

When the iciness didn't come, she looked up and saw he was surveying her cheek. They took a moment for her to have his blood. Her cheek was better immediately.

They teleported to Ramsey's living room. She lost her breath but that was the worst of it. The living room was empty. Victor still had her hand as he lead her into the hallway and up the wide staircase.

As they walked down the hall, a door at the end opened. Ramsey and Elizabeth emerged from the dim room. They met Celia and Victor halfway, in front of a closed door. The close proximity to the other vamps started a tingling inside Celia that she tried to ignore.

Victor gave Celia a measuring look, probably as one last effort to change her mind. In response, she raised her chin in the air, determined. Deep down, under the arousal at seeing Ramsey and Elizabeth, she was shaking. She hoped they couldn't tell.

Victor's hand tightened on hers. He knocked on the door with the other.

"Come in," came a male's voice.

Victor turned the knob and the four of them entered. This room was small. The full-sized bed was next to the door. There was a dresser, a nightstand and chair. That was about all it could house comfortably. The closet door was shut but she was sure it was paltry. She would be correct.

The man on the bed was sitting, propped up by two pillows, a blue cup in his hand. He lowered it from his mouth when the door opened. He had short, spiky hair that was light brown on top and darker around his ears and nape.

He wasn't really handsome, with his hooded eyes, broad nose, and thick goatee. His skin was ashen, but was probably normally a nice olive tone. Thanks to his vampire state he was still kind of alluring. The most remarkable thing about him, however, was the long scar that started halfway across his right cheek, then curved over his jaw and along his neck, stopping at his collarbone. The scar hadn't healed well; the skin was puckered and wrinkled.

Of course Celia's eyes went there first. The vampire brushed his fingers along the scar.

"This happened in eighteen thirty-two," Charlie replied.

She forced herself to look him in the eye, embarrassment flooding her cheeks and neck. He hissed softly at the rise in her pulse and she saw his hand clench around his cup. It was made of a hard plastic but his grip looked deadly.

The other vamps had stiffened as well. She thought that was because Charlie was still on the mend and may not have been in complete control. Victor took a step in front of her, ratcheting up the tension even more as Charlie regarded him with a predatory glare. Celia took a deep breath to calm herself seeing as how she had been the catalyst.

Charlie actually looked disappointed when she got a hold of herself. He was one of those that loved the chase; loved the fear he could inspire. He took a sip from the cup. His fingers were still on his scar.

"I was accused of stealing," he went on as if there had been no interruption. "The vendor decided to punish me himself. I was seventeen then. Doctors were scarce and you needed money or barter to pay for the service. I was poor, hence the stealing."

His voice was tinged with a Spanish or Italian cadence; she couldn't tell which. She wasn't concerned or interested either.

Charlie looked her over—the parts of her he could see around Victor—and when he finished, seemed intrigued.

"They tell me you wanted to speak with me," he opened.

Celia licked her lips, giving herself an extra moment to ensure she was composed.

"Yes," she said softly. "My name is Celia. I knew Ashleigh, but only casually." It was best to be cordial.

His eyes closed at the mention of her name. "Ah, my Ashleigh." His hand went to his chest where his heart used to beat. "This breaks my heart. When I woke up, I knew she was gone. She had much potential. She was so beautiful, so graceful."

"She tried to kill me," Celia said hotly, throwing away the whole civility thing at the blink of an eye.

He opened his eyes to stare at her. She felt the lick of his magic—a rush of heat warming her face like she was suddenly standing in front of a heat lamp—and she quickly dropped her gaze to his chin. That way she was still facing him, just not affording him the opportunity to do anything to her.

"You did not like my Ashleigh?" he asked and he actually sounded curious.

She decided to be honest. "No, I did not."

"How did she perish?"

Certainly one of the vampires crowded in the room with her had already told him.

"You know how," Victor interjected before she could answer. His voice was cold, prompting that death stare from Charlie. Then they were both hissing. It sounded like someone had just released a couple of snakes in the room.

"She attacked me when I was leaving work," Celia told Charlie, her voice even. She didn't want Victor's hostility to interfere with what she was trying to accomplish. "And some wolves came to my aid."

His gaze returned to her. "Wolves." He spat the word like it was rotten. "There is a pack upstate, near Syracuse. Vile animals."

"They saved my life," she informed him.

"Do you know these animals personally?"

She pondered that for a moment. She didn't think it wise to admit that one of them was a sometimey friend. That would give Charlie more leverage.

"No," she answered simply. Luckily, Victor made no indication that she was lying. He kept up his guarded watch of Charlie impassively.

Charlie nodded but his features were unreadable. Damn vampires and their blank expressions. It was frustrating.

"You are very beautiful," Charlie commented, triggering that jumpy nervousness she was trying to forget. "Of course anyone would want to save you. Except now I am without one of my own."

His eyes suddenly grew cold—Celia had hazarded a glance since she was used to looking people in the eye when she was speaking. He did seem truly troubled by his loss, which caused a brush of guilt inside her. She shook that away real quick. Her encounters with Ashleigh had been enough for a lifetime. Besides, she hadn't killed her.

"I just wanted to ask you, in person, to spare the wolves," Celia said. "Please."

He considered her a moment, taking in Victor's stance as well. Ramsey and Elizabeth were by the door—out of the way but not out of sight. Silent reinforcements. It was comforting since Charlie's gaze was giving her the creeps.

"Your human is something," Charlie said, obviously addressing Victor though he was still studying Celia's throat. "She wants mercy for a couple of wolves who mean nothing to her." Something about his tone made it seem that he hadn't believed her for a second.

"I figured you'd want revenge and innocent people shouldn't

die."

Anger clouded Charlie's face. She resisted the impulse to take a step back. "Are you saying Ashleigh wasn't innocent? That she deserved to die?"

"No, of course not," Celia said hurriedly, which was mostly true. She hadn't wanted her dead, just . . . away. Plus, Ashleigh had helped find Annie, which gave her, oh, maybe four cool points in Celia's book.

"It is normal practice to seek justice for our dead," he plowed over her.

"Yes, I know—"

"Do you?" he snapped. "It appears that I am to just leave without my Ashleigh and go on as if life has not changed."

"I didn't mean to imply—"

"How is that fair, eh? Do you know how long it takes to find the right human to bring over? The qualities you have to seek out? Then you wait in anticipation of them surviving the change."

Celia looked down. That was something she did not want to know.

"I had been watching those two all summer. They came to the mountains like clockwork for hikes. He was dispensable. She was . . ." He smiled. "She was all that I could want."

Great. Now he was making her feel bad for Ashleigh.

"How about this?" Charlie asked and she lifted her head again. He was grinning now, and she saw his fangs slide down. His scar seemed to smile at her, too. Victor took another step in front of her. She had to lean to the side to see Charlie.

"You come with me in her place, back to New York."

"I don't think so," Victor hissed. He interrupted so quickly that Celia hadn't even had time to process that request. She didn't want to picture what would be in store for her if she had to go with him. She wished she could say this, along with Rafael's request, was the most she'd ever been propositioned in so many days. Working in a bar precluded that.

"Then she can stay with me a few days. We'll work something out," he added vaguely, sending shudders of fear up and down her spine.

"Stay with you where?" she asked before Victor could intercede. Not that she was considering this, she was just curious if he was going to do whatever he had in mind under Ramsey's roof and if Ramsey would allow it. Was that one of the bylines in the Vampire Book of Rules?

Pursuant to the resolution of the litigation, the two parties shall resolve such matters within the confines of the location where such litigation has taken place . . .

Talk about a headache.

Charlie's grin was still firmly positioned under his goatee. "I have a place. Where Ashleigh and I were originally going to stay."

"What're you asking of me?" She needed him to be a whole lot more explicit than *we'll work something out.* She tried not to wince as Victor's hand tightened around hers. He was telling her to stop but she had to know, to figure out what she'd need to do to protect Michael.

Charlie seemed impressed that she had asked. "Well, my dear, you would have to submit yourself to me wholly. You would do whatever I tell you." Again, that blast of warmth as he tried to enthrall her. Her cheeks began to redden, as if he were actually aiming a space heater directly at her face. His power was different from Michael's engulfing blanket of comfort. Beneath the vampire's heat, goose bumps erupted as if he were touching her with probing fingers. Their goal was her eyes. The eyes were how they caught you.

"Stop that," she said without thinking. He blinked in astonishment and the warmth disappeared.

"That's intriguing, indeed," he said, more to himself since he spoke in an undertone.

"By 'whatever you tell me,'" Celia said to get the conversation back on track, "that means . . . what, exactly?"

Charlie was no longer grinning after she stopped his magic but he was definitely regarding her with interest.

"Light cleaning. Accompany me to a few meetings and parties I still need to attend in the area. Sex, of course." His expression never wavered however his lust was evident in his eyes—and fangs.

Yuck. She knew he had been insinuating so much but hearing him say it outright made her stomach toss with repulsion. Victor's hand loosened slightly so he must've felt that and was pleased. She almost pinched him. Like he really needed to be concerned.

Oh, gross, now she was imagining being cooped up in some house somewhere with Charlie kissing her and touching her. And then visions of her hanging on his arm at clubs, on display as his latest sex toy. Too bad he wasn't around when Serena was here. She'd probably love the opportunity to meet new vampires.

Celia shook her head to push the thoughts away. She hoped her disgust hadn't been displayed on her face. Charlie took the gesture as her answer. His shoulders jerked up then down in a resigned sort of way.

"Then I cannot help you."

She tried not to let her disappointment show. There was no way in hell she was going to stay with him. Michael was cool and all, but it just wasn't going to happen. And he surely wouldn't appreciate her putting herself in an awkward and demeaning position to help him. Look how upset he'd gotten about her relationship with Victor. He'd kill her if he found out she was mingling with vampires on his behalf.

Why was it that negotiations with vamps never seemed to go the way she wanted?

Charlie was still eyeing her.

"She's mine," Victor said in a harsh whisper. He was too incensed to speak any louder. He wanted to make it perfectly clear that Charlie was not to go after her. Of course Celia's inner feminist wanted to protest. She told her to shut the fuck up because now was so not the time.

Charlie waved his hand dismissively. "I have no interest in your human. These wolves, however . . ." He licked his lips lewdly and ran his tongue along his fangs. "They may be just the adventure I need to get back on my feet."

Celia's mouth opened to object. Ramsey spoke first.

"No."

Charlie turned to him in utter disbelief. Celia looked, too. Ramsey had been leaning casually against the door. She'd released her anger about Cillian, or so she thought. Now, with him standing up for her, and when he came to her aid with Ashleigh, she realized Ramsey had her best interest at heart.

"What's that?" Charlie cried. "You are denying me?"

"That's right," Ramsey drawled lightly, folding his arms at the chest. "This here's my territory. You may not hunt on these grounds without my permission, as you're well aware."

The vampire leader's eyes narrowed dangerously. It was the first time she'd ever seen any kind of ferocity in him. She was glad it wasn't directed at her.

"Is that so?" Charlie asked darkly. Hey, he didn't have to know about Milo and Clarice.

"There's a delicate balance here. I won't have it disrupted any further. We've already discussed your indiscretion with Ashleigh and her friend."

"You'll protect wolves?" he sputtered incredulously.

Ramsey nodded once. Charlie's furious eyes flashed back to Celia, like this was all her fault. Maybe it was.

"You better tell your friends not to leave this area," he warned. At least he respected some rules. Obviously he had to hear that killing humans was a no-no from the leader directly. Celia didn't respond though, at least not outwardly. Inside, she was screaming with relief.

"Leave me now," Charlie grumbled. He turned away from them so that only his profile was in view. "I will be out of your way tonight."

"Very well," Ramsey said and the four of them left. Celia waited until they were downstairs in the living room before addressing Ramsey.

"If I had known you could prevent him from killing them, I would've come to you instead." She shivered as she recalled the conversation. "Now for the nightmares," she muttered under her breath.

Ramsey smiled a little. He reached out to squeeze her shoulder. "You're a good friend," he commented. Celia assumed he was referring to her stepping in for Michael. She only shrugged sheepishly, though she was going to make sure Michael didn't forget it. If she asked for a favor and if he started to waver, she'd just go, "Hey, remember that time I made us even by saving your life? Are you sure you can't fold these napkins for me?"

Elizabeth cleared her throat. Celia glanced her way. She was directing a pointed look at Ramsey. Ramsey sighed.

"I wanted y'all to know that Cillian didn't act by himself."

Celia's mouth dropped slightly.

"You know how he tends to talk in circles," he said to Victor. "He mentioned Celia and how sweet her aroma is and Ashleigh caught on." His eyes went to Celia. "She told him she knew where you lived. Cillian said that I told him you were not his. But Ashleigh was insistent. She told Elizabeth she was with Bryce and Bryce she was with Elizabeth. She let him out the room. She told him how to find you. He said he caught your scent and knew it was the right place."

Celia's free hand tightened into a fist. "That fucking bitch."

She couldn't be too mad at Cillian. That fucking bitch had sent the deadly vampire after her. He had been a missile once he had his target. And when he failed, Ashleigh tried to finish the job. She would've succeeded, if Celia didn't have the backup that she did. She found herself appreciating the people in her life ten times more.

"Ashleigh caused a lot of damage with that stunt. Cillian's regressed."

"Ramsey can only feed him with the IV bags," Elizabeth added.

"I'm sorry, brown eyes."

Ramsey and Elizabeth glided from the room. Victor was still riled.

"It's okay, honey," Celia whispered, rubbing the hand that was still clamped around hers. She mostly wanted him to loosen up because she was losing sensation.

"I'm going to make sure he leaves the city," Victor said after a while. He was the opposite of Celia when it came to anxiousness. Instead of pacing the room (which he would've been dragging Celia along for the ride), he stood absolutely still, his face as smooth as granite. He looked down at Celia.

"You are to stay in the apartment until I come back."

She shook her head gently. "I have to tell Mi—him," she corrected herself.

Victor scowled in frustration. "You can't just call him?"

"I don't have his number."

He closed his eyes, and to her amazement, he started to laugh. It was small at first, softening his face. Then it bubbled out of him in loud gasps. He clutched his stomach with his free hand while Celia stood there staring at him like a screw just came loose.

"Was it something I said?"

He waved his hand. "Sorry. I'm just relieved."

"That I don't have his number?"

"Yes."

She waited for more but he was chuckling to himself. "O . . . kay . . ."

Victor couldn't possibly think that Michael was a threat to their relationship, could he? She normally would've pried more except there were too many ears in the house.

"Come on," he said, still smiling. "I have enough in me to get us out of here."

And then they were in her living room. He cradled his head, sinking to the sofa like a rock. She sat across his lap, put her arm around him, and rubbed his back until he was no longer grimacing in pain. He peeked up at her with black eyes and that serious look.

Celia leaned forward and kissed his lips. His fangs came out at her touch. He shifted so that he was lying on top of her, his hands exploring everywhere, warming her up. She wasn't really in the mood for sex so she didn't mind when he got straight to business and bit her neck. His fingers had slid into her pants and parted her lips while he sucked away. He grunted, his breath rustling the little hairs on the back of her neck in a pleasant sort of way. She was sighing too when he pulled away.

They lay together for a few minutes, their legs intertwined and her fingers in his soft, dark hair. Celia listened to crickets and cars rattling down the street. Two women passed under the window, laughing.

"What was Ramsey talking about back there? What was Charlie's indiscretion?"

"Killing Ashleigh and her boyfriend. Ramsey doesn't allow that. New Hampshire is a part of his territory."

"The whole state?"

"All of New England."

"Oh." She studied him a moment. "How come you're not a

part of his nest?"

Victor glanced away. "I like my freedom. Ramsey's not as demanding as most leaders are but I don't want someone controlling my actions again."

"Again?"

His voice was tight. "I was stuck with a despicable maker."

He didn't elaborate but she got the picture. "And Ramsey's okay with you being on your own?"

Victor considered her. She could sense his surprise at her interest. "For now. I don't know how long that will last."

He heaved a regretful sigh. "I have to go."

"Mmm," she replied.

He lifted up so he could look her in the face. "Come straight home after talking to your little friend."

"Yes, dear," she said dryly.

"I love you, Seal."

She smiled. "I love you."

He gave her a kiss, climbed off, and vanished.

***

Celia strolled down Bay State Road with her hands in her pockets. She was wearing her black North Face fleece and was glad she thought to wrap a yellow scarf around her neck because it was brisk tonight.

September had come and gone. Now October was nearly done. She couldn't believe it. That meant holidays were around the corner. Her anniversary was coming up as well, she just realized. Next month. Hmm. They never did make it to Seattle . . .

She spotted a dark figure sitting beside the silver wave sculpture. Celia crossed over and dropped down next to him on the damp grass. More cars traveled on Storrow Drive tonight, kicking up the waves of BU Beach.

Michael's eyes were closed like last time. The moon was just as bright as it neared its fullness. He didn't move, though she was sure he heard her, especially since she had tripped on a tiny divot and cursed out loud.

"I guess I owe you a big-ass thank you," Celia began. She stared straight ahead at the passing cars.

"There's gonna be a full moon, day after tomorrow."

He took a deep breath, letting the night air fill his lungs to capacity. He held it for a few seconds and blew it out from his mouth.

"That vampire you guys killed," she said carefully. "Her maker will be looking for you. He can't fight you here because Ramsey, the leader of this area, said so. You and your friends need to keep an eye out."

Michael was silent beside her. She looked over to him. His eyes were still closed but now a small smile pulled his lips upward.

"Did you hear me?" she asked. "I know you get caught up in your little . . . moon song but this is important."

"I heard you," he said simply.

His lighthearted answer and carefree manner were incredibly inadequate for her. After all the shit she went through—discontent from arguing with Victor, nervousness and fear from meeting with Charlie—she expected more.

"Well, you could give me a little more emotion than that," Celia snapped. "I've been through hell trying to make sure this guy didn't come after you. I've never felt more like a prized pig I'll have you know. So, some kind of appreciation would be excellent."

He finally faced her. She was greeted with his warmth. She actually had to loosen her scarf. Michael's eyes blazed golden and her muscles relaxed immediately. Like when you settled into a steam room after a long workout and all the warmth absorbed into your skin and bones, down to your soul. Yes, it was that dramatic. And the only reason she didn't lay back was because she didn't want grass stains on her fleece.

She opened her mouth a few times but she couldn't form complete thoughts. She had wanted to ream him out some more. She had wanted to ask about the two other wolves, to relay what Victor had told her about werewolves. The words fizzled before they were comprehensible. This was twenty times more potent than the combination of vamp blood.

"I can't remember what I was going to say."

His smile deepened. "That's okay. Just enjoy the ocean."

So, she did, for a little while at least. It was very nice being in his company. She didn't have to worry about vampires at her heels. If she had closed her eyes, she could've fooled herself into thinking she was on a sunny patch of beach somewhere, with the water lapping at her feet.

Sense came back to her sluggishly. She needed to get home. "I should go," Celia whispered, sounding as wistful as she felt.

"Thank you, Celia. And I apologize," Michael said. At this admission, his blanket of warmth rescinded a bit. She watched his face, the different emotions flitting across. "I've been kinda rude to you, which wasn't fair."

He stared at her earnestly, his tone firm. "I want to be friends, I really do. I'll try to keep my . . . issues in hand." He did a half shrug, conceding. "Anyone lucky enough to be your friend can't be all bad."

She smiled, touched. She reached over to squeeze his hand. His skin felt like it was on fire. Using his shoulder as a prop, she got to her feet. She left his warmth and headed home, where her boyfriend was waiting for her. Her boyfriend who cared for her, loved her, and protected her. Her smile widened at the thought and, tightening her scarf, she hurried off.

Just as Celia reached out for the door handle of her car, a sudden breeze whipped past the back of her neck. She looked up with a frown because she thought she felt fingers graze her skin.

Across the street, beside a bench, Milo paused long enough to smirk. His left arm was longer than last she saw him. He'd pinned the sleeve of his SpongeBob shirt back to conceal the stump.

Before the tremor of fear could make every one of Celia's hairs stand on end, the vampire streaked off along the grass, around a building and out of sight.

Celia and Victor's relationship has reached the one-year mark.

A vacation to Vegas couldn't be dangerous . . . right?

An exclusive excerpt:

Bitter

Book Three

of the

Bitten Series

Bitter

"Do you have anyone at home who could help you?" Leilani asked.

Celia opened her mouth to respond . . . only, no words came out. The room tilted slightly to one side. She looked around in surprise.

When her eyes met Leilani's, she saw the witch was smiling widely. "I think we're ready." She finished her own glass and stood. "Let's go out back."

She took Celia's hand. Celia followed without realizing. When she looked back, she saw herself sitting on the chair, laughing hysterically. Outside, the air was still hot. Leilani's backyard was an open field, surrounded by high trees to afford them privacy. In the center of the yard, a circle of torches were already burning. There were five mason jars on the ground, filled with a clear liquid.

Leilani released Celia's hand and shrugged off her robe. As she undressed, so did the others.

"What . . . what's going . . . on?" Celia managed to utter. Her tongue tasted like copper.

The women were humming as one. The four of them began skipping around the open space.

"Join us, Celia!" Leilani called.

Celia took a step forward but that was as far as she could go.

Her legs didn't seem to want to work.

The women danced and hummed as they made circles around the torches. Leilani was first to pick up a mason jar. Once the others had one in hand, she held her jar to the sky.

"We take of the ocean, to give back to the earth."

They others repeated in unison, "We take of the ocean, to give back to the earth."

After drinking all of the liquid, they opened their circle and traced between the torches. Celia stood in her spot, swaying in an invisible wind. The women suddenly slowed to a crawl though they were still laughing and frolicking. Large bursts of orange and blue shot up from the torches. Celia's palms were becoming slick with sweat.

A golden haze began to surround each of them. Leilani had the brightest glow. This couldn't be right. Celia looked down at the glass she still held in her hand. It slipped from her grip. The red liquid splashed on the grass. The dripping green blades turned their faces to her.

"We take of the ocean, to give back to the earth."

What the fuck had they done to her?

"Psst!"

She glanced to her right. A vision of herself stood beside her. Her hair was loose around her shoulders. The light breeze swished it around. Her steady gaze reflected cool confidence. The vision's hand was stretched out to her, her palm to the sky. A round, golden ball rotated slowly. It was brilliant and beautiful and Celia didn't understand.

She looked to the women. Did they see the vision? Instead of the slow pace, their movements had sped up to warp speed. She could barely keep up with them.

"We take of the ocean, to give back to the earth."

Celia wiped at the sweat leaking from her temples. Suddenly, she wasn't watching the nude witches. Everything was black. She thought maybe she had gone blind. Just as the panic began to rise and overtake her, the darkness vanished.

The women had stopped, and were staring at her curiously.

"Did you see something?" Thomasina asked. They approached her with excitement in their eyes.

"She saw something," Makala cried breathlessly.

"What did you see?" Leilani asked.

They were too close, asking too many questions at once. Celia shook her head and tried to step back but she stumbled in the grass. Four sets of hands reached for her to make sure she didn't fall. She had to get away.

About the author

The *Bitten* series offers Uzuri a chance to explore the paranormal. It first came to fruition in 2009, and continues to grow in her mind. Uzuri currently resides in Boston, Mass.

Find out more at: www.uzurimwilkerson.com
Follow her at: www.twitter.com/uzuri_iruzu
Friend her on: www.facebook.com/uzuriwilkerson